Romantic Suspense

Danger. Passion. Drama.

Witness Protection Breach
Karen Kirst

Sabotaged Mission
Tina Radcliffe

MILLS & BOON

WITNESS PROTECTION BREACH
© 2022 by Karen Vyskocil
Philippine Copyright 2022
Australian Copyright 2022
New Zealand Copyright 2022

First Published 2022
First Australian Paperback Edition 2024
ISBN 978 1 038 90270 2

SABOTAGED MISSION
© 2022 by Tina M. Radcliffe
Philippine Copyright 2022
Australian Copyright 2022
New Zealand Copyright 2022

First Published 2022
First Australian Paperback Edition 2024
ISBN 978 1 038 90270 2

MIX
Paper | Supporting
responsible forestry
FSC® C001695

Published by
Harlequin Mills & Boon
An imprint of Harlequin Enterprises (Australia) Pty Limited
(ABN 47 001 180 918), a subsidiary of HarperCollins
Publishers Australia Pty Limited
(ABN 36 009 913 517)
Level 19, 201 Elizabeth Street
SYDNEY NSW 2000 AUSTRALIA

Cover art used by arrangement with Harlequin Books S.A.. All rights reserved.

Printed and bound in Australia by McPherson's Printing Group

Witness Protection Breach
Karen Kirst

MILLS & BOON

Karen Kirst was born and raised in East Tennessee near the Great Smoky Mountains. She's a lifelong lover of books, but it wasn't until after college that she had the grand idea to write one herself. Now she divides her time between being a wife, homeschooling mum and romance writer. Her favourite pastimes are reading, visiting tearooms and watching romantic comedies.

But the God of all grace, who hath called us unto his eternal glory by Christ Jesus, after that ye have suffered a while, make you perfect, stablish, strengthen, settle you.
—*1 Peter* 5:10

DEDICATION

To my mum, Dorothy Kirst.
I couldn't have asked for a better mum and friend.
I love you.

Chapter One

Serenity, Tennessee

Somewhere in the square, a truck engine back-fired, and Jade Harris choked on her steamed vanilla milk. The gunfire-like blast hauled her back in time to the seedy streets of Gainesville, Florida, and a life the US Marshals had erased in exchange for testimony against her drug-trafficker boyfriend. Jenny Hollowell—college cheerleader turned drug addict dropout—had been declared dead.

She wiped the whipped cream from her nose and resumed her stroll past the festive window displays that lit up the night. Serenity's town square had been transformed for the holidays, and residents and tourists alike had come out for the Victorian Christmas Extravaganza. What wasn't to like about twinkling lights, free treats in every shop, hayrides and carolers dressed like

Charles Dickens's characters? She had about twenty minutes to finish her shopping before her five-year-old son, Henry, returned from the hayride with his part-time babysitter, Tessa Reed, and her daughter, Lily.

She crossed to the central, picturesque square. Wreaths hung on the lampposts. Lights sparkled like fireflies in bushes of various sizes and shapes, and tree trunks had been wrapped with bulbs that winked red and green. There were fewer people here, but those she passed smiled in greeting. Thanks to her job at Serenity's only vet clinic, she was a familiar face to many in town.

The brick path took her into an isolated, shadowed copse, and unease pinched her spine. She picked up the pace even as she scolded herself. The path curved, and she almost collided with a stranger. She yelped and jerked away. The man lifted his brows and, sidestepping, continued on his way.

There's nothing to fear here, remember?

Axel Ward was locked away in a Florida prison. What was more, he thought she was dead, taken out by the car bomb he'd had one of his associates plant.

The path curved again, and she emerged into an open area facing another line of shops. She stopped and inventoried her surroundings. Some people conversed outside the general store, enjoying the fudge and hot cider owner Bill was giving away. Others walked with purpose, shopping bags swinging from their arms. No one paid her any attention. In the distance, near the courthouse and library, she glimpsed a mounted police officer astride his horse. Could've been Mason Reed or Cruz Castillo. The shadows made it impossible to discern the horse's coloring.

Her irrational fears calmed by the sight, she entered the bookstore and found a book about trains for Henry. After making the purchase, she walked to the spare lot at the end of the complex to stow the gifts in the trunk before meeting up with Tessa and the kids.

Because she was envisioning Christmas morning and her little boy's reaction to her gifts, she didn't perceive the impending danger. By the time she heard the gravel dislodge and smelled the pungent odor of sweat and cigars, it was too late. There wasn't time to turn and confront whoever was behind her. A man's wide, callused hand smothered her mouth and nose. His other one clamped around her waist, one muscled arm lifting her off the ground and half propelling, half dragging her between the nearby trees.

Mounted Police Officer Cruz Castillo wasn't paying attention to the rumbling tractor near the courthouse or the families waiting for the next hayride around town. He had his eye on a group of rowdy teenagers whose playful shoving and taunts threatened to become a real brawl. He arched his back to relieve the stiffness brought on by a day in the saddle. His partner, Renegade, shifted his bulk and flicked his ears as if to say he, too, was ready for the event to end. The harness bells jangled as Cruz nudged the Tennessee Walker in the teenagers' direction. Sometimes all it took to ward off trouble was the arrival of a thousand-pound horse in official police gear.

The boys noticed their approach, and the roughhousing began to subside. Cruz's attention shifted to a pint-size figure off to their left, and his gaze narrowed. A towheaded boy darted in between the cluster of people, his elfin face twisted in worry as he stopped and turned first one way and then another.

Henry Harris, the only child of his closest neighbor, Jade.

Although much of Cruz's police work was accomplished from the saddle, he dismounted and guided Renegade to the boy.

"Hey, buddy." Cruz crouched down and touched his shoulder.

"I can't find my mommy, Mr. Cruz."

Jade must be out of her mind with worry. She was devoted to Henry, attentive and nurturing while being firm in discipline. In that aspect, she reminded Cruz of his own mother.

Beneath the mop of tousled blond hair, Henry's big green eyes were shiny, a sure sign waterworks were inevitable if Cruz didn't act fast.

"I'll help you search. Wanna ride with me?"

The boy sniffled and tilted his head to get a good look at Renegade. "Is he nice like Gunsmoke and Old Bob?"

Henry had ridden Cruz's personal horses on several occasions. His pasture abutted Jade's rental property, and, shortly after they'd moved in, Henry had sneaked in to get a closer look at the horses. Cruz had been inspecting the paddock gate and had spotted him. He'd introduced him to the horses and given him a ride.

"Renegade's sweeter than baby's breath." Cruz lifted the boy onto his partner's back and climbed on behind him. He took the reins in hand and curled his arm around Henry's middle. "Did your mom go for a snack? Or to the bathroom?"

He shook his head vehemently. "She's shopping."

Henry's fingers clamped onto Cruz's wrist, and he was struck by his size and vulnerability. Good thing they'd crossed paths. The event was packed. A long-standing tradition, the Victorian Christmas Extravaganza drew people from surrounding towns, as well as tourists visiting the Smoky Mountains for the holidays.

Cruz searched the crowd for the petite vet tech, whose long snow-blond locks, pale skin and vivid green eyes made her stand out. "Do you remember what color coat she's wearing?"

Henry thought about it. "Uh-uh."

"That's all right." Cruz signaled Renegade forward. They hadn't gone far when he heard his name being called. He turned his head and saw his sergeant's wife, Tessa, hurrying toward them with their four-year-old daughter, Lily, in tow. Her stricken expression crumpled when she spotted the boy.

"Henry!" Her breath came out in a whoosh. "I've been looking everywhere for you!"

"I have to find my mommy."

Beneath the halo of black curls, Tessa's hazel eyes were troubled when she looked at Cruz. "I took the kids on a hayride. There were a lot of people waiting to take the next ride, and I lost track of Henry. I thought maybe he'd gone to the courthouse steps to meet Jade. She's not there. I've texted and called her several times."

He patted Henry's middle. "Change of plans, buddy. I want you to go with Tessa and Lily."

He stiffened. Tessa must've noticed the brewing protest, because she placed a hand on Henry's leg. "Let's go get those gingerbread cookies we talked about. We'll pick one out for your mom, too."

The starch went out of him, and Cruz lowered the boy into Tessa's waiting arms.

"Text me her contact information, will you?"

Tessa fished her phone from her coat pocket. His phone chimed, and he attempted to reach Jade as he and Renegade passed a group of carolers and entered the square. He used his police radio to alert his sergeant, Mason, and the other unit officers of his plans. While there was no reason to suspect trouble, his partners agreed to join in the search. Raven Ferrer was near the Black Bear Café and would have a look around as soon as she handed off an inebriated customer to a patrol officer. Silver Williams and Mason would start at opposite ends of the square and work their way along the shops.

From his vantage point, he could see Mason near the Mint Julep Boutique, but the trees in the center blocked his view of the daycare and the shops on the other side. He continued on, looking through the store windows for a glimpse of Jade. Had she decided to duck into Spike's for a burger? Or gotten caught up in conversation with someone?

He observed a pair of adult males conversing outside the restrooms, which capped the end of this row. He would ask if they'd seen Jade and, failing that, knock on the women's restroom door. Next on his list was the temporary parking area roped off behind the shops.

A shout broke into his thoughts, and Renegade was leaping into action almost before he gave the cue. The men raced into the trees. He couldn't make out their words, but he sensed their urgency. He activated his heavy-duty flashlight and navigated to the other side. The chaotic scene he encountered in the thickest part of the copse hardened his gut and released a flood of adrenaline through his system.

There was no denying the woman the two

men were helping off the ground was Jade. Her hair gleamed like an iridescent pearl against black sand. The flashlight beam glanced off her disheveled clothing and bloodied lip. Heat flushed through his veins, and his muscles quivered with the need to avenge her. Violence against women and children never failed to trip his temper. He scoured the area for a target to zero in on.

After relaying his status over the radio, Cruz nudged Renegade closer.

"What happened, Jade?"

"Someone grabbed me from behind and dragged me here." She brought her hand to her mouth and winced. Her moss-green eyes were stark in her pinched face.

"Officer, we heard the scuffle and came running." The taller of the two men spoke up. He pointed in the direction of the main road. "The guy took off that way."

"Did he speak to you? Communicate his intent?" Cruz asked Jade.

"No." She wrapped her arms around herself, and he noticed her knuckles were cut up.

Mason arrived on his horse, Scout, and radioed the suspect's possible escape route to the others. The patrol officers would take charge of the search.

"You all right, Jade?" Mason inquired, his brown eyes somber. "Do you need a ride to the clinic?"

Her arms still wound tightly around her upper body, she shook her head. Pale threads of hair had escaped her braid. "I'm fine."

The sleeve of her black coat had been ripped free of the shoulder seam, evidence of the force of her attacker's grip.

"I'll take these gentlemen's statements." Mason gestured to Jade. "Cruz?"

They'd worked together long enough to develop a sort of nonverbal shorthand. He understood his sergeant's wishes without being told.

Cruz dismounted and approached Jade. She dropped her arms and took a step back, lips parted, eyes wide. He stopped, surprised by the reaction. He wasn't a stranger. He certainly wouldn't ever hurt her.

He took his time scooping up her discarded packages and held out his other hand.

"Walk with me?"

She glanced at the spot on the ground where she'd been attacked, and a shudder racked her body. Ignoring his hand, she started walking. "I need to get to Henry."

Cruz took Renegade's lead rope and used the flashlight to illuminate their path. "Henry was worried. I found him searching for you. He slipped away from Tessa."

"What?" Her stride lengthened. "Where is he now?"

"With Tessa and Lily."

She would've burst into a jog if he hadn't lifted his arm as a barrier. "Hold up a second. I know you're eager to see him, but I have to get your full statement. More importantly, we need to address your wounds."

"But—"

"You don't want him to see you like this, Jade." He lightly touched the rip in her coat sleeve, and she jumped. "We'll get those scrapes bandaged, okay?"

Her fingers worried the silver cross dangling from a thin chain at her neck. "Okay."

Cruz worked hard to bottle his anger. He suspected what the perp's likely intent had been, and he was grateful Jade had been spared. He would do everything in his power to run this guy to ground and make sure he didn't hurt anyone else.

Chapter Two

Jade couldn't stop trembling. This wasn't the first or even the second time she'd been roughed up, but it had been years since she'd escaped Gainesville's criminal underbelly. She'd gotten used to people treating her with kindness and respect. She'd gotten soft. The attack had rattled her to the core, a harsh reminder that violence exacted a mental toll. She felt as if the stranger's hands were still on her, his breath on her neck, his malicious intentions infusing her with dread.

The hair that escaped her French braid dangled limply around her face. Her attempts to weave the strands into place failed, so she removed the elastic band and used her fingers to comb out the tangles.

Cruz crouched beside the folding table closest to the police tent's entrance and riffled through a duffel bag. It was impossible not to notice the ripple of taut muscles beneath his blue-black uniform shirt. Her gaze moved upward to the tanned, smooth skin above his starched collar. He'd removed his helmet, and his short black hair was damp at the temples, the longer top strands in disarray. He retrieved a navy blue Serenity Mounted Police sweatshirt and brought it to her.

When they'd entered the white canvas tent, he'd set a metal chair next to the snack table for her. Now he placed a second chair facing her, lowered his body onto it and slid the first aid kit closer to himself.

She murmured her thanks and, after shucking her torn coat, pulled the sweatshirt over her head. His cologne clung to the material—a sultry, musky scent perfect for a heart-stopping cowboy type. But she couldn't separate his Texas roots from his current career. Police in general made her antsy, even though she was no longer on the wrong side of the law.

Cruz Castillo's profession wasn't the only reason he got under her skin. Over six feet tall with a strapping build, he was the kind of man you didn't dismiss or forget, whether in uniform or in his usual shirt, jeans and cowboy boots. His jet-black hair and short goatee enhanced his wide forehead, defined cheekbones and angular jaw. His cocoa-colored eyes were sharp with intelligence and seemed to cut through lies like a laser.

Twisting the lid off a water bottle, he reached for her hand. She sucked in a breath when his warm, callused fingers wrapped around her palm. A pleasant sensation tickled her skin. The contact was nice.

His eyes flashed an apology. "I'll be as gentle as I can."

Holding her hand above the grass, he poured water over the busted knuckles and pressed a clean cloth to them. She stared at his bent head, at the hint of wave in his thick locks. This was the closest she'd ever been to him.

"I fought to get away from him," she blurted, thrown off-kilter by her reaction.

He lifted his head. "Good thinking. You delayed him long enough for those men to intervene."

Framed by his beard, his lips were full and beautiful. Mortified and confused by the thought, she pressed her own together and experienced a shimmer of pain.

His forehead creased. "I'll get you a wet cloth for that lip."

"How bad does it look? Will Henry notice?"

"Henry's as bright as a new penny. You may want to prepare a tactful answer in case he does."

He was still holding her hand carefully. She'd seen his gentleness with her son on multiple occasions. She hadn't experienced it for herself, however. Thankfully, he made quick work of doctoring her wounds with antibiotic cream and bandages.

"I need you to walk me through what happened." He took a small notebook from his uniform pocket and held his pen aloft.

He looked somber but also riled. He was angry on her behalf. Imagine that, from a cop.

Cruz's polite manner would disappear if he learned of her sordid past. His loathing for drugs was no secret. He'd made it his personal mission to drive them out of Serenity and to convince students not to succumb to peer pressure or curiosity. He wouldn't learn her secret, though. The locals thought she'd led a run-of-the-mill, standard American life, which was the truth—up until she'd struck up a fateful friendship with the wrong man.

Jade ran her palms over her pants and, noticing a slight tear, began to pick at it.

"I went into several shops and purchased gifts for Henry. I headed to my car to put them in the trunk before meeting up with Tessa and the kids. As I was passing the restroom, he grabbed me from behind and dragged me into the trees."

"Did your attacker say anything?"

"No."

His silence had unnerved her. It was as if she was less than human and didn't deserve to be spoken to.

"Did you get a look at his face? Notice any features?"

"He was behind me the whole time. I struggled and got free, but I tripped and fell. As I was trying to get up, he struck me." She touched her busted lip. "I crawled away. He seized the back of my neck. The next thing I know, the men were shouting and running, and he fled."

A muscle in his cheek twitched. "Are there any details you can give me? Height? Build?"

Jade closed her eyes. "He was quite a bit taller than me."

"You're, what? Somewhere around five-four?"

She nodded and continued with her description of her attacker. "His muscles were exaggerated, like he spends a substantial amount of time in the gym."

His hand had seemed powerful enough to snap her neck like a toothpick.

"Do you recall any specific smells?"

"Cigar. Sweat."

"He didn't try to take your purse, phone or jewelry?"

"No." Fear jolted her as her mind landed on what he might've wanted with her. She quickly stood. "That's all I remember. Can I go to Henry now?"

Cruz got to his feet as well, and tucked his notebook in his pocket. He towered over her, and she had to tilt her head to meet his gaze.

"Did you notice anyone suspicious around you tonight?"

"Everyone I encountered was in happy spirits."

He hooked his thumb over his shoulder. "I'll walk with you."

She didn't try to talk him out of it. The big Texan's presence was exactly what she needed right now.

"I'll compare my notes with Mason's. But I want you to be prepared in the event we don't locate this guy. We have very little to go on."

She swallowed her nervousness and gathered her shopping bags. "I understand."

"This is what I'd call an attack of opportunity. You were alone. The noise and activity made him bold. I don't foresee you having this kind of trouble again." His brows crashed together. "I am sorry this happened to you."

He swept open the tent flap and greeted Renegade. "You remember Jade, don't you? She's the one who gives you extra treats after your shots."

"You noticed?" She ran her hand along the horse's neck, wishing she could hug him until the ordeal faded from memory.

He untied the lead rope. "I'm trained to notice important details. Renegade is your favorite, isn't he?"

"I can't confirm nor deny."

"Don't worry, your secret is safe with me."

She shifted her gaze to her tennis shoes. If he only knew her entire life was a secret. Sometimes, she felt the urge to tell someone. She felt so alone in this giant, extravagant lie. Her one consolation? It was keeping her and Henry safe.

Cruz accompanied her to the bakery and waited with Renegade right outside. Henry's face lit up when he saw her. "Mommy!"

He launched himself forward, and Jade crouched to catch him, almost tipping over backward in the process. His hug was fierce. He smelled sweet and gingery, like the cookie crumbles around his mouth. She held his slight body close, tears welling up.

What if he'd gotten lost looking for her? What if the stranger had gotten her into a vehicle?

Thank You, Jesus, for watching over me and my boy.

He broke the hug, his adoration shifting to accusation in a blink of an eye, five-year-old style. "Where were you?"

She tenderly brushed the scruffy bangs off his forehead. "I got delayed." Trying to distract him, she motioned to the table he shared with Tessa and Lily. "Did you save me a cookie?"

Lily called his name and urged him to go look at something in the bakery case with her. Quick as a blink, he forgot their conversation and left with his friend.

Tessa leaned forward, her eyes apologetic. "Jade, I feel terrible. He melted into the crowd while I was helping Lily off the tractor. I called his name, but he was already gone. I guess searching for you. I'm sick over it, truly."

Jade put a hand on her friend's arm. "It could've happened to anyone. In fact, he's done it to me at the park a time or two. I'll have a talk with him tomorrow."

Tessa noticed her bandaged hand, and her frown intensified. "Where's your coat? And why is Cruz guarding the door?"

"Not here." There were too many people around who could overhear. "Let's get the kids into the truck first."

It wasn't easy to pull the kids away from the colorful array of desserts, but they gathered up their cookies and finished them off as they exited.

After greeting Tessa, Cruz put on his helmet and adjusted the strap. Inserting one boot into the stirrup, he effortlessly seated himself in the saddle.

She and Tessa walked directly behind the kids, with Cruz bringing up the rear. Jade felt better once Henry was buckled into his booster seat and Lily was bouncing on the seat beside him. Cruz stationed himself at the hood of the truck, affording her and Tessa a modicum of privacy. When she'd relayed the news, Tessa hugged her with a fierce protectiveness that again had Jade fighting emotion.

Lord, thank You for second chances, for blessing

me with this new life and friends who love and support me.

"Do you want to stay at our house tonight?"

"Don't tempt me." She shook her head. "We'll be fine."

"Call if you change your mind. Or if you can't sleep and need someone to talk to."

"I will."

"I mean it, no matter what time."

"All right."

Tessa and Lily bade Cruz good-night and went in search of Mason.

Jade lightly gripped the truck's door handle. "Thank you, Cruz, for everything."

He inclined his head. "You'll see my number on your phone. Store it. And remember, if you need me, I'm right next door."

She averted her face, hiding her surprise. Although they'd been neighbors for a long time, he'd kept his distance. They certainly didn't swap cups of sugar and juicy bits of news across the fence.

Jade told him good-night, and he signaled Renegade to back up. She felt the weight of his stare as she got behind the wheel, started the engine and eased out of the space. During the ride home, Henry chattered about the hayride.

Jade made adequate noises in response, but her mind whirled with tonight's events, touching repeatedly on Cruz Castillo.

His opinion of her was a mystery. Although their social and professional lives overlapped, he hadn't initiated a friendship with her. He was clearly uninterested in getting to know her better. Was it because she was a single mom? He stuck with his fellow officers and close buddies, often hanging out at the Black Bear Café listening to live bands and playing cornhole on the patio. He wasn't known to date locals...and not due to lack of opportunities. She'd seen women flirting with him. Overheard them ask him out. She'd also heard him politely decline.

Tessa had let it slip that he'd left an ex-wife behind in Texas, but she hadn't shared details. Apparently, Cruz was closemouthed about his past. Jade could commiserate.

Thoughts of the enigmatic Texan scattered as the white Craftsman house they called home came into view. The single front porch light no longer seemed adequate. Parking beneath the live oak tree that hugged the paved drive, she studied the darkened side windows. As her anxiety ramped up, she gave herself a stern scolding. She'd been on her own for years, and she'd managed to keep herself and her son safe. Cruz was right. The attack was a random, isolated event. This night, she told herself firmly, would soon be nothing more than an uncomfortable memory.

Still, she rushed Henry inside, flipping on lights and testing the doors and windows. While he splashed and played in the bath, Jade stepped into the hallway and connected with her friend Leslie via video chat.

Leslie Harding was the first friend she'd made after entering the protection program. Jade had been relocated to Knoxville and had gotten a job at a convenience store as a means to support herself while pursuing her degree. The older and wiser Leslie had seen the lonely, bruised heart behind her bravado and befriended her. She'd showered her with love and compassion. She'd taken her to church. And when Jade had learned of her pregnancy and become overwhelmed, Leslie had prayed with her, encouraged her, supported her. Most importantly, she'd introduced her to her Savior, Jesus Christ.

"Jade." Leslie's brown eyes sparkled behind her paisley-print glasses. Her vivid red blouse was the perfect foil for her luminescent black skin and hair. The room around her buzzed with music and laughter.

Jade had forgotten tonight was her friend's annual Christmas party and apologized for interrupting.

"I'm happy to hear from you," Leslie told her. "How was the extravaganza?"

Jade rushed out an explanation in a wobbly voice. Immediately, Leslie's features shifted into motherly concern. "I'll come over."

"I don't want you to leave your party." Leslie and her husband had two grown sons and a wide circle of friends. It was an hour's drive from her home in Knoxville to Serenity. "I just wanted you to know. To pray."

Leaning against the wall across from the open bathroom door, she peeked at Henry. Coated in bubbles, he held action figures in each hand and was carrying on a conversation with an imaginary companion.

"You have my prayers, of course. But you can have me there, too. Gerard can handle hosting duties."

"I'm fine, Leslie. Just rattled."

"You're sure?"

"Positive." Her attacker didn't know her name or where she lived.

They made plans to meet the following weekend and ended the call.

Jade got Henry into pajamas and under his covers. Thanks to the day's excitement, he wasn't ready for sleep. She turned off the overhead fixture, and the bedside lamp bathed the room in soothing light. She got comfortable beside him, the padded headboard supporting her back, and retrieved the stack of books from the bedside table. They just might make it through all of them tonight before he dozed off.

Jade was halfway through the second book when she heard the telltale creak. The top step of her back deck was warped and always made a distinctive noise. Her heartbeat kicked into overdrive.

"What is it, Mommy?"

Schooling her features, she handed him the book. "I'll be right back."

Gripping her phone in her palm, she tiptoed through the living room and into the kitchen. The wicker light fixture above the round white table and chairs cast odd patterns through the room. Ahead, flanked by a storage closet and laundry room, the back door was shut and the lock engaged. The door seemed solid enough, but for the first time she was aware of the glass insert. Suddenly, she was viewing her home through a security lens. Working up her courage, she walked to the door, flipped on the porch light and drew the curtain aside.

The deck furniture hadn't been disturbed. The stairs were empty.

False alarm.

She let out the breath she'd been holding in one short burst. As she started to turn away, she saw someone standing between the trees and fence that marked Cruz's property line. Someone was out there.

Her phone slipped from her fingers and clattered to the floor.

Chapter Three

"I'm sorry, Jade. I didn't mean to frighten you." Cruz closed and locked the back door, shutting out the biting cold. She'd called him in a panic, not realizing he was the one who'd spooked her. "Gunsmoke wandered down this way and wouldn't respond to my calls. He can be stubborn sometimes."

Jade was stationed in the galley kitchen near the stainless steel stove, both hands worrying the cross pendant at her throat. A gold ring adorned her right ring finger, and the jade stone glinted in the overhead light. She still wore his sweatshirt. The casual garment didn't mesh with her usual elegant style. Even when on vet duty, she wore crisp collared shirts with floral or geometric prints and dainty buttons. Her nails were always painted, her jewelry minimal and her hair held back either in a braid or with a barrette. Now her hair cascaded around her shoulders like a drift of freshly fallen snow, and his heart kicked like a wily stallion each time he looked her in the eye. Not a pleasant state of affairs.

Walking around the table, he stopped and leaned against the farmhouse sink. "I should've called and let you know I'd be out there."

She ran her tongue over her busted lip. "I thought I heard someone on the deck and over-reacted."

He hated that someone had shattered her peace and that he'd compounded the problem. He didn't know her well enough to guess how long this would affect her.

The patter of feet in the living room behind her heralded Henry's arrival. "Mr. Cruz, will you read me a story?"

Henry's hair was damp and combed off his face. The traces of dirt, sweat and treats had been wiped away, and he stood there, fresh and clean in striped cotton pajamas. The boy had his mother's moss-green eyes, pale hair and rounded chin. Did he resemble his father at all? Cruz's curiosity flared to life, and he suddenly had a burning desire to know more about Jade's pre-Serenity life.

"Will you?"

Jade didn't offer any objections, and Cruz couldn't deny him. "Sure. What's it about?"

"A Christmas donkey." Henry snagged Cruz's hand and tugged.

"A donkey, huh?"

Their two-bedroom bungalow had the living room and second bedroom at the front of the house. Henry's bedroom was a spectrum of blue, from powder to navy, with white walls and white furniture. His lamp was shaped like a star. There were toy bins, a dresser and a rug made to look like a racetrack. Jade had certainly infused the older house with charm and warmth.

Henry snuggled under the covers and patted the mattress. Following the boy's lead, Cruz removed his boots and found a spot on the bed. He noticed Jade hovering in the doorway, observing, and felt a nervous quiver in his belly. Jade wasn't out to snag a husband. She hadn't ever given off that vibe. Why, then, did he wish she wouldn't listen to him read?

Henry leaned against him, and he automatically curved his arm around the boy. An odd ache gripped him. If he and Denise had found a way to make their marriage work, would he have a son of his own by now?

Licking his dry lips, he turned the page and

mustered on. When he'd finished that one, Henry scrambled for another.

Jade held up her finger. "You said one, Henry." Her pale pink lips curved slightly in Cruz's direction. "Around here, one can easily become a dozen."

"You don't mind, do you?" Henry entreated.

"I don't mind, but Gunsmoke and Old Bob probably do. They're waiting on me to put them to bed."

"Will you read to me tomorrow night?"

Jade blushed to the roots of her hair.

Cruz chuckled and ruffled the boy's pale locks. "Good night, Henry."

She admonished Henry to remain in bed this time and, pulling the door almost closed, trailed Cruz into the living room. The furniture was mismatched and well loved. There were candles and books set about and a geometric-pattern rug on the oak floors. A white artificial tree was tucked between the couch and an armchair, and it was decorated like a package of gumdrops in tones of pink, green and blue.

He wandered to a collection of picture frames on a side table. "Who's this?"

"My dear friends, Leslie and Gerard Harding. You may have seen them around. They visit us from time to time. They like the Black Bear almost as much as you do."

"Too much of my paycheck goes to that place, but it seems pointless to cook for one." He liked to use his smoker and grill, but he didn't have the patience for any sides other than rice. He was sure his mother didn't count the green peppers and onions in his *arroz verde*. She would say he needed more vegetables in his diet…if she wasn't too busy interrogating him about his love life. "Where did you live before Serenity?"

"Knoxville."

"That's your hometown?"

"No. Florida."

"Where in Florida?"

Her smile seemed practiced, and his internal alarm ticked a warning.

"An insignificant town on the Gulf Coast. You wouldn't know it."

Her evasiveness bothered him. "No photos of your folks?"

"We're not on good terms." She twisted the jade ring round and round. "Leslie and Gerard are my family now."

Her firm tone cautioned against more questions. When she covered a yawn, he moved to the door. "You've got church in the morning. I'll get going."

She leaned her hip into the couch and cocked her head, her hair spilling over one shoulder. "I haven't seen you there in a while."

Distracted by the play of light in her lustrous hair, he said, "I figured going because it's expected wasn't benefiting anyone."

Questions flitted over her face that he chose to answer—in part.

"My relationship with God isn't what it used to be."

His mom and grandmother were heartbroken over it. Bothered his father, too, but he didn't ask Cruz weekly if he was going to church.

"I'm sorry to hear that. I put my trust in Him in the early days of my pregnancy, and I've never once regretted it. He's everything to me."

The peace and confidence wrapped up in her words were alluring, and, for a moment, Cruz yearned for the closeness he'd once experienced with God. But then he remembered how God had allowed his nineteen-year-old brother to be gunned down by drug runners, how God had allowed his wife to walk away, to give up on their marriage. Bitterness, anger and regret were rooted deep inside him, and he couldn't see past them to the hope and optimism he used to have.

"Good night, Jade."

Striding to his truck, he scanned the darkened yard, the road and the Lambert farm across the way. If he was still a praying man, he'd ask the Lord to keep Jade and little Henry safe. But praying hadn't helped Sal. Hadn't helped his marriage. God wasn't listening to him anymore.

Jade parked her truck outside the farmers' co-op the next day. Brief bursts of wintry air rustled the bushes hugging the bright red buildings laid out in a linear fashion. Overhead, woolen clouds stretched across the sky. She'd allowed Henry to go home with Lily after the morning service and would soon be joining him there for the mounted police unit's Christmas party. Mason and Tessa had become dear friends, and she was happy they treated her and Henry as part of their extended family. The other officers didn't seem to mind when she horned in on unit functions. Mason's mom, Gina, and sister, Candace, were frequently in attendance, as well. The group was expanding in other ways, with both Silver and Raven having gotten married this year. She wondered how Cruz felt about being the last single one in the group, but she wasn't going to pose that question to him. He'd think she was asking because of a romantic reason and give her an even wider berth.

His expression as he'd walked out her door last night was imprinted on her brain. What had driven a wedge between him and God? She knew very little about his family, only that he'd lost his older brother as a teen to drugs. Her heart grew heavy at the thought. She'd seen too many people die during her time with Axel— either to overdoses or to the violence of associating with drug pushers. She'd been too wrapped up in her own addictions to care that much then. Now that she was living a clean, redeemed life, she grieved the unnecessary losses.

If Cruz knew about her past, would he have even answered her call last night?

Through her windshield, she watched an old Oldsmobile cruise slowly past on the two-lane road. The car had pulled out behind her at the Mountain Side Inn, but she hadn't given it any thought. Her hand clenched around her phone, fingers poised to call for help. But the car continued down the road, and she relaxed. She hoped this hyperalertness would fade soon.

Looping her purse strap over her shoulder, she

walked inside the co-op at a purposefully slow pace. She wasn't in danger. There was no need to act like she was.

Gary, the part-time clerk, was half draped over the register, staring at his phone. He offered a limp wave. She was the only customer in this main section, which housed home goods, apparel and pet supplies. Sunday afternoons were slow, even during the holiday season. Taking a cart, she left the building and traversed the covered walkway bordered by small-engine tractors. She entered the warehouse portion, bypassing industrial feed and fertilizer. The fresh wreaths and garlands her boss wanted for the clinic were stored in the deep recesses of the warehouse. The cart wheels bumped along the cement floor as she traversed the wide aisles between tall metal shelves.

Jade located the greenery and began stacking wreaths in the cart. Her body was sore in odd places, a reminder of last night's tussle with a stranger. As she was reaching for the last wreath, she was bumped from behind. Before she could turn around or speak, something hard looped around her throat and cut off her air supply.

Panicked, she clawed at the unyielding object.

The attacker's hot breath wafted over her cheek, and she shuddered.

She stomped on his foot, but he only grunted. He tugged her against him and pinned her arms to her sides, never letting up on the garrote.

Air. She needed air.

Her lungs strained. Her heart thundered.

She kicked her heel up and back, catching him in the inner thigh. He growled and cinched the object tighter around her throat. Her skin burned. Her head felt lighter than her body.

Gray static danced in her peripheral vision.

Before she lost consciousness, she asked God to watch over her son.

Chapter Four

The smell of pungent earth invaded Jade's nostrils. She lay on something soft and damp, and her body was being gently rocked. Her eyelids were heavy and unresponsive at first. When she finally coaxed them open, her surroundings didn't make sense. Metal coated with orange rust surrounded her. Above, there was nothing but gray sky. Frosty air washed over her skin. Her fingers curled into the foreign material beneath her and came away trailing bits of mulch. The grunt and strain of a truck engine registered, and everything came at her at once.

She'd been abducted from the co-op. This wasn't a random crime of opportunity. Someone had an agenda, and she was the target.

Terror pushed her into action. Where was she? Where was he taking her? She crawled on her hands and knees to the back of the dump truck. The driver downshifted, knocking her forward, and she smacked her forehead on the metal gate. Blood trickled down her nose. Grasping the top edge, she gained her footing and peered over at rolling fields and a barn. Jade recognized the country road. In a few miles, the sporadic farms would give way to uninhabited land and a garbage dump. She wasn't about to stick around and find out what her abductor had in mind for her.

She had to escape, for Henry's sake.

The dump truck wasn't able to travel at a high rate of speed here—a point in her favor. She studied the pavement shunting past and gauged the risks. A broken bone was the least of her worries. It took her several tries to hook her knee over the top ledge and climb over. Her grip wasn't as sure as she'd thought, and she fell to the ground before she was ready. The impact jarred the breath from her lungs and wrenched her shoulder. The momentum rolled her into the ditch, among discarded trash and a child's sneaker.

Jade lay in the weeds, panting, taking stock of her injuries and praising God she'd made it out. She checked her coat pockets before remembering her phone was in her purse. Had she dropped that at the co-op? The truck's brakes squealed, and her relief disappeared like a vapor. Had he seen her escape?

She got up and ran. Ran until her head pounded, her lungs screamed for mercy and her injured shoulder couldn't endure another jarring step. Bent at the waist, her hands braced against her knees, she gulped mouthfuls of air that felt like ice shards in her throat. Sweat mixed with the blood from her head wound and dripped down her face.

A car approached, and she waved both arms. The teenage girl behind the wheel slammed on the brakes and stared, jaw hanging low. Jade rapped on the passenger window. The girl rolled it down an inch.

"Please, I'm in trouble. Can you take me to the police station?"

Her head bobbed, and Jade didn't hesitate. Buckling her seat belt, she introduced herself while peering through the foggy windshield. If her abductor had noticed her escape, he would've had to find a suitable place to turn the cumbersome vehicle around.

"I'm Sarah." The girl hung on to the wheel, wide eyes taking in Jade's appearance.

"I appreciate your help, Sarah."

With a nod, she removed her foot from the

brake and did a U-turn in the middle of the road. Sarah let her borrow her cell phone, and Jade called the Serenity Police Station and explained the situation so they could send an officer in search of the dump truck. She also reached out to her WITSEC handler, Alan Prescott, and got his voice mail. That wasn't unusual. Although a busy man, he typically returned her calls within forty-eight hours. With Sarah in the car, Jade couldn't leave a detailed message, so she simply asked him to call her. Prescott would've already been in contact if there'd been a change in her case, of course, but she couldn't help worrying.

Axel Ward was a notorious drug trafficker whose influence and reach wouldn't be diminished by his incarceration. Back in Gainesville, the mere mention of his name was enough to incite fear. He not only pushed product that resulted in people's deaths, he ordered the murders of rivals, officials and anyone else who dared cross him. If he ever found out she was alive, he'd come after her. That was why she was very careful to follow the US Marshals' instructions.

At the station, she was met in the parking lot by Officer James Bell. He accompanied her inside and pointed her to a corner office. She sank gratefully into the cushioned chair across from his desk and accepted the paper cup he offered. Didn't matter that she hadn't had a drop of coffee—or any caffeinated beverage—in years. The rich, hot brew soothed her parched throat.

"Tell me what happened," he said gently. "Try to include all the details. Nothing is too small or insignificant."

Holding the cup between her palms, she replayed the events in her mind and got the words out in stilted bursts. James's head was bent over his desk while he copied them down. She wished it was Cruz taking her statement, but he worked out of the mounted police stables.

The station door opened, and the man himself ambled through it. His fleece-lined black canvas coat was open to reveal a plaid button-down shirt. The top buttons weren't fastened, revealing a startling white T-shirt underneath. He spoke to the receptionist, who must've pointed him in her direction. When he turned his head, his chocolate gaze widened. His leather boots pounded on the chipped tile floor. After a swift inventory of her person, he barked James Bell's name.

James's pen clinked onto the desk and rolled off. At the reprimand in Cruz's voice, the dark-haired man looked at Jade with fresh eyes and flushed. "Sorry, Ms. Harris. I didn't think." Palms on the desk, he pushed back his chair. "The first aid kit's in the break room—"

"I'll handle it. Come with me, Jade."

She set the cup down and stood, unsure where this rush of warm feelings was coming from. His hand settled on her lower back as he guided her down the hall, deeper into the one-story building. His closeness was reassuring, but the blended scents of leather and musky cologne clinging to his clothes and skin sent her pulse reeling again.

"How did you know I was here?"

"Bell contacted Mason."

"Why would he do that?"

"You're part of the mounted police family," he said matter-of-factly. "I took a smoked brisket over to Mason's for the party. Lily was having a fit about something, so I came without him." He pointed to the restroom door. "Go ahead and wash up. I'll bring the kit."

One look in the mirror explained Cruz's consternation. Dirt and dried blood streaked down her face. The cut on her forehead, above her right eyebrow, was about an inch wide. There was a scrape under her chin. She removed her coat and gingerly massaged her shoulder. Although it ached deep in the joint, she was able to move it without severe pain.

Cruz returned with the kit, his body filling the doorway. "Need anything else?"

"A hug and a promise this isn't going to happen again."

"I don't make promises I can't keep. Not anymore. As for the other—" Clearing his throat, he stepped forward and started to lift his arms.

She put her hand on his chest and, feeling his muscles flex, jerked it away. Heat entered her cheeks. "I didn't mean for you to actually..."

"Right." The tips of his ears turned red, and he ducked his head to knead the back of his neck. "I'll be in Bell's office."

He spun on his heel and walked away. Jade shut the door and made a face at her reflection. "Why did you say that, to him of all people?"

She quickly washed her face, neck and hands and placed a bandage on her cut. Without a comb, there wasn't much she could do about her bird's nest hair. Her coat was dirty, with bits of mulch attached, but it was in one piece. Good thing, since she couldn't afford to buy another. This one was her backup.

She rejoined the men, who stood up. "Did you locate the truck?"

Bell nodded. "Abandoned at the dump entrance. Our guys are searching the surrounding area as we speak, but we're at a disadvantage without a physical description."

"I'll take you to the co-op for your vehicle," Cruz said. "We'll inquire about security cameras while we're there. Maybe we'll get a glimpse of this guy."

The inside of Cruz's truck was immaculate. Of course, he didn't have a young child who liked to travel with toys and snacks. The newer model had heated seats, and she sank into the cushion with a sigh.

His radio was tuned to a country station, and a husky voice crooned about lost love. He punched the knob with his finger, blanketing the cab in silence. "Bell told me you jumped out of a moving vehicle."

"I didn't have a choice."

"I can think of a few seasoned officers who wouldn't have done what you did."

Pleasure spread through her at his admiring tone. "I'm all Henry has."

"What about his father?"

Axel's face flashed in her mind, and she grimaced. The drugs had inhibited her judgment. If she'd been thinking clearly, she wouldn't have stayed with him. "He's not part of our lives."

"Could he be behind these attacks?"

"What? No, he's—" She stopped short, having almost blurted the truth. Axel not only thought she was dead, he was also locked up.

Cruz arched a brow as he turned into the co-op lot.

"He doesn't want anything to do with us, trust me."

Axel didn't know about Henry. She'd wondered how he'd react to the knowledge he had a son. He wasn't capable of compassion or selflessness. However, he was the king of exploiting people. He'd use Henry as a pawn to get his own way, if given the chance.

A police cruiser was parked beside the main co-op entrance, the same one she'd entered earlier believing the danger had passed. How wrong she'd been. Cruz stayed close as they walked inside, his eyes alert and his mouth grim. She wished he'd put his hand on her back again. Returning here so soon after her ordeal was creating a serious attack of nerves.

Gary's greeting was different this time around.

He looked spooked. The officer left the payment counter and met them near the shopping carts.

"The clerk didn't see or hear anything. They do have security cameras, but not in the warehouse area where Ms. Harris was abducted. I'm going to review the footage to see if we can spot him elsewhere on the property."

Cruz thanked him. "Jade, take me through what happened."

"I came to buy greenery for the vet clinic, so I grabbed a cart and headed this way." She retraced her steps, and he kept pace beside her.

"Were there any other customers or employees?"

"Just Gary."

Her heart rate picked up as they entered the designated aisle. Her cart was there, with her purse, and the final wreath she'd chosen was angled between the bottom shelf and cement floor. Those terrible moments rose up to torment her. Cruz walked to the end of the aisle, turning in a slow circle, obviously considering her abductor's approach and retreat. Had he dragged her from the building? Carried her over his shoulder?

She shuddered. Who was this man? Why had he targeted her?

And when would he strike next?

★ ★ ★

Cruz's thoughts were jumping around like hot grease on a skillet. He didn't like that Jade's attacker was acting with escalating boldness. A crowded public event was one thing. The hustle and bustle and cloak of darkness had acted in his favor. A store in the middle of town, in broad daylight, carried more risk.

Unable to quell his concern, he flipped the steaks he was grilling, then removed them to a plate. Mason opened the door for him. He appreciated the shift from chilled, pine-scented air to the warmth of Mason and Tessa's farmhouse kitchen. The tangy, smoky smell emanating from the plate he carried mingled with the aroma of fresh-baked sourdough loaves and made his stomach rumble with anticipation. As Cruz slid the plate in between sweet potato casserole and macaroni and cheese, his ears picked up Jade's velvet-soft voice.

He shifted to search the adjacent living room and watched as she boosted first Lily and then Henry up to hang their homemade ornaments on the tree. Her movements were stiff, and she was favoring her right shoulder. She hadn't told him she'd injured it. His gut said she hadn't told him a lot of things.

After leaving the co-op, he'd followed her home so she could change clothes and comb the debris from her hair. Now her green sweater deepened the color of her eyes, and her hair hung in a shimmering pearl curtain to the middle of her back. The bandage above her eye spoiled the illusion of holiday cheer.

He turned back to Mason. "What do you know about Jade's past?"

He scratched his beard. "Not much. Why?"

Cruz peeled the aluminum foil off the brisket and got a waft of steam. "She was evasive about her family. Clammed up when I asked about Henry's father." He hadn't exactly given her a reason to confide in him, though, had he? He hadn't gone out of his way to be a friendly neighbor.

"I figured she'd gotten burned." Mason studied her, his dark eyes contemplative. "She's close to Leslie and her family. Hasn't spoken about her own. I've sensed deep rifts. She's a compassionate person. Sensitive. Trauma would affect her deeply and make it difficult to discuss."

Cruz began to slice the meat. He couldn't shake the feeling that Jade was being intentionally deceptive. He'd developed a radar for that sort of thing while working with the Texas narcotics unit. He'd gone undercover to ferret out the men who'd killed his big brother, Sal, and had rubbed elbows with liars, thieves and murderers.

"Is she capable of hiding her child from his own father? Could she be a noncustodial parent on the run?"

"No."

There was a whole lot of conviction in his sergeant's voice. The notion was far-fetched, but it wasn't impossible. A burst of laughter brought his attention to her once more, and he saw her shaking her head at something Henry was saying. Her disquiet had temporarily dissolved, and she looked as she usually did—as serene and inviting as his favorite childhood swimming hole.

That scene in the station flooded back, and his chest burned where she'd touched him. He'd almost held her. Women had flirted and cajoled and tried to rope him, and he'd had no problem rebuffing them. One request from Jade Harris had him reaching for her. She'd certainly looked in desperate need of a hug, but she'd merely been venting her frustration.

Tessa, who'd retreated upstairs a while ago, returned to the kitchen. She walked with less than her usual pep, her watery gaze riveted on

Mason. At his raised brows, she shook her head and walked into his waiting arms, resting her cheek in the curve of his neck. He whispered into her ear and stroked her back.

Concern kicked him in the ribs. When Tessa joined Jade and the kids, he glanced at Mason. "Is she okay?"

He shoved his hands in his pockets, his expression pensive. "She will be."

If Cruz thought the Lord would heed his pleas, he'd say a prayer for the couple. They'd walked through fire to get to where they were today, and he hated to think they were facing more trouble. Tessa and Jade embraced. Did Jade know what was going on?

Silver Williams and his wife, Lindsey, arrived with their arms full of gifts. Although they'd married in February, they still had the honeymoon glow. Had he and Denise ever looked at each other like that? Their marriage had imploded before their first anniversary, so he kind of doubted it. When Raven and her new husband, Aiden, arrived a short time later, Cruz experienced a familiar and unwelcome pinch of envy. Their unit dynamics had changed dramatically. He didn't belong to anyone. Hadn't in a long time. He'd convinced himself he liked it that way, because he'd tried commitment and failed. But now that his three partners were married, he was reevaluating his bachelor life.

Raven leaned past him to get a whiff of the brisket. "Smells delicious, Cruz. I'm starving."

Her joy had been on full display ever since Aiden had resurfaced, and Cruz couldn't be happier for her.

He handed her a small slice. She popped it in her mouth and made a humming noise. "Any progress on Jade's case?"

"Not yet." Last night, he'd been positive her attack was a random event. He'd even convinced her of it. If the stranger had been successful today, the blame would fall squarely on Cruz's shoulders.

A knowing tension entered Raven's face. "I thought the trouble was over for good."

Their unit had been bombarded with personal trials lately. Although Jade wasn't a mounted police officer, she was important to them. They wouldn't stand by and let her face danger on her own.

Tessa walked over and assessed the spread. "Grab a plate, everyone." She pointed to the plates and silverware on the counter. "We'll do this buffet-style."

The distressed white table situated between the island and patio doors was decorated with greenery and white candles. He'd helped Mason put in the extensions in order to have enough space.

The kids raced over, and Henry tugged on Cruz's shirt. "I want to sit next to you, Mr. Cruz."

He gently ruffled the boy's hair. "You got it, buddy."

Henry also wanted to sit beside Lily, which left Cruz in between the boy and his mother. Of course, Mason asked for everyone to hold hands during the prayer. It was tradition. Jade avoided his gaze as she slipped hers into his. A blush splashed across her cheeks. Cruz's focus swerved away from her and landed on Silver. He was watching them, his violet eyes speculative. His gray brows lifted a fraction, and a goading smile tipped his lips.

Cruz glared, hoping to forestall an inquisition later. The man had a way of pushing his buttons, much like a sibling would. Like Sal used to. The grief wasn't as breath-stealing as it used to be, but he felt his older brother's absence deep inside, like a wound that never healed.

Mason asked Aiden to do the honors, and the

architecture professor happily agreed. As they prayed, Cruz found himself distracted by Henry's wiggling on his left and Jade's utter stillness on his right. He liked the way her hand fit into his, her fingers wrapped around his in a trusting way.

Conversation erupted around him as everyone began to dig in. Jade leaned close.

"Would you prefer to switch places with me? Henry will need some help."

He'd eaten enough meals with Mason, Tessa and Lily to know how it worked. "I'll manage."

"You're sure?"

"This ain't my first rodeo," he said, winking.

Her lashes swept down as her cheeks pinked. He could've kicked himself. If Silver or the others caught the exchange, he'd be in for it. He stuffed a roll in his mouth and turned to Henry, expecting to have to cajole him into eating his vegetables. He had no idea what sort of meals Jade prepared. He'd never given her personal habits and preferences much thought before today. But Henry tucked into the array of choices on his plate. Score for Jade.

The conversation touched on the literacy tutoring center Raven had opened and Aiden's return to teaching college students. They avoided the topic at the forefront of their minds—the attacks on Jade—out of consideration of the children. It wasn't long before Henry and Lily lost interest in their meals and scampered back to their makeshift craft table close to the tree.

Cruz received a phone call and excused himself. When he returned, everyone looked at him with questions in their eyes. He zeroed in on Jade. "The suspect's in the wind, and the security footage didn't capture anything useful. I'm sorry."

Her gaze darted to Henry. Her son was always her first thought, wasn't he?

Lindsey tossed her napkin beside her plate. "So what are we going to do to keep Jade safe?"

Everyone looked to him for direction. Why did they assume he was taking point on this?

Chapter Five

Ironic how a group of police officers had come to her defense the moment she encountered trouble. In her former life, she'd been the suspect. The guilty one.

Beside her, Cruz shifted in his chair, and she realized they were waiting for him to impart a brilliant plan of action. Was it because they were neighbors? Were the others under the impression that he and Jade interacted on a regular basis?

"Our suspect pool is empty." He turned to her. It took effort to concentrate on the words coming out of his mouth instead of how handsome he looked in his red-and-white-plaid shirt. "Has anyone come to mind? I was originally thinking tourist, but this second attack changes things. A majority of victims know their attackers."

Mason sprinkled salt and pepper on a second helping of potatoes. "What about the vet clinic?

Is there a client whose behavior toward you has recently changed?"

She mentally ran down the short list of men in her life who made her uneasy. "Jeremiah Taylor. He's pestered me for months to go out with him. I was nice in the beginning, but then I had to get firm. His manner turned icy after that, bordering on rude."

"He's in the singles class at church, right?" Tessa said, tucking her curls behind her ear. "You mentioned him a time or two. I haven't crossed paths with him very often. We sit in different sections during the service, and afterward I'm off to pick up Lily. Mason, does he have history with the police?"

"Not that I'm aware of."

Beside her, Cruz's hand fisted on his thigh. Their knees brushed, and her stomach tightened. Having all his scrutiny and intensity focused on her at close range was unsettling.

"Has he threatened you, Jade?"

"Not in so many words." She twisted the paper napkin into a tight roll. "I don't want to cause trouble for him if he's innocent."

"We'll be subtle. If we find anything linking him to the attacks, then there will be trouble."

His gaze promised retribution for hurting her.

Why did he care about what happened to her all of a sudden? Why did her heart leap with anticipation every time he came close?

"You and Henry are welcome to stay with us until this guy is caught," Lindsey said, nudging her glasses farther up her nose.

"Or us," Raven chimed in, waving a hand between her and Aiden. "Although we don't have an indoor pool to offer." She winked at Silver.

"Nor do you have Lindsey's baking skills," he added, grinning.

"You're welcome here, too," Tessa said with feeling. "We have plenty of space."

Jade was overcome with gratitude, and it took her a few moments to speak. "Thank you. For now, I'd like to stay put and not upset Henry's routine."

Mason and Tessa were dealing with a serious issue, and the other two couples were practically newlyweds. She couldn't bring herself to accept their offers. Besides, this guy had tried twice and been foiled twice. He had to know he'd gotten law enforcement's attention. Surely, he'd abandon his plan in order to stay out of jail.

"Who's ready for dessert? I brought peppermint brownies and cranberry-orange shortbread cookies." Lindsey scooted back her chair and popped to her feet. She immediately put her hand to her forehead and swayed. Silver shot out of his chair and caught her as she slumped sideways.

"Lindsey!" Worry reflected in Silver's eyes. "Guys, she's unconscious."

Everyone abandoned their seats. Jade remained on the fringe of the group, heart pounding with dread. Cruz helped Silver ease her to the floor, taking a pillow from Mason to slide beneath her head. "Has this happened before?"

"She's been having blood sugar issues lately." Silver's jaw was tight as he knelt beside her and checked her pulse. "Sometimes feels lightheaded."

Aiden put his hand on Raven's shoulder. "Should I call an ambulance?"

Before anyone could answer, Lindsey's lashes fluttered behind her lenses. "No ambulance."

Silver had a tight grip on her hand. "How are you feeling, Linds?"

"Other than a slight headache, fine and dandy." She started to sit up, and Silver curved his arm around her shoulders.

"Take it easy."

She belatedly noticed everyone huddled around her. "I'm fine, I promise."

"We'll let the doctor have the final say on that. We're going to the walk-in clinic."

"But dessert—"

He kissed her lightly on the lips. "They'll save you some."

"I want one of each, Tessa. Don't let the guys eat all of your coconut cream pie, either."

Silver kept her tucked close to his side as they made their way outside.

After dessert, Tessa suggested they postpone the gift exchange until a later date, and everyone pitched in clearing the dishes and storing leftovers. By the time they were done, exhaustion settled heavily on Jade's shoulders. She'd need a good night's rest if she was going to tackle the patient load tomorrow with a clear head.

"I'm going home, Tess. Keep me updated."

Tessa's hazel eyes assessed her. "Are you sure you don't want to stay here tonight?"

"Positive."

"I'll come with you and check things out," Cruz said, washing and drying his hands.

Jade didn't argue, partly because she didn't have the energy and partly because she would feel safer knowing he'd cleared the house. Henry wasn't ready to leave, but his protests died down when he learned Cruz was coming, too. He clearly liked the officer, and she worried that he'd get ideas. He'd been asking why he didn't have a father like Lily and his other friend Kai, and she'd struggled to find a suitable answer that would satisfy him.

The sun was on its downward slide when they parked in her driveway. Cruz came to her truck window and got her keys. A few minutes later, he emerged from the house and gave her a thumbs-up. He waited on the porch for them. Henry hopped along the pavers and up the steps.

"Catch me, Mr. Cruz!"

He jumped, and Cruz caught him and swung him up into his arms with a laugh. "Aren't you tired yet, cowboy?"

He shook his head with fervor, wavy locks falling into his eyes. "Can we ride Gunsmoke?"

"Not tonight." His gaze landed on Jade. "Your mom has had a busy weekend, and she needs her rest."

A lump formed in Jade's throat. How wonderful it would be to have a partner who looked out for her best interests, who supported her on the hard days and made her laugh when she took life too seriously. A man who'd be a good role model for Henry and would love him as much as she did.

"Why does she need rest?"

"She has to work tomorrow, and so do I. You're on school break, so all you have to do tomorrow is play."

"Sometimes I stay at Lily's house and sometimes Kai's."

"Good deal. You get to play with different toys."

"Kai has a ball pit."

The pair looked comfortable, like a real father and son. Cruz didn't seem to mind Henry's natural exuberance.

Cruz smiled at Henry, and his features went from handsome to breath-stealing. His gaze shifted to her, temporarily including her in his good humor.

She felt a pang of sharp disappointment.

To love and cherish someone required honesty. As long as she was playacting at life, she didn't have her whole heart to give.

Cruz Castillo had been on Jade's mind when she'd fallen asleep and when she'd woken up. Probably because Henry wouldn't stop talking about him. Now she was in his workplace, ears straining to detect his deep, smooth voice, turning at every sound to see if he was nearby.

Thanks to her unusual weekend, she'd forgotten about the clinic's scheduled visit to the mounted police stables.

Would Cruz stick to his normal routine and steer clear of her? It would be best if he did. Mooning over a police officer was the definition of foolishness.

"Four down, two to go." One of Jade's bosses, Dr. Belinda Lisle, gestured to Lightning's stall. "I'll tackle this big guy."

Jade smiled, pleased Belinda had let her have Renegade. He was the largest of all their horses and, in her opinion, the most likely to grace a magazine cover. He could be mischievous and rambunctious but also sweet.

Inside his stall, she set her supplies down and greeted him. "There's my handsome guy. How have you been? Missed me?" She rubbed his nose, and he bobbed his head. "It's time for your deworming and shots. I promise I'll be quick."

"Told you he was your favorite."

Jade whipped her head around, her stomach jumping. "Cruz."

He entered the stall and stood next to her, his attention on his equine partner. She detected his pleasing cologne amid the myriad smells of horseflesh, hay and leather. He wore the same informal uniform as the other officers—a collared, long-sleeve navy shirt, featuring the Serenity Mounted Police emblem, tucked into black utility pants. Unlike the military-style boots the others favored, Cruz sported his cowboy boots.

He reached to stroke Renegade's neck, and his shoulder muscles bunched beneath the fabric. "Did you get any rest last night?"

She was distracted, studying his neat goatee and how it accentuated his cheekbones and square jaw. Would it be soft or prickly? He turned his head and caught her staring.

She averted her gaze. "I did, thank you."

He'd made her promise to call him if she felt scared or anxious. He'd also had her text him when she left the house and when she arrived at the clinic.

She cleared her throat and went to work, hoping he'd return to his. But he stayed and watched, muscular arms crossed over his chest, as she cleaned Renegade's neck with alcohol in preparation for the injection.

"And Henry?"

"He wasn't cranky when he woke up this morning, so I'm guessing he slept well. You should know that you're his favorite topic at the moment. Although I didn't have much information to impart."

His mouth eased into a smile. "Is that so? You can tell him I grew up on a horse and goat ranch near Bandera, Texas."

"Are your folks still there?"

"My parents and younger brother, Diego. He's taken over most of the day-to-day operations."

She heard pride and maybe a little longing in his voice. "Ranching wasn't your calling?"

"I used to think I'd live and die on that ranch. My priorities shifted, and I decided law enforcement was it for me."

She removed the cap and checked the needle. Inserting it, she pulled back to check for blood. Seeing none, she injected the solution and then massaged the muscles.

"Did you work with a mounted police unit in Texas?"

"Narcotics. I did multiple undercover stints."

Of course he had. Jade didn't want to hear about it. Memories of those days made her cringe inside. Even though she knew Jesus had forgiven her for her sins, she couldn't help feeling sad about the things she'd done.

After dosing Renegade with the dewormer paste, she didn't linger. Cruz followed her into the wide aisle. Belinda was already walking toward the offices. "I'm going to speak to Mason. Meet you at the truck."

When the veterinarian was no longer within hearing range, Cruz said, "Does she know about the attacks?"

"Seems everyone knows." One of the downsides to living in a small town, she'd learned.

"She's obviously okay with you working."

"Why wouldn't she be?"

"Officers Bell and Weiland spoke with Jeremiah Taylor this morning. He adamantly denies involvement. While he doesn't have anyone to substantiate his whereabouts on Saturday night, he has a rock-solid alibi for Sunday afternoon. Multiple people have verified he wasn't at the co-op."

Jade's hopes that this would be solved quickly evaporated. "What now?"

He tugged on his earlobe. "You think of anyone else, you let us know. Until then, don't let your guard down."

"You think he'll come after me again?"

"I can't rule it out."

"Cruz, I'm your neighbor. Your horse's favorite vet tech. Level with me."

His chest expanded on a sigh. "He's taken

big risks trying to get to you. To answer your question, I suspect he won't be swayed from his goals."

Despite the balmy warmth of the stables, cold swept through Jade. Her phone vibrated. "It's Elaine. Henry's at her house today. I have to take it."

He nodded and started to step away.

"Hey, Elaine. What's up?"

"A man was here, at the house. O-outside. Kai and Henry were playing in the tree fort, and I noticed him in the field." Her voice was high and wobbly.

Jade's heart slammed against her ribs. "The boys. Where are they?"

Cruz pivoted back, brows lowered.

"In the kitchen. They're safe. I may have over-reacted, but after what happened to you…" She trailed off, and Jade could almost see her friend twisting her auburn hair into knots.

"You did the right thing, Elaine. Is he still there?"

"I don't know."

"I'm coming over." She ended the call.

"What is it?"

"There was a man in the vacant field behind her house. He was watching the boys." She walked as fast as her wobbly legs would take her. He fell into step beside her. "I have to see Henry. Make sure he's okay."

She found Belinda in Mason's office and explained the situation.

"Let's go back to the clinic so you can get your truck," Jade's boss said.

She clenched her teeth. The clinic was in the opposite direction of Elaine's. Returning there would delay her by at least thirty minutes.

Mason pushed out of his chair and opened his mouth.

Cruz spoke first. "The paperwork on my desk can wait a while. I'll take her."

Jade wasn't sure how she refrained from hugging him.

Jade's nervous energy radiated in waves through the cab. Her hands were in constant motion, twisting, furling, splaying, palms rubbing over her hot-pink scrub pants. He extended his arm across the bench seat and rested his hand on her shoulder, hoping to impart comfort. The only acknowledgment of his gesture was a hard swallow. She kept her eyes on the leafless trees, brownish-green grass and brittle blue sky, probably calculating the remaining distance based on familiar landmarks.

They didn't know who this stranger was or why he was on Elaine's property. But Cruz wasn't discounting anything.

He wanted to see for himself that Henry was okay. Besides, he was the only one with a free morning. Mason had a lunch date with Tessa— and they clearly needed uninterrupted time together. Silver had accompanied Lindsey to the lab for bloodwork. Raven was trying to hire more tutors for the literacy center.

It occurred to him that no one depended on him outside this job—besides Gunsmoke and Old Bob.

He gave her shoulder a squeeze. "Hey."

She seemed to remember she wasn't alone. Pushing her hair behind her ear, she looked at him. The stark fear in her eyes was like a kick in the stomach. He didn't have to be a father to imagine the thoughts and emotions she was dealing with. Twice in the span of two days, she'd been violently attacked, and now she suspected this man had switched his sights to her only child.

He glanced between her and the road. "Henry is sitting at Elaine's kitchen table, probably eating Popsicles or cookies or something else he wouldn't normally be eating for a midmorning snack. He's fine."

She nodded slowly, trying to hold tightly to his reassurance. "Elaine does keep a secret stash for when the boys get too rambunctious."

"How did you and Elaine become friends?" He had to distract her from her musings.

"Story hour."

"I don't know what that is."

"The library has story hour for the kids every Saturday. A librarian reads them a book. Sometimes it's followed by a craft. Kai and Henry got on well together, and Elaine and I began chatting. We scheduled a playdate, and it became a regular thing." She leaned forward, the seat belt digging into her shoulder. "There's her road."

Cruz made the turn and shifted his focus to their surroundings. Elaine and her husband, Franklin, lived on a quiet lane. The homes sat on several-acre plots. Some were wooded, and some were gently rolling fields dotted with cattle. They were closer to the foot of the mountains here, and the high, rounded ridges—brown and dark this time of year—hemmed them in. Because it was a Monday morning, many of the homeowners were at work. There was little activity that he could see.

The Latimer home was the fifth one down, and Jade unbuckled as he reached the drive. She bailed before he could switch off the engine. He hurried to catch up with her. The front door of the stately brick home opened, and Elaine ushered them inside.

"Did you see anyone?" Her complexion wan, she rolled the hem of her shirt and released it. The material was wrinkled from what he guessed was constant bunching. "I've been watching from the windows and haven't seen him again."

"There wasn't anyone on the road," Jade told her, craning her neck toward the kitchen.

Elaine gestured behind her. "They're working on a puzzle."

They progressed across the tile floor through the living room and around a corner to the kitchen, which spanned the rear wall. The boys were side by side on the table's bench seat, heads together as they considered the puzzle pieces. Empty pudding cups had been pushed to the side.

When Henry spied Jade, his face lit up. "Mommy!"

He scrambled off the bench and threw his

arms around her waist. Jade bent over and returned the hug. Her hair swung forward like an ivory silk curtain, enveloping them in their own safe world. Cruz had a feeling she would've preferred to hold her son longer, but Henry squirmed out of her hold. Her eyes were suspiciously bright when she straightened.

"Look at our puzzle, Mr. Cruz."

Cruz moved behind Kai and Henry and inspected their work. "Good job, boys."

"Franklin's at a dentist appointment this morning," Elaine informed Cruz. "I tried to reach him, but his phone's turned off. He listed a bicycle for sale, and I thought maybe he'd arranged for someone to come out and look at it. But most people would come to the door, not just wander around the property. Plus, the guy was fixated on the boys. It occurred to me that it could be the same man who…" Her voice trailed off, obviously not wanting to continue out of consideration for the children.

"What did he look like?" Jade asked, smoothing her hands over her bright scrub shirt. Now that she'd seen Henry for herself, she seemed more in command of her emotions.

"Tall. Muscular. He had a baseball hat on, so I couldn't make out his features or hair color."

"What about clothing?" Cruz asked.

"Um, jeans, I think. Tan shirt with a picture on the front."

"Are you in contact with your closest neighbors?"

"I have their numbers."

"Call them."

While she did that, Jade paced between the windows. He was about to tell her to move away when Elaine spoke.

"The Griggses aren't home. Betsy Campbell is, though, and she hasn't noticed anyone lurking around."

"I'm going to take a look around outside."

Elaine explained the layout of the property. He walked the length and breadth of it, searching for footprints or other clues left behind. The warehouse garage was set back from the house, some distance away from the in-ground pool. The garage doors were open—an invitation for mischief in Cruz's mind.

There was a red fishing boat on a trailer in the first bay and a Chevy Silverado in the second. The third bay was empty. Silver utility shelves and red tool cabinets lined the side walls. There was valuable equipment sitting around, and none of it looked disturbed. He spied a door and wondered if it led to a storage closet or outside.

He turned the knob, nudged it open with his boot and caught sight of paint cans and cardboard boxes. The hairs on the back of his neck stood to attention, and he tensed.

Something heavy connected with his skull, and excruciating pain ripped a moan from his throat. He stumbled into the room, his knees refusing to support him, and slammed into the concrete. His breath wheezed from his lungs. He tried to reach his gun and earned another blow to the middle of his back before he could. Shadows danced at the edge of his vision.

Something clattered to the floor, followed by retreating footsteps. The perp was getting away—and he could be heading straight for Jade and Henry.

Chapter Six

Out of habit, Cruz reached for his radio to call for backup. But he wasn't in his official uniform. It took immense effort to get to his feet. As soon as the swirling sensation passed, he gave chase, pulling his phone from his pocket and contacting dispatch. His aching skull screamed in protest, and his stomach threatened mutiny. Gritting his teeth, he flew by the boat, only to stumble to a stop before sprinting into the open.

Get a grip on yourself, man. Unholstering his weapon, he checked his sight lines while maintaining cover and spotted the suspect fleeing toward the neighbor's woods. Not going for Jade, then. Good.

His pace wasn't fast or efficient. The perp put increasing distance between them and ducked into the woods. Moments later, Cruz heard an engine rev. Sounded like an off-road motorcycle. He slowed as he entered the woods. He wasn't going to catch up with him, but at least he could give patrol a description.

There was a flash of blue and white between the trees, and then nothing.

A frustrated growl rumbled through his chest. Returning his weapon to its holster, he jogged back the way he'd come. The women must've been watching from the windows, because Jade was waiting by the door.

"You should take the boys upstairs," he grunted, adrenaline wearing off and pain demanding to make its presence known.

Her green eyes went wide as, chest heaving, he leaned against the wall. He was trying not to pass out.

"Elaine?" Jade spoke her friend's name without looking at her.

The other woman hustled over to the table. "Boys, let's go play LEGOs."

"What about our puzzle?" Kai asked.

Cruz closed his eyes and focused on drawing air in and letting it out. When Jade took his hand, he reopened them and found they were alone.

"Sit down before you fall over." He allowed her to lead him to a chair at the table and gently push him into it. "Where are you hurt?"

"Head. Back."

She moved behind him. Leaning close, she lightly parted his hair, her fingers gentle. "You're bleeding, and a knot is already forming." Her hands rested on his shoulders, and he was tempted to lean against her. "What did he hit you with?"

"A metal bar of some sort. We'll test it for fingerprints."

"I'm concerned about a possible concussion." As she listed off the symptoms, she bent her head forward and her hair tickled his ear. "I'm going to lift your shirt."

He tensed as her fingers trailed across his back, just below the line of pain. He couldn't remember the last time he'd been treated with such tenderness, and uncomfortable emotion filled him. Instead of analyzing it, he homed in on the anger he felt toward the man who was targeting an innocent woman and child.

"His hair was black."

He stood up, needing distance between them. His head swam for a moment.

"What?" She looked at him quizzically.

"Our guy. His hat was knocked sideways by a branch, and I saw his hair. It's black. Cut short.

There's a tattoo on his right forearm, but I was too far away to make out the details."

His phone pressed to his ear, he updated dispatch and strode to the front porch to await the patrol units. He breathed deeply of the brisk air, hoping it would clear his head.

Jade followed him. "I'll go with you to the hospital if you'd like."

"Hospital?"

She held his gaze. "Your injuries need to be checked out."

Mason would come to the same conclusion. He took the welfare of his officers seriously. "Later. Right now, I have a dangerous criminal to catch."

Jade dropped her keys on the kitchen counter, opened the overhead cabinet door and pointed to her selection of herbal teas. "Want some?"

Raven smiled and lifted her monogrammed travel mug. "I've got coffee."

Henry's high-pitched singing carried from his bedroom, and the officer's smile widened. Raven and Mason had converged on Elaine's not long after the patrol officers arrived. Cruz had jumped into the front seat of Officer Bell's cruiser, and they'd taken off...but not before he'd rolled down his window and basically ordered Raven to accompany Jade home.

Jade selected her tea. "Will you make sure Cruz sees a doctor?"

Raven leaned against the counter and ran her hand along her braid. Her wedding rings winked in the afternoon sunlight streaming through the sink window. "Cruz has a stubborn streak, but Mason outranks him." She smirked. "He'll go."

Jade was surprised by the depth of her concern. Cruz had been a constant factor on the fringes of her life since she'd rented this house in Serenity several years ago. They may not have had much interaction, but she'd known he was next door in case of an emergency. He was a visible presence around town, strong and tall in Renegade's saddle, ready to protect Serenity's citizens. She'd seen him in action. Once, he'd chased a robbery suspect through the square and, leaping from the saddle, tackled the man to the ground. In a matter of seconds, Cruz had had the man in handcuffs.

She'd begun to think of him as invincible. When he'd come inside at Elaine's, she'd been alarmed by his pallor and the weakness he'd allowed her to see.

Raven must've guessed the direction of her

thoughts, because she said, "Don't worry. It would take a lot to derail that tough-as-nails cowboy."

She filled the kettle with water. "Do you think they'll find this man?"

"Hard to say. There are lots of secluded coves, trails and wooded areas for him to hide in. Even an outsider would find it easy to slip away."

Jade chose a mug and got out the honey while the water heated. She would reach out to Alan Prescott again. This time, she'd make sure to relay the details. When she'd received Elaine's phone call that morning, she'd had the fleeting, terrifying thought that Axel might've escaped prison. But Axel had auburn hair, not black, and he'd avoided tattoos, saying they made it too easy for cops to identify him. Not to mention Prescott would've alerted her to any trouble. If Axel had somehow gotten out, the US Marshals would've swooped in and whisked her and Henry away.

The thought was incomprehensible. She'd put down roots here. She couldn't bear to imagine leaving her friends, her church, her job.

Raven consulted her watch. "I've got to get back to the stables."

Jade walked with her through the living

room. Raven poked her head into Henry's room and told him goodbye. Henry stopped playing with his trains long enough to wave and smile shyly at the officer.

"You've done a wonderful job with him," the other woman told Jade.

Raven didn't stick around for her response, so she missed the tears gathering in Jade's eyes. *Thank You, Lord, for bringing me out of the pit I dug myself into. Thank You for Your salvation and that Your mercies are new every morning. Thank You for letting me be Henry's mom.*

She left another message for Prescott and attacked the never-ending laundry pile. Later that evening, she was preparing a salad and grilled chicken when her phone rang. Her heart performed a backflip when she saw Cruz's name on the screen.

"I'm afraid I don't have the news you wanted," he began without preamble. "One of our guys spotted the dirt bike leaving Serenity and heading toward Pigeon Forge. We're coordinating with their law enforcement agencies. The metal bar he used will be examined for trace evidence."

Disappointment leaked into her. "How are you feeling?"

"You'll be happy to know I went to the clinic. I've got a mild concussion, but I'm cleared to work."

Relieved, she considered inviting him for supper but dismissed the idea. She liked him and wanted to get to know him. But given all she was hiding, she had to keep her distance.

She heard talking in the background.

"I have to go, Jade. I'll be home in an hour or so. If you see anything suspicious or just feel like something's off, call me."

He hung up, and she stared off into space. Why did it seem natural for him to call her? And why did she have to stow her phone in the drawer to keep from texting him a supper invitation? It wasn't fair that the first man to capture her interest was a cop. She'd been on a total of maybe five dates in as many years. The prospect of being vulnerable made her twitchy. What if she chose the wrong man again? This time, she wouldn't be the only one to suffer.

After she and Henry finished eating, she stored the leftovers and settled him on the couch to watch *Frosty the Snowman*. She went to start another load of laundry and realized she was out of detergent. This house was charming but seriously lacking in storage. Her extra supplies had to be stored in the shed.

"I've got to get something from the shed, Henry. I'll be right back."

Nodding, he pulled his feet onto the cushion and propped his chin on his knees.

Out on the deck, she searched the yard and the pastures beyond the fence. Cruz's horses grazed nearby. Birds chirped and looped between the pine and the oak. From the top step, she could see a slice of Cruz's barn. His house was on the far side of that, however, so she couldn't know for sure if he was home or not.

Jade hurried across the yard. She entered the darkened shed and tripped over something just inside, catching herself on a stack of plastic bins. A foul smell unlike any she'd ever encountered wound around her, making her gag. Had a sick animal crawled in here and died? She turned to see what she'd tripped over, hoping a shovel or rake had fallen across the threshold. Hoping it wasn't a poor stray cat or dog.

Her blood turned to sludge. Was that a man's shoe?

Moving as if in slow motion, she took two steps closer and touched the foot with the tip of her tennis shoe.

It was real, all right. And unmoving.

Sweat rolling between her shoulder blades, she crouched and lifted the blue tarp. Then she screamed.

Chapter Seven

Cruz never made it into the barn. He dropped the sack of carrots in the dirt and sprinted for Jade's the minute she called him.

"Dead body," she'd said, her panic practically reaching through the speaker to claw at his throat. "In my shed."

"Are you safe?"

"I—I think so. Henry's in the house."

He passed a giant magnolia tree in the field between his barn and her house. "Almost there," he told her now. "Stay on the line."

"Okay."

He heard her talking to Henry, urging him to stay inside. He pushed between two Douglas firs and emerged in her well-tended yard. The evergreens flanking the backyard created a dark green vista, and her pink scrubs stood out like a brilliant summer bloom. She leaned against the shed, one arm hugging her middle and the other hand flat against her mouth. Her eyes were large in her pale face, and they fastened onto him with relief and a hefty helping of trust.

She lifted her fingers a fraction. "Behind the door. Under the tarp."

Cruz entered, careful to disturb as little as possible in this crime scene. The stench was enough to make him rethink that day-old burrito he'd scarfed down a few minutes ago. He eyed the victim's leather shoe. Good quality, practically new. Lifting the tarp, he unleashed another wave of powerful, eye-watering odor. Cruz noted crucial details—plain clothing, wedding ring, expensive watch. Male, short brown hair. Dried blood and such heavy bruising a facial ID would be impossible. No obvious method of death.

After summoning assistance from dispatch, he stepped outside. Jade sprang away from the wall as if it seared her.

"Who is he? What if Henry had discovered him?" She gasped. "Were we home when it happened?"

Cruz settled his hands on her shoulders and ducked his head to be closer to her eye level. "Breathe, Jade. Close your eyes and breathe."

She instantly obeyed. Then her eyes popped

open, and she grimaced. "All I can see is his face. His features are beyond recognition."

Her body was trembling. Shucking off his jacket, he draped it over her shoulders and turned her toward a black metal bench near the base of one of the live oaks. "Let's go sit for a minute."

Guiding her over, he waited until she'd gotten settled before crouching in front of her, one knee in the crisp grass. She anticipated his questions, because she launched into a play-by-play of her evening, even mentioning almost inviting him over for supper. Had she meant to reveal that detail? The admission startled and intrigued him to the point he had to ask her to repeat a few things.

Corralling his unruly thoughts, he studied her. Her pulse flittered in her neck. Her gestures were erratic, her hands not quite steady. Her alarm was genuine. Anyone would be unnerved by a deceased person on their property. But why did he have a feeling she knew more than she was letting on? Was she somehow involved?

He would be remiss in his duty if he didn't consider the last three days' events from all angles. While he trusted Mason and Tessa's judgment, what did any of them really know about

Jade? It would be easy to believe she was as pure as the driven snow, with her guileless green eyes and angelic features, framed by that glorious white-blond hair.

She'd wanted him to sit at her table and share a homemade meal with her and her son.

If she *had* invited him, what would've been his response?

Cruz stood. "I'm going to look around."

Her brow creased, tugging at the small bandage above her right eye. Her busted lower lip looked sore and tender. There were scratches and bruises on her neck. He reined in his suspicions. He would do well to focus on the villain who'd targeted her and whether or not this suspicious death was connected.

He approached the shed, surveying what he could see from a distance. If there were drag marks or footprints, he didn't want to disturb them. The patrol unit arrived with Detective York, who immediately set up a perimeter and peppered Jade with questions. Then he inspected the scene without touching the body. They had to wait for the medical examiner.

Standing beside Jade, Cruz saw her look toward the house. Henry was plastered against the glass door leading to the deck. The height and

angle prevented him from seeing the shed—
Cruz had checked.

Jade clutched the lapels of his jacket close to
her throat. "I need to be with Henry."

"Gather your things," he found himself saying. "You two are staying with me tonight."

Her hands dropped to her side. "I don't know
if that's such a good idea."

He arched a brow. "Will Henry sleep peace-
fully in there after seeing uniforms crawling
over his yard? Will you?"

Her teeth came out to burrow in her lip, and
she winced. "I'll get our things."

The headache he'd earned that morning had
lessened throughout the day. It returned with
greater intensity as he waited in the darkening
yard. He could've contacted Mason or suggested
she sleep at Elaine's. Probably should've. But she
looked ready to drop from exhaustion—more
mental than physical—and Henry's bedtime was
fast approaching. Cruz had a perfectly adequate
spare bedroom next door. There was no reason
why he shouldn't offer them protection and a
sense of security.

Detective York had told her not to leave town.
His inscrutable look had made her uneasy. Did

he suspect she'd had something to do with that man's death?

"I'm hungry, Mommy." Henry bounced on the bed in Cruz's guest room. His normal routine had been obliterated, and he was in a different house. He wasn't showing any signs of winding down for the night.

Jade pinched the bridge of her nose. She'd forgotten to pack a snack.

"I've got apples," Cruz said from the doorway.

She jerked, her heart thudding. "I didn't hear you come in."

He hadn't given them a tour. He'd shown them directly into this room, pointed out the bathroom and then hurried out to the barn.

He leaned against the doorjamb, hands in his pants pockets. Other than a streak of dirt across the chest of his official collared shirt, he looked pristine. His posture was relaxed. She sensed he was far from it. His eyes were watchful. Wary. Did he suspect her of foul play? What was his true motive for offering his home as refuge?

"Do you have peanut butter?" Henry hopped off the bed, sock-covered feet hitting the carpet with a thump.

Cruz was a bachelor accustomed to solitude at

the end of his workday. How would he handle having an energetic child around?

He cocked his head to the side. "No, but I'm pretty sure I have peanut butter crackers. Will that do?"

Henry nodded and skipped past Cruz into the hallway.

Jade placed his pajamas on the bedside table. "He's usually not this energetic at night. I'm sorry if we're keeping you from something. Or someone."

One brow arched, and she blushed. She wasn't fishing for information. If Cruz Castillo had finally deigned to date a local woman, every Serenity resident would hear about it.

"I haven't had an overnight guest since Diego visited last year, so my skills are rusty. You'll have to speak up if you need something."

She recalled seeing the younger man around town. The Castillo men had similar golden-brown complexions and coal-black hair, only Cruz was taller and stockier.

"That won't be a problem for Henry. Most kids his age announce their wants and needs to anyone who will listen."

They went into the kitchen, where Henry was already taking inventory of Cruz's cabinet contents. Jade intervened, explaining why that wasn't considered good manners. Cruz smiled, seemingly unbothered by the intrusion.

"I like this color," she said, skimming the basil-green bottom cabinets. A stained wooden countertop ran the length of two walls and was offset by white subway tiles. Matching wood shelves stood in for the upper cabinets. There was a generous island in the middle.

"The previous owner redid it before putting the house up for sale. I use the smoker and grill more than the appliances in here. As long as the kitchen functions, I'm happy."

He'd brought them in via the back door, and she'd glimpsed his outdoor-cooking setup on the deck.

"You use those year-round?"

"Pretty much."

He extracted a box of prepackaged crackers and set it on the island. Then he tapped a glass bowl piled high with apples and told Henry to pick one. Henry made his choice, and Cruz helped him wash it beneath the spray of water. Then he sliced it into fat quarters and arranged it on a plate.

His dark eyes flashed up, blunt fingers resting on the bowl. "Want one, Jade?"

She shook her head, unable to consider eating anything. "Just water."

He retrieved a glass and inclined his head toward the fridge dispenser. "Make yourself at home."

Henry asked to watch television. Because it would be futile to put him to bed yet, she got him settled on the couch while Cruz found children's programming. He returned to the kitchen, and she followed him.

"How long before we hear anything on the dead man?"

"Hard to say. And we can't build a list of suspects until we know the victim's identity." He tossed the apple core into the garbage and washed the knife. "Have you spoken to your landlord?"

"I have." Kevin had been understandably shocked. "He's probably over there now."

He dried off his hands and returned the knife to the butcher block. "He didn't have any meaningful information?"

"He's in the dark, like me."

His phone rang, and he glanced down at the screen. "That's Detective York now."

His responses were one syllable, so she didn't glean much from his side of the conversation. A strange expression gripped his features. When he ended the call, he stared at the screen for long moments, as if he was reluctant to look at her.

"They found a badge."

"An employee badge?"

His gaze finally lifted. His brown eyes could be at times warm and inviting. Other times, they were friendly but distant, warning her to keep her distance. Now, they were hot with confusion.

He shook his head. "US marshal."

Numbness entombed her. Could it be? No. *Please, Lord, no.*

But Prescott hadn't returned her messages. Her thoughts whirled, round and round, slamming against her skull.

She was tempted to slump to the floor until the weakness bled out of her body. The ramifications were too huge, too frightening to process.

"Jade?"

Most people wouldn't connect the seemingly random attacks with the death of a US marshal. Cruz was a seasoned officer with years of undercover work under his belt. His mind would go where others' wouldn't.

Somehow, she pushed all the emotions deep

inside, imprisoning them. "That's terrible," she said, her voice sounding almost normal. "Do they know his name?"

"Not yet. His identification and credentials are missing." He stared hard at her, dissecting her reaction. "But they will."

She pressed her hand against her stomach, praying she didn't throw up. "I, uh, am going to get Henry ready for bed. See you in the morning."

She pivoted on her heel, expecting him to forestall her. She didn't breathe freely until she and Henry were closed inside the guest bedroom.

If the downed marshal was Prescott, it could mean only one thing—her sweet life in Serenity had come to an end.

Chapter Eight

Restorative sleep was all but impossible. Jade got snatches of rest, but mostly she stared at the gleaming drapes on the windows. Her chest felt heavy, and she couldn't get the deceased marshal out of her mind. The wedding ring, specifically. He had a wife somewhere who was wondering why he hadn't come home. Did he have children?

Lord, did that man give his life trying to warn me?

Until his identity was confirmed, she couldn't know for sure.

Why else would he be here? Face it, Jade. Axel is at the root of this nightmare.

A great trembling started deep inside her and pulsed through her limbs. Had Axel pulled her into those woods? Had he followed her into the co-op, strangled her and tossed her into that dump truck?

The unanswered questions prevented her from

sleeping. The moon's glow behind the sheer curtains gradually gave way to the pink blush of dawn. Unable to take the inactivity a minute longer, she eased out of bed and tucked the cover around Henry. She changed into the only outfit she'd packed—black pants, a white blouse printed with Dalmatians and a black sweater—and pulled a brush through her hair until her scalp tingled. She tiptoed along the hall, glad it was a split-bedroom floor plan. A confrontation with Cruz was inevitable. He'd want answers... and she had to figure out what those would be. Continue the charade or confess everything?

Jade punched in the alarm code he'd given her and, praying he was a heavy sleeper, stole outside. The scene was pretty enough to grace a calendar. Fog hugged the pastures. The red barn formed a dramatic backdrop for the trees' gnarled branches. Nearby ducks honked a morning serenade.

The barn blocked the view of her house. According to Cruz, the police would be there until every scrap of evidence had been collected... even if it took all night. She couldn't sleep and didn't want to wake Cruz. Why not check to see if a member of the crime scene unit was still there? Or a patrol officer? They might have valuable information.

She descended the stairs and strolled through the yard. When she reached the back side of the barn near the paddock, she noticed the free-standing lights had been removed and the yellow caution tape was intact. There weren't any voices or activity. Movement in her peripheral vision startled her. But it was only Gunsmoke coming to greet her.

She walked over to the slatted fence and ran her hand along the horse's face. "Good morning." There was a slight scar where she'd patched up a nasty cut he'd sustained last year.

He nudged her shoulder. "I suppose you think I'm out here to feed you, huh?" Spying Old Bob lumbering toward them, she gestured to the barn. "Meet me inside, boys."

Cruz had gone above and beyond for her. Crossing some of the chores off his list was the least she could do. Especially since he would probably refuse to speak to her once he learned the truth, much less provide protection.

Having treated both horses before, she was familiar with his tack and feed room setup. The horses ambled into their respective stalls, which had been left open to the pastures overnight.

She measured out the sweet feed and dispensed it into their buckets.

Turning toward Gunsmoke's exit, she halted midstep. The bucket she held crashed to the dirt.

"Hello, Jenny."

His voice was raspier than she remembered. He was also larger than she remembered.

Axel had bulked up in prison. His sweatshirt stretched over his rough-hewn upper body, barely able to contain the overblown biceps and ropy neck muscles. He wouldn't need a weapon to subdue her.

"Like what you see?" His lips curled into a sneer, and his blue eyes were surly. His auburn hair had been dyed black, and it was shaved close to his head.

She darted toward the pasture opening. He blocked her, his meaty hand snagging her throat and shoving her up against the enclosure partition. His mouth crushed hers, and she whimpered. He smelled like alcohol, stale cigars and sweat.

Desperate to escape, she kneed his inner thigh. Axel growled and ripped his mouth from hers, glaring down at her. She braced herself for a blow that didn't come.

"Still feisty, I see." He suddenly laughed,

tweaking her collar. "The clothing has changed, but inside you're the same street-savvy fireball."

"How did you find me?" Her heart quivered like a frightened rabbit.

"Your photograph was on the news." When she didn't respond, his brows inched up. "The kid who saved his little sister from a fire? The story is popular online. One of my guys saw it and got word to me."

The memory clicked into place. The story had been big news in Serenity. Several news outlets had come to town and featured the boy. She hadn't known she'd been caught on camera.

"How did you get out?"

His ire returned full force, and the pressure on her neck increased. "Took time and planning. A few bribes, too. While you were living it up here in Serenity, I was locked away in that cement box." His gaze blazed over her face. "I daydreamed about this reunion, you know. I thought of all the ways I'd end you. But watching you this week has changed my mind."

"You've been here a *week*?"

"I've learned patience, Jenny. I've also learned to be flexible. I don't believe I'll kill you. At least, not at first."

Her throat was so dry she couldn't speak.

"You've created a prim and proper life for yourself and your son. We both know it's a sham. I'm going to enjoy stripping it away. Everything you think you gained by turning on me will be gone with one slide of the needle." He snapped his fingers near her ear, and she flinched.

Then his words registered. She shook her head from side to side. Denial was a sour taste in her mouth.

With his free hand, he traced her inner elbow to her wrist. "I'm going to remind you how much you used to love getting high."

"No."

His grin was pure evil. "Oh yes, lovely Jenny. I'm going to strip away the sweet, pure veneer and return you to your true self. A couple of days strung out on my supply, and you'll forget this place exists. You'll be dependent on me again. I'll be the center of your world, just like old times." He slid a strand of her hair between his fingers. "Who knows? Maybe I'll decide to keep you around for a while."

Jade's knees buckled, and she would've sunk to the ground if he wasn't imprisoning her.

Axel obviously hadn't guessed Henry was his

child, and she would do anything to keep it that way. Even if it meant leaving Serenity without her son.

Cruz braced a hand on the kitchen sink and stared out the window. He'd heard Jade leave the house and, quickly dressing, had tracked her petite form across the yard.

He decided coffee was necessary to fuel the coming confrontation. His gut churned. She'd duped him. Not only him, but the rest of the team.

The instant York told him their victim was a US marshal, his mind had made the leap to witness protection. Her evasiveness about her past. Her "break" with her family. The utter lack of information about Henry's father. Everything fit.

If he was right, it could mean she was a family member of a person in WITSEC, a witness to a crime or a criminal who turned on a bigger criminal.

Judging by her reaction last night, he was going with criminal. The fear that flashed in her expressive eyes had been mixed with the dread of discovery.

Slamming the mug into the sink, he shook

off the hot liquid that splashed on his hand. He was almost to the door when he remembered the sleeping boy. Had his fit of pique awakened him?

Cruz walked lightly around the table and down the hall. He peeked inside the guest room, his chest squeezing at the sight of Henry's face under the halo of white-blond hair. Criminal acts almost always exacted a price from the innocent. What had Jade done to warrant government protection?

He snagged his coat from the hook by the door and put it on, then shoved his feet into his boots. As he approached the barn, a spontaneous prayer formed in his mind. *Help me keep my temper in check, Lord.*

His stride slowed. He'd had a strong relationship with God as a teenager, buoyed by his parents' faith and a close-knit church youth group. Sal's death had made him question everything, including God's goodness. Even though his faith had wavered, there were times he longed for a renewed intimacy with the Lord, when he knew he couldn't make it on his own strength. This was one of those times.

As he entered, he heard a man's voice. Jade's response communicated her terror. His hackles rose. He hadn't brought his weapon or his phone.

A stranger emerged from Gunsmoke's stall before he had a chance to formulate a plan. Big guy. He outweighed Cruz by at least fifty pounds. His hair was obviously dyed, because it looked unnatural against his pale, freckled skin. His blue eyes locked onto Cruz, and his brows slammed down. He yanked Jade against him and held a long, deadly blade to the underside of her chin.

"Axel, don't." With both hands, she gripped his thick wrist.

This man wasn't a stranger to her. Had she tossed his name to Cruz on purpose?

"I'm unarmed." Cruz lifted his hands in a placating gesture. "Let's make a deal. Leave her, and I'll wait an hour before alerting the police. Plenty of time to get out of town."

"No deal." His upper lip curled, and he dragged her toward the opposite exit. "Jenny and I have unfinished business."

Cruz ground his teeth together. Her real name was Jenny. Confirmation she was living and working in his town under an assumed name. But at that moment, he didn't care what her story was. He was afraid for her. Axel's eyes were soulless.

He slowly advanced. "I can't let you take her."

"You don't have a choice, Officer."

Jade cried out, and blood dripped from her neck.

Cruz's chest rumbled with an utterance that didn't sound human. His fingers furled and unfurled, and he mentally cataloged the items in his tack room in search of a makeshift weapon. He kept his gaze fixed on Jade, silently communicating he wasn't going to abandon her.

Tears streamed down her cheeks. "Let me go," she whispered.

The words weren't directed at her captor. They were meant for him.

He rejected them outright, giving a small shake of his head.

"She gets another slice with each step you take," Axel warned, continuing his retreat.

Jade's eyes were pools of misery. She pressed her lips into a thin line. She didn't protest. Didn't plead for mercy. She was resigned to her fate. Why?

They backed out of the barn and took measured steps, the knife still poised for maximum damage, closer and closer to the woods. Sweat poured off Cruz. The inaction was killing him. Axel shifted his bulk, seized her upper arm and forced her into a run.

Cruz spun on his heel, raced into Gunsmoke's stall and hauled himself onto the horse's bare back. It had been a while since he'd ridden without a saddle. Gunsmoke wasn't thrilled, either, but he obeyed his commands. Axel and Jade had already been swallowed up by the woods. Axel was sure to have a mode of escape stashed in the trees. Cruz had to reach them before it was too late.

Gunsmoke's hooves pounded the earth. Cruz ducked to avoid getting whacked by low-slung branches. He had to rescue her. For Henry's sake.

He spotted them, surprised at the amount of ground they'd already covered. Axel heard his approach. Glancing over his shoulder, he scowled, his features hardening. Cruz saw the glint of the knife blade. Saw it cut into Jade's side.

Axel shoved her to the ground and fled.

She clutched at the wound and scrambled on her hands and knees toward Cruz. He dismounted and helped her stand.

"Can you ride?"

At her nod, he boosted her onto Gunsmoke and hauled himself up behind her. At the barn, she sagged against the wall, bent over and panting, while Cruz quickly returned the horse to his stall.

Cruz scooped her into his arms and carried her inside the house. The bloodstain on her shirt was growing. He debated where to take her and, in an effort to shield Henry, decided on his own room. He laid her carefully on the bed.

"I need to check the wound."

She didn't acknowledge him. Her eyes were closed, mouth clamped tightly. Against the backdrop of his maroon-and-navy bedding, her skin was nearly translucent, the delicate blue veins visible.

He slid the torn and bloody material up. The slicing wound was right above her waistband.

"It's not deep, nor is it a puncture wound. I can patch it temporarily here."

"All right." Her lips barely moved, and her eyes remained closed.

While fetching the first aid kit, hot water and cloths, he called dispatch first and Mason second. When he returned, he found Jade sobbing into his pillow.

Apprehension slithered through him. Had he misjudged the severity of her injury?

"Jade, talk to me." He crouched by the bed and instinctively held her hand. "I'll take you straight to the hospital if that's what you want. I've got over-the-counter pain reliever—"

"It's not that."

Her tears gutted him. "He's gone, Jade. You're safe. Henry's safe. Police are searching for him now."

Her shoulders quaked with the force of her sorrow. Cruz sat on the mattress and tucked her hand against his chest.

If it wasn't the pain, then what—

He recalled the moment she'd urged him to let her go, and a thought formed in his mind. Henry. She must have thought he would be safer if she left with this Axel person. But why? He hadn't attempted to abduct the boy. The boy…

If this Axel was Henry's father, Jade would do anything to keep him away from him. She'd even be willing to sacrifice her life for the sake of her son.

Her eyes popped open. "Leslie. I need to talk to her. Tessa, too."

"Not now. We have to clean you up before Henry comes looking for you."

Her eyes were red, her nose pink and her lips trembling. "There's a good chance I'm not going to make it through this. I have to be sure someone I know and trust will raise my son after I'm gone."

Chapter Nine

Cruz looking startled was new to her. His grip on her hand tightened. His mouth opened. Closed. Then resolve settled over his features, and he was the self-assured police officer once again.

"Our unit is going to protect both of you."

You don't know what I've done. She didn't say the words aloud. Not yet. He would have to be told. If she didn't offer the information, he'd ask questions. That much she knew.

Jade swiped at the moisture on her cheeks. He released her hand to fetch tissues, and she instantly missed the connection.

After disinfecting the cut and applying a bandage, he rummaged in his dresser and returned with a plain shirt the color of magnolia leaves. He hovered by the bed as she sat up, hands waiting to catch her if she swayed. She hadn't counted on the Texan having a nurturing, compassionate side.

"Any light-headedness?"

"No, just feeling weak."

He curled his arm around her upper back and helped her stand, then guided her to the bathroom door. "I'll wait here."

Jade switched out the shirts, amazed at the flimsiness of her limbs. Her side pulsed with pain, and the nick under her chin smarted. When she opened the door, Cruz arched a brow. The soft cotton shirt engulfed her, hanging almost to her knees. His arm came around her again. As they made their way to the kitchen, she leaned into his side, greedy for the strength and sturdiness he offered. She didn't meet his gaze as she settled into a chair facing the kitchen. He poured a glass of orange juice and placed it in front of her, along with a bottle of pain reliever and a package of oat biscuits.

While she nibbled on the snack, he poured himself coffee and heated water in the microwave. Snagging the single box of tea she'd brought over, he dunked one bag in the mug and brought it to her. He removed his coat, replaced it on the peg and lowered himself into the chair directly opposite her.

"Is Axel Henry's father?"

The reprieve was over. She prayed for courage. She prayed for Cruz's understanding.

"Yes."

"He's the reason you're in witness protection?"

Her stomach flip-flopped. She wasn't surprised he'd guessed the truth, but she hadn't admitted it to anyone outside the USMS. "Yes."

He ran his hand over his hair and kneaded the back of his neck. She waited while he processed the information. "What happened?"

"You mean, what did I do? You're sure you want to know?"

His gaze remained steady, his expression a blank canvas.

"I was attending university in Gainesville, Florida, and living the standard student life when I met Axel at a club. He was attractive. Older. Had a hard edge that intrigued me." The laugh that escaped was harsh and grating. "I was looking for excitement, and he delivered."

"In the form of drugs."

Embarrassment flooded her cheeks. "It started with the cheap stuff and progressed to addictive substances. Soon enough, the drugs dictated my everyday choices. My good grades tanked. I got placed on academic review and kicked off the cheer team. I stole from my roommates. Begged friends for money."

She dug her fingernail into a scratch in the table. Speaking of that time brought the painful, shameful memories to the surface.

"I burned all my bridges until Axel was my only person. A dangerous position to be in, but that's how he liked it."

Axel's threat thrummed through her, making her lungs squeeze until she thought she'd suffocate. Death would be preferable to what he had planned for her.

"I became an addict and a dealer. I chucked any morals I might've had and sold product to anyone with green to spare. I robbed grocery stores, pawnshops, you name it…all to subdue the monster inside me. I stood by while Axel beat his best friend to the point of death, and I couldn't find it in myself to care."

Cruz offered nothing but stoic silence. It was hard to look at him and even harder to stomach the loss of his regard. Although his facial muscles were arranged into a controlled mask, he couldn't hide the anger and disdain in his molten brown eyes. Did he wish he'd let Axel take her?

"I understand this is as difficult for you to hear as it is for me to say. I've heard about your brother."

Beneath the table, his knee bobbed incessantly. He shoved his chair out so fast that she jerked back. He stalked to the island, rested his balled fist on the counter and stared out the window.

"Then you're aware of my hatred for drugs and the havoc they cause."

"I am."

"Sal got sucked into that life thanks to one of his football teammates. He became uninterested in school. Quit his part-time job. I was sixteen at the time and didn't understand what was happening. All I knew was my hero older brother had changed. He went from a likable, outgoing guy with promise to a sullen, sulking shadow. My parents were beside themselves. They didn't know how to help him." Twisting, he speared her with his gaze. "He owed people money and couldn't pay, so they made an example of him. He was only nineteen."

"I'm sorry, Cruz. When you're deep into it, you don't think how your actions affect other people."

He looked away, presenting her with his stone-faced profile.

"I was fortunate," she continued. "The officers who arrested me wanted to net a bigger fish. They offered me a deal—protection in exchange for my cooperation in capturing Axel. That day was a critical turning point."

"Yeah, well, my brother didn't get the chance to turn his life around."

His hurt was a living, breathing thing crowding out the light in the room. He'd be glad to know she was leaving town. It would be easy for him to forget her and her sordid past. She wouldn't forget him, though.

Jade went to him and laid her hand on his arm. His muscle twitched, and she let her fingers slide away. "I appreciate everything you've done for us. I have to ask for one more favor, though. Will you go to the house with us while I pack some of our things? I don't feel comfortable going alone."

His brow furrowed. "You've already been in contact with the marshals?"

"I'm through with the program. Henry and I will be better off on our own."

Cruz stared at Jade, wishing she'd told him anything else but this. Her past was stained with the scourge of society, the same illegal lifestyle that had cut short his brother's life and broken his parents' hearts. He respected the fact that she hadn't sugarcoated her actions or offered excuses, but he was sorely disappointed.

Still, he had to convince her that leaving without marshal protection was a mistake. A potentially deadly mistake. "Striking out on your own? Not a smart move."

She hiked up her chin. "It's not ideal, but I can't rely on the marshals to protect us. They didn't tell me Axel escaped prison, and the marshal they finally sent to warn me was murdered steps from my door."

The program was voluntary. If she refused protection, they wouldn't force her, especially considering her part of the deal was done. "If you won't accept help from the marshals, at least stay in Serenity," he urged. "You have the full support of SPD. The mounted unit will be your protection network."

"I can't stay. He knows where to find me, and he wants revenge. But if we leave, he'll have to start fresh. We could go anywhere in the country. Somewhere he won't find us again."

Cruz was surprised at how much he disliked the idea. Why did he feel a personal stake in their safety? "Do you know how to cover your tracks? It's not as easy as it used to be. What about money to support yourselves?"

She pulled the cross pendant from beneath the shirt and pressed it between her fingers. "I've been careful. I have savings."

"I don't like it, Jade. Money doesn't last long when you're traveling, staying in motels and eating out. Putting a deposit on an apartment. What happens if your truck breaks down on the side of the road? Or you get sick?"

Her gaze darted toward the guest bedroom.

"Think about what I'm saying, Jade. Axel's obviously good at getting his needs met while evading authorities. He's crossed several states to reach you and is most likely responsible for the marshal's death. Don't you see you'd be safer here where you can be protected?"

Before she could formulate a reply, Officer Bell arrived to take their statements. Henry was still sleeping when he left around eight o'clock. When Cruz voiced concern, Jade checked on him and reassured Cruz he sometimes slept in.

Mason and Tessa pulled in bearing a box of fresh-baked pastries. The women hugged, and Tessa guided Jade into the living room, where they settled close together on the couch. Cruz watched them. Was Jade planning to ask Tessa to raise her son in case she wasn't around to do it?

"You have a strange expression," Mason said. "Care to share what's on your mind?"

Cruz hadn't noticed his sergeant had come to stand beside him. "Let's go outside."

Out on the back deck, he leaned against the house and crossed his arms. The rough bricks leached their cold into his body. "Her name isn't Jade Harris. It's Jenny something. Don't know the surname."

Mason's brows shot up. "I didn't see that one coming." He took a similar position at the opposite railing and waited for him to explain. Cruz relayed what he knew, which didn't feel like a lot.

Mason grunted and scraped his hand along his bearded jaw. He didn't speak for a while, and Cruz knew to wait him out.

"What are her plans?"

"Not WITSEC. She wants to make a run for it. On her own. I'm trying to convince her to stay and let us handle it."

"And?"

"I don't know."

"Tess and I will take them in."

Cruz thought about keeping his mouth shut.

Mason's solution would make things easier for him. He wouldn't have day-to-day interaction with Jade. But he couldn't be selfish and put Mason and Tessa to the trouble. Plus, they had Lily to think about.

"Let me take point on this," he said. "She's my neighbor, after all. If they stay here, they'll be close to their belongings, should they need anything. Henry will probably take comfort in that."

"Her past won't be a problem for you?" Mason's voice rang with doubt.

"I'm a professional. I can separate my private feelings from this task. Besides, I noticed something was wrong the other day between you and Tessa. Whatever's going on, you don't need the extra stress."

His sigh was weighted with sadness. "We're hoping to give Lily a sibling, but Tessa's had several miscarriages."

Cruz's arms dropped to his sides. "I'm sorry, brother."

Mason's devotion to his wife and daughter were well-known around town. He and Lily were as thick as thieves, belying the fact he hadn't known about her until she was three years old. Of course, he must be anticipating being with Tessa throughout the whole process and supporting her through pregnancy. For the first time, he'd get to witness the birth of his child and experience everything he'd missed with Lily.

Surprisingly, Cruz's instinct was to offer to pray for them. He knew they prayed for him, because they'd told him so. They asked him to come back to church at least a few times a month.

"All the more reason for them to stay with me. Focus on your family and provide backup when I need it. Enjoy what's left of the season."

Christmas was eleven days away. Mason and Tessa had family living in Serenity, and they were involved in church programs. Cruz didn't have parties or gatherings to worry about.

"Thank you."

"Also, I probably won't make it in today. Jade will get more rest here than at the stables."

"No problem. We'll handle the patrols without you."

"Any news on Lindsey?"

"Not yet."

Once inside, Mason veered to the island and helped himself to a pastry. Cruz peered into the living room and discovered the women praying.

To his right, he heard a creak. He shifted and spotted Henry's towhead in the thin opening. The boy was staring at him.

Cruz beckoned him over, and Henry ran-hopped to his side. "I'm hungry." A loud rumble from his midsection punctuated the claim.

Smiling, Cruz boosted him into his arms. "You'll be happy to hear we have pastries." Setting him on the countertop, he slid the box over and flipped up the lid.

Henry appeared doubtful. "Mommy makes me oatmeal for breakfast. Sometimes a smoothie."

Mason chuckled softly from across the counter. "Cruz doesn't keep that stuff around."

"That's true. I don't often eat breakfast. It's oat biscuits, peanut butter crackers or one of these."

Henry eyed the selection and pointed to a cream cheese Danish.

"Good choice." While Mason tucked it into a napkin and handed it over, Cruz poured milk into a mug.

Cruz was working on his second croissant when the women joined them.

Henry's face lit up. "Look, Mommy!"

Jade's smile was like the sun breaking through rain clouds. "Good morning, sweet boy."

Coming to stand beside Cruz, she ran her hand lightly over Henry's hair. "Did you sleep well?"

He nodded. "Try this."

She sank her teeth into the flaky pastry and made a humming noise. "Very good."

"I didn't want crackers again." His dubious expression made both Mason and Cruz laugh.

He'd have to stock his pantry with more care if his houseguests decided to stay. The prospect of having Jade and her son here was unsettling for various reasons, but he wasn't a rookie cop. He had years of experience under his belt. He could protect them while keeping his personal views out of it.

Her gaze settled on Mason. "Cruz told you everything?"

He nodded. "It doesn't change anything for me. You're important to us, Jade."

Tessa leaned into her husband, and he anchored her there with his arm. The couple presented a united front.

Her revelation didn't change anything for them because they hadn't lost a loved one to the criminal world she'd inhabited. Their family hadn't been destroyed. Their faith hadn't suffered.

Jade turned to regard him with an expectant

expression. What did she think he would say? Words failed him, so he put the ball in her court. "What have you decided to do?"

Chapter Ten

Jade grimaced at her reflection in the bathroom mirror. She hadn't brought her hair dryer with her, because she hadn't counted on being gone long. She hadn't counted on a lot of things.

Why is this happening, God? I like Serenity. This is the only home Henry has ever known. Did I not express my gratitude often enough? Did I take my new life for granted?

She yanked the comb through her wet hair until it hung in a straight, damp curtain past her shoulders.

Was she making the right decision to stand her ground? To stay and fight? She was counting on the mounted police to keep them safe. On Officer Cruz Castillo, specifically.

After Mason and Tessa had left, he'd explained why he was taking lead on her case. Everything he'd said made sense, but she had reservations—chiefly her reaction to the man.

Nursing an infatuation with him was a ridiculous endeavor, yet her heart surged ahead like a bloodhound tracking a scent.

It had to be loneliness. A yearning for love had started creeping into her days. When Henry was a baby, she hadn't had the energy or brain space to think about the future. Now, she found herself envisioning a special someone to share her dreams, hopes and fears with. A godly man who'd pray and discuss Scriptures with her. A kind, noble-hearted man who'd love Henry as his own. And, yes, a strong, capable man who'd mow the lawn sometimes and kill the really hairy spiders.

That man is not Cruz Castillo. Sure, he was the dreamy cowboy type who spent his days putting his life on the line for others. But she was the last woman he'd be interested in.

Leaving the bathroom, she went to the living room where she'd left Henry watching television and stopped short. Where was he?

"Henry?" Heart hammering, she veered into the kitchen. "Henry, where are you?"

"Downstairs," Cruz's muffled voice called out.

She approached the open door across from his bedroom and descended the carpeted stairs to a bright, open space below. The walls had been painted a neutral caramel and were bare save for a painted wooden American flag. A comfortable sitting area dominated the rectangular room. The couch was obviously a hand-me-down. A pillow and handmade quilt were stacked on one end, telling her Cruz probably stretched out there while watching the flat screen affixed to the wall.

A chair creaked, drawing her attention to the far end, where Cruz sat in a comfy leather rolling chair before a polished walnut desk. Henry was perched on his lap, a well-loved baseball hat dwarfing his head.

"His show ended," Cruz informed her. "He got bored."

This was obviously where he took care of personal business. His laptop was there, along with an organizer stuffed with unopened mail and a book of stamps.

"Mr. Cruz is a good drawer, Mommy. See?" Her son held up a cutout drawing of a goat.

As she got closer, she saw there were multiple cutouts of various animals, as well as a barn. Cruz had gathered markers, computer paper and scissors. She was stunned that he'd made the effort to keep her son entertained. He could've easily brushed him off or tried to distract him with another show.

"Those are quite good."

He shrugged off the compliment. "How are you feeling?"

Her skin itched beneath his gaze. "Better, thank you."

Her side was beginning to ache again. After her shower, she'd applied butterfly bandages and antibiotic ointment and prayed infection wouldn't set in.

"Did you speak with Belinda or David?"

The married couple who operated the Serenity Vet Clinic had expressed concern for Jade. However, Belinda and her husband had to balance their employees' and patients' needs. "While they sympathize with my situation, they can't afford for me to miss work again tomorrow. We're short-staffed as it is, and Belinda needs me to assist with surgeries."

Jade didn't want to jeopardize her job. She had to support herself and Henry.

Cruz frowned.

Henry twisted slightly and laid his hand flat against Cruz's cheek. "Will you draw me another horse? Like Renegade, this time?"

He didn't act bothered by the overfamiliar gesture. "Sure thing, cowboy."

Jade moved closer until the desk pressed into her leg. She was close enough that it would be natural for her to rest her hand on his broad shoulder. Then he could wind his arm around her waist and hold her against his side.

Stop that. "Are we keeping you from anything?"

He considered which marker color to use. "I'm having groceries delivered before lunch. Until then, I'm a free agent."

Henry tapped one of the myriad photos spread across the desk. "That's Castillo Ranch."

Jade picked it up. "Beautiful property. Do you visit often?"

His fingers worked with efficiency as he sketched out the horse. "Once a year. Twice, if I can manage it. My folks try to come up here sometimes, too."

She inventoried the photos of people who must be his extended family. She zeroed in on an image of Cruz as a young teenager. He was sandwiched between two other boys.

"Is that you with your brothers?"

"Yes."

"Do you ever think about moving back?"

His hand stilled, and his head remained bent. "I like it here. Fresh start, you know?"

"Yes, I do know."

He finally looked at her, his expression inscrutable.

Henry wriggled to get down. Cruz sat back, watching silently as the little boy shuffled several of the cutouts into his hands, carried them over to the couch and began to concoct imaginary conversations.

"You're good with kids," she said.

He'd been the epitome of patience with Henry since the day they'd met. He was the same way with Lily. He'd once sat for an hour with the pair and played Play-Doh.

"My mom and dad are the eldest of their siblings. Thanks to large age gaps, most of my cousins are much younger than me. Our family has a tradition of frequent gatherings, and the task of minding the kids fell to Sal and me." He pressed his lips together, as if regretting mentioning his brother. He returned the marker to its box and leaned closer to whisper, "Does Axel know he's a father?"

She glanced over her shoulder to be sure Henry was engaged with the cutouts and wouldn't overhear. "I didn't learn of the pregnancy until I was in the program."

Using the toe of his boot, he rotated the chair until he was facing her. "Did you undergo drug testing?"

Jade told herself it was a fair question. "I submitted to testing throughout my pregnancy and for a year after his birth. The marshals provided the resources and counseling I needed to get and stay clean. Leslie was key in my success, though. We worked together at a convenience store in Knoxville, where I first settled. She became my mentor, cheerleader and mother figure, all in one. I don't know if I'd be where I am today without her. I freaked out when I discovered I was pregnant. I was alone in a new city. Taking it one day at a time, trying to make the right choices. Suddenly I had a baby on the way who would depend on me for everything." Her throat threatened to close with remembered panic.

Cruz's brows tugged together. "You couldn't contact your folks."

Her shoulders drooped beneath the weight of sadness. "They have no idea they have a grandson. My younger sister would be an amazing aunt."

Jade had scant information about their lives.

She'd been warned not to try and learn things through social media or other online sources, because it could be tracked. She'd obeyed, yet Axel had found her anyway.

"Did you have a chance to say goodbye?"

"The marshals advised against it, and I wasn't in a place mentally to argue my side. They probably think I was killed in the car bomb Axel planted."

Cruz shot to his feet. "He blew up your car?"

The sudden movement brought his chest an inch from her nose. She stepped back so she wouldn't have to wrench her neck to see his face.

"I managed to get a copy of his contacts network for the police. I also wore a wire and asked the questions they told me to. After he got arrested, he figured out it was me and tasked one of his associates to get payback."

The veins at his temple pulsed. "How did you avoid the blast?"

"It malfunctioned when a garbage truck smacked into the bumper." Her stomach clenched. "I'm grateful no one was injured in the explosion, and that I wasn't anywhere near it."

He stared down at her, hands on his hips,

and she could practically see him puzzling out something.

"He's had you in his grasp three times now. Why didn't he finish you?"

She winced at his bluntness. "He wants to see me suffer first."

She didn't share the details. It was too terrible to think about, much less put into words.

His phone buzzed. Frowning, he checked the screen. "Groceries are here."

"I'll help Henry tidy your desk."

Cruz studied her for a minute more, obviously reluctant to abandon his line of questioning. When he left, her body sagged with relief.

Seated astride Renegade the next morning, Cruz followed the steers' progress around the arena's outer ring. The mounted unit had come early to the neighboring town's fairgrounds complex for training with the Twin Pines farm. The horses were learning to work a herd. It was a different experience for them. He'd grown up on a ranch, of course, but it gave the other officers a chance to work on their horsemanship in new ways. The farm owners, Jacob and Leah, called out instructions.

Outside the covered pavilion, an unrelenting drizzle licked the earth. His cheekbones and ears ached, and his breath came out in a vapor. Cruz couldn't find his usual enjoyment in training, and it had nothing to do with the miserable weather. Jade was miles away in Serenity. Officers Bell and Weiland had promised to do numerous patrols around the vet clinic, but he couldn't help feeling as if he'd abandoned her. Couldn't stop replaying yesterday morning's close call.

Axel hated Jade. He knew she'd helped authorities put him away and had probably spent a lot of his time in lockup planning his revenge. He wanted her to pay...on his terms. Cruz wasn't about to let that happen.

The officers had also promised to keep an eye on Elaine and Franklin's place. Since Franklin was ex-military and worked from home, Cruz didn't have qualms about Elaine continuing to babysit Henry.

Raven and her mount, Thorn, slowed to a halt in front of him. Cruz guided Renegade alongside them and tried to concentrate on the farmers' words. She shot him a sideways glance full of questions he'd eventually have to answer. When they dispersed for lunch, they dismounted and walked the horses to the nearest stock tank.

She removed her helmet and smoothed her braid. "How's it going with Jade and Henry?"

Jade had agreed it was important to share her story with Raven and Silver. Since Cruz had been busy getting his guests settled yesterday, he'd asked Mason to bring them up to speed.

"She's hanging in there." Jade was proof positive that appearances could be deceiving. She had the appearance of a delicate Southern bloom, but she had grit. "Henry hasn't seemed to pick up on any of the tension."

"He's a great kid."

"Agreed." He hadn't turned out that way by accident. Jade was a good mother, plain and simple. Cruz was still having trouble reconciling the responsible, caring person he knew with the ugly picture she'd painted of her younger self.

"Is having them with you going to be problem? Aiden and I will be happy to take them in. You *say* you've gotten over Denise—"

"Why are we talking about my failed marriage? Jade is nothing like my ex-wife."

An adventure seeker, Denise was bold and brash. Together, they'd burned bright and hot, often clashing on issues both big and small. The discord had eventually outweighed the good times. She'd blamed their demise on his absences. He'd blamed it on her unwillingness to fight for their marriage. She was, after all, the one who'd walked away.

Jade was very different. Patient and easygoing, she exuded contentment. Her sweet manner drew others to her.

"She's a lovely woman in all the ways that matter," Raven said, watching him closely. "She's also in a vulnerable position."

"Are you suggesting I'd take advantage of her?"

"No, of course not. But she's going to need a gentle hand and a hefty dose of compassion."

His phone vibrated. Removing it from his uniform pocket, he saw Officer Bell's name and gritted his teeth.

"Bell, what is it? Are Jade and Henry okay?"

"They're fine." Cruz's chest released. "We've had a robbery at Jim's Pawn Shop. Suspect fitting Axel's description ambushed Jim early this morning, tied him up and got away with several rifles, a pistol and ammo."

Cruz dug his fingers into his forehead. Axel had clearly decided to upgrade his weapon collection. "How's Jim?"

"Shaken up. A customer who had an appointment found Jim's car out back but the doors locked. He decided to contact us. Thought Jim might've had a medical emergency."

"Thanks for the heads-up."

"One more thing. The feds and marshals are setting up shop at SPD. We'll have to run our information and movements through them."

Cruz grunted in response. Those agencies didn't play well with others—or each other. The US Marshals would be champing at the bit to get justice for Prescott, whose identity had been confirmed late last night. He wasn't sure how the power play would work itself out, and he didn't care—extra help running Axel to ground was appreciated. He was just glad they were camping out at the police station and not the stables.

Raven lifted her brows expectantly, and he filled her in. "This isn't good," he finished.

"Axel's illegally acquired arsenal or our law enforcement guests?"

"Both."

After they got the horses loaded, they climbed into the truck cab and accessed Axel's information on the laptop.

He slowly scrolled through the records, his gut clenching. "He's a cold one. He's rumored to have killed or given orders to kill over a dozen people. Nothing that can be confirmed, of course."

"He's good at keeping his hands clean."

"He's good at inspiring fear in everyone around him." Why else hadn't the Gainesville PD gotten someone to testify against him in these murder cases?

Raven stared out the rain-splotched window. "Has Jade talked about the time she spent with him?"

"Not much." Granted, he hadn't asked for more. He wasn't sure he wanted to know the details. "We have to find this guy soon, Raven."

Patrol officers had been canvassing neighborhoods, and they'd alerted local businesses to the potential danger. So far, they'd received tips that led nowhere. It was frustrating. Axel had to eat and sleep, and Cruz doubted he had contacts this far north of Florida.

"With people flooding in over the next few days for the car show, that might not be as easy as we'd like."

He groaned. "I forgot about that." Classic car enthusiasts converged on the Smokies several times a year. Great for the economy, but sometimes the crowds created challenges for law enforcement. "Let's get back to Serenity."

He texted Mason and Silver that they were heading out. Mason responded that they'd be leaving in another half hour. The rain became heavier the closer they got to Serenity. He and Raven were soaking wet by the time they got the horses inside the stables.

"I'm going to be late picking up Jade." He consulted his watch, wishing he had time for a hot shower.

"Go on," she said. "I'll see to the horses."

Cruz hurried back into the onslaught. On the way to the clinic, he wondered if they would be called back out tonight to help with accidents. Already there were places of standing water. At least the ground was warm, preventing the roadways from freezing.

In the clinic parking lot, he texted Jade. Five minutes passed without a response. Impatient, he dashed inside, almost colliding with the receptionist at the door.

Gloria held a key ring in her hand. "Oh, Officer Castillo. I was just about to lock up."

"I'm here to pick up Jade."

"She and Belinda went out to the MacGregor farm."

"When did she leave?"

"About two hours ago. They were supposed

to have been back by now, but sometimes house calls take longer than expected." She gestured to the door, keys jingling.

"Thanks."

Out in his truck, Cruz tried to reach Jade. It went straight to voice mail. The MacGregor farm was about fifteen miles away and isolated.

He didn't like that she'd left the clinic without protection and hadn't bothered to contact him. More than that, he didn't like that he was beginning to view her as more than a routine case.

Chapter Eleven

"The trailer's stuck," Belinda announced over the sound of spinning tires. Easing her foot off the gas, she sank against the worn seat. The wipers swooshed across the windshield, sloshing water around without actually clearing the glass.

They'd finished treating Winston Mac-Gregor's mare and had been on their way out when their mobile supply trailer's rear tire had gotten sucked into the muck.

Jade inspected the sky. Gray clouds were stretched out like a dirty blanket, blocking the light. She checked her phone again. Still no reply from Cruz to her texts, which was odd.

The rain turned the MacGregor farm into a bleak, gray landscape, and she couldn't distinguish the shapes in the distance. If Axel did know her location, this would be a prime time to strike.

"Maybe Winston can use his dually to pull us out," Belinda said.

Headlights slashed across her vision, and she recognized the truck turning into the gravel drive. The relief flooding her wasn't specific to the officer behind the wheel. She would've been as happy to see Mason, Silver or Raven.

Liar. You have a personal interest in Cruz.

After entering her new life, she'd determined not to lie to herself. She'd ignored the internal warnings about Axel, had told herself he wasn't that bad. When his actions proved otherwise, she'd told herself she could change him. When she'd gotten in deep, she'd told herself she couldn't survive without him. Without the drugs. All lies.

Belinda sat up straighter. "Is Cruz here on account of you?"

Jade knew she was on rocky ground with her boss, not because of her skills or job performance, but because of the danger surrounding her.

"Probably checking up on me." She strove for nonchalance. He'd stressed the need for her to take it easy at work today and not strain her injury.

He parked his truck beside them and, before she could unbuckle, rounded the hood and wrenched open her door. Water splattered on her jeans, and she shivered.

"You okay?" The hood of his police raincoat had fallen back, and his hair was plastered to his head.

"I sent you multiple texts, but you know how the signal can be up here. You didn't get any of them?"

"No, I didn't." His gaze flicked past her, and he nodded. "Belinda. Looks like you need some assistance. I've got equipment with me. I can get you out."

He shut the door and quickly worked to get them unstuck.

"The most eligible bachelor in Serenity is at your beck and call, it seems," Belinda said, smiling over at Jade. "Are you finally ready to jump into the dating pool?"

She gave the same answer she always gave when asked why she wasn't dating. "Henry's my priority right now. I'll think about romance when he's older."

"Are you telling me you'd turn down an invitation from him? Cruz Castillo is a responsible, stand-up guy with a good career. He'd be good to you both."

She thought about the smoothie ingredients he'd ordered from the store. When she'd asked about it, he'd said Henry had mentioned she liked to make fruit and spinach smoothies every day. He'd even gotten the ground flax. When she'd tried to pay him, he'd refused. It had been a kind gesture.

And her main reason for not dating was no longer an issue. Her most dearly guarded secret had been exposed.

He will never see you as anything other than a former drug addict.

The thought was harsh and ugly, but she feared it was the truth. The others in the mounted unit knew her better than he did, and they didn't associate her former choices with a personal tragedy.

Cruz yanked open her door again. "Ready?"

She glanced over at Belinda, who wore a knowing smirk. "See you in the morning."

Pulling up the hood of her coat, she snagged her purse and followed him into the downpour. The lower half of her jeans was soaked through by the time she shut herself inside his truck. Mud splattered her yellow rain boots decorated with chickens.

His cologne enveloped her, and she surreptitiously breathed it in. A country song provided a soft, crooning backdrop to the rain pelting the truck roof.

"I'm glad you showed up when you did," she said, holding her hands near the vent blasting hot air. "Saved us from trekking through the rain and muck back to Winston's house."

Grunting, he backed out onto the road and put the gear into Drive. "To Elaine's, right?"

"Yes, please." A call from Belinda came through, and she glanced into the side mirror to see the clinic truck poised at the gravel drive's edge. The call was brief.

"Belinda's not heading back to town just yet," she told him when she disconnected. "She has a quick stop to make. A friend's cat is recovering from surgery and has ongoing lethargy." When he didn't comment, she said, "How was training?"

"Good."

She got the feeling he was annoyed with her. "I did try to reach you. I would've called if I hadn't gotten busy with Winston's horse."

His knuckles went white on the steering wheel. "I was worried."

Her stomach went into free fall. "I'd be lying if I said I wasn't worried, too. I'm aware of the risks, but I have to pay the rent and feed and clothe my child."

"I know."

"So, how was training?" she repeated, staring him down.

After a beat of silence, he gave her a rundown of what they'd done with the Twin Pines owners and their cattle.

"What do you like about the mounted police?"

He didn't hesitate. "The horses. People react differently to us when we're on horseback. They're curious and much more likely to approach us than if we're in a patrol car. Every day is different, which I like, and most of our time is spent outdoors."

He'd grown up on a ranch, so that made sense. The road wound through heavily wooded areas. He routinely checked the rearview and side mirrors.

"Why did you choose to be a vet tech?"

His interest surprised her. He wasn't the type to make small talk for the sake of filling silence. "I was one of those kids who could've opened a small zoo and charged admission. I had ferrets, iguanas, parrots, rabbits, dogs, cats…you name it."

"All at the same time?" He guffawed. "Did you live in the country?"

"City." She laughed. "We had a sprawling house with more space than we knew what to do with. My parents allowed me to have as many animals as I wanted, as long as I kept them downstairs in the basement and took care of them. Dad grumbled about the upkeep costs, of course. I eventually got a part-time job scooping ice cream because I was afraid he'd change his mind and make me get rid of them. I did eventually have to find homes for them before I moved into the college dorms. Except for Pete. He was an African gray parrot, and my dad found him amusing. I wonder if he's still with them. They can live between forty and sixty years."

An almost overwhelming yearning to see her mom, dad and sister seized her. She'd essentially buried her family the day she entered the witness program, and she continued to grieve what she'd lost.

"Your parents sound nice."

"I guess you're wondering how I messed up so badly. Bottom line... I didn't appreciate how good I had it until I lost everything. I don't let mistakes go to waste, though. My priorities are in order now."

He slowed and drove around a branch blocking the road. "You didn't finish college in Florida, right?"

"I was forced to drop out because I simply stopped going to class. Once I settled in Knoxville with a fresh start handed to me, I realized I wanted a career. I loved animals, and science wasn't a problem for me, so I chose vet tech. I signed up for classes before I learned about Henry. Leslie convinced me not to drop out."

"Couldn't have been easy to juggle raising a child with college courses and a job."

Again, he stole her breath. That sounded suspiciously like empathy. "Some days were brutal. I lost track of how many times I cried myself to sleep." The words slipped out unbidden.

"You're a survivor."

Her head whipped around. At her shocked expression, he lifted a shoulder, the raincoat sounding like paper rustling.

"I don't like what you did, Jade. That world you got yourself involved in stole my brother's future. Every day, drugs destroy lives across this country. But that doesn't mean I can't see how you've turned your life around."

He returned his attention to the road and braked. An orange-and-white A-frame barricade blocked it. His brows clashed. "I suspected flooding would be a problem. The road crew will be out in full force tonight." He turned the truck around and took the road they'd just passed.

Jade's mind was full of what he'd said. It was refreshing to be able to talk about her real life with someone, even if the truth was difficult for them both.

"There's something in the road."

Cruz applied the brakes. The windshield wipers swooshed back and forth, and in between the swipes, she tried to make out what she was seeing.

"Is that a person?"

His face was grim as he killed the engine and unbuckled his seat belt. He pointed to the left side of the road, where the rear end of a sedan was visible between the overgrowth. "Looks like he hydroplaned and hit the tree. Stay here."

He exited the cab, shut the door and approached the man. Crouching next to him, he felt for a pulse.

Jade held her breath, praying he would be all

right. Then a sound she knew too well ripped through the night, and she screamed Cruz's name.

At the sound of a gunshot, Cruz flattened himself against the pavement and whipped out his weapon. He was in serious trouble. No sight of the shooter. Nothing to hide behind. The truck's headlights were acting as a spotlight.

Another bullet whizzed through the rain near his head.

An engine revved, and his truck lurched forward between him and the sedan. Jade threw open the passenger door.

"Get in!"

Staying low, Cruz dragged the victim over and boosted him into the cab. As Jade reached over to assist him, the driver's side window exploded. Her scream mingled with the sound of breaking glass. Cruz pushed her down while simultaneously shielding the victim, who stirred and moaned.

"Jade?" he called.

"I'm okay." Her whisper was barely audible.

Thank You, Lord. The bullet must've exited the open door without hitting him, because he hadn't heard it enter the truck body.

"Start driving."

He jerked the passenger door closed after they were in motion. Sheathing his weapon, he called dispatch and reported the incident.

"Where to?" she asked.

"Walk-in clinic. They can assess if this guy needs ambulance transport." He wasn't going to ask her to drive forty-five minutes to the nearest hospital.

Rain and wind whipped at her hair. In the glow of the dash lights, he could see she had a viselike grip on the wheel.

"I should've checked with the highway department before taking the detour."

"You think Axel set up the roadblock to lure us here?"

"And caused the accident," he surmised. "To make sure we stopped."

The victim was slumped in the seat between them, head lolled toward Jade. He was probably in his early twenties. The wound on his head was the only obvious injury. Cruz knew he shouldn't have moved him. Leaving him on the road in the freezing rain, at the mercy of Axel's plans, hadn't been an option, however.

"He maneuvered us exactly where he wanted us." Cruz wasn't happy. Why couldn't Axel be one of the duller criminals? "How could you have gotten involved with someone like Axel?"

She winced at the bite in his tone. "Don't lay guilt on me. I've accepted God's forgiveness and grace, and it's unproductive to try and pick up old sins again. I'm a new creation in Christ."

His conscience pricked, he fell silent and mulled over her words.

After the clinic took custody of the victim, Cruz and Jade switched places, and he drove to Elaine and Franklin's. They lent him a tarp, and he fashioned a makeshift covering for the window to keep out the elements. Henry's chatter broke the adults' silence during the ride home, not taking a break even when they picked up pizzas for supper. As they neared his house, Cruz noted a pair of vehicles with government plates in his driveway. Jade must have seen them, too, because she gasped.

"What's the matter, Mommy?" Henry strained against his seat belt.

She tossed a tumultuous gaze at Cruz, and he reached out and grasped her hand without thinking. "I forgot to tell you we have federal agencies in town." He glanced in the rearview mirror. "Henry, how about you and I have a picnic in your bedroom?"

"In my house?" Henry said, confused.

"The room you and your mom are staying in."

"Mommy doesn't let me eat in the bedroom."

Jade clung to Cruz's hand. "This is a special occasion," she said in an overly bright tone. "Just be careful not to get pizza sauce on Cruz's carpet."

"I'll be careful," he vowed.

Cruz parked behind the SUVs, and two men emerged, wearing windbreakers with the words *US Marshals* across the back.

"Who's that?" Henry asked.

"Someone who wants to talk to your mom for a few minutes." Cruz squeezed her cold fingers and turned in the seat. "Henry, I haven't had a chance to put up my tree. It's a miniature version of yours. Will you help me decorate it?"

Henry's big eyes shifted to Cruz, and he grinned. "Yes, sir!"

Cruz squeezed her hand again. "You've got this," he said softly.

The marshals were grim-faced. They'd lost one of their own thanks to this case. No doubt they would strongly encourage her to continue with the program. Would she change her mind and go with them? He acknowledged that if she did, she and Henry would leave a big hole in his life. He'd gotten used to knowing she was next door. He'd gotten used to seeing her smiling face at the stables, unit barbecues and the Black Bear Café.

He didn't want her to leave, and that troubled him. If he committed his heart to someone again—and that was as unlikely as a white Christmas in Texas—he wouldn't, *couldn't* love a woman who was a constant reminder of the biggest tragedy of his life.

Chapter Twelve

Cruz sat on the guest bed and consumed one slice of meat lover's pizza after another. The boxes were stacked on the bedside table, the top one flipped open to the plain cheese Henry had requested. The five-year-old had a seemingly endless supply of energy. He would take a bite and dart back over to the tree that wasn't much taller than him. A plastic container on the floor next to it held an assortment of sparkly ornaments, and the boy delighted in choosing each one and then finding the perfect spot to hang it.

On this return trip, he eyed Cruz's pizza. "Are you going to save Mommy some?"

He nodded and showed him the contents inside the bottom box. "See? I've left her half. Think that's enough?"

Henry took a sip of clear bubbly soda. According to Jade, he wasn't allowed to drink the caffeinated stuff. He glanced at the closed bedroom door. Occasionally, he heard murmurings or the slide of a chair across his kitchen floor, but he couldn't hear what Jade or the marshals were saying.

To distract himself and Henry, he posed the universal question kids heard this time of year. "What do you want for Christmas?"

His green eyes sparkled. "I asked Mommy for a cat. I want an orange one. They're my favorite. And a gray one and a black one."

Cruz couldn't help but laugh. "Is that so? What did she say?"

"Maybe." He danced back over to the ornament box.

It was odd that a vet tech who loved animals didn't have any of her own. Perhaps she was waiting until Serenity felt like her forever home. Had she lived with her eyes on the rearview mirror, always looking back and never quite letting herself enjoy the present, wondering if her past was going to catch up to her?

A shame some man hadn't come along to be a father to little Henry. Jade juggled all the responsibilities of a single parent—holding down a job, running a household and raising a child— and she did it beautifully without complaint.

"I want race cars, too. A rocket ship and a stuffed Brachiosaurus."

"A what?"

Henry launched into a speech about the different dinosaurs, and Cruz was amazed at the extent of his knowledge. He couldn't verify the information, of course, but Henry sure did sound convincing.

Cruz heard a door close, followed by engines humming to life out front. A minute later Jade swept into the bedroom.

Cruz rose to his feet.

Henry darted over and threw his arms around her legs.

She smiled down into his upturned face. Framing his cheeks with her hands, she said, "I love you to the moon and back, Henry Wade Harris."

"I love you, Mommy Harris."

A soft laugh escaped, and she lifted her gaze to Cruz. "They're gone," she said unnecessarily.

"Are they coming back?"

He held his breath. Would she and Henry be ripped from everything they knew and plunked into an unfamiliar town?

"Not unless I ask them to." A crevice dug between her brows. "I hope I made the right decision."

He didn't dare examine the reasons for the relief sweeping through him.

Henry tugged on her hand. "Come look at the tree."

While she was admiring his work, Cruz pressed a soda and plate piled with generous slices into her hands.

"How hungry do you think I am?"

"As my mama would say, you need to eat to keep up your strength." Taking her shoulders, he turned her toward the bed. "Have a seat while I assist young Henry." Leaning in, he whispered, "That boy of yours is smart as a whip. He just gave me a fifteen-minute lesson on dinosaurs."

Some of the strain receded, and her eyes sparkled with pride. "He surprises me every day with some new tidbit he's learned."

"Is there room in your life for someone special?"

Her jaw sagged.

He held up his hands, ears burning. "I was just thinking you seem to be as gun-shy about relationships as I am. Surely you get lonely."

Instead of answering, she sank onto the bed and stuffed pizza into her mouth.

"Sorry. I was out of line. I certainly don't like when people ask why I haven't found a wife and settled down yet."

She washed down the bite with soda. "I

couldn't bring myself to enter a relationship based on a lie."

He sat on the bed beside her and thought about that. The admission told him a lot about her character. Maybe that was why he felt comfortable to share some of his truths. "My first wife left me. Didn't even make it a year."

She didn't act surprised. He'd kept his past close to the vest and initially only told Raven. Eventually, he'd shared it with Mason and Silver.

"Tessa told you?" he guessed.

"She didn't have much to say on the subject."

"That's because I didn't share details in the first place." He studied her. "You were talking about me with Tessa, huh?"

He watched the flush spreading across her face with fascination.

She stuffed another bite into her mouth, and he chuckled. They turned their attention to Henry, who had become absorbed with his task.

"You don't plan to try again?" she said, wiping her mouth with a paper napkin.

He thought how easy it was having her and Henry in his home. He'd been apprehensive at first, but they'd filled the place with conversation and energy he didn't realize he'd been missing.

"I want kids," he admitted without thought.

"But you're not sure you want to risk trusting someone and having them walk away like your first wife."

"Something like that."

"How old were you?"

"Twenty-four when we got married, but we dated for several years before that."

"You're thirty-two now, right? You're surely a different man than you were back then. You've learned, stretched and matured. You won't make the same mistakes you did before."

He searched her face. Jade's outward beauty reflected her heart. She was kind, gentle and loving. Grounded and mature, something his ex-wife hadn't been.

Jade was taking advantage of his inspection to do one of her own. He saw her gaze lock onto his mouth, saw the interest stir to life in the mossy depths. His heart reared, then galloped against his rib cage. Shock shuddered through him. Was she attracted to him?

Excitement rushed through his veins, and he struggled to rein it in. He'd promised Mason and the others he could separate his personal feelings from his professional duty. That included foolhardy impulses—like wanting to kiss Jade Harris.

★ ★ ★

Belinda sat behind the desk and her husband, David, lounged beside the dry-erase board posted with surgery dates and patient names. They shared expressions of consternation.

Gloria had pounced on Jade the minute she stepped foot in the clinic and informed her the bosses wanted to see her in Belinda's office. Her stomach was tighter than a drum. She felt hot and flushed.

"We heard what happened last night," Belinda began, leaning forward and folding her hands on the desk. "I'm glad you're okay."

"I am. Okay, that is." She rubbed her damp palms over her scrub pants. "I'm fully capable of performing my duties." Granted, her knife wound was still healing and prevented her from lifting large animals onto the operating table or carrying heavy stuff like pet food or litter bags. But reminding them of her stabbing wouldn't help her case.

David cleared his throat. "The thing is, Jade, we have a responsibility to our patients and their owners. We understand none of this is your fault, but we can't put them or our other employees at risk."

"You're firing me?"

Belinda shook her head. "No, no. You're a valuable employee, Jade. We don't want to lose you. However, we've hired a temporary replacement until your troubles are over. She's coming from middle Tennessee and will be here Monday. You can work the remainder of the week."

Jade stared at the shiny tile floor and pressed her hand to her mouth. What now? How would she pay her rent? Buy groceries? She had savings, but it wouldn't carry them for long.

David pulled an envelope from his pocket, looking both discomfited and sympathetic. "Here's your Christmas bonus."

She accepted the envelope but didn't open it. Usually, they received their bonus on Christmas Eve. "Thank you."

Barking erupted in the reception area. Patients were waiting.

Belinda stood, her chair creaking. "I'm sorry, Jade. Hopefully this situation will be resolved soon."

"Sure." She exited the office and retreated to the break room, where she absentmindedly poured Gloria's strong-as-nails coffee and drank without thinking of the caffeine.

Jade made it through back-to-back appointments, performing her tasks with the constant refrain buzzing in the back of her mind. *No job.* Not even a visit from her favorite standard poodle could dissipate the cloud of anxiety. By lunchtime, she was a mess. She buttoned up her coat and carried her insulated bag to the large enclosure at the rear of the clinic. At this time of year, only the indoor kennels were in use. Grateful for the solitude and quiet, she sat at the picnic table and ate her soup.

What am I supposed to do, Lord? My life is unraveling.

Hard to believe less than a week ago, she'd been reveling in the holiday whirl, anticipating her Sunday school party and trying to decide what to cook for Leslie's Christmas Day gathering. Henry had a role as a sheep in the church play, and she had yet to purchase gifts for Tessa and Elaine. Those things seemed trivial now.

But without faith, it is impossible to please Him. The verse was one of the first Leslie had encouraged her to memorize. "When problems arise, cling to that verse," Leslie had said. Jade had repeated it to herself during those early days of her pregnancy when she'd been overwhelmed with uncertainty and tempted to withdraw from her classes.

I know You love me, Father. I know You're in control. Help me to remember that, no matter what happens.

The rest of the day was easier, although her heart was sad. She told herself she'd get her job back when this was all over, but there was always the possibility Belinda and David would prefer her replacement and decide not to bring Jade back. By the time she sat in Cruz's truck at the end of the shift, her emotions were all over the place.

He let the truck idle and turned off the radio. "What's wrong?"

She wrapped her hand around her cross pendant. "I've been placed on a leave of absence starting Monday," she choked out.

A heavy sigh left him. His hand came to rest on her shoulder. "I'm sorry."

"I don't blame them. They have to do what's best for the clinic. I wouldn't dream of putting others at risk, of course."

She felt bad enough about that young car accident victim. He'd been treated and released with minor injuries, but his car had been totaled. She'd purchase him a new one if she had the money.

"You're not in this alone."

She finally braved a glance in his direction and was stunned to see the depth of his concern.

Unable to voice her gratitude without risking tears spilling over, she merely nodded.

As he backed out of the space, she belatedly noticed the tarp was gone. He must've gotten the window fixed on his lunch break.

"I got a call from Detective York during my drive over. They located Axel's hideout. Law enforcement has received a number of tips in recent days, but this one actually paid off. They're searching for clues and trying to establish his pattern of movements. Want to ride along?"

She texted Tessa, who responded that she was happy to let Henry stay longer.

As they drove through town, they shared tidbits about their days. Everything about Cruz intrigued her. He was no longer a distant individual on the fringes of her life. He was becoming a friend. Someone she counted on and trusted. Did he consider her a friend, too? Or was her past too much of an obstacle?

Leaving the center of town behind, they drove down roads flanked mostly by farms. He eventually turned down a wooded street with identical cabins.

"These look like vacation rentals," she said.

"This street connects to a residential neighborhood up ahead."

They progressed through a series of stop signs, passing older homes on postage-stamp lots. On the last street, the yards were bigger and the homes neglected. A few were almost buried beneath a blanket of brown kudzu. Police cruisers and unmarked vehicles were parked on either side of the street in front of a drab gray house with black shutters. Local officers and federal agents milled about.

"Why did he pick this one?" she mused aloud.

"Either the owners aren't around, or he coerced them to help him."

They exited the vehicle, and Jade eyed the candy-colored sky. The pink and yellow splashes would soon be absorbed by darkness.

Detective York met them in the driveway.

"Good news. We intercepted the owner a few minutes ago and are interrogating him inside. Name's Nick Turner. He's been busted twice for possession of marijuana. He'll crack like an egg, I'm sure of it." He gestured to the house. "There's something I'd like to show you."

At the mention of Turner's crimes, Cruz's face hardened to marble. Jade could practically feel his distaste heating the air around him.

The house was sparsely furnished, and little light filtered through the dirty windows. The floors hadn't seen a broom or mop in some time. Jade could hear men conversing in another part of the house. Detective York led them down the hallway to a large bedroom. A mattress was on the floor, along with a table and one camp chair. Chinese takeout boxes and bags containing ramen noodles and tuna cans littered the room.

York picked up a folder from the bed and dropped it on the table, tapping the sleek cover with one finger. "Our man is thorough, to say the least."

Cruz opened it. He stared down at the contents without moving. Jade's feet reluctantly brought her to his side. Photos of her. Dozens of them.

She spread them out with shaking fingers. They depicted her at various times and on different days. Dropping Henry off at Elaine's. Leaving the clinic after a shift. In the grocery store parking lot, loading bags into her truck. Talking with friends on the church steps.

She didn't realize she was close to passing out until Cruz gently pressed her into the chair and curved his broad hand on the back of her neck.

"Put your head between your knees and breathe," he instructed softly, standing behind the chair.

His fingertips gingerly brushed her hair to one side, strand after strand after strand. His other hand came to rest on her shoulder. She closed her eyes and focused on the reassuring contact.

Axel wasn't here, but he had been. He'd stalked her. Taken the time to have the photos printed so he could study her and imagine ways to exact his revenge.

Footsteps clipped along the hall. "Sir? We're done with Turner."

"Thanks, Bell."

Jade slowly sat up, thankful the dancing black dots had disappeared from her vision. Cruz moved to stand beside her, his dark eyes soft and inviting. "You okay?"

She thought fleetingly that she could get used to him looking at her like this. Like he cared. "I'm good."

"What did you find out, Bell?" York asked.

Officer Bell's gaze touched on Jade before returning to his notepad. "Axel broke into the home about ten days ago. He issued an ultimatum. Either Turner helped him, or he'd kill him. He's rattled."

"When did he see Axel last?" Cruz asked.

"This morning. He doesn't know where he

went. Axel didn't keep him apprised of his comings and goings. Sometimes he'd task Turner with getting food or other supplies." He lifted his gaze. "Oh, the blue and white motorcycle you saw at Franklin and Elaine Latimer's place is registered to Turner and is parked in the shed."

"What's Axel driving now?" York asked.

"Turner doesn't know."

"Or he claims not to know," Cruz muttered. "We've collected all the guns Axel stole from the pawnshop except for a semiautomatic rifle and a handgun. Also, several boxes of ammo."

Bell returned to the other part of the house, and York walked around until he was facing them. His eyes rested on her. "Ms. Harris, is there anything you can tell me that will aid this investigation?"

"Nothing that you don't already know. Axel doesn't care who he hurts as long as he gets what he wants."

York nodded. "The reports are in from CSU. We were able to positively link evidence at the murder scene to Axel. He's responsible for the murder of US Marshal Prescott."

Jade could only nod in acknowledgment. An innocent man's blood was on her hands. Fear chewed up her insides and spit them out. What if Cruz met the same end?

Cruz's brows tugged together. "What exactly did Axel say to you in the barn that morning? There could be some detail we overlooked."

She bit her lip. Both men stared at her, waiting.

"He plans to get me hooked on drugs again."

Fury surged in his eyes. He visibly fought to control his reaction, his fingers clenching and unclenching. When he spoke, his words were underscored with icy resolve.

"I refuse to let that happen."

Jade wanted to believe that. The alternative was too terrible to contemplate.

Chapter Thirteen

Cruz had encountered all sorts of criminals during his career. On a scale from annoying to evil, Axel dipped toward the worst of the worst. He *enjoyed* other people's misery. He'd watched Jade for days and had seen how she'd turned her life around. The best way to exact his revenge was to rip away her freedom and reduce her to the dependent addict she used to be.

His stomach churned.

Axel had lost his hideout and errand boy, but he'd proved he was resilient. He'd find a way to meet his needs.

The piano at the other end of the fellowship hall abruptly stopped, halting his thoughts. The children's voices that had filled the hall for the past hour faded uncertainly. Mason's sister, Candace, was the choir leader, and she gave them instructions in a singsong voice. Sandwiched between Lily and Kai, Henry stood on the second row of the makeshift bleachers, his blond hair shining beneath the bay lights overhead.

The airy room was abuzz with activity as volunteers pitched in to help prepare for the upcoming Christmas pageant. This was the last place he'd expected to come tonight. As they were leaving the Turner residence, Jade had informed him that Henry had practice. His first instinct was to argue against it, but she'd explained that he'd been practicing for months, learning the songs and accompanying hand motions, and he would be devastated if he didn't get to participate. So Cruz had gotten on the phone and asked some buddies from patrol if they'd stand watch outside the church for a few hours. Mason would be there, as well.

Cruz had planned to remain on the perimeter and keep watch. Instead, he'd been roped into painting sets with the other parents. He and Jade were working on a storefront. They were in the farthest corner from the choir, in a dead zone of activity. He was painting a faux-brick exterior. She was painting windows, adding realistic details like frost, sparkle, garlands and ornaments. She worked with painstaking care, as if this was going in an art gallery.

He put his paintbrush in the can and arched his stiff back. "You're good at this."

A becoming blush splashed across her cheeks, and he surmised she wasn't used to getting compliments.

"I did set design for the high school drama club. My favorite production was *Beauty and the Beast*. The backdrops were ornate. The schedule was demanding, but I loved every minute."

"Why didn't you pursue art as a career? Or theater?"

"I considered it. My parents convinced me to consider other options. I entered as an undecided major and never did narrow it down." She contemplated her work and leaned in to add swipes of silver to the ornaments. "I was involved in the university theater department my freshman and sophomore years, but I stopped when I had to choose between that and volleyball."

"Did you play in high school?"

"Yes. We were a tight-knit group."

"Artistic and sporty," he drawled. "Were you voted most popular, too?"

Her green eyes flashed in surprise, and she laughed, a husky, pleasant sound that warmed him. "Not quite."

He didn't have any trouble picturing her as

a teenager. She had probably been one of those students who didn't belong to any one group, someone who was friendly to everyone, regardless of social standing.

"Someone as beautiful and kind as you must've had your fair share of admirers."

Her lips curved sweetly. He was tempted to reach out and skim his thumb over them. Test their softness. Lean in and—

"I had a steady boyfriend my senior year."

Shocked by his thoughts, he forced his gaze to roam the room. "Let me guess—the star quarterback."

"Point guard. He accepted a basketball scholarship in a different state, and we decided against the long-distance thing. I didn't date again until Axel. If I'd been in a relationship, I wouldn't have noticed him that night. But then, I wouldn't have Henry."

The hitch in her voice brought his focus back to her. He longed to make things right for her. He even wanted her to experience a sincere, loving relationship with a stand-up guy.

She gestured to his half-finished brick wall. "You're not so bad at this yourself. Were you in drama club, too?"

"Me? No way. Ranch operations dominated my after-school hours."

"You weren't involved in sports? I pictured you as a football player."

"That was Sal. He made it clear ranching wasn't in his future. He was hoping for a football scholarship as his ticket out of Texas."

"Did your other brother play?"

"Diego? Nah, he was like me. More interested in being with the horses. My parents wouldn't have let us play even if we'd expressed interest. Sal got introduced to drugs by some teammates, and they were petrified of losing another son to that life."

"What are your parents like?"

"They're firm believers in hard work. God and family are their foundations. Mom and Dad grew up on neighboring ranches. Their parents were friends and occasionally had dinner together. Dad likes to say he fell in love with her *sopapillas* before falling in love with her."

"Ah, the girl next door," she teased. She stopped and ducked her head, blushing again.

Was she thinking that she was *his* girl next door? He shook his head, stunned he'd go there.

"Will you spend Christmas with them?"

"I typically go to Texas after Christmas. We

have a late celebration, and I stay through New Year's. What about you?"

"Henry and I go to the church's Christmas Eve candlelight service and spend Christmas Day with Leslie and her family. They've basically adopted us at this point."

He'd seen them at the candlelight services before he'd stopped going. "What were your holidays like growing up?"

"My mother was big on volunteering, so we served at various organizations throughout the year. The weeks leading up to Christmas were busier. We wrapped presents for charities, helped at soup kitchens and delivered food donations to shut-ins. My parents, sister and I exchanged gifts on Christmas Eve because we had several stops to make on the twenty-fifth. Two sets of grandparents, as well as an elderly aunt and uncle."

"Sounds hectic."

"It was a whirlwind, for sure. I might've complained a time or two." Her smile didn't last. "I know what I'm missing now. I'd give anything to hug my grandma Hazel. She and I were especially close."

"Do you know how she's doing?"

Her expression was pained. "If she's alive, she just celebrated her eighty-first birthday."

"Now that Axel knows your location, there's nothing stopping you from contacting your family."

It was obvious she'd contemplated it. "I'm scared to reach out. Will my parents want a relationship with me? Will they reject Henry because of who his father is? I don't know what to do. The decision will have to wait. Either Axel will be captured, or…" She trailed off, probably picturing in her mind's eye the other scenarios. "Or he won't."

Without thinking, he slid his hand beneath the silken curtain of her hair and cupped her cheek. Her eyes were sad and troubled, and he wished he could promise everything would be okay. "No matter what happens, you can count on me. I won't leave your side."

She turned her face into his palm, reaching up to hold his hand in place. His nerve endings fired, jolting him. "I don't know how I'll ever repay you."

His mind emptied of all thoughts but one—he was not immune to Jade Harris, after all.

The noise around her faded to a low hum. Cruz's espresso eyes invited her closer. His mouth, which could be so stern and forbidding, was soft and relaxed. She could see the proof in his face—he felt the same pull as she did. If they were alone, she felt sure this moment would mark a turning point. But was that wise? For either of them?

"Cruz. Jade." Mason's voice snapped the connection. They dropped their hands simultaneously. She turned to face Mason and Tessa.

Mason's gaze was sharp, watchful. Tessa, on the other hand, looked like a cat with a bowl of cream.

Cruz's face was angled away, so it was hard for her to gauge his thoughts.

"Mason decided it was time for punch and cookies. Want to join us?" Tessa gestured to the snack table in the opposite corner. Several people had congregated there to chat.

"I could use something to drink," she said, getting to her feet.

"I'll pass," Cruz said.

Mason crossed his arms. "Tessa, can you bring me some?"

"Sure." She linked her arm with Jade's as they walked away. "I have a feeling Mason's going to grill Cruz."

"Why would he do that?"

Tessa's hazel eyes veered to her, laughter in

them. "You aren't aware of how cozy you two looked just now. In fact, I'm sure you forgot where you were for a while."

Jade glanced over her shoulder. Cruz was standing, arms folded across his chest, mirroring Mason's stance. Their conversation was obviously a serious one.

"He was merely reassuring me." She attempted to dismiss the emotionally charged moment.

At the table, Tessa poured them each a cup of bright green punch. "I'm not buying that. You like him, don't you?"

She sipped the chilled lime-flavored drink and grimaced. "Liking him would be a very bad idea."

"He's a great guy. He has deeply held convictions and a strong thirst for justice. His intensity intimidates some people. Is that what has you worried?"

"Didn't even cross my mind. I admire his passion."

"Then what is it?"

"He's a cop. My past disqualifies me."

Tessa touched her arm. "Forget your past. It's what you do with your present that matters."

She knew that, but she wasn't sure Cruz saw it that way.

"Your ex's return has likely stirred up memories of a bad time, but don't forget who you are now. Whose you are."

After years of searching for peace in all the wrong places, she had found meaning and belonging in Christ. She was loved and forgiven.

"Cruz hasn't shown an inkling of interest in a woman since he moved here," Tessa continued. "But he's different around you."

Jade ignored the hopeful leap of her heart. She had to be responsible. She had to do what was best for Henry. For Cruz, too. He'd been hurt and abandoned by his ex-wife. His next relationship should be with someone who didn't come with baggage.

Candace released the kids, and they streamed through the room. Lily and Henry were already with Mason and Cruz by the time she and Tessa reached them. Tessa handed Mason a napkin full of cookies, which he proceeded to share with the kids.

Cruz met Jade's searching gaze and gave her a tight smile.

"Is Lily coming to my birthday party?" Henry spoke around a mouthful of cookie.

Jade frowned. She'd forgotten about her own son's party. She'd scheduled it months ago and sent invitations to ten kids. The arcade was an overwhelming experience on a good day. During the holiday break, when the weather outside pushed the kids indoors to cure their boredom, it was over-the-top. Certainly a security nightmare. Too much activity and noise and places to hide.

"Of course Lily is invited."

Henry and Lily hopped around the group of adults, whooping and laughing. Kai and others joined in.

Jade looked between Mason and Tessa. "I have to cancel the party."

She'd felt guilty enough asking Cruz and the other officers to babysit them for this final practice and the upcoming performance. She couldn't expect them to put their life on hold every time she had an event on her calendar.

"Where's it supposed to be?" Cruz asked.

"The arcade."

His forehead furrowed. "That would be tough to contain."

"Maybe you should tell him you're going to postpone the party instead of outright canceling it," Tessa suggested.

Henry was going to be upset, either way.

"Let me give it some thought before you decide," Cruz said.

Tessa corralled the kids so that Cruz and Jade could finish their project. Mason was enlisted to help carry the wet set pieces into the hallway to dry.

After they'd been painting in silence for some time, Jade stopped and watched him work. He must've sensed her attention, because he sat up and raised his brows.

"Something on your mind?"

"Is everything okay between you and Mason?"

He thought about his response. "The line between personal and professional gets blurred sometimes."

She parted her lips to ask for specifics.

He held her off. "We're okay. Our unit functions like a family. We have differences of opinion, snipe and squabble, but we always make up in the end."

She'd been around the officers long enough to know he spoke the truth. "I don't like being the cause of discord, though."

"Please, don't worry about it."

The word *please* didn't come out of Cruz Castillo's mouth often, which made her sit up and pay attention. "I'll try not to."

"I guess that will have to satisfy me." He winked, his mouth curving in a toe-curling smile.

She returned to her painting, although there was a slight quiver in her fingers. They finished almost an hour later and carried the pieces to the hallway. By that time, Henry's energy was flagging. Mason accompanied them to Cruz's truck, his mood solemn. She appreciated that he cared about her welfare, but she truly didn't want to cause trouble. Before she could think of something to reassure him, Officer Weiland drove up and said there wasn't anything unusual to report. Weiland followed them home, waiting at the end of the driveway as they exited the vehicle.

Henry had fallen asleep in his car seat. Without a word, Cruz unbuckled him and hoisted him into his arms. He handed her the house keys and, as soon as they were through the door, waved to Weiland and pivoted inside to disarm the security system.

He'd left the end table lamps on in the living room, as well as the hood light above the stove. The white wall tiles and the farmhouse sink gleamed in the semidarkness. The heater kicked on, chasing away the chill they'd carried inside. His extra coat hung on a peg beside the door, and she smelled his cologne each time she walked past it. His home was becoming familiar. Comfortable. A welcoming haven of rest and security.

Cruz carried Henry into the guest room, laid him gently on the bed and removed his shoes. Henry stirred and mumbled something about peanut butter crackers.

Cruz aimed a quizzical smile at Jade. "How can he have room after all those cookies?"

"Anything to postpone bedtime," she murmured, removing clean pajamas from the dresser drawer. "Come on, Henry, let's go to the bathroom and brush your teeth."

To her surprise, Cruz was still in the room when they returned.

He tousled Henry's hair, his face softening with fondness. "Sweet dreams, cowboy."

Henry snuggled beneath the covers. "Will you read to me, Cruz?"

"It's late. Maybe tomorrow night."

"Will you pray with me?"

Cruz hesitated a moment before kneeling beside the bed. Jade's heart skipped a beat. Once Henry had Cruz's hand in his grip, he turned his big eyes toward her and extended his other hand. "Mommy, it's time to pray."

She scooted onto the bed on his other side and sandwiched his hand between hers. Her gaze locked with Cruz's, and she felt something shift inside her. He bowed his head and began to haltingly beseech God for His protection and mercy. As the prayer continued, his voice became stronger and filled with conviction—proof Cruz hadn't walked away from his faith forever.

Longing consumed her. What woman wouldn't want a dreamy, honorable cowboy cop as her own? A man who fought for justice and protected the innocent and vulnerable? A man who loved Jesus as much as she did?

Longing for something with all her heart didn't make it achievable. This feeling that she, Henry and Cruz were a family was deceptive, a lie she could easily let herself believe. A dangerous lie for them all.

Chapter Fourteen

Cruz and Silver walked out of the stables to-gether at shift's end the next day.

"You heading to the clinic?" Silver asked, pulling the collar of his black jacket up when a stiff wind blew through the parking lot. The building lights lit up the entire space, as well as part of the paddock.

"It's gonna be a long night." Jade had called him an hour ago and said the night-shift vet tech had called in sick, leaving her to fill the slot. Animals recovering from surgery needed round-the-clock care. Henry would sleep at Mason and Tessa's.

He was relieved Jade wouldn't be at the clinic after this week. While he understood her concerns about lost wages, he couldn't help feeling uneasy when they were apart.

"I considered picking up her favorite meal from the Black Bear, but she's been alone for half an hour at least. I'll have something delivered instead."

"You know her favorite meal? This is getting serious."

"Don't start."

"What's her favorite color? Espresso, like your eyes?" Silver grinned and waggled his brows.

Cruz rolled his eyes. Inwardly, he wondered about the answer to that question. The more he learned about Jade, the more he wanted to know. Silver couldn't discover that, however. He'd be relentless.

"Jade and I are too preoccupied with her ex-boyfriend to worry about individual preferences. We just so happen to have eaten several meals together. That's the only reason I know she orders the strawberry spinach salad every time. She's a healthy eater." His mom would like that.

Silver cocked his head to the side. "You like her."

"Don't you have somewhere to be? Like with your wife?"

"You don't deny it, then." Triumph gleamed in his eyes. "Lindsey thinks you two are perfect for each other, you know."

He grunted. "How is Lindsey?"

"Trying to distract me, huh?"

They reached their trucks, parked side by side, and Cruz hit the unlock fob on his key ring. His truck lights flickered in response.

"She hasn't fainted again. Around the holidays, she gets busy and forgets to eat. She's taken a larger role in the Christmas with Cops children's program this year, on top of everything else." He opened his truck door and tossed in his duffel bag. "I text her throughout the day and ask if she's eating. I've become a nag."

Silver had changed. He no longer tried to hide his scars or pretend his past hadn't happened. He was less guarded. He smiled more. Joked more. He was happier. Because of Lindsey.

Cruz thought about how Jade and Henry had changed his life in such a short time. Last night, when Henry had asked him to pray, Cruz had been knocked for a loop. The boy's innocent request had humbled him. And as he'd prayed, he realized the futility of holding on to bitterness and anger. He was only hurting himself. Plus, he'd really missed being close to God.

He'd gone to his own room, pulled out his Bible and had a long talk with the Lord. He'd asked for forgiveness and help healing his stubborn heart.

"Another fault to add to your already lengthy

list," Cruz quipped. "I don't know how she puts up with you."

"Because I'm lovable and handsome, that's why."

"See you tomorrow."

Their work schedules weren't always Monday through Friday. Occasionally, they had an event or training on the weekends. Tomorrow, they would complete drone training. Jade had promised him use of a cot for tonight, but he didn't plan to sleep. His job was to watch over her while she watched over the animals in her care.

When he pulled into the clinic lot, he surveyed the property and its surroundings. He didn't particularly like what he saw. The clinic was located on a lonely stretch of road, out past the underground caverns tourist site, and backed up to woods. A car mechanic business was across the street. The building had been neglected, and the signage for Bob's Garage had all but succumbed to time and weather. There were cars in the closed bays, however, and the tall privacy fence bordering the adjacent lot looked relatively new.

He texted Jade and climbed out of the truck, duffel bag in hand. She met him at the door, her petite frame outlined by golden light deeper in the building.

Her smile was shy, sweet and only for him. He entered, unable to keep from brushing against her as they traded places in the hallway. Beneath the smell of dog hair, pet food and disinfectant, he detected her flowery shampoo. She turned the lock and tested the handle.

Her Christmas scrubs matched her eyes. When she'd climbed into his truck this morning, her unbound hair had gleamed like strands of moonlight. She'd pulled it into a makeshift knot at some point during the day.

"I didn't think to ask if you had pet allergies."

He shook his head. "But I am allergic to Valentine's Day, erratic drivers and fancy coffee concoctions."

As they passed the exam rooms, she tilted her head in his direction. "I don't drink coffee often, as you know, and I agree with you that bad drivers should stay home. But what's wrong with Valentine's Day? You don't like stuffed bears and chocolate truffles?"

"Forced expressions of love? Inflated flower prices? High expectations no man can meet? No."

She chuckled. "Don't hold back."

He rubbed the back of his neck. "My ex-wife was picky," he confessed. "Any gift I brought home—whether for Valentine's, birthday or just because—wasn't good enough. I guess that's tainted my view."

Her sneakers squeaked against the tile as she led him into a room that was the hub of the clinic. Christmas lights were strung around the doors, flashing in patterns of vivid colors.

"For me, it's not the gift that matters," she said. "I appreciate when someone takes the time to pick out something special. That they thought about me, you know?"

Of course, Jade would have that outlook. He thought about what she'd said before. "Chocolate truffles, huh? I thought you didn't do dessert."

"I do healthy versions of dessert," she corrected, smiling. "I do have one weakness—dark chocolate and orange. That's a combination I can't resist."

He filed the information away along with other tidbits he'd collected about her during this week of close contact. For what purpose? As soon as Axel was in handcuffs, their obligatory connection would be severed. They'd return to normal life. He'd be busy with his work and his antidrug campaign, and she'd continue raising her son and caring for Serenity's animals.

She opened a door in the corner. "This is Belinda's office. I've already set up the cot. You can put your duffel in here."

A cat's pitiful mewling caused her to frown. He counted ten kennels built into the wall on their right.

"Excuse me for a second."

After stowing his duffel on the floor beside the desk, he took a moment to familiarize himself with the T-shaped building. The front section housed the lobby and reception desk, as well as the exam rooms. This back section held two offices—one for Belinda and one for her husband—a large supply room, a closet-size break room and an operating room.

A stainless steel table dominated the middle of the space. Glass-fronted cabinets lined the wall opposite the kennels.

There were three exits. The main one, a second between the exam rooms and bathroom, and a rear one leading to an enclosed kennel area. There wasn't an alarm system, which bothered him.

Jade held an orange cat tucked against her chest. The cat's eyes were droopy and bloodshot and appeared to be smeared with a clear, goopy substance. He'd stopped crying the moment she picked him up. Smart cat.

Cruz went closer. "What's he in for?"

Her nose scrunched. "You make it sound like he's in jail."

"He is. Vet jail."

"Pumpkin snuck out of his owners' house and got attacked by a stray dog. We were able to save his leg, but he has to stay here for observation for a couple of days."

"Poor fella." He reached out his hand. "Can I?"

"Sure."

He let the cat sniff his fingers before stroking the downy fur.

"Don't worry," she cooed softly to the feline. "Cruz may look big and scary, but he knows how to be gentle."

Cruz realized he'd spent more time alone with Jade than he had with any woman since moving to Serenity. He liked being around her.

Lowering his hand, he drifted to the cages and peered in the occupied ones that didn't have blankets covering the doors.

"Why does this beagle have photos taped up

in there?" he asked softly. The dog's eyes were open, but she didn't lift her head.

"Sadie is recovering from pneumonia, and she's anxious without her family." She came to stand beside him. "Her mom and dad provided the pictures and that chew toy, which is her favorite. Believe it or not, things from home calm them."

"How many overnighters do you usually have?"

She shrugged. "As you can see, we're not equipped to handle a lot of patients. Tonight we have six. Most of these patients are here because they had a scheduled surgery. We refer emergencies to the larger clinic in Maryville."

"You love what you do, don't you?"

"I do. Sometimes it gets stressful, like any other job, but I like that each day is different." She cuddled the snoozing cat closer and kissed his head. "It's rewarding when we help them feel better and in turn make their humans happy."

"I feel the same about my work. There are challenges, and some days I want to strangle someone, but I wouldn't change it for the world."

"You like it better than the narcotics unit?"

"Night and day difference. I'm not operating

on a private vendetta here. Not that I regret my time with that unit."

Opening up to Jade felt natural. She made everything easy.

"The narcotics officer who discovered Sal's body delivered the news to my parents. That wasn't standard protocol. His name was Oliver Frank. Sal's death impacted him. He said he was tired of seeing kids dying before their twenty-first birthdays. He vowed to personally run down his murderer. To our grieving family, the fact that he cared about Sal meant a lot. He's the reason I decided to go into law enforcement."

"Did he find your brother's killer?"

His gut hardened. "He was gunned down in the line of duty before he could. I was in the patrol unit at the time. Once again, Frank impacted my career. I worked my way into narcotics and eventually started undercover gigs. I became obsessed with finding the men who'd taken both Sal's and Frank's lives and making them pay. After Denise and I were married, I was home maybe two months. She got fed up and left the week before our anniversary."

Jade's expression was difficult to read. "You never considered trying to win her back?"

"She remarried and has a kid."

"And what about you? Is your heart broken beyond repair?"

"Don't get me wrong. Her decision to quit, to walk out, tore me apart. Instead of fighting for our marriage, I went harder after revenge. I lost myself in that world. One night, I almost killed a man. Woke me up in a hurry. I felt like God was telling me that if I didn't give up this vendetta, it would destroy me. So, I walked away. Turned in my badge and service weapon and returned to the ranch. I worked from dawn until dusk for weeks on end, trying to stay busy so I didn't have to think about my failures."

Reliving the memories brought the disappointment and regret to the surface, and he had a scary thought.

He'd failed to get justice for Sal and for his own family. He'd failed to do the right thing for Denise. What if, after being so careful not to put himself into this sort of situation, he failed Jade and Henry, too?

After Jade had entered WITSEC, her handler had set her up with counseling sessions. The first thing her counselor had taught her was to take ownership of her mistakes. Cruz had been up front about the ones that had cost him his marriage and almost cost him his career. It was difficult to envision him living in the same world she'd inhabited, pretending to be ruthless and making terrible decisions in order to blend in. She understood how it must've torn him apart... craving justice for his brother but hating every minute of his false existence. And in the middle of that, his wife had walked out.

Jade was relieved he wasn't pining after Denise. The inconvenient truth? She wanted him for herself.

She returned Pumpkin to his cage. "How long did it take you?"

He cocked his head to one side. "For what?"

"To stop blaming yourself."

The skin around his eyes bunched, and he lowered his gaze. That was answer enough.

"You weren't there when your brother and that officer were killed. You didn't pack your wife's bags and ask for the house keys."

He caught his breath. "That's what my mom said. She gave me space initially, but that didn't last long. The woman has practically made lecturing into an art form."

Jade would like to meet the woman who'd raised this courageous, passionate, bighearted man.

"How long before you came to Tennessee?"

"I continued my undercover work for close to nine months after Denise left before resigning that first time. The department wanted me back, and I agreed, as long as no undercover was involved. But truly, my heart wasn't in it. I couldn't shake the disappointment. After another eighteen months, I saw the job opening for Serenity's mounted patrol officer, did some research into the position and the area, and cast my name in the pool."

"Your mom doesn't ask you to come back?"

"She's accepted that I'm content here. She says this is where God wants me."

His phone beeped with a text alert, and after reading it, he told Jade, "Officer Weiland just patrolled this area, and everything is quiet. He'll come this way again in another hour. Meanwhile, I'm hungry. What about you?"

"I could go for a salad."

"You don't want to take a walk on the wild side and have a burger?"

She tucked stray ends into the messy knot at

the back of her head. "I will have some vegetable soup along with the salad."

"Can I talk you into chocolate mousse cake? We could share."

The image of them sharing a slice with one fork made her skin tingle. "I brought dessert."

He looked dubious. "Those things you made last night in the food processor?"

"Date balls."

"You put chia seeds in there. Along with other things I've never heard of. That's not dessert. What are cocoa nibs, anyway?"

Laughter bubbled up and spilled out.

"What's worse is you have poor Henry eating that stuff."

She laughed harder. Eventually his mock scowl gave way to amusement, and it reached his eyes. Oh, those eyes. They could turn her bones to jelly.

While he ordered their food on the Black Bear's website, she consulted the patient charts. The first round of meds was due to be administered soon.

As she read Pumpkin's dosage, the room was thrust into darkness.

"Cruz?"

He activated his phone light and no doubt saw

the fear that had suddenly taken hold of her features. "Does the clinic have a generator?"

"No."

She tried to remain calm, but this had Axel's name written all over it.

"I want you to lock yourself in the bathroom." His hand closed over hers.

She resisted. "I can't leave the animals."

"This is just a precaution. Someone probably plowed into an electric pole."

"And if that isn't the case?"

"Axel doesn't care about the animals." His tone was grim.

She heard what he didn't say—Axel only wanted her.

He led her into the hallway, his phone light bouncing along the walls. They were almost to the bathroom when something was launched through the front door. Glass shattered, followed by a thud.

Cruz let go of her hand and unsheathed his weapon. "Change of plans."

They retraced their steps, turning right at the end of the hall and heading for the outdoor kennel. Already, some of the dogs were whining. Poor things. She couldn't act on her urge to comfort them.

He paused at the door. "Stay close to me."
Turning the lock, he pushed the door open.
"Evenin', Officer."
Axel greeted them with a rifle and a nause-
ating smile.

Chapter Fifteen

Axel's weapon dwarfed his own, but Cruz wasn't going to lower his. That would leave him and Jade at this man's mercy.

He shifted sideways to block her. "Appears we have a problem."

"I don't have a problem. You do."

The hair on Cruz's arms stood to attention. He reached behind him to pull Jade closer, but his fingers met empty space. Her gasp was accompanied by a fourth person's grunt.

"Go ahead," Axel taunted. "Have a look."

Sweat beaded on his forehead. Taking his eye off a loaded weapon pointed right at him went against common sense. Keeping his weapon trained on Axel, he peered over his shoulder.

A second man whose features were distorted by hosiery held a gun on Jade. Her eyes pleaded with Cruz to do something. He ran through various scenarios. Each and every one had a likely outcome—a bullet in Jade or himself, or both.

Fury bubbled like volcanic lava in his gut. He couldn't let Axel win. *Think, Cruz.*

"Where are the drugs you promised me?" the man holding a gun on Jade asked Axel. He sounded young and uncertain. Definitely inexperienced at the crime game. Cruz could use that to his advantage.

"When I'm done with you," Axel snapped. "Officer Castillo, toss your weapon in the grass."

Cruz didn't have a choice. As soon as he'd done so, Axel dug the rifle barrel into his chest and shoved him back a step. "Inside."

The turning of the lock felt like a death sentence. Axel had the upper hand. Weiland wouldn't be patrolling this way for another half hour, at least.

"Move."

Axel marched everyone into the surgical room, and Hose Man set a flashlight upright on the cabinets, illuminating the center of the room. The animals moved restlessly in their cages, and Pumpkin started mewling again.

Cruz and Jade stood side by side between Belinda's office and the hallway door.

"Get their phones."

Hose Man tucked his gun in his waistband and took Cruz's phone. Jade's was on the desk. He started to pocket them, but Axel snorted.

"Do you *want* the police to track you?"

He put the phones in the desk drawer. "Now what?"

"You brought the tape."

"Oh, yeah." The younger man reached into his pocket and produced a roll of silver duct tape. "You want me to tape their hands?"

"No, I want you to make a tape sculpture," Axel retorted, his hold on the rifle steady and assured. When Hose Man hesitated, Axel growled, "Tape their wrists as tight as possible."

Cruz observed him as he taped Jade's wrists together. He was short and thin, an amateur. This was probably his first rodeo. He'd be easily bested.

Axel was another story. He'd had little else to do in prison other than pumping iron and learning to fight dirty. His distaste for law enforcement was exceeded only by his hatred for Jade.

Hose Man finished with Jade and turned to him.

"You sure you know what you're doing, kid?" Cruz murmured. "Helping an escaped felon?"

He hesitated. Cruz's muscles trembled with

the need for action. He heeded that need, lodging his elbow in the man's Adam's apple and kicking his kneecap in one quick move. The man's howls bounced off the walls as he doubled over.

Cruz rushed Axel. He grabbed the rifle with both hands and pointed it to the ceiling. Axel refused to let go, and they wrestled over the weapon. Their momentum carried them into the cabinets, cracking the glass fronts and rattling the contents. Axel chopped the side of Cruz's neck with his flattened hand. He choked, and his eyes watered. A second blow in the same spot was enough to dislodge him.

In a blink, Axel brought the barrel sideways. When it connected with Cruz's skull, he saw stars bursting in the darkness and hit the floor on all fours. He almost vomited. Blackness swirled around him.

Lord, please don't let me lose consciousness.

Jade cried out for him, but Hose Man had recovered and held her back.

"Get up." Axel landed a swift kick to Cruz's ribs. He was pretty sure he felt one crack.

He sucked in short bursts of air, trying to rise above the pain and regroup. He couldn't give up.

He grasped the surgical table and climbed to

his feet, leaning against it when his knees threatened to buckle.

"Stop! Just stop!" Jade pleaded, tugging against Hose Man's hold. "Do the right thing for once in your life, Axel. Forget this vendetta. Go live your life. Leave us alone."

"Forget?" he retorted. "Forget that my main girl played me for a fool? You know me, babe. No mercy, remember? I can't go back to my crew and tell them I let you off the hook."

"You could always lie," she challenged dryly.

"And miss out on the fun? I don't think so." He turned to his crony. "Take care of him."

Although clearly not the brightest bulb in the box, Hose Man bound Cruz's wrists tightly enough to cut off the blood supply to his hands. Having his hands fixed behind his back ramped up the pain in his side. Good. He needed the pain to keep him awake and alert. On the lookout for any opportunity to get Jade to safety.

Hose Man turned to Jade, who was leaning against the office door. "Where's the ketamine?"

"Cabinet closest to the desk."

He bounded over, busted out the glass with the butt of his gun and began stuffing the bottles into his pockets. Cruz shouldn't be surprised that the man had handed over human lives for a quick fix. Ketamine was popular in the drug scene. Since it couldn't easily be manufactured, users stole from vet clinics. Disgust coated his mouth.

"Leave one for me," Axel ordered, placing his rifle on the desk.

The implications of that command sent a shock wave through Cruz. His head whipped to Jade, whose features were horror-stricken.

"No, Axel." Jade edged toward the hallway.

He ignored her. Joining Hose Man, he told him to load a syringe for him.

Cruz started moving, too. If they could somehow get outside and flag a passerby, they might have a chance.

Axel happened to glance their way, and he muttered a string of expletives. Barreling across the room, he seized her arm and dragged her over to Hose Man. Cruz's blood boiled. He charged after them without a plan.

Axel snagged his cohort's gun and leveled it at Cruz. When Cruz halted, he went to the desk, hooked his foot around the chair leg and dragged it over.

"Sit."

Although every cell in his body rebelled, he did as ordered. If he got himself killed, he couldn't be of use to Jade. Axel kept the gun trained on him while Hose Man taped his ankles to the chair legs.

"Now can I go?" he whined.

With one clipped nod from Axel, the other man dashed out of the room, apparently uncaring that he'd left his weapon behind. The back door slammed shut. While Cruz liked that one foe had been removed from the equation, the situation was grim.

Axel shoved Jade to a seated position on the floor opposite Cruz and, stuffing the handgun in his waistband, crouched beside her. He wielded the syringe.

"Don't." Cruz's upper body strained forward, and the chair tipped over. He landed on his side, his cheek and temple glancing off the tile. The pain coursing through his body was nothing compared to what was unfolding before his eyes.

The brute trailed his fingers down her face. She cringed away from him, and he seized her chin, forcing eye contact. "Beautiful, feisty Jenny. You and I could've built an empire together. We could've been the king and queen of Gainesville. If only you hadn't ruined everything." His voice sharpened. "I wish I could stay and watch the show. The good officer here will be your only spectator."

She shook her head, her features a mask of terror. "Don't do this."

He shushed her and, maneuvering her head to one side, slid the needle in her neck and injected the liquid.

Cruz knew what God said about hating your enemies, but that was the only emotion he could manage at the moment. Hate and helplessness. He had never felt so helpless in all his life, not even when his parents had told him about Sal's death. What could he have done to change the outcome? Sal's cold, lifeless body had already been in the morgue.

Jade was still alive.

But for how long? an insidious voice prodded.

Axel pivoted and sneered at Cruz, his eyes tombs of evil. "You were a fool to think you'd beat me. Everyone who stands in my way will pay the price, one way or another."

He snatched his rifle from the table and used the same exit his partner had moments ago.

"Talk to me, Jade." He squirmed and shifted in an effort to reach her. "What can I do?"

Tears streamed down her face, and her eyes were closed. "Watch over my son," she whispered, each word punctuated with agony. "Tell him…" Her breathing was becoming labored. "Tell him I loved him."

"Look at me." He continued to try to get to her. The wooden chair was cumbersome and heavy.

She shook her head. "I can't." A sob quaked her shoulders, and her chin touched her chest, her hair streaming forward. "I can't bear it."

His chest squeezed, and his heart nearly ripped in two. She thought he would judge her? Condemn her for something out of her control?

"I want to help you. Is there anything I can give you? Some medicine to counteract the ketamine?"

She didn't answer him. Instead, she slid slowly onto her side and pulled her knees up. "I can't think right now, Cruz. I'm going to sleep for a while."

Her voice had taken on a dreamy note, and he ground his teeth together. Even if there were something in this clinic that could help her, how would he reach it?

He kept going, desperate to get to her. It seemed to take ages, but he finally got within inches of her. Their heads were close together.

He couldn't see her face, though, because of her hair.

"Hold on, Jade. Weiland will be here soon. Hold on for Henry's sake. For me, too."

It killed him to be this close to her and unable to touch her, rock her in his arms and promise her everything was going to be okay.

A soft sigh left her lips. "You're cute, you know that? My fiery Texan."

Cruz squeezed his eyes shut. He didn't want to hear that from her unless she was in her right mind.

"I'm going to try and reach the phones."

"Don't leave me," she murmured, unmoving.

"I wouldn't dream of it, darlin'."

He started praying for stamina and guidance. This was going to be nigh on impossible. Before he'd made the first move, he heard the crunch of glass.

"Cruz? You in there?"

He recognized the Black Bear waitress's voice. "Paige!" he called out. "Call an ambulance!"

Thank You, Lord. He'd ordered the food right before Axel got there. *Thank You for sending help.*

Paige entered the room and promptly dropped the paper sacks.

"Call 911," he repeated. "Then look in that desk for scissors or a knife you can use to free us."

Her mouth opened and closed. She fumbled for her cell phone and contacted dispatch. He told her what to tell them. Without ending the connection, she placed the phone on the floor and riffled through the drawers.

"Found it." The college student dashed over, her eyes as huge as the plates they used to serve their onion blossom appetizer. "What now?"

Cruz relayed his wishes, urging her to act quickly. "I don't care if you nick me. Time is not on our side."

Paige managed to slice through the tape with only a few minor cuts to his wrists. As soon as he was free, he flexed his fingers to get the blood pumping. He dispensed with the tape around his ankles and, kicking the chair away, went to work on Jade's restraints.

When her arms were free, he tucked her hair behind her ear and cupped her face.

"Help is on the way, darlin'."

Her mouth curved in an exaggerated smile. She tried to lift her finger to his nose but couldn't. Her eyes were glazed, her pupils dilated.

Her unfocused gaze bounced around the room. Did she recognize him or her surroundings? Or had her mind succumbed to the substance coursing through her veins?

He'd heard of people dying from a ketamine overdose on rare occasions. Had Axel given her a lethal amount? His heart quaked with denial.

Jade couldn't die. She couldn't. Henry needed her.

He told Paige to stay with her. Grabbing both their phones from the desk, he retrieved his gun from the outdoor kennel and returned to Jade's side. He sat on the floor and held her hand, wishing he could pour his strength into her.

"Is she going to be okay?" Paige asked, hovering nearby.

"The effects aren't long-lasting. Maybe an hour or two, depending on a variety of factors." Depending on how much was in her system.

The helpless feeling returned. He wanted nothing more than to rewind time and handle things differently. He'd failed her, just like he'd failed Sal and Denise.

The ambulance's siren was the sweetest sound he'd heard in hours.

"You came at the right time, Paige. You're an answer to prayer."

Jade didn't flinch as the sirens permeated the building, stirring the animals into a frenzy. She was unresponsive as the paramedics strapped her to the gurney. Cruz was literally shaking by the time they got her loaded into the vehicle. They rejected his request to ride with her. He could've pressed the issue, but she wouldn't know he was there anyway. He needed the solitary ride to the hospital to calm down.

Powerful, soul-shaking emotions bombarded him. He fought to regain control. He didn't want to care this deeply. Wasn't ready to risk his heart again. Not for anyone, not even Jade.

She was being pulled deep under the waves, a manacle around her wrist holding her fast. Her lungs begged for relief. Startled awake, she found herself in a dim, sterile room. The whoosh and whisper of the ocean rolled from a speaker. Out of place here, yet it explained her dream. Her skin was tight and itchy, and her head throbbed. When she tried to lift her hand, she met resistance.

The manacle. Was she handcuffed to the bed?

Her heart fluttering in panic, she tugged harder. Something—no, someone—shifted in the chair. The fingers around her wrist began to stroke her sensitive skin. She got a whiff of

Cruz's distinct scent and turned her head on the thin pillow.

The expression on his bruised face was hard to decipher. The memories of what happened at the clinic slammed into her, making her gasp. She bolted upright. Her stomach swooshed sideways.

"Are you in pain?" He stood, one hand cradling his ribs.

"I'm not taking any more drugs, legal or not," she said hotly.

Humiliation and denial crawled over her skin like tiny spiders. She'd vowed to herself that she wouldn't ever lose herself like that again. Lose time. Lose control.

For this to happen at all was her worst nightmare. For Cruz to witness it? Beyond words.

She buried her face in her hands.

The tears didn't come. She felt hollow. Her hope? Gone.

Why did this happen, God? You know my struggles, how difficult it was to rise out of the ashes. You remember my commitment to a clean, upright life. All I wanted was to raise my son in this peaceful mountain town and leave Axel and my bad choices behind.

He cleared his throat. "The doctor said it's unlikely you'll experience cravings. Ketamine isn't as addictive as other substances."

She lifted her head. He'd backed away, almost to the door, and he stood with his hands at his sides. He looked miserable. Or was he uncomfortable being around her?

Her heart thrummed with indignation. "The day I had my first ultrasound and saw my baby, I vowed I wouldn't put anything in my body that would harm him. I checked out library books and read blogs about nutrition. I traded coffee for smoothies, sugary cereals for oatmeal, candy bars for date balls. After he was born, my convictions strengthened. He was entirely dependent on me, and I wouldn't have jeopardized his well-being for anything. I've stuck to that vow." Her hands twisted the crisp, abrasive sheets. "I refuse to let Axel or anyone else derail me."

His expression shuttered even more, and his gaze slid to his boots. She suddenly wished him gone. In the clinic, he'd risked his life to try and save her. He'd obviously had time to mull over what happened. He was acting as if she was the girl she used to be...

She squeezed her eyes shut, gripped with embarrassment. While under the influence, how had she acted? Looked? Talked? All she knew was that, more than anything, she'd craved this man's approval.

Be real. You wanted far more than that.

Clearly, from his body language, she would be getting neither.

"Why are you still here, Cruz?"

His forehead furrowed, and something sparked in his eyes. "Where else would I be?"

"You obviously want to be anywhere else but here."

"That's not true—"

A knock announced a nurse's arrival, and he clamped his mouth shut. The pretty young brunette checked her vitals and announced she was free to leave.

Jade was tempted to call Tessa and ask her to pick her up. Tessa would be happy to take her and Henry in, as would Lindsey and Raven. But that would invite questions and potentially put Cruz in a tough spot with his sergeant and fellow officers, not to mention confuse and upset Henry even further.

She was resilient. She could handle his silent condemnation.

This was a timely reminder that caring for the Texan wasn't wise. He would never reciprocate her feelings. Besides, she didn't need a man who lost faith in her so easily.

She swung her feet around to the floor, and

the room tilted. He moved to assist her, but she held him off. The sensation gradually faded.

"Who's caring for the animals? They need meds and fluids, not to mention lots of reassurance. They can't be left alone. Did you get my phone? I have to contact Belinda."

"Already taken care of. I called her on the way here and explained everything. She was heading straight over to the clinic."

Jade kneaded her forehead. "Those poor animals…"

"The important thing is none of them were hurt."

He was right. "Can you wait out in the hall?"

Surprise flickered across his face. "You might not be steady on your feet after…"

His words trailed off, riling her.

"After I was pumped full of ketamine?"

He grimaced and looked away.

"Just go."

He turned on his booted heel and closed the door softly behind him. It was wrong that she felt disappointed, that she had wanted him to ignore her words, take her into his arms and hold her. When she glimpsed her reflection in the bathroom's unforgiving lights, she almost broke down. She'd looked the same after a night of partying.

Messy hair. Bloodshot eyes. Smeared mascara. Dry, cracked lips.

She gripped the porcelain sink and willed the tears away.

"I didn't choose this," she said aloud.

She couldn't let the creeping shame take root. Couldn't let Axel destroy her.

Refocused, she donned her dirty scrubs because they were all she had and stepped out into the hall.

Cruz was silent during the long walk through the hospital. Once inside his truck, he blasted the heater and turned on the radio but still did not speak. The tension inside the cab was almost unbearable. She wanted to rail at him. How dare he condemn her?

The fact he'd opened his home to her and Henry without complaint and had risked his life for hers kept her silent.

Her relief was significant when his house came into view. Outside fixtures lit up the yard, and the living room windows gleamed a soft yellow. He ushered her in—close but not touching, fortunately—deactivated the alarm, and offered her drinks and food. She declined and ducked into the bathroom, desperate to wash away the grime. If only she could wash away tonight's events with soap and water.

When she emerged, he was waiting in the hallway with an oversize mug of hot herbal tea.

"Better?"

She wrapped both hands around the mug and inhaled the scents of honey, lemon and ginger. He watched her sip the tea, his unwavering focus doing strange things to her equilibrium.

"Much better." She held the mug close to her chest and ordered her body to behave. "Did a doctor check your injuries?"

"Nothing major. Bruised ribs."

Lights flashed through the living room windows, followed by a car door slamming.

Uneasiness swirled through her. "Who's that?"

"I hope you don't mind," he said, hesitating. "I asked her to come."

She trailed him into the living room, curiosity warring with dread. She wasn't up for company.

He opened the door and moved aside. Her best friend stood on the porch.

"Leslie!"

Leslie enveloped her in a hug, and the dam holding back Jade's emotions crumbled into bits. Tears flooded her cheeks, and sobs shook her body. When Leslie led her to the couch and offered her a package of tissues from her purse, Jade noticed Cruz had disappeared.

"What did Cruz tell you?"

"Only that you needed me." Leslie's eyes brimmed with concern and questions.

"He's right. I do." She blew her nose and swiped at her cheeks.

She couldn't believe he'd done this for her. It didn't change anything between them, however. He wasn't the man God had in mind for her, and she certainly wasn't his new lease on life.

Chapter Sixteen

"You've made my taste buds dance in anticipation," Leslie said as Cruz slid a plate in front of her Saturday morning. She took a big whiff. "What's this called again?"

"*Machacado.* Shredded dried beef, scrambled eggs and *pico de gallo.* I added shredded cheese. It's the only breakfast my mom taught me to make. She had to twist my arm to get me in the kitchen. Now that I don't have frequent access to her cooking, I regret my laziness."

His smile was strictly for Leslie's benefit. Jade's friend was astute. Did she sense the undercurrent of tension passing between them?

"Yogurt and granola for you, as requested." He set a bowl before her.

"I would like to try your dish," she said, determined to be pleasant. She was a guest in his home, after all. An unwanted guest. "But I'm not sure what my stomach can handle this morning."

She'd wakened with a slight headache and a general feeling of unwellness. That could be due to the ketamine's lingering effects or lack of sleep. She and Leslie had talked for hours last night, crying, hugging and praying.

His gaze lingered on her. "I'll fix it again another day."

Leslie took a bite and hummed loudly. "Okay, now my taste buds are doing the salsa. You could charge for this, you know."

Over at the stove, Cruz scooped a hefty portion for himself. "I'm glad you like it."

He returned to the table, wincing as he sat in the chair across from them, and picked up his fork. Mottled bruising covered his cheek. Jade had a flashback of him bound to the chair, of it crashing to the floor, of Axel's boot aiming for his ribs.

A lump formed in her throat.

"You should be resting today," she blurted. "Not waiting on us."

Cruz didn't look up from his plate. "I'm not letting you loose in my kitchen," he quipped. "You're likely to sneak dates in my food."

Laughter shook Leslie's shoulders. "Smart man. If you're not careful, she'll have you eating hockey pucks for breakfast."

Jade elbowed her. "You're being melodramatic. My pumpkin-oat muffins are tasty and good for you."

Leslie pointed her fork at Cruz. "Hockey pucks."

He changed the subject by inviting Leslie to talk about her family. He exuded an interested air, but his gaze repeatedly returned to his phone and occasionally to the windows. Clearly, he hadn't forgotten the reason he had guests to feed.

Jade's stomach tightened. She swirled the granola through the yogurt, her appetite nonexistent. Where was Axel? It was too much to hope he'd left town, satisfied with his victory. Knowing him, he'd stuck around to make sure he'd finished the job. Or maybe this was his way of toying with her.

"I had plans to visit Texas between Christmas and the new year," Cruz was saying, "but I'm not sure if I will go or not."

Jade looked at him, and he covered the moment with a long sip of coffee.

"If you go," Leslie told him, "I'll pay you to bring back some of your mama's cooking. Or even better, her recipes."

Leslie launched into a conversation about

her own family's favorite foods, all of which Jade had sampled at one time or another. When they'd finished eating, Leslie received a call from her son and excused herself. Jade carried the dishes to the sink. Before Cruz could start rinsing them, she put her hand on his arm.

His dark eyes all but consumed her, causing her heart to trip over itself.

She withdrew her fingers as if his skin was a hot griddle. "You knew exactly what I needed. I can't thank you enough."

"She's important to you."

"Leslie is a special woman, and I'm grateful God brought her into my life."

She was grateful for Cruz, too, despite how things stood between them.

The doorbell rang. "That will be Mason and Tessa," he said, drying off his hands and letting them in.

Henry raced straight for Jade, his face beaming. "Mommy, guess what? We had blueberry pancakes for breakfast!"

She knelt and enveloped him in a hug, overwhelmed with gratitude. Henry could have been without a mother this morning, had God not kept His hand of protection on her.

He wouldn't have been alone, however. Every

single person in this house would have made sure he was loved and cared for.

Unaware of her deep thoughts, Henry wiggled out of her arms. "Lily's going to get a hamster for Christmas," he claimed. "And I got to sleep in her tepee."

"Is that right?"

Mason and Tessa were in conversation with Cruz. Lily was tucked in her daddy's arms, her head on his shoulder and big eyes surveying the room.

Leslie emerged from the bedroom and greeted Henry with a giant smile. He ran into her open arms, and she dispensed with an exaggerated bear hug.

Mason and Tessa had met Leslie before, and they came over to greet her.

Henry tugged on her blouse sleeve. "Are you going to be at my birthday party?"

Her dark eyes met Jade's in question. "I haven't missed one yet, young man."

Jade sighed. She would have to speak to Henry today and explain that the arcade party he'd begged for wasn't going to happen, after all.

Cruz stepped close beside her, his fingers skimming her back. She shivered, his touch shimmering up and down her spine. It wasn't enough. It was never enough.

"Can I talk to you for a moment?"

"Uh, sure."

They moved into the hallway near his bedroom. "I have an idea for an alternative birthday celebration and thought I'd run it by you before I take it to Mason."

Surprised, she gestured for him to go on.

"Henry loves horses. What if we decorated the stables and set up cake and presents in the break room? Ten kids and their families would be too many, but I thought Lily and Kai could be there. Security wouldn't be an issue. The horses don't mind noise or balloons, of course." He shifted his stance, his expression somber. "What do you think? Not as exciting as an arcade, but it could work."

"He does love horses."

"He'd be the first kid ever to have his birthday party at the mounted police stables."

She shouldn't be surprised that he'd given thought to her son's happiness. Throughout this whole ordeal, Cruz had been wonderful with Henry. Of course, Henry wasn't the one he had a problem with.

"It's perfect. Thank you, Cruz."

For a brief instant, sadness shone in his eyes.

He recovered quickly, though, inclining his head and returning to the group.

What did he have to be sad about?

Cruz felt like he'd been stomped on by an angry bull. He walked stiffly between the trees behind the vet clinic, his gaze scanning the carpet of dead leaves and pine needles, hoping to find something linked to Axel's accomplice. Hose Man was probably a local. Running him down just might lead them to their man.

He turned to glance back at the clinic, his ribs angry at the inconsiderate movement. Raven stopped her search lower down the hill and raised her brows. "You should be at home with Jade."

That was the last place he should be. After the others had left, she and Henry had settled on the couch, cozied beneath a blanket, and turned on a Christmas movie. Henry had asked him to join them. Jade's eyes had been telling. She didn't want him to stay.

He knew exactly what she thought of him. And even though it was eating him up inside, he wasn't going to correct her assumptions. This distance between them was necessary. He couldn't let his feelings for her grow any more than they already had.

Desperate for a reprieve from the cozy living room scene, he'd called Bell and asked him to guard the house so he could help SPD with the search. Mason had decided to postpone the drone training scheduled for today.

Raven bent to examine a broken branch, her thick braid swinging forward over her shoulder. "Jade seems to be doing okay."

Leslie hadn't been gone ten minutes before the rest of his unit and their significant others had descended on his house. Jade had gotten teary-eyed amid all the hugs and encouragement. His friends had rallied around her, and he appreciated that more than he could say. It was as if, by supporting her, they were supporting him, as well. But he and Jade weren't a team or a couple. Never would be.

"She's a fighter."

Raven straightened. "I'm glad you took lead on her case."

"Why?"

"You need her."

Hands hanging at his sides, he stared at her. "Why?"

"If you have to ask, you've been alone too long, my friend."

"Here's the problem. The three of you are

thick in the middle of marital bliss, and you want me to drink the same punch. I'm not getting married again. Period." He didn't care how beautiful, sweet and loving Jade was or what kind of reaction she caused inside him each time she came near.

"Who said anything about marriage?" Her eyes sparkled.

He rolled his eyes and started walking again. His head throbbed with each step.

Raven wasn't done, though. "Your personalities complement each other beautifully. She's grounded, calm and smooths your rough edges."

He grunted. Calmness wasn't the reaction she aroused in him.

"Young Henry has taken a shine to you. You'd make a wonderful dad to him and any other kiddos that came along."

"How about you focus on your own relationship?" he snapped, irritated that her rambling created images of dark-haired, green-eyed babies. He was *not* going to daydream about having children with Jade. "When are you and Aiden going to start a family?"

Her cheeks pinked. "I'd like to have him all to myself for a while before we start our family."

Cruz's ire cooled. He supposed he could understand why his friends wanted him to find love. If he had what they had, he'd want the people he cared about to experience similar happiness.

"Castillo! We got something!"

He and the others converged on the far corner of the fence line. Weiland held an evidence bag aloft. Inside was the hosiery Axel's accomplice had been wearing.

Raven touched his elbow. "Think he was smart enough to wash it first?" she asked sarcastically.

"If only we could get the DNA results in hours rather than days." Or even weeks.

"We're not gonna sit on our hands while we wait," she reminded him. "Between SPD, the sheriff's department, and our FBI and marshal friends, we'll identify this guy, and he'll lead us to Axel."

"I wish I had your confidence."

"I know God's on our side. Remember my favorite verse."

"'But without faith it is impossible to please Him, for he that cometh to God must believe that He is, and that He is a rewarder of them that diligently seek Him.'"

She had it plastered on her locker and framed on her office desk.

Cruz found himself praying for faith. The faith to trust in God's plan. He prayed for strength and wisdom to protect Jade. And to guard his heart until this case was over.

Chapter Seventeen

Monday morning, at last. Five days until Christmas. Jade stared out the window at the passing houses adorned with cheerful ribbons, wreaths and snowmen, her fingers combing through her scarf fringes. Normally she'd be making the trek to town alone on a weekday. After dropping Henry at a sitter's or school, she'd head straight to the clinic. But the clinic was closed today for cleaning and repair work, and, she reminded herself, she had been put on leave. Belinda and David had brought flowers to her at Cruz's on Saturday evening and apologized profusely for not having an alarm at the clinic. They were understandably shocked that the robbers had injected her with ketamine. Of course, they didn't know about her past or her connection to Axel. And she'd kept it that way.

Cruz had excused himself during that portion of the conversation. Her heart squeezed painfully.

Turning her head, she observed his profile. If he sensed her gaze, he didn't show it. He kept his attention on the road ahead, gloved hands propped on his thighs and fingers on the wheel. His black jacket collar was turned up, skimming the underside of his chin.

He'd avoided her most of yesterday. After watching online church services with her and Henry—because attending in person carried too much risk—he'd shared a hastily assembled lunch and then descended into his downstairs retreat. Henry had gotten curious and ventured down there. She'd heard conversation and, later, a television program. She hadn't gone to investigate.

The chasm between them shouldn't hurt this much. She regretted giving him the power to hurt her. Her fault, of course. Cruz hadn't let on that he had feelings for her. He'd been the consummate professional.

Though she suspected he'd rather be far from her, he kept her at his side today as they rode toward town.

Up ahead, right before a mom-and-pop gas station, a cruiser with flashing lights waited on the road's shoulder. A beat-up hatchback sat at an angle, partly on the asphalt and partly in the yellowed grass. Cruz slowed the truck and parked behind it. She could see a man's silhouette in the back.

Officer Bell had called and informed Cruz that he'd discovered a bottle of ketamine during a routine traffic stop. Since they'd already dropped Henry at Elaine's, they'd driven straight over.

Tucking her scarf deeper into her coat, she exited the truck. The morning air was brisk and scented with pine. The thick cloud cover hung close above their heads, blocking the sun.

Officer Bell met her and Cruz in the space between their vehicles.

"I pulled him over for a broken taillight. He was agitated, and his car reeks of weed. I conducted a search and found this."

Bell held a bottle in his gloved hand. "The prescription label has been scratched off. I tested the contents. Positive for ketamine."

Cruz looked at Jade. "Is this from the clinic?"

"It looks like ours."

Bell's gaze tracked a passing garbage truck. "I already checked with vets in surrounding towns, and none of them have had recent thefts."

Cruz gestured to the cruiser. "He tell you where he scored this?"

"He hasn't said much."

"Because he's under the influence?" Cruz said sharply.

Bell shook his head. "Seems relatively sober to me. It's more of not wanting to snitch."

"Has he been in trouble before?" Jade asked, shivering when the wind gusted and whipped at her hair.

"This is his first offense." Bell set the ketamine on the trunk beside a test kit. "His name is Kent Myers. I'm sure you know his mom, Cruz. She's a waitress at the Black Bear. Been there for years."

"Vickie?" Cruz squinted at the rear window.

"That's the one."

He groaned. "Vickie's a sweetheart. She brags on her son every chance she gets. She's gonna be devastated. Why do these kids continue to make dumb decisions?"

"For a lot of reasons," Jade shot back. "Or none at all."

Bell's gaze bounced between them before he opened the rear door and assisted the young man outside. His clothes were disheveled, and his honey-blond hair hung in his eyes.

Jade bit down hard on her lip. He couldn't have been more than twenty. If not for the dark circles under his eyes and belligerent glare, he would've been handsome.

"I'm not a squealer," he snarled.

His gaze snagged on her, and his brow furrowed, no doubt confused by her presence. She offered a tremulous smile. His eyes widened before sliding to his feet.

"You scratch our back, we'll scratch yours," Cruz said.

There was no response.

"We need a name. Who sold you the K?"

Kent scuffed his untied shoe against the pavement.

Cruz folded his arms over his chest. "What are you? A senior in high school?"

"Yeah. So?"

"Your record is clean. Adding a drug charge is going to make it harder to get into college or the military."

"Who cares?"

His tough attitude was belied by the hint of worry in his voice.

"You think Patrick in the gas station here will be eager to hire you? How could he trust you to run the cash register? You'd be fortunate if he trusts you to clean his bathrooms."

When he didn't respond, Cruz shrugged.

"Have it your way. We'll take you in and call Vickie. Or should you be the one to tell her? You do get a phone call."

Kent's head whipped up. "You know my mom?"

"Sweet lady. I'm a regular at the café. She talks about you a lot. Of course, she probably won't want to share this with the customers."

The boy licked his lips, his expression panicked. "I scored it off a guy who comes around the high school. He used to go there."

Bell pulled out his notebook. "Name?"

"Scott Pelt."

"He's on our radar," Bell told Cruz.

"Thought it sounded familiar. Where does he live, Kent?"

"I don't know, I swear. He hangs out in the athletic park near the school. That's where students meet up with him."

Cruz's eyes were black with outrage. A rock thrown at his jaw would bounce off, it was so rigid.

Kent shivered beneath that glare. "You're not going to tell him who told you, are you?"

"No, but I will be having a talk with your mom."

"Hey—"

"And giving another speech at the high school. Looks like I'll have to up my game."

Bell unlocked Kent's handcuffs. "Don't let me catch you with drugs in your possession again. No more second chances, you hear?"

The boy nodded shakily and, with one last glance at Cruz, hurried to his car. The engine sputtered to life, and he drove away. Bell got into his cruiser to access his computer, leaving her and Cruz alone for a moment.

"I can talk to the students," Jade offered before fully thinking it through.

Cruz turned to stare, his lips parting.

The more she thought about it, the more she was convinced she could help. She should at least try. "What good is my past if I don't use it to point others in the right direction? If I can stop one kid from taking the same path, it would be worth it."

Why hadn't he thought of this before? Not Jade, specifically, but someone who could speak from personal experience. The students were much more likely to listen to a civilian who'd overcome poor lifestyle choices than they were a cop.

Before he could answer, Bell returned with Scott Pelt's address.

"How do you want to play it?"

"We'll need backup on the off chance Scott's not alone. I'll ask Mason to meet us there."

"I'll reach out to Weiland," Bell said. "What about our FBI and marshal friends?"

"We'll contact them if this pans out."

Distracted, he placed his hand against Jade's back as they returned to the truck. Her sharp inhale reminded him of his place.

I'm a cop. She's a citizen in trouble. A case number. Nothing more.

He climbed behind the wheel, careful not to tax his sore ribs, and texted Mason. Pulling onto the road behind Bell, he told Jade, "Mason's set to meet us at the Wingate apartment complex. You'll have to stay in the truck until we secure the suspect."

"All right."

Her voice was soft, almost sad. He glanced over. Her charcoal-gray peacoat and multicolored scarf enhanced her eyes. Sparkly silver clasps were tucked into her hair above her left ear, while the rest flowed unchecked down her back. Miniature silver tree earrings winked in her earlobes. Her fingernails shimmered a forest green.

He was used to seeing her in scrubs. While those weren't boring—some were neon hues and some had playful prints—this outfit was dressy. Festive, even.

Celebrating the holiday season was far from her mind, he was certain. Did she, like him, keep replaying Friday's chaotic scenes? Did she relive the helplessness and frustration? The not knowing if they would live to see another sunrise?

Gritting his teeth, he turned up the radio and studied the passing scenery. Weiland was already at the complex when they parked. Mason joined them ten minutes later.

Bell showed them a photograph of their guy. Cruz wasn't able to positively identify him, thanks to the hosiery disguise Axel's accomplice had worn, but Scott did fit the body weight and height categories.

Cruz scoped out the complex. Should he leave Jade in the truck? She would be far from the action. Vulnerable, though. He was second-guessing his decisions, and that didn't bode well.

He opened her door. "Come with us. You can hang back, out of sight."

The group hemmed her in as they crossed the lot, bypassing the office and several buildings to reach the last one on this row. Each two-story section was comprised of eight apartments, with a central, outdoor staircase. Pulling their weapons, they climbed the metal stairs to the second story and approached the right rear unit.

Cruz motioned to Weiland to stay back and guard Jade. The officer nodded and maneuvered her close to the building.

Bell pounded on the door, referred to as a cop knock—one that could alert the neighbors.

They heard muttering and footsteps. The door cracked open to reveal a bleary-eyed, sandy-haired man. "What do you want?"

"Scott Pelt? My colleagues and I have some questions for you."

The authoritative tone, along with the uniforms and guns, jolted the man awake. He shoved on the door. Bell stopped it with his foot and advanced into the apartment. Cruz was right behind him, and Mason held up the rear.

Scott tripped over a garbage can and sprawled on the carpet. "You can't do this. I haven't done anything."

Bell held his weapon aloft while Cruz and

Mason cleared the rooms. When they deemed it safe, Bell holstered his gun and hauled Scott to his feet. He pointed to the couch.

"Sit."

Mason began to look around the kitchen. "Bingo."

When he held up three bottles of ketamine, Scott paled.

Cruz's pulse thundered in his ears. Stepping between the coffee table and the couch, he loomed over Scott. "Where were you Friday night between the hours of 6:00 and 8:00 p.m.?"

Scott looked up, for the first time seeming to notice the mottled bruising on Cruz's cheek. His lips pulled back in fear, revealing uneven front teeth. He visibly swallowed.

Mason cleared his throat. "Holster your weapon, Cruz."

"I was here, man," Scott said. "Some friends came over to party."

"Don't lie to me." The clinic attack fresh in his mind, he started to lean in.

"Cruz," Mason barked. "Your gun."

Scott stared up at him with wide eyes. Cruz blew out a breath, counted to ten and obeyed his superior officer's command. Weapon secured, he leaned in.

"We found the hose disguise outside the clinic. It's only a matter of time before the DNA results are in. Let's try this again. Where were you Friday night?"

Beads of sweat popped out on his forehead.

"I was there, okay? I needed the score. But I didn't hurt you or your lady friend, remember? I didn't lay a hand on you."

"No, you helped the man who did hurt us." Fury built inside him. Jade could have died. "Between that and the ketamine, you're going away for a very long time."

Cruz kicked the coffee table leg. Bell and Mason stared at him, brows raised, silently asking if they needed to take over.

"I didn't know what he had planned, you know."

"You didn't care," Cruz growled, glaring down at him. "Where is Axel now?"

"I swear, I don't know."

"Where'd you meet him?"

"The Rusty Nail. He approached me. Asked if I wanted to make some money and score some K."

"When?"

"Thursday night. He told me to meet him

Friday afternoon at the bar. When I got there, he gave me a handgun and explained what he wanted. I haven't seen him since that night."

Mason propped his boot on the couch cushion. "Did he say where he's staying?"

"No."

"Did you see what he was driving?"

"A black truck." He gave them the make and model. "The windshield was cracked."

Mason immediately got on the phone with dispatch.

Bell got the handcuffs ready. "Anything else you can think of that will help us locate him?"

"Can't we make a deal here or something?" Scott whined. "I told you what I know."

Cruz swallowed his retort and stalked outside.

"Nothing unusual out here," Weiland said before handing off Jade and heading inside.

Jade pushed off from the wall, her expression hopeful. Cruz wished he had more to offer, to keep her hope alive.

"We got a make and model, so we're putting out a BOLO for the vehicle Axel was using Friday," he told her.

Her expression fell. "He could've already ditched it."

"It's a possibility. But if he doesn't think we can track down his buddy Scott, he'll keep using it."

A breeze teased the ends of her platinum hair. She put her hands together and blew on them. He pulled his gloves off.

"Take mine."

She stared at the gloves, then lifted her gaze to his. "No, thanks."

He hadn't realized she had a stubborn streak. Or maybe she wasn't in the mood to accept any kind gestures from him. "Please?"

She took the gloves and put them on. They engulfed her small hands, of course, but they'd keep her fingers warm. "What happens now?"

"The feds and marshals are going to be all over this new info. They'll search for Axel."

"He's managed to evade authorities this long. What makes you think that will change now?"

"We have to stay positive, Jade. If not for ourselves, for Henry."

She bit down hard on her lip, shook her head and stared at nothing. He yearned to comfort her with more than words. Instead, he stuffed his hands in his pockets.

He was not what she needed or what she wanted, he reminded himself.

The rift he'd allowed to grow between them would have to remain intact.

Chapter Eighteen

Her baby was six years old.

That evening, Jade placed the decorated cake on the table and watched Henry's smile stretch from ear to ear, his big green eyes reflecting the shimmering candles. As the birthday song swelled in the stables' break room, the deeper, smoother adult voices blending with the children's high-pitched ones, she was overwhelmed with God's goodness.

Although she didn't deserve the blessings He'd showered upon her, she was deeply grateful. *Thank You, Jesus.*

Jade carved the cake into slices and placed them on colorful paper plates. Elaine doled them out to the kids first and then the officers and other adults. When everyone had cake, Jade retreated to the drinks station at the back wall and poured herself a glass of lemon water. The break room was outfitted with a fridge, upper and lower cabinets, and a sink. A microwave and coffee maker sat on the counter.

"You forgot to serve yourself." Tessa joined her, holding out a plate of cake. "You have to try this."

Jade accepted the plate and dutifully took a bite, even though she had zero appetite. The chocolate cake with fudge glaze had the perfect amount of sweetness. When she'd called the bakery to order Henry's cake, she'd asked for something that wouldn't make their teeth ache. "This is good."

"It's delicious," Tessa agreed. "I might have to order this for Mason's birthday."

They could see the entire room from their vantage point. The adults had to wade through the bobbing balloons and repeatedly bat them away. Streamers dripped from the walls. Every color of the rainbow was represented in the tablecloths and coordinated plates, napkins, cups and forks.

"Sending Mason, Cruz and Silver to the party supply store might've been a mistake," Jade said, smiling wryly. "Do you think they left anything for the other customers?"

"According to Mason, this is all on Cruz. He

had no self-control." Tessa laughed. "They all want Henry to have the best birthday ever."

Cruz was crouched beside Henry's chair and listening intently to whatever he was saying. How odd it was that, in such a short time, Cruz had become integral to her happiness. He'd come to matter to her and her son.

She allowed herself to appreciate how his navy-hued SMP shirt enhanced his golden skin and midnight hair and molded to his strong shoulders and muscular back. Then she cut the thoughts off and turned her focus to her son.

"I can't believe he's six. I still remember how he looked when he was first born. He was crying when the nurse placed him in my arms. I was terrified." She paused, remembering all the birthdays since then. Some had been easier than others. "The years seem to have gone by in a blink."

"I know how you feel."

Jade and Tessa had both had their babies without the support of family. Both had raised their children alone under stressful circumstances. Tessa's story had a happy ending—she'd reconciled with the father of her child, and they were raising Lily together. That wasn't possible for Jade.

"I have big hopes for my boy," she said, shoving the futile thoughts away. "I want him to follow his dreams. I want him to be happy and fulfilled. Most importantly, I want him to love Jesus and follow Him with all his heart."

Tessa squeezed her arm. "You're doing it right, Jade. He's precious. I confess, I sometimes like to think he and Lily might wind up together."

Jade grinned. "Then you and I would officially be family."

Tessa's brow creased. "You already are my family."

"Stop that. You're going to make me cry."

She'd spent so much time crying during this season that was supposed to be joyful. Tears of fear, frustration, anger and sadness. Today was a celebration.

Leslie separated from the group and ventured over. "I need your baker's name."

Jade finished off her last bite and told her about the bakery. "I'm glad I took Lindsey's advice and went there."

"Henry doesn't seem upset about the change in his birthday plans," Leslie said, watching him.

"The Serenity Mounted Police aim to serve and, in this case, save a little boy's birthday."

"Cruz instigated this whole thing," Tessa said, pouring herself a decaffeinated soda.

They watched as Cruz grinned at Henry and patted his arm.

Leslie let out a satisfied grunt. "He cares about Henry as if he's his own son."

Jade pressed her lips together. He was clearly fond of Henry. But he wasn't looking to be part of a family again, and definitely not with her.

"Can we open presents now, Mommy?" Henry called out to her.

Jade nodded. She pasted on a smile and chose the first paper-wrapped box from the gift table she passed.

"That one's from me," Cruz told Henry, his dark eyes fastened on Jade.

Did he realize how he looked at her sometimes? Like she was a source of fascination? Like he couldn't decide if he trusted her or not?

Henry ripped open the paper and cheered. Cruz had gotten him an art set with markers, crayons, colored pencils and stickers.

Henry peered up at him. "Can we draw more animals?"

"You can count on it, cowboy."

Kai and Lily pressed in on either side of Henry's chair, exclaiming over each gift he opened.

When he'd revealed the final one, Cruz clapped his hands together.

"Who's ready to give the horses treats?"

The kids jumped up and down, each eagerly taking an apple and trailing Cruz out of the room. Jade got her phone ready to take pictures. In the stable area, everyone waited along one side while Cruz, Silver and Mason led the horses out of their stalls.

Jade's jaw dropped. Each horse looked like they were about to take part in a royal parade. Their manes and tails were woven with ribbons of all shades. Pinks, yellows, greens, blues. The kids gazed at them in awe.

Raven nudged her shoulder. "Stunning, isn't it?"

"Did you do this?"

Her black brows winged up. "Me? I don't have the patience. While you and Henry were hiding out in the meeting room earlier and Silver, Mason and I were decorating the break room, Cruz was out here prettying up the horses."

She blinked. Cruz grinned as he boosted Henry onto Renegade's back. She'd never seen him this relaxed before.

"Are you sure?"

"Why is it so difficult for you to believe? He

adores your son. He's good with kids in general. I keep telling him to find a wife already and start a family. He's hardheaded, though."

There was something in her tone that brought Jade's gaze back to her. "What aren't you saying?"

She shrugged, her honey-colored eyes twinkling. "I don't know what you mean."

"You don't think that he and I…"

"Why not? It's obvious you care about each other."

The caring was one-sided. "It's not that simple."

"Love doesn't have to be complicated." Raven caught her husband's gaze from across the way and winked. He immediately started making his way through the crowd to get to her.

"You can forget about a happy ending for Cruz and me. He will never be able to see beyond my past mistakes."

His response to Axel's latest attack was proof. Yearning for a different outcome didn't make it reality. She'd accepted that her energies had to be directed to her son's happiness and well-being, not her own.

"You're wrong—"

Raven was cut off by Aiden's arrival. He

wrapped his arm around her, tugged her close and dropped a kiss on her hair.

"I have to take pictures," Jade said, unwilling to finish the conversation.

For the remainder of the party, she focused on Henry, which was as it should be. But as they loaded the presents in Cruz's truck, drove to his house and carried them and the leftover cake inside, a storm brewed inside her. An irrational anger suffused her like a bonfire.

While she got Henry washed up and ready for bed, Cruz went out to the barn to see to Gunsmoke and Old Bob's needs. She read several books to Henry, but her mind was on the man of the house. Henry had fallen asleep by the time she heard the back door open and close, Cruz's boots thud to the floor, one by one, and him lumber through the kitchen to his bedroom.

Without thinking through what she would say, she left Henry's room and strode after him, catching him before he closed his bedroom door. He'd removed his coat and, tossing it onto the bed, returned to the hallway. His tall, broad frame seemed to fill the entire space. She'd never felt intimidated by his size, but right now he was too much for her to handle.

"What's wrong?"

"Why are you doing this?" she demanded, her voice harsh and shaky.

He splayed his hands. "Doing what, exactly?"

"Opening your home. Babysitting us 24-7. Risking your life."

His brows lowered. "You've been in a strange mood all evening. What's really bothering you, Jade?"

"That party was over-the-top." Her eyes filled with hot tears. "Why are you being so nice?"

His lips parted on a breath. "Um…"

"Why act like you care when, deep down inside, I disgust you?"

Anger chased disbelief across his face like thunder after lightning. "Stop."

"Can't handle the truth, can you? Can't handle what I once was?" she lashed out, poking his chest.

"Stop talking, Jade," he growled. His fingers gripped her shoulders.

"You see me as broken and weak and shameful—"

His mouth came down on hers. She gasped. Delight quickly eclipsed her shock.

His lips were firm and smooth, insistent and greedy.

He pressed her against the wall, his chest imprisoning her. She wasn't going anywhere, not when the man her heart cried out for every second of the day was single-handedly tipping her world upside down.

Her fingers curling into his sides, holding him fast, Jade kissed him back with all the fervor he dished out.

Jade Harris was going to be the death of him.

He submerged his fingers into her platinum hair. The strands felt like silk against his skin, as he'd known they would. Her flowery shampoo scent enveloped him, transporting him to an oasis, a safe place where no obstacles existed between them.

She was sweeter than Texas sheet cake and spicier than a ghost pepper.

He cradled her head. Jade was all woman in his arms. So soft. Warm. Loving.

Something clicked into place, and the need to protect Jade at all costs—even from himself—overtook him. He hit the brakes, gentling the kiss until it became a reverent, tentative voyage of discovery.

He didn't want to end it. He had to end it.

Lifting his head, he gazed down into her

beautiful eyes that swirled with a new knowledge. A new power.

He cleared his throat. "What you said—"

"Later," she whispered. She brushed her lips against his once. Twice. A third time. Scattering his thoughts.

Cupping her cheek, he softly kissed her temple, her cheekbone and the spot at the corner of her mouth.

She sighed, and he felt that sigh shimmer through him. It spoke of wistful dreams and star-bright kisses. There was a sad quality to it, too.

Jade knew this didn't change anything between them. He knew it, too, and hated it.

"Mommy?" Henry's voice wafted through the house. "I can't sleep."

"Be right there." Her gaze locked onto his, blazing with longing. She stroked his face with such tenderness that he had to close his eyes against the pain.

She left him there in the hallway.

His phone buzzed. Mason.

"What?"

A pause. "You sound weird."

He disregarded his sergeant's comment. "Do you have news for me?"

"As a matter of fact, I do. The black truck was found ditched on the far side the county."

Their county was huge. "You think Axel's headed out of town?"

"I'm not sure. Did he accomplish what he wanted? Is he the type to change plans when the heat is on? He knows federal, state and local agencies are hunting for him."

Cruz didn't have answers. On the surface, the news that Axel might be leaving the area was positive. Jade wouldn't be in immediate danger. But they couldn't be sure what Axel was doing. Cruz wished he knew, but the only thing he was certain of was that Jade couldn't live under lock and key—couldn't stay here indefinitely.

She had to resume her normal life, and so did he.

Chapter Nineteen

Memories could be both a blessing and a curse. Jade scraped diced carrots, onion and celery into the heated oil and sprinkled in a variety of spices. It didn't help that *the incident* had happened in this house, where she spent half of her time, only steps from the kitchen. She and Cruz were together day and night. How was she supposed to remain logical and impartial? How was she going to purge him from her system?

"Look at my puzzle," Henry called out.

Setting the burner to low, she put the spoon on the counter and crossed to the table. He'd hauled out this puzzle, a gift from Leslie, when they'd returned from another day at the police stables an hour ago.

"Good job, sweetie."

He smiled, feet swinging, as he contemplated

his progress. He picked up another piece. "I miss my toys. When can we go home?"

She didn't have an answer to that. No one did.

It had been less than twenty-four hours since *the incident.* She'd yet to let herself dwell on those delightful moments, which meant snatches of the kiss would catch her off guard and send her senses into a tailspin. His strong hands in her hair... Those lighter-than-spun-sugar kisses on her face...

"Mommy?"

She swallowed and, refocusing on her son, caressed his cheek. "I'm not sure, Henry."

He cocked his head to one side, his blond hair slipping into his eyes. "Is this our home now?"

An ache she couldn't explain bloomed inside her. She was content with their rental home next door and had worked hard to put her stamp on it. She and Henry had shared many happy memories there. But this home had one thing theirs didn't—Cruz.

"We're just visiting."

"I like Mr. Cruz." He turned his attention back to the puzzle. For him, the matter was forgotten.

She liked Cruz, too. Liked sharing her days with him.

Popping up from the chair, she returned to the stove. "Are you ready for your performance tonight?"

"I'm going to be the best sheep ever!"

She smiled at his enthusiasm. Cruz had arranged for the unit, in addition to Officers Weiland and Bell, to be at the church tonight so that Henry could take part. Cruz had told her that they'd found the truck and it could mean Axel had decided to lie low or leave the area altogether, and the feds and marshals agreed. She wanted to believe them.

What if they couldn't locate him? She couldn't continue to live here much longer. It wasn't fair to Cruz. Henry was also affected by the unusual situation.

Cruz's bedroom door opened and closed, and he entered the kitchen with damp hair and a neatly trimmed goatee. The smell of his cologne evoked forbidden images.

His dark eyes locked onto her, sending a frisson of longing across her back.

He poked the bag of red lentils. "What's for supper?"

"Lentil stew. I'm in the mood for something hearty and comforting."

"Lentils are not what I'd consider comforting." He picked up the leftover stalk of celery and frowned. "The last time I ate celery, it accompanied a platter of spicy chicken wings."

She burst out laughing, and it startled them both. Their gazes locked across the counter, and she felt a current pass between them. A knowledge that they'd endured trauma together and survived. They'd shared an experience no one else could understand.

How could she find humor when their situation was so dire? Because he was in this fight with her?

She swallowed against the emotions, lowering her gaze to hide her longing. He didn't need to know she would like him to walk around the island, tug her against his broad chest and kiss her senseless again.

"Everyone who's had my stew said it's satisfying. You'll see."

"They were probably just being nice," he mumbled, causing her to chuckle again.

After supper, during which Cruz conceded the stew wasn't terrible, they hustled Henry into the truck and drove to church. Trees in the lot had been wrapped with twinkly lights, and giant wreaths adorned the front doors. People were already parking and making their way inside.

Silver and Raven greeted them, bundled in their police jackets and thick gloves, their cheeks and noses pink and breath fogging in the crisp air. They would remain outside, along with Bell and Weiland. Cruz hurried Jade and Henry through the side entrance, where Tessa was waiting for them.

"Mason's already in the auditorium. He's saving seats for you." She touched Henry's shoulder and pointed behind her. "Lily's over by the window."

He raced into the kindergarten classroom housing the costumes.

"I'll stay with them until they go on stage," Tessa said, smiling. "Then I'll join you."

Jade could see their choir leader, Candace, and several young moms assisting kids into their costumes.

"Everyone, we have half an hour," Candace called out.

Jade and Cruz made their way to the auditorium. Mason waved them over to the middle section, three rows from the front. The stage had been transformed into a holiday scene, complete with the trees and storefronts the parents had built and decorated.

She turned off her phone ringer and slid the

device into her coat pocket, content to listen to Mason and Cruz talk about work.

Cruz sat close beside her, his shoulder and thigh rubbing against her when he moved. He looked dashing in his green-white-and-blue-plaid shirt, crisp jeans and cowboy boots. Like her own personal Christmas present. Her tummy did a dance. If only that were true.

The lights dimmed, and a hush fell over the auditorium as Candace came onto the stage and addressed the crowd. Tessa ducked into the seat between Mason and Jade just as the kids filed onto the stage and launched into their first song. Lily waved at Mason and Tessa. Henry tapped her arm and shook his head.

Cruz chuckled, and Jade was filled with wistful warmth. *Why can't he be the one, Lord? Why can't we be a family?*

If only Cruz didn't have a personal tragedy in his life that made it impossible for him to love her. If only he hadn't been soured on marriage.

Ignoring him was impossible. She was aware of everything…his smell, his breathing patterns, his habit of popping his knuckles and picking at loose threads.

Near the end of the performance, both Mason and Cruz received phone alerts. She felt their moods shift as they read the messages and then exchanged glances.

"What is it?" she whispered.

He shifted to whisper in her ear. "Accident victim in the national park. They need our help extracting him. I'm afraid Henry won't be able to stay for the party. Bell will take you home and guard you until I return, which could be as late as tomorrow or the next day. We never know the timelines on these things." His hand rested on her knee, and her skin flushed hot. "Tell Henry I'm sorry."

"The performance was the important part."

The music swelled and, after a standing ovation, the kids trundled off the stage. Parents, siblings, grandparents and other audience members crowded the aisles.

"Mason and I will wait for you outside the same entrance we came in. We have to relay the change in plans to Bell. Weiland might be able to follow you to my house, as well."

His hand skimmed her neck, once again inducing longing.

He's protecting you because he drew the short straw, not because he wanted to. He's taking one for the team.

He'd kissed her because of emotions gone

wild. Her frustration had spilled over and onto him, and he'd reacted without thinking.

The progress to the kindergarten room was slow. By the time she and Tessa reached it, half the kids had been claimed by their parents. Lily ran over to Tessa.

"Was I a good sheep, Mommy?"

Tessa laughed and tweaked her curls. "You certainly were, ladybug."

Jade scanned the room, expecting Henry to be close behind his friend. Kai wasn't there, which meant Elaine had gotten there before her.

"I don't see Henry."

Tessa's smile vanished. "I'll check the restroom."

Candace wasn't here. She'd been caught by parents wanting to praise her hard work. Jade approached one of the assistants. "Have you seen my son? Henry Harris. Blond. Green eyes."

The young woman's forehead furrowed. "He went with his father."

Jade's heart turned to stone. "That's not possible."

"I'm sorry?"

"What did he look like?"

"I—I didn't speak to him. We were in the hallway, walking in a long line, and I looked back and saw him. He waved and nodded, and I assumed—" She paled. "Was that not his dad?"

Cruz wouldn't have picked up Henry without informing her. She quickly described Axel, and the woman nodded.

"He had a hat on, but that sounds right."

She had to remind her lungs to draw in air. "Which way did they go?"

"The far side exit."

Jade bolted from the room, not responding to the woman's apology. She nearly knocked Tessa over.

"Jade, he's not in there—"

She gripped Tessa's arm. "Find Cruz. Axel has my son."

Brushing past her friend, Jade raced along the hall and burst through the exit door and into the cold night. People startled and stared as she darted between them. Rounding the building's rear corner, she yelled her son's name. This area wasn't as well lit, and shadows were thick in the children's play area.

There, close to the tree's edge, she saw a flash of white. Henry had been wearing a white shirt.

"Henry!"

She ran as fast as she could. She didn't see the cement curb and tripped, almost falling face-first onto the pavement. Windmilling her arms, she managed to stay upright.

"Henry!"

Surely if he was out here, he'd respond.

She dashed around the dumpsters and entered the woods. An iron hand seized her arm, and she whirled in a circle.

"Hello, Jenny." In the shadows, she made out Axel's hulking figure. With his other hand, he held tightly to Henry's arm. "Welcome to the family reunion. It's time I introduced myself to my son."

He knew something was wrong the moment he saw Tessa's stricken expression.

"Henry's missing." She jogged across the grass to Cruz with Lily in tow. "Axel has him, and Jade's gone after them."

Mason, Silver and Raven pressed in closer. To keep him from losing it? To keep him upright and breathing?

"Where?" Cruz demanded.

She pointed behind her, indicating the opposite corner of the church. He would've taken off running if Mason hadn't thrown his arm across his chest, stalling him.

"Tess, tell us what you know."

"Jade and I got to the costume room, and Henry wasn't there."

Cruz's gut was a ball of nerves. Sweet, vulnerable Henry at the mercy of a hardened felon? He could only imagine Jade's reaction. Her state of mind.

"Where was Candace?" Mason asked.

"Your sister got waylaid. One of the helpers said she saw a man take Henry's arm and wave in greeting from the other end of the hallway. She assumed he was Henry's father. I—I think she's fairly new to town and the church." Her tormented gaze bounced between her husband and Cruz. "Please, you have to find them."

Still blocking Cruz, Mason barked orders. "Silver—you, Bell and Weiland get these people inside. Raven, go back in there and work on gathering everyone into one location. Don't let anyone else leave."

"Yes, sir."

They hurried to carry out his orders.

"Tess, get Lily inside."

She nodded, her gaze lingering on Cruz. "Be careful."

Cruz shoved Mason out of the way and jogged along the building, leaving the activity behind and heading for the woods. Mason soon caught up.

"Hold on, Cruz. We need a plan."

He kept running. "If I were Axel, I'd stick to the woods," he tossed over his shoulder. "I'm going in there."

"I'll search that section." Mason kept pace beside him, indicating the trees spreading out to their right. His hand shot out and snagged Cruz's shirt, and his eyes were fierce. "We do this by the book, you hear? Sound the alarm if you spot them. Don't go in alone."

Cruz couldn't promise anything right now. Pulling out of reach, he pounded past the slides and swings, praying God would orchestrate Jade and Henry's rescue. He wouldn't let himself consider any other outcome.

Chapter Twenty

"How did you find out?"

"The news did a nice little report on the clinic break-in this morning. Included an interview with one of your patients, and she mentioned your son was about to turn six. I did the math, Jenny."

Enough moonlight filtered through the trees that she was able to see Axel's and Henry's faces, as well as the forest floor they trod upon as they went deeper into the woods.

"I want Mommy," Henry cried, reaching for her.

She lunged for him, but Axel held him away.

"Shut up," he said roughly.

Henry's obvious fright, combined with Axel's callousness, made her eyes sting. She also got angry, a desperate kind of anger that didn't include logic.

"Leave him here," she begged. "You don't want to be saddled with a child."

"And miss out on a chance to get to know my only son?"

"You're a career criminal, Axel! An escaped felon. You can't be a father."

"Don't tell me what I can and can't do," he growled.

Their pace was punishing. When Henry tripped and hurt his knee, Axel had no patience. "Stop crying," he commanded, which only made the boy cry harder.

She clawed at Axel's shirt. "Let's go without him. Just you and me. L-like old times."

He pushed her away, swung Henry into his arms and kept marching. His ominous silence told her everything she needed to know. He didn't want her around. He would kill her the first chance he got. And then what would happen to Henry?

Axel would soon realize that staying under the radar would be impossible. What then? Would he hurt their son?

The trees opened to a gravel parking lot. Spotting a lone car, she panicked.

Jade tried to wrest Henry from Axel's arms. Frightened, the boy started crying in earnest.

"I won't let you take him!"

She kicked Axel as hard as she could in his left kneecap, and he howled in pain and rage.

"Mommy!"

When Axel bent to grab his knee, she managed to get Henry free and, with him in her arms, started to run. They didn't get far. Axel's meaty fingers wrapped around her upper arm, squeezing until she cried out. He yanked her to the car and, ripping Henry from her arms, shoved him into the back seat and slammed the door.

When he removed a gun from his rear waistband, all the blood in her body pooled in her feet. She put up her hands.

"No, Axel. Not here." Her gaze slid to the rear window, to where Henry's face was pressed against the glass. "Don't do this."

Please, God, do something.

He advanced on her, the veins bulging in his temple and neck. "*I said*, stop telling me what to do." He called her a few choice names. "I should've wasted you the day I stepped foot in this town."

The sound of movement in the trees had them both spinning around, but she saw no one, heard nothing…until a gun fired. Axel yelped and, clutching his arm, fired into the dark woods.

Cruz emerged from the shadows, his gun held aloft. Mason advanced from a different direction.

"Drop your weapon!"

Axel dashed around the hood and dived for the driver's side door.

Jade threw herself at the car, opening the rear door and scooping up Henry as the engine rumbled to life. She couldn't run very fast with him in her arms, and her muscles were taut, expecting to be shot or run over.

The car sped out of the lot, spraying gravel in every direction. As Mason fired at the vehicle, Cruz ran to her, taking Henry and putting his arm around her. He hustled them back through the dark woods and into the church. Once inside, he ushered them into the first room they came to—the pastor's office—and locked the door.

She threw her arms around him and Henry, knocking him back a step.

Tears leaked from her eyes unchecked, and she couldn't stop shaking.

Cruz rubbed her back. "Let's sit."

On the couch, Henry scrambled onto her lap. "Who was that bad man, Mommy? Is he going to take me away?"

Her body trembling, she framed his face with her hands. "No, baby. I won't let that happen. Cruz, Mason, Silver and Raven will keep us safe."

Her son wouldn't detect the thread of doubt in her voice, but would Cruz? She'd been seconds away from death, she was sure of it. Axel had reached his patience's limit.

Cruz snagged a tissue box from the pastor's desk. She used the tissues to mop up Henry's face first, then her own. Mason arrived and informed them that they had put out a BOLO for Axel's car. The FBI agents and US marshals would join the sheriff's department in the search. Everyone was to stay put until they gave the all clear. Then Mason went in search of Silver and Raven.

Henry announced he needed to use the bathroom, so Jade and Cruz escorted him to the nearest one. The hallways were empty and quiet, because the adults and children were gathered in the auditorium.

While Henry was in the bathroom, Cruz took her hand and threaded his fingers through hers. He didn't say a thing. Didn't have to. His brown eyes throbbed with worry.

They both knew this had been too close. Worse than the clinic.

"No more public places," he stated.

She held tightly to his hand. "Okay."

"How did he know about Henry?"

"He said there was a news report."

Cruz's brows crashed together. Releasing her, he pulled out his phone and brought up a local news channel's website. The video recording began with a reporter standing outside the vet clinic and discussing the break-in. The shattered door was visible, as well as an SPD cruiser. When a recent photograph of Jade and Henry flashed onto the screen, she gasped.

"A vet tech employed here at Serenity Vet Clinic was working when the break-in occurred," the female reporter stated. "Jade Harris sustained injuries and was taken to the hospital. While we don't have details, we've been told she was treated and released."

The video switched to a recorded interview, and Jade recognized one of their patients' owners, Bobbie Polanski. "Jade is such a kind young woman. It's a shame she was hurt. She has a young son… He's about to turn six. Cute as a button. Anyway, she's wonderful with our rottweiler, and I hope she gets well soon."

Jade's ears buzzed. "Henry's small for his age, and he has my coloring. But when Axel heard he was turning six, he figured it out."

His face had hardened into a marble-like mask, and his eyes smoldered. "This should never have been put out there for the public. I'm of a mind to pay the news station a visit."

"The damage has already been done. What would that accomplish?"

"It would make me feel better."

Her fiery Texan was fiercely protective of her and her son, but he couldn't control the flow of information any more than he could Axel's movements. None of them could anticipate the final outcome...whether or not they'd come out the other side of this alive.

Henry woke up multiple times throughout the night, crying and reaching for her. Her heart broke every time. All she could do was pray and hold him until he drifted off again. She heard Cruz pacing in the living room at times, but he didn't come to their door.

He was in the kitchen ahead of them the next morning.

He gifted Henry with a big smile. "Mornin',

cowboy. There's a stack of chocolate chip pancakes with your name on them."

Henry didn't react with his usual good humor. Instead, he pressed into Jade's side, his arms locked around her upper legs. Cruz's brows drew together. She shrugged, uncertain what to expect. Her son had been traumatized, and she couldn't guess how he would process what had happened.

"There's whipped cream, too," she told him, stroking his hair. "I don't know about you, but I'm hungry."

He peeked up at her. "*You're* going to eat pancakes?"

She smiled. "I am. Want to put the whipped cream on mine?"

He nodded. They sat side by side in the chairs facing the kitchen. She served up the pancakes, and Cruz brought Henry a glass of milk.

When Cruz had seated himself across from them, he held out his hands. "Let's pray."

His prayer was brief and to the point. Afterward, he talked about his family and the ranch, trying to draw out Henry. But Henry remained subdued. He did eat one whole pancake, along with several strips of bacon. When he'd returned to the guest room, Cruz put down his fork.

"Our work calendar is clear of public engagements until after the new year. With the abundance of law enforcement in town and considering what happened last night, Mason decided against our neighborhood patrols on horseback. Silver called and invited us over. He thought Henry might need a distraction. There's the indoor pool. The animals. The others are coming, too. What do you think?"

"Henry had a blast the last time we were at Silver's." The officer had once called her to check on one of his macaws, and Henry had accompanied her.

"He'll have fun swimming with Lily. Mason and I can hang out in the pool while you and the girls chitchat. You need a distraction, too."

"You sure you feel up to it? I don't think you got any more sleep than we did."

His face tensed. "I wasn't sure what to do, so I prayed. I don't know if you've noticed, but I've squared things with the Lord. I can't do life without Him any longer."

"I'm happy to hear that." She reached across the table and covered his hand. "I'm grateful He put you in our lives. I don't know what we would do without you."

"I wish I could be what you both need...for

the long haul." His throat convulsed. His gaze on his mug, he ran his finger along the rim.

He was talking about the impossibility of a future together.

His gaze met hers, daring her to argue. "I'm not cut out for family. My past is proof of that."

This wasn't news, but it hurt to hear him say it.

"At some point, you have to forgive yourself, Cruz."

He slipped his hand free. "I'm no good for you or Henry or anyone else. I'm meant to be alone. That's what I've resigned myself to. It's what I want, Jade."

Although she didn't believe him, she didn't challenge him. The stubborn cowboy had made up his mind. Only he could change the way he saw himself.

He carried his plate to the sink. "Can you be ready to leave in an hour?"

"We'll be ready."

Jade was weary in heart and body. This situation was painful for them all.

The change of atmosphere was a good idea. Silver and Lindsey's home was the epitome of Christmas cheer, and the presence of their friends was the perfect distraction. Lily's playfulness melted Henry's reserve, and the children hurried to the dining room to interact with the macaws.

Cruz and the men were clustered around the long kitchen island, evaluating the various appetizers and sneaking bites when they thought the women weren't looking. The women were chopping vegetables and arranging them on a tray.

Raven pointed at her husband. "Aiden, I see you."

Aiden froze, a sausage ball halfway to his mouth. He shrugged and popped it in his mouth. "What do you expect, woman? You're the reason I slept late and missed breakfast."

Raven blushed and acted flustered, and Aiden winked at her.

"Men," Raven muttered. "Watch this." She nudged Jade's shoulder. "Lily? Henry? Are you ready to swim?"

The guys groaned as Lily and Henry dashed over to them, begging them to take them to the pool.

Silver placed several ham rolls into a napkin and stuffed a cookie in his mouth. "Let's go," he said, his mouth full.

The kids thundered down the stairs behind him. Aiden and Mason followed.

Grabbing the backpacks, Cruz sent Jade an inscrutable look. "They forgot their gear."

When he was out of earshot, Raven propped her hands on her hips. "Is he being difficult?"

"I don't want to talk about it."

Her face full of compassion, Raven nodded. "Understood."

"Was it your idea to have us over?" Jade asked Lindsey.

She pinked. "We all know what you're going through. I thought being together would help. Silver agreed."

Jade was touched by their thoughtfulness. They'd all set aside their own plans during the busy holiday season to make her and Henry feel better, and she was incredibly grateful.

Tessa pointed to a corner where stacks of white gift boxes and rolls of sparkly ribbon awaited. "You're delivering your traditional gingerbread cookies today, aren't you?"

"Today or tomorrow."

Jade had heard of their tradition of gifting cookies to their cabin rental guests right before Christmas. As owners of Hearthside Rentals, they went above and beyond for their customers.

"Have you already baked them?" Raven asked, smoothing her long black hair behind her shoulder.

"Not yet."

"I don't mind helping," Jade said.

"I'm no cook, but I can follow directions." Raven laughed.

"The kids could help decorate," Tessa suggested.

Lindsey looked surprised. "You don't have to do that."

"You didn't have to host this gathering, either," Jade said. "We *want* to."

"We'll make a day of it, then," Lindsey announced. Her smile faded, and she pressed her hand to her stomach. "That breakfast casserole I ate earlier isn't agreeing with me."

Tessa wiped her hands on a towel. "Have you had any more fainting spells? Been more tired than usual lately?"

"No more fainting spells, but I am exhausted. Sometimes, when I sit down to watch television, it feels like someone unplugged me."

Jade and Tessa exchanged a glance.

Lindsey's big brown eyes touched on each of their faces. "What?"

"Lindsey, it is possible you're pregnant?"

Her mouth opened and closed, and color surged and waned in her face.

"Let's sit." Jade steered Lindsey into the living room, close to the crackling fireplace and Christmas tree.

"I've been so busy, I haven't paid attention to the calendar…" She pressed her hands to her cheeks. "A baby never occurred to me. What will Silver say?"

Tessa softly laughed. "I know what he'll *do*. Go into protective overdrive until the baby is five. He'll be impossible, but you're accustomed to dealing with him."

"You need see your doctor to confirm," Jade added.

Raven popped to her feet. "And wait a few days for her to get an appointment? No way. I'm going to the pharmacy."

Jade caught Tessa's eye and gave her knee a commiserating squeeze. Tessa's smile had a tinge of sadness.

Lindsey looked at Tessa. "Is something wrong?"

Raven sat back down. "Out with it."

Tessa took a deep breath. "Mason and I have been trying to get pregnant for a while. I've had miscarriages, and my doctor doesn't know why."

"Oh, honey," Raven clasped her hand between her own. "I'm so sorry."

Dashing away a tear, Tessa put her arm around Lindsey. "I don't want to focus on me right now. We may have a miniature Lindsey or Silver on the way."

Lindsey still wore a dumbfounded expression. "A baby. With Silver."

Jade was thrilled for her friend. She took to heart the verse that instructed her to rejoice with others. Part of her was sad, though, because a baby with the man she loved was out of the question.

Cruz couldn't see past his mistakes and refused to try for a second chance.

Chapter Twenty-One

Silver snapped his fingers in Cruz's face. "Wake up, Castillo."

Standing in the corner of the formal dining room, deep in thought, Cruz dragged his gaze to his friend.

"What's got you distracted?" Silver asked him.

"I have a favor to ask of you."

Silver's violet gaze probed his, one gray brow arched in sardonic question. "Shoot."

There was little risk anyone would overhear them. Everyone was busy decorating cookies.

"It's time to pass this case to someone else. You have the most secure setup of us all, and Henry wouldn't lack for things to do." His chest felt tight, and he tugged at his shirt collar. The thought of telling Jade about the switch made him break out in a cold sweat. He dreaded hurting her. But he wasn't the best option for her. He should've seen that in the beginning. Could've saved them all a heap of heartache.

"That is, if you're still willing."

He braced himself for one of Silver's wise-cracks. They'd perfected the art of riling each other simply for the fun of it.

"Of course." Silver stared at him. "I have to ask why, though."

He chose honesty. "I've lost my ability to remain professional."

Silver's lips pursed. "Is this truly what's best for them? Or are you doing it because you care too much?"

Before Cruz could speak, Henry ran over. The boy's small hand slid into his, and his big green eyes—so like his mother's—looked expectant.

"Will you decorate a cookie with me, Cruz?"

He couldn't say no, especially knowing he was about to boot him and his mother out of his life. Plus, he didn't really want to answer Silver's question.

"Show me the way, cowboy."

Grinning, Henry led Cruz to the table, then clambered onto his lap and launched into the instructions. Cruz could feel Jade's gaze on him, but he didn't look up.

Coward.

They decorated too many cookies to count. Lindsey and Raven entered the dining room, and he could tell something was up. Raven was about to burst, and Lindsey's eyes looked brighter than the Christmas tree.

Tessa and Jade exchanged private smiles, while Raven called out, "Fun's over, everyone. Let's clear out." Aiden returned from the kitchen, a towel thrown over his shoulder. "We're leaving this for them to clean up?"

"Yep." Raven linked arms with her husband and turned him toward the door.

Everyone evacuated as if the house was on fire.

As Cruz drove the truck out of the driveway, he asked Jade, "What was that about?"

"Why would you assume I know?"

The dash lights illuminated her features, allowing him to see the hint of a smile.

"Because you're not asking me. Therefore, I think you know something."

She paused. "It's not my news to share."

Judging from her tone, it was good news. He thought through recent weeks and landed on the obvious conclusion. "They're expecting?"

She held up a hand. "That hasn't been confirmed by a doctor."

Watching the road, he absorbed the news. Silver deserved this happiness. He and Lindsey would make wonderful parents.

Cruz's heart felt like a stone inside his chest as he thought of all he and Jade could've shared. He learned from his mistakes, however. He couldn't bear to disappoint Jade.

He glanced at Henry in the rearview, then studied her profile, unable to resist asking the question burning in his gut. "Have you ever thought of giving Henry a sibling?"

Sorrow tightened her features. "Don't ask me that, Cruz."

He was silent the rest of the ride.

When his property came into view, he leaned forward in his seat, and his hands tightened on the wheel.

"Light's on in the barn."

She stiffened. "You don't leave the lights on."

"No, I don't." Parking close to the house, he grabbed his weapon from the glove box. "Stay here."

"Wait—" She put her hand out.

"If I'm not back in five minutes, call Mason." The cold night air seeped into his bones as he exited and closed his door. The hair on the back of his neck stood to attention. With one final glance inside the truck, he hurried around the house, straining to detect if anything felt off. The silence blanketing his property didn't seem sinister.

Had he forgotten to turn out the light? His schedule hadn't been normal lately, his mind preoccupied.

Gun in hand, he jogged to the barn. His horses came to the stall doors and whinnied. They didn't act out of sorts. He cleared the building. The tack room was as he'd left it. As he emerged, a little boy's cries shattered the illusion of normalcy.

Axel used the butt of his rifle to bust out the driver's side window. He reached in and unlocked the door.

"Get out, Jenny, or the boy is toast."

Her head felt swimmy thanks to the sudden dump of adrenaline. Axel had appeared out of nowhere. The gunshot wound he'd received from Cruz must've been minor, because he wasn't favoring his arm.

In the back seat, Henry was crying and reaching for her.

She turned to him. "I love you, baby."

She scooted across the seat toward Axel, dislodging bits of broken window. He yanked her out and wedged the barrel of the gun into her spine. "Get in the car."

Spying the darkened sedan at the end of the drive, she quivered inside. If she got in that car, she'd never see Cruz or Henry again. She was certain.

Her heart vibrated against her ribs, and her whole body shook with the need to flee. One step. Another. And another. She cast her gaze to the fields across the road. The woods to her right, just beyond her rental house.

The fields were too open. It would have to be the woods.

At the last second, she darted away, dodging his grasping hands. If she could lure him into the woods, there was a chance Cruz could catch up to them.

"You can't outrun me," Axel yelled, huffing close behind her. "This ends tonight."

She veered around trees, got whacked in the face with branches, tripped.

Keep going. Don't stop.

The moonlight glinted off a stream Henry liked to explore. She glanced over her shoulder.

Big mistake. Her foot caught on a rock, and she went sprawling. The icy water soaked into her pants and sweater.

Axel's heavy steps registered seconds before a hand clamped on her neck. "Gotcha."

Before she could speak, he thrust her face-down into the water. She choked. Thrashed. Fought to stay conscious.

The pressure eased, and she shot up, gasping and sucking in precious air.

He chortled and thrust her under the water again. This time, the blackness seeped in, robbing her brain of life-giving oxygen. Terror coiled in her middle.

Was this the end?

Would Cruz find her limp, lifeless body in these woods?

God, I'm not ready to say goodbye. Cruz doesn't know I love him. Henry needs me, Lord.

Axel hauled her out again, twisted her onto her back and loomed over her. Her chest heaved, her desperate gasps breaking the silence.

She tried to scramble back, anything to get away from him.

His massive hand gripped her cheek. His grin was evil in the moonlight. "I'm going to end you, Jenny, and then I'm going to kill your cop boyfriend just for fun. Then I'm going to take our son back to Florida. I think he'll thrive in the family business."

"No!" She gripped his wrist, fingernails digging into his flesh.

He flinched, and she landed a kick to his inner thigh. Jade squirmed out of reach and, somehow getting to her feet, began running again.

His laugh trailed after her. "Still feisty, aren't you, babe?"

Her wet hair slapped against her cheeks, and goose bumps covered her exposed skin. Her neck and knees throbbed.

Please, God, give me strength. Lead me out of here.

"I like games, Jenny," he called, still coming for her. "And I always win in the end."

Chapter Twenty-Two

Raven and Aiden careened into the driveway long, excruciating minutes after Cruz witnessed Axel chase Jade into the distant woods. He'd called her and the others from the barn, and Raven had been the closest.

They rushed onto his porch, their faces grim but determined.

"I've got Henry," Aiden stated. "You two, go."

Cruz crouched in front of Henry, who was seated on the couch hugging a stuffed bear to his chest. Tear tracks marred his face.

"I'm going to bring your mom home, Henry. I promise."

Raven shot him a startled look. He'd broken a cardinal rule. This was one promise he planned to keep, however.

Stepping off the porch, Raven paused. "Walk or ride?"

Cruz didn't want to waste another minute, but they'd cover more ground in the woods on horseback.

"Ride."

They hurriedly saddled up Gunsmoke and Old Bob.

"You armed?" he asked.

"Always."

He knew that, but he had to make sure. He couldn't worry about Raven, too. Aiden would skin him alive if anything happened to her.

Cruz's stomach felt like it was in continuous free fall. Dread settled in his bones. He knew exactly how Aiden felt.

Raven put her foot in the stirrup and swung her leg over the saddle. One look at him, and she jutted her chin. "She's scrappy. For one, she didn't get into that car with him."

"I can't…" He swallowed down emotion and ground his teeth. "I made a promise to that little boy in there, and I intend to keep it."

"Let's go get our girl."

The saddles creaked, and the horses' hooves struck the earth in an uneven beat. How much of a head start did Axel have?

Too many minutes for his peace of mind. They slowed often, using a flashlight he'd grabbed from the barn to search for clues. At the stream's edge, he saw Jade's scarf floating half in the water. His eyes burned, imagining what had happened.

They continued to pick their way through the shadowed woods, and he lost track of time. Every minute was torture, because he knew she was facing a monster alone.

The first gunshot startled him. He jerked as if the bullet had slammed into him. A second round blasted through the silence.

"Jade," Cruz whispered.

Kicking Gunsmoke's flank, he urged the horse to go faster than was probably wise. Raven followed close behind.

A third shot raked his ears, and he hunched forward in the saddle. Up ahead, a break in the trees allowed moonlight to filter in, and he saw her.

Jade was on the ground. Looming nearby, Axel shot a fourth time. The bullet scattered the earth near her foot. She screamed and scuttled out of the way.

The brute was toying with her.

Training and protocol went out the window. He called out.

Axel spun and aimed at them. Raven fired

her weapon, striking Axel in the shoulder. He stumbled to the side. Lowered his weapon. For a moment, it looked as if he would surrender. Then he glanced at Jade, his murderous intent tattooed on his face. He lunged for her. She screamed and tried to roll out of reach.

Cruz dismounted and raced toward them. Axel grabbed her arm, yanked her onto her back and pointed his gun at her forehead.

"No!" Cruz yelled.

A shot rang out.

Axel thundered to the ground, clutching at his throat and making gurgling noises. Raven had shot him a second time.

Cruz ran to meet Jade. She hurtled into him, sopping wet and shivering. Sobs shook her petite, freezing body.

He anchored her to him, emotion clogging his throat. Over the top of Jade's head, he watched as Raven carefully approached Axel. He had slumped onto the ground, eyes and mouth open.

Jade spoke into his chest. "Is he dead?"

Raven checked for a pulse and grimly nodded.

He rubbed her back. "He's gone."

She went limp. "Henry?"

"With Aiden."

Raven was already on the phone. She waved him on, wordlessly urging him to get Jade home while she waited with the body.

The return ride was accomplished in total silence. In the barn's bright lights, he could see the scrapes and scratches on her skin, her bloodshot eyes, her torn clothing.

"Is it truly over?" she whispered.

He nodded, barely able to speak. His emotions were all over the place and too much to handle.

"You're finally free," he managed, his voice rusty. "You can go anywhere you like. Live anywhere."

She stood with her arms at her sides, her big green eyes locked onto him. Waiting.

He stared back.

She sighed. "I don't know how I'll ever repay you, Cruz." She licked her lips. "Maybe free vet care for life?"

He continued to stare at her, not knowing what to do with the sudden freedom that Axel's death had given them.

"Well, I'm going to pack our things." Her eyes were shiny, and the brave smile she gave him was watery.

She walked past him, and he let her.

Cruz closed his eyes. His life would be empty without Jade and Henry. Joyless. Sad.

But they'd be better off without him.

At the house, Aiden stood off to the side as Jade reunited with her son, his eyes demanding answers from Cruz. *Are you really going to let her walk away?*

He couldn't bring himself to stop her, not even when Henry hurtled into his arms and burrowed his head in Cruz's neck.

Later, Aiden was the one who carried their belongings out the door. Cruz watched from the porch as the trio trudged through the yards. His heart heavy, he returned inside, locked the door and retreated to his bedroom. The police statement could wait until tomorrow. Tonight, he had to come to terms with the dismal future awaiting him.

Sleep didn't come. After a long shower, he thought the post-case crash would catch up to him. He was wrong.

Tossing off the covers, he padded through the house to the guest bedroom. He turned on the bedside lamp and sank onto the bed, feeling forlorn. Broken.

His heel bumped against something hard. He bent and picked up one of Henry's books.

Cruz had read this one to him several times. He leafed through the pages of vibrant pictures of the planets. The text reminded the reader that God had spoken the universe into being, had created the Earth and everything on it.

Cruz sat up straight. God was all-powerful, and His strength was available for any Christian to access.

I've come at this all wrong, Lord. I was worried about hurting her, failing her, and I would do those things if I relied on my own strength. I forgot that Your grace is sufficient. Your power is made perfect in weakness. I'm weak, but You're strong.

He had to tell Jade how he felt.

He was on her back deck at eight o'clock the next morning. She pulled open the door, her expression troubled. She wore an oversize sweatshirt over green leggings and fuzzy socks. Her hair streamed past her shoulders.

"Cruz, what's wrong?"

"I missed you."

Her brows shot up. "You saw me less than twelve hours ago."

"That's a problem, don't you think?"

She bit her lip, then pointed to the basket he cradled in his left arm. "Is that for me?"

"Yes."

"I didn't know Serenity had an Edible Arrangements store."

"We don't," he admitted sheepishly. "I went to the twenty-four-hour store and bought the fruit and these stick things. Uh, this is heavy. Can I come in?"

Scooting back, she waved him inside. He set the basket on the dining table and glanced around. Not much had changed since he'd been here last.

She touched one of the cantaloupe pieces. "You did this all yourself?"

He stuffed his hands in his pockets to keep from touching her and rocked on his heels. "Turns out dipping fruit in chocolate is a little harder than I thought, but it's easier than trying to carve it into something resembling a flower. You should see my kitchen."

She didn't say anything. Just kept staring at the bouquet.

"Um, is Henry sleeping?"

"It took him a while to go to sleep last night."

"I didn't sleep at all."

Jade looked sadder than he'd ever seen her, and he couldn't help himself. He closed the distance between them and lightly gripped her upper arms. "I don't want you to leave."

Her brow creased. "I know you can't stay at my house, of course. What I meant was I don't want you to leave me."

Her gaze was cautious. "I can't change my past, Cruz."

"After the clinic attack, I let you believe that your past was a deal breaker. That wasn't the problem. I failed you that night, just like I failed Sal and Denise. I was already falling for you, and I couldn't forgive myself for letting Axel hurt you like that. I've realized that I will fail you. I'm not perfect. I'll make mistakes and act like an idiot sometimes. I'll disappoint you and make you want to pull your hair out. But that doesn't mean we can't be together. With God as our foundation, I'll love you how God wants me to love you. I'll be the husband and father that I'm supposed to be, as long as I let Him guide and strengthen me."

She blinked up at him. "Husband?"

"I want to marry you, Jade, if you'll have me. First, I'd like to go on a real date, and not just to the Black Bear Café. To a swanky place where you can order the biggest, freshest salad in town, with homemade dressing."

She giggled.

"I also need to see how good you are at mini golf and go-kart racing."

"That's important."

"We'll have to take turns cooking. I can only handle lentils fifty percent of the time."

Jade ran her hands up his chest and around his neck, almost causing him to lose his balance. The look in her eyes made him want to kiss her senseless.

"I can switch things up and serve pinto beans, instead," she teased huskily.

When her fingers delved into his hair, he groaned. "I'll eat beans every day for you, woman."

Cruz lowered his mouth to hers, catching her cinnamon-flavored lips and expressing exactly what he hadn't allowed himself to feel or think or say. She clung to him, kissing him sweetly and intently, as if she couldn't exist without him.

Long minutes later, they resurfaced. She hugged him, pressing her cheek to his galloping heart.

"I love you."

He buried his face in her hair. "I love you, too."

Epilogue

"He's going to spoil her, you know." Tessa sank into the lawn chair beside her and pressed the frosty can to her forehead.

Jade smiled. Her husband held their daughter in his arms and was gazing at her with pride and wonder as Mason looked on. Bella Marie Castillo had been born two weeks ago. She'd surprised them early, and they'd had to postpone the baby shower.

"He's so sweet with her," she said. "He's been patient with Henry, who has a tendency to smother his new baby sister."

"Henry's at a good age to help. Lily's jealous. She can't wait to meet her sisters." Tessa rubbed her swollen belly.

"I'm eager to meet them, too." After trying for so long and suffering several miscarriages, the couple was finally growing their family. "I'm glad our children are going to grow up together."

"The mounted police unit looks very different than it did when I first arrived in Serenity," Tessa said.

"God has been generous with His blessings."

Pink and gold balloons strung between the trees danced in the light breeze. At the snack table, Aiden balanced Jaxon—one of the two foster placements in his and Raven's care—on his shoulders while Raven helped Adelaide fill her plate. They were hoping to adopt through the foster care system before adding biological children to their family.

Silver and Lindsey were seated at one of the round tables, a high chair between them. They were trying to cajole their brown-haired cherub, Alec, into eating pureed squash. He wasn't having it.

Lily and Henry chased each other around the yard with water guns, whooping and hollering, enjoying a carefree day. As childhood should be. Jade was grateful Henry wasn't dealing with issues related to Axel's campaign of revenge.

Cruz and Mason ambled over.

"Ready to eat?" Mason asked his wife.

"I could go for cake," Tessa said.

He grinned and turned to Cruz. "She's as bad as Lindsey these days. Always searching through the cabinets for sweets and grumbling, like I hid it or something."

She held up a finger. "Don't play innocent. You did hide the doughnuts."

"After you ate mine and left me nothing for breakfast."

Cruz chuckled and nodded to Jade. "This one swore off smoothies three months into the pregnancy. Can you imagine that?"

Jade shrugged and held out her hands. "Bella must take after her daddy."

Cruz carefully placed their daughter into her arms. He'd been overly cautious with her in those first few days, but his confidence was growing by leaps and bounds. Jade touched a fingertip to her daughter's silken cheek. She had a cap of dark hair and a bow-shaped mouth. This pregnancy and birth had been so different than Henry's. Fear and uncertainty had been replaced with love and support from Cruz, as well as her circle of friends.

When she lifted her gaze, Tessa and Mason were already ambling toward the snack table, and Cruz had filled the vacant seat beside her. His gaze was warm with admiration and boundless love.

They would celebrate their first wedding anniversary next month, and he still had the power to make her knees go weak with a single look. He leaned in and pressed a tender kiss on her lips. Her pulse quickened.

He shifted away with regret. "I have to go to the airport soon and pick up your parents and sister."

Jade was excited to introduce them to Bella. This was their fourth trip to Serenity in the year and a half since Axel's death. She wished Grandma Hazel could make the trip, but she was too feeble. She, Cruz and Henry had made the trip to Florida twice, however, and she'd been able to visit with her. Her family had been shocked to learn she was alive and eager to resume their relationship. They hadn't made her feel ashamed for her poor choices. They adored Henry. They'd also welcomed Cruz into the fold without hesitation.

The Castillos had treated her and Henry with similar openness. When they'd made the trek to Texas, she and Cruz had sat down with his parents and brother and explained everything. There had been many tears and hugs and much love shared during that visit. Hope for the future, as well.

"I'm glad the house next door was available.

Between your family and mine, we'd be bursting at the seams."

She and Cruz had gotten married the summer after their fateful Christmas together, and when they moved, her landlord had turned the bungalow into a short-term vacation rental.

He cupped Bella's tiny head. "We'll probably have to add on anyway, considering the number of kids we're planning to have."

"You indicated you wanted two. Three at the most."

"I've changed my mind." His gaze found hers, and he gave her a heart-melting smile. "I'm thinking five or six."

Jade grinned. "You won't get any arguments from me."

She'd walk with confidence into the future—whatever it might bring—with her husband at her side and the Lord guiding her steps.

★ ★ ★ ★ ★

Sabotaged Mission
Tina Radcliffe

MILLS & BOON

Tina Radcliffe has been dreaming and scribbling for years. Originally from Western New York, she left home for a tour of duty with the US Army Security Agency stationed in Augsburg, Germany, and ended up in Tulsa, Oklahoma. Her past careers include certified oncology RN, library cataloger and pharmacy clerk. She recently moved from Denver, Colorado, to the Phoenix, Arizona, area, where she writes heartwarming and fun inspirational romance.

Visit the Author Profile page
at millsandboon.com.au.

But they that wait upon the Lord
shall renew their strength; they shall mount up with
wings as eagles; they shall run, and not be weary;
and they shall walk, and not faint.

—*Isaiah* 40:31

DEDICATION

Dedicated to the many encouraging writers
who helped birth the original concept for this book
years ago, including Vince Mooney, Rhonda Starnes,
Connie Queen, Terri Weldon, Jackie Layton,
Sharee Stover and Stephanie Dees.
It really does take a village.

To Tom Radcliffe, who kept asking if I was ever going to
write that suspense book. A huge thank-you
goes out to my deadline buddies, Melanie Dickerson
and Josee Telfer, for early morning
writing accountability sessions (really early, it turns out,
because I'm in Arizona).

Thank you to my editor, Dina Davis, for this opportunity
and my agent, Jessica Alvarez, for her support.

Chapter One

Winston growled, the feral sound low and drawn out, then it morphed into a snapping bark. The bulldog's barking continued, loud enough to nearly drown out the banging on the front door.

Mackenzie Sharp grabbed the Glock from the coffee table long before it registered that she'd fallen asleep on the couch again. She glanced at her watch and tensed.

It was well after 10:00 p.m. on a Friday night.

Whoever was at the door had guts. They kept knocking, and Winston kept barking. The dog was in a frenzy now, his nails clicking on the tiled floor as he raced back and forth.

"Winston. Come."

The cacophony immediately ceased. The animal crossed the living room to her.

"Good boy." She praised him as he shoved his nose against her shoulder and licked her cheek.

The animal's fierce devotion had only increased since she'd returned from the CIA assignment that nearly claimed her life.

Mac slowly sat up. Gripping the handle of her ebony cane, she stood and grimaced at the stab of intense pain that shot down her left leg. She wiped a bead of sweat from her forehead.

Flying into action was no longer an option. Instead, she methodically tucked the Glock she kept for protection into the waistband of her jeans and hobbled to the door.

"No more than I can handle," she muttered. "Wasn't that our deal, Lord?"

She pulled up the security cam on her phone to assess her visitor. Framed by the silhouette of a huge palm tree that filled the horizon and backlit by the haze of a full moon, the man on her stoop faced the street.

When he turned toward the camera, she gasped.

Gabe Denton, a mistake from her past. From the days when she'd foolishly believed she could have a normal life. One that included a relationship.

Despite her careful attempts to stay off the grid, trouble had found her. He stood on her doorstep in a dark suit and tie that screamed "government-issue." Mac released a groan.

She disarmed the security system, turned the dead bolt and withdrew her Glock. When she cracked the door as far as the chain allowed, the hot, dry, desert breeze seemed to whisper as it moved past.

Fully aware that the screen door and chain lock were all that stood between her and the man on her stoop, Mac leveled the gun at her visitor and slid her index finger into position. Meanwhile, Winston nosed his way into the doorway. The muscular animal bared his teeth, all too eager to reach out and touch.

Unfazed, Denton's gaze flicked to Winston and then met hers and held. Black-framed glasses emphasized hazel irises that were warm like honey, with flecks of forest green. They offered something she hadn't expected.

Compassion.

"Hello, Mac."

Mac shivered. His voice, both smooth and husky at the same time, stirred memories she thought had been buried five years ago. "What are you doing here?"

"Shipman sent me," he said.

CIA Senior Officer Todd Shipman. Her boss

and handler on the Toronto mission that had gone so very wrong.

Mac frowned, confused. Gabe Denton was a close friend and protégé of Shipman. The presence of this particular man meant something serious was going down.

"How did you even find me?" she finally asked.

He didn't answer, but his expression said that if he could find her, anyone could. Anyone. Like the unknown shooter who slid through her memory in flashes that kept her awake at night.

"I'm not operational. Shipman is well aware of my status," she continued.

"He hoped you'd make an exception."

"An exception? To what? Shipman decommissioned the task force. Which leaves me unassigned as well." Lips clamped tight, she met his gaze again. She wouldn't address the obvious physical limitations that kept her from returning to the Agency anytime soon.

He looked past her into the house. "May I come in?"

Mac didn't try to hide her frustration as she released the chain, opened the solid metal door and then the screen, careful not to lose her balance.

As he moved past her, his jacket inched back,

revealing a leather shoulder holster and a SIG Sauer. Mac tensed at the sight. Sent by Shipman and carrying a weapon? It certainly was not protocol.

Denton stared pointedly at the gun that still targeted his upper torso. She tucked away her own weapon as he stepped into the room and looked around. He frowned and evaluated her living space, leaving no doubt that he was as thrilled with her generic rental as he was with being here.

That made two of them.

Hiding out in suburbia was not part of her planned career path. Nor had she expected to find herself in the middle of a mission that had gone south. The assignment eight weeks ago had left her injured and her fellow agent Liz Morrow presumed dead.

The physical healing from Mac's injuries was slow. Her mental and emotional healing even slower. Mac had finally reached the other side and was able to sleep a few restless hours at a time. She'd been on her way to becoming whole again. But all that had been destroyed when she'd been compromised by an unknown gunman at the rehab facility. She'd left her condo in Denver and arrived at this rental two weeks ago to try yet again to get back on her feet, literally and figuratively.

Now this man's arrival threatened to toss every scrap of that hard-won progress out the window.

"Off the beaten path, isn't it?" he commented.

Mac shrugged. That was the point. The place sat on a cul-de-sac on the edge of the desert, along with six other identical one-story stucco homes with red-tiled roofs. The grounds consisted of decorative gravel and cacti. Spartan. Like the inside. Cell service could be counted on to be spotty, but traffic at this end of the residential development was nil. All good, since she was trying to be inconspicuous.

Mac leaned back against the closed door and released a long breath. "Why are you here?"

Denton shoved his hands in his pockets and faced her. He was silent for a moment, as if deciding how much information to share. Mac couldn't help but assess him. Nothing had changed. Gabe Denton still looked good in his nerdy GQ kind of way.

He cleared his throat. "There's a situation, and Shipman needs you."

"The man has an entire organization at his disposal," she said.

"He wants you."

And that sealed the deal. Mac couldn't and wouldn't refuse her boss. Even Denton knew that. They went way back. Todd Shipman had been her father's best friend. The Shipmans had taken her under their wing when she was fifteen—the year her parents died.

Still, Mac had made the decision to go to ground, locking out even Shipman, in a last-ditch effort to keep herself alive.

Yes, she'd do anything for the man, but in her current condition, her assistance on an assignment would be more a hindrance than a help.

The look in his eyes since Denton had stepped into her home said he agreed.

"If you expect me to leave Phoenix, you're going to have to do better than that," she said. "I had protection in Denver, and that didn't stop someone from trying to put a bullet in me." She paused. "Or should I say, another bullet?"

Denton offered a short nod that let her know he was well aware of why she'd fled Colorado.

"The Agency has intel that Elizabeth Morrow is alive and being held hostage."

"What?" Mac's stomach took a hit, and her knees threatened to buckle. She gripped her cane tightly.

Liz was alive? Goose bumps shot up her arms.

For eight weeks she had been grieving the loss of her partner on the mission. Grieving and heaping guilt upon herself for Liz's death.

Mac worked to calm the rapid beating of her heart. "I assume they're acting on that intel." She barely got the words past her trembling lips.

"The intel is being verified. In the meantime, Shipman feels that the threat to your personal safety has escalated and he wants you to come in."

"You said he needs me. This is a different story." Mac shook her head. "Thanks, but no. I've done a pretty good job keeping myself alive up to now."

"He wants you to come in." The words were resolute, his gaze unwavering.

Dread washed over Mac. She swallowed. "I'm going to need more. Who has Morrow?" This time her words were barely a whisper as she shoved back the fear that nearly strangled her.

"I don't have that information."

"Someone has Liz," she murmured, the words unbelievable.

Then she did the math. Eight weeks. Where had Liz been all this time? Mac shook her head, clearing away the images and questions slamming into her. If only she could figure out why the Toronto mission went sideways and why she was on someone's hit list, she might be able to get ahead of the situation. Thus far, she had no clue, and to her knowledge, neither did the Agency.

"There's a plane waiting for us at Sky Harbor," Denton continued. "From there, we'll head to the Denver office, where Shipman is waiting to brief you."

Mac nodded slowly again, digesting the information. Liz was alive.

She was afraid to be relieved. Her mind swirled as her gaze narrowed to focus on Denton and his plan to take her to Denver International Airport.

"Okay. Now we know why me," she said. "Why you?"

"He trusts me." Denton paused. "And he hoped that you would, too."

She stared at him for a moment, sorting her thoughts. Of course Shipman would use her history with Denton as leverage to gain an advantage. While they hadn't parted on contentious terms, the current situation was nothing less than awkward.

"Then you can read me in," Mac finally said.

She'd prefer to get the details from her boss, but the sooner she could begin processing, the better.

"My job is to get you to Denver. Period."

Not surprised at his response, Mac offered an annoyed grunt. Gabe Denton was a letter-of-the-law sort of guy. If he did know more than he'd let on, he wouldn't break protocol.

"Fine. I'll get my ready bag and Winston's supplies." She was only agreeing because Todd Shipman had made the request. Not because she wanted or needed the Agency's protection.

Denton's gaze went from the dog to her. His expression said he wasn't pleased.

That wasn't her problem. The bulldog would make up for the fact that she wasn't functioning at 100 percent yet. He'd also have her back. Because until the assailant who'd put half a dozen bullets in her in Toronto and tried again in Denver was found, she didn't trust anyone else to keep her alive. Not even Gabe.

Gabe Denton did his best to keep his face impassive. Though he tried not to show concern, he couldn't deny an unexpected surge of protective emotions when he looked at Mac. She'd lost at least ten pounds since he'd seen her last, and the haunting blue eyes were underlined with dark smudges, indicating she slept little, if at all. But there was something else, besides lack of sleep. Mac was functioning by rote. The spark that used to be in her eyes was gone.

While they hadn't kept in touch since their breakup five years ago, he'd made a point of subtly asking about her whenever he met with Shipman. There was something about Mac that touched him in a way that no one else ever had. He hadn't realized he'd had a heart until she'd broken it.

Gabe had read her file before he left Colorado. It was filled with heavy redactions regarding her disastrous assignment in Canada. Removed from the duty roster for postoperative recovery in Denver, she'd been compromised at the facility where she'd been receiving outpatient rehab. The agent assigned to protect her had been shot and killed.

Mac had gone to ground. He'd have done the same thing. The Agency was tasked to protect its operations officers. What went wrong?

Guilt tore at him. He should have visited her in the hospital, but he'd been convinced she would refuse to see him. Mac loathed anyone, especially him, seeing her vulnerable. As it was, she was less than happy to find him on her door-step tonight.

He shook his head. What was Todd Shipman thinking? And why had Gabe agreed to be the liaison for this mission? Right now he ought to be fly-fishing in Montana. So why wasn't he?

Because Shipman said that with the uncertain intel on Liz, Mac would be safer if she came in, and he was sure that Denton could convince her to come back to Denver. Then there was the fact that Denton owed Shipman his life and his career. So, yeah, agreeing was a no-brainer.

As he walked around the small living room, his gaze fell on a framed photo facedown on the coffee table. Gabe flipped it over. It was a younger and markedly less thin Mac standing with her parents, smiling at the camera. He'd seen the picture of her parents before, though she had never talked about the embassy bombing that had left Ambassador and Mrs. Sharp dead.

He'd lost his own mother to cancer since he'd last seen Mac. The fact that he and Mac had a lot in common failed to comfort him. Two loners recruited into government service, living lives that were lies for the greater good.

About once a year, he considered a line of work in the private sector.

Once this assignment was complete, he vowed to seriously give a career change more thought. He found himself shaking his head.

Who was he kidding? He was a company man, and he probably always would be, if only to keep his father happy.

When Mac returned to the room, her chin-length straight blond hair had been tucked behind her ears, mostly hidden by a black ball cap. A cane was in one hand and a black duffle in the other. She'd strapped a messenger bag across her chest. Again, he noted the dark circles around her eyes and the awkward movements.

He was headed on a mission with a woman who was in no way ready for the field. Dread left a sour taste in his mouth.

As if reading his mind, she lifted her face in challenge.

For a moment, he stared, more than a little intrigued by the proud tilt of her chin and the fire in her eyes. She was a beautiful woman, despite her current issues. Almost unconsciously, he stepped back. Yeah, and he'd been burned by Mac once before. He still cared, and that was a dangerous thing.

"How's the leg?" he asked. "You had surgery?"

She nodded. "A bullet tore a chunk of muscle from my hip. They grafted replacement tissue from…elsewhere and put a metal rod in my lower left leg, where another bullet fractured the tibia." She raised an eyebrow. "Any other questions?"

Denton eyed the bulldog with concern. "Can I trust that he's not going to take a piece of me?"

She patted the animal's head. "You never were a dog person, as I recall."

"Nope. Never had a dog." Dogs were complications, and his father, the general, didn't do complications.

"Winston's bark is much worse than his bite," she said.

"If you say so." He glanced around the room. "What kind of dog is he?"

"American bulldog."

"And does he have a crate?"

"He prefers a harness."

Gabe opened his mouth and closed it again. Great. Just great. The fact was, now he was escorting two bulldogs to Denver.

He opened the front door and assessed the cul-de-sac's perimeter while Mac dropped her bag to clamp a leash on the dog. The brown-and-white animal trotted out the door, eager for an adventure. Though his owner stood in the open doorway digging in her messenger bag, Winston kept moving down the paved walk.

His leash continued to stretch until the dog suddenly stopped and stiffened. Winston stood on the edge of the walk, staring across the gravel yard to the curb, at the black Yukon that Gabe had rented at the airport. Ears perked, tail raised, Winston offered a low menacing growl.

Gabe froze.

The hair on the back of his neck stood up.

His gut said to get away from the vehicle.

In a split second, his brain agreed.

"Back! Get back in the house!" He grabbed the dog's leash and yanked hard to get Mac's attention. Eyes wide, she complied and pulled Winston toward her.

Gabe glanced over his shoulder in the same second that the vehicle exploded. He raised his arms to protect his head.

The bright light of a fireball turned the darkness into day. Shrapnel and glass flew, accompanied by a deafening boom that ripped the night.

There was no way to escape the wall of heated force that slammed into him. Gabe flew through the air toward the house. A painful jolt resonated down to his bones as his body thudded into the frame of the screen door, and he slid to the warm cement.

Car alarms sounded for a few moments.

Then nothing.

Silence.

With a hand, he pushed himself to a half-sitting position.

Whoa. Dizzy.

His head spun, and he collapsed back down to the ground. Gabe stared at the sky, mesmerized by fragments of the wreckage that floated through the air. A hot ember shot into the darkness, glowing like a fiery ruby.

When something warm and wet touched his face, Gabe jerked back. Turning his head, he met the bulldog's concerned eyes.

Then he assessed the house. The aluminum door had crumpled with the impact of his body. The dog stood inside, his head poking through the flaps of the torn screen.

Mac? His heart clutched with desperation as he tried to look around.

Where was she?

Gabe called her name. The words registered as a dull, muffled sound. Almost as if he was underwater.

Once again, he called out.

Then he stopped and fell back to the cement.

He couldn't hear.

Couldn't hear and wasn't certain if Mac was dead or alive.

Lord, help us, he prayed.

Chapter Two

Mac blinked and refocused. She was lying on the tiled floor of the entryway. With a groan, she rolled to her side and sat up, trying to make sense of what just happened.

"Winston?" Panic choked her as she searched for the bulldog. "Winston!"

The dog barked. He raised his head from where he stood with his body halfway through what was left of the mangled screen door.

Mac picked up her cane and struggled to a standing position as realization hit. Denton had pushed her and Winston back into the house. He'd saved their lives.

On the other side of the door, Gabe Denton lay motionless. Mac worked to slow the quick, shallow breaths that accompanied her racing heart. Though she willed herself to focus and tried to push back emotions, she couldn't get past the sight before her.

"No. No. No. Not Gabe. Please, not Gabe," she whispered on an agonized breath.

Metal on metal screeched as she used her shoulder to bend the doorframe far enough out of the way to get to him.

Stepping outside, behind the cover of a large bougainvillea bush, Mac gasped at the sight of the smoldering metal that used to be a black SUV. The thick, acrid odor of burning oil and melted rubber hung in the air.

Her hands shook as she eased to the ground and placed her fingers against Denton's carotid artery. His pulse was strong and regular.

Relief surged through her.

There was no way she could take responsibility for another death. Especially not this man. She'd ended their relationship so this wouldn't happen.

"Denton?"

When he didn't respond, she spoke louder. "Denton!"

He moved his head a fraction and groaned.

Nothing had ever sounded so good. For a moment, Mac closed her eyes and said a prayer of thanks.

Then, she assessed the scene around her, grateful that the vehicle had been parked at the curb of the cul-de-sac, between her house and the empty one next door, and not in her drive. Heated embers from the explosion sizzled on the ground around what used to be the SUV.

Across the street, a few unknown elderly neighbors gathered, clutching their bathrobes closed. They stared and whispered beneath the streetlamps, yet didn't dare move closer. Most of the houses were empty, waiting for the snowbirds who would return to Phoenix in late autumn.

Mac carefully scanned the area, but saw nothing amiss. The desert beyond the houses remained dark, with a few regal saguaro cacti visible in the distance.

Someone had triggered the explosive on the SUV from afar. In the desert, perhaps? Were they still watching? A shiver ran over her at the thought.

Mac took a deep breath before assessing Denton for injuries. The cuts and scratches on his face were superficial. If those were the worst of his injuries, the man was fortunate. No doubt his shoulder was bruised from plowing into her door, and she could only pray there were no serious internal injuries.

When she ran her fingers over the lump at the

back of his head, he opened his eyes and winced. He was in pain. But he was alive.

Ignoring the fire that shot up her leg, she staggered to a standing position once more and froze. The wail of emergency vehicles echoed in the distance, getting closer and closer.

"We have to get out of here," she murmured. If not, they'd be caught up in bureaucratic red tape for hours instead of heading to Denver.

Denton groaned again, his lids drifting closed. Beneath the glow of house lights, his skin reflected an eerie pallor.

Take him with her or leave him here? Could she trust him? The question hammered at her, along with a dozen more. Had she been targeted, or had he? It was unlikely he'd set a device that harmed himself, yet…

Her mind raced with possible scenarios. Not one of them was good and her concerns escalated. There was a fine line between suspicion and paranoia. She was letting fear take over instead of her training.

Mac took a deep breath, and in a split second, the decision was made. Denton was coming with her. But caution prevailed, so she reached into his jacket and took his service weapon.

Denton's eyes popped open, and his hand shot

out to circle her wrist. His gaze moved from her face to the SIG Sauer in her hand.

"Easy," Mac murmured. She pulled out of his grip and put the weapon in her messenger bag.

Jaw clenched, Denton grimaced and moved to a sitting position.

"Are you okay?" she asked.

He didn't answer. Instead, he palmed the ground until he found his glasses in the gravel. After straightening the bent frames, he slid them on his face.

"Denton? Are you okay?" She said the words louder this time.

He turned to her, head cocked, confusion on his face. "Say something." His words were spoken much louder than necessary.

"You saved my life," Mac returned.

"I can't hear you." He cupped a hand to his ear.

"How…about…now?" She enunciated with exaggerated slowness, her voice as loud as his.

"That's better, except you sound like you're underwater and far, far away." He offered another grimace as he shifted position.

"Are you okay?" Mac repeated.

"Your house hit me."

She nearly laughed aloud at the comment and

the crooked smile that transformed his face into the endearing man from so long ago.

Except there was nothing amusing about the situation.

Yet, when he met her gaze and something connected between them, she paused at the humor that lurked in the depths of the hazel eyes.

Lighten up, Mac. It was as if he'd said the words aloud. Like he had so many times in the past.

She forced herself to look away. "Do you have any idea who did this?" she asked.

"Not a clue."

She should believe him—after all, he'd been injured. But once again, paranoia whispered in her ear and told her not to take anything at face value.

Denton stood and then suddenly swayed. Mac stepped toward him, and he grabbed her arm.

"Careful there." Thoughts whirling, she continued to evaluate him.

Possible concussion, with hearing impairment and vertigo. She'd seen auditory fatigue in the field. No way were they flying to Denver until his ears had recovered. The shift in air pressure driving to the higher elevation would be painful enough. Flying? Out of the question. It could permanently damage his hearing.

"Call Shipman," Denton said. "He'll extract us."

"No. I'm not calling anyone yet."

"Why not?" He asked the question with his eyes fixed on her mouth, obviously reading her lips.

Mac didn't answer. She didn't tell him that she'd been putting together theories since the events in Toronto and Denver. Little things that didn't add up. She'd managed to stay alive in the past by trusting her gut. That's exactly what she'd do now. She would stay far away from the Agency until she was certain of whom she could trust.

Once again, she pushed back the twisted metal of the screen door with her shoulder, so both of them could get inside the house. Out of habit, Mac locked the dead bolt behind them.

"Let's go." She picked up her bags and cane, then faced her dog. "Winston. Come!"

"Where?" Denton asked. He leaned against the couch, as if steadying himself.

"Denver." She nodded toward the kitchen. Dropping what was in her hands, she grabbed a bag of dog food and took her keys from the wall.

Mac opened the door to the garage. A nondescript 1997 navy Crown Victoria gleamed in the half light. She opened the trunk and tossed in the dog food before grabbing a case of plastic water bottles from the shelf behind her. Attempting the transfer without putting weight on her leg proved more difficult than expected.

Denton appeared behind her. He took the water from her hands and shoved the pack into the trunk.

"Thanks." She reached for an emergency-medical-supply tackle box from the shelf and slid it onto the floor of the front passenger seat.

Turning to Denton, she spoke slowly. "How's the head?"

"Sore."

"First-aid kit is in the front seat. Get in the car."

He stopped her with a hand on her arm. "We need to talk."

When she stared at his fingers circling her arm, he released her and stepped away.

"Sorry."

"We can talk in the car." Mac headed to the kitchen, slammed supplies into an insulated tote and picked up her ready bag. When she returned to the garage, Denton stood in her path.

"You're driving to Denver?" he asked.

"That's right. You can't fly. You'll permanently damage your ears." She took off her messenger bag and placed it and her ready bag behind the driver's seat. "You've had a noise-induced threshold shift. Hopefully temporary," she added. "Winston! Come!"

The dog rushed into the garage at her command, his leash trailing behind. A red plastic food dish was gripped between his teeth.

"He's done this before," Denton observed.

Yes. She and Winston had taken drives to nowhere over the last few weeks. Long drives to help clear her head so she could think. She'd been preparing for today. The day when she'd be on the run again.

Mac removed the leash and tossed it and the food dish into the back seat. She grabbed her cane and limped to the other side, then pushed back the passenger seat. "Come."

Winston jumped in, and she fastened his harness.

Once she and Denton were settled, Mac pressed the garage-door opener. With a heavy foot on the gas, the Crown Vic shot into the cul-de-sac. She wasn't going to wait around for another explosion.

"Ouch." Denton's hand shot out to grip the dashboard. He reached for his seat belt as she made a hard right.

"Sorry." She grimaced with regret at the necessary move. Mac well knew what it was like to feel every bump in the road, and she hurt for him.

Once they'd turned the corner, she eased off the gas pedal but kept the headlights dark while directing the vehicle to an exit. Less than a minute later, a police car's flashing lights reflected between the crowded subdivisions of homes several blocks over.

"Code three," Denton murmured. He slid down in the seat.

He was correct. Law-enforcement code three indicated lights and sirens activated as a response to the emergency situation. Mac flipped on her headlights and steered into traffic, where they passed more police cars, lights flashing, headed to the neighborhood.

"We got out of there just in time," Denton said. "The last thing we need is to spend hours explaining who we work for and why."

She nodded and glanced in the rearview mirror. "We're out, and so far without a tail."

"Does anyone else know you were staying in the rental house?" Denton asked.

"No. What about the SUV?" she asked him. "Can it be traced back to you?"

"I used an Agency alias. The trail will dead-end."

Several blocks away, she slowed for a red light in front of a twenty-four-hour urgent care. The facility's name in neon heralded the entrance. Mac glanced at her passenger and again noted his abrasions. He'd always reminded her of Clark Kent with those glasses and his perpetual shadow of stubble. Gabe had always been a good guy. Straight as an arrow and chivalrous. Had that changed? She hoped not.

For a moment, her mind wandered to five years ago.

No.

Mac gave a slight shake of her head. She couldn't—wouldn't—allow herself to think about their past. Not now. All she knew was that he didn't deserve the beating he'd taken on her account. The right thing would be to drop him here and drive to Denver alone.

Mac raised a hand and pointed toward the building as the signal changed to green.

"Not necessary," he said. "Hearing is improved."

"That's because I've been yelling. You could have internal injuries and most likely a concussion."

"Tomorrow, I'm going to hurt in places I didn't know I could hurt. As for right now…" He shrugged. "My bottom line is that Shipman said to escort you to Denver, and I'm going to do that."

"Your call." She glanced in her rearview mirror, then drove in and out of the side streets a few more times to be sure they weren't followed before hitting the on-ramp to the expressway.

"Cell-phone detonating device?" Denton asked.

She nodded. "Most likely. There are miles of desert behind the cul-de-sac. And plenty of dead zones."

"Which threw off the timing."

"That's my guess," she said. "And there's no way they'd have planned for Winston standing between me and the vehicle."

He offered a slow nod, eyes on the road, clearly deep in thought.

"How did you know?" Mac finally asked the question burning in her gut.

"The device?"

"Yes."

"God's had my back for a long time. I try to listen to what He's telling me." He paused. "Your dog's behavior outside your house only confirmed things."

God? Her gaze moved from the road to the man in her passenger seat. She'd never heard anyone at the Agency make that kind of admission, except Shipman and Denton. For the first time in a long time, she found herself without a comeback. She admired his transparency about his faith and always had.

"You've got my phone and my weapon," Denton continued.

"You don't need either at the moment. But for the record, I don't have your phone."

"I must have left it in the rental. Which means it died in that explosion. Accounting is going to kill me. That's the third phone I've destroyed this year."

"You're alive. They'll get over it, and at least I don't have to consider that someone is tracking us using your cell." She shot a quick glance in his direction and froze. "That was presumptuous. Sorry. Is someone expecting your call?"

"Huh?"

"Wife? Girlfriend?" She raised her voice with the questions she really didn't want the answers to.

"Yeah, right. I think we already proved that this job doesn't make for sustained relationships."

"Merely asking." Mac quickly closed her mouth before she said anything else awkward. She couldn't help but recall that they'd managed a mostly long-distance relationship for nearly a year before she'd ended it. Things were mostly good, except she kept waiting for the other shoe to fall.

They were in a line of work with risks, and she couldn't handle it if someone else she cared about died. It wasn't until Gabe had left that she realized how much she already cared. That part surprised her.

"Compromised-agent protocol requires us to check in and update them on our location and status," Denton said.

"What?" Mac shot him an annoyed glance. Surely he wasn't spouting Agency regs right now.

"Comprised-agent protocol. You must have a burner phone."

"Nothing is required of me. I'm not active." She kept her eyes on the road, without mentioning the ready bag behind her seat that held not one, but two burner phones, along with everything else she needed to survive off the grid.

"You don't trust Shipman?" Gabe asked.

It was time to make herself perfectly clear. Mac turned and met his eyes in the dim light of the vehicle. "I was compromised in Toronto and then in Denver. It's in my best interest if I don't trust anyone at the Agency at this point."

"Why did you agree to go to Denver if you don't trust Shipman?"

"I owe it to Liz," she said grimly.

A few minutes later, Denton swiveled in his seat as they passed a sign pointing in the other direction, toward Flagstaff. "Where are you going?"

"Next stop is Tucson," she said loud enough to ensure that he heard her.

"Why aren't we going north?"

"We're heading to Las Cruces."

"Las Cruces!" Denton slapped a hand on the dash and stared at her. "That's an additional hour and forty-five minutes at least."

Mac leveled him with a cold stare, surprised at the uncustomary outburst. "Your ears can't handle the rapid elevation change. The drive to Las Cruces will give you a little more time to adjust." And she hoped that anyone who decided to check the highways wouldn't consider a detour to New Mexico.

"They'll be searching for us when we don't show up at Sky Harbor Airport," Denton said.

Mac scoffed and shook her head. "That's the least of my worries."

"And what about Morrow?" he asked.

"I can't help Liz if I'm dead. Right now, the only thing that I'm certain of is that someone tried to blow me up."

"Ah, you forget that I was nearly killed, too."

"Sorry, but I'm guessing you're collateral damage to whoever is behind that explosion." She assessed him for a reaction, but he failed to deliver. "Maybe it's time you shared what you know."

"I told you. Shipman will read you in. I'm just your escort to Denver."

"Right. Stick to the script."

"Protocol," Denton muttered. "Not a script."

Silence stretched, taut with unspoken concerns.

Gabe glanced around the Crown Vic. "Whose car is this? My briefing indicates you own a hybrid."

"I bought it off of a Craigslist ad. It's a vehicle. Reliable, and it has a twenty-gallon gas tank. The Vic, like the house-rental agreement, is in the name of an alias."

"An Agency alias?"

Mac shook her head. "Let's call it my safe identity."

"Follow the rules much?" he asked.

"Nope. And that's probably why I'm still alive."

For a few minutes, she silently reviewed tonight's events in her mind. Why did she open the door to Denton? It went against all her self-preservation rules. Something automatic had kicked in when she saw his face. An emotional response based on their history that said Denton could be trusted, though she wouldn't tell him that. Now, she could only pray she hadn't made a fatal mistake.

Mac looked at him. "How did Shipman find me, anyhow?"

"Not Shipman. I found you. I remember you once joked about Phoenix in July being a great place to disappear because no one comes here in the summer. I called rental agencies and had them cross-check all the leases from around the time Shipman said you left Denver. Yours was the only one paid for in cash. Secured with a prepaid anonymous credit card under a name I was unable to trace."

Mac didn't have a response. The admission

caught her off guard. There was some small pleasure in the realization that he'd remembered anything she'd said five years ago.

"You were right." Denton frowned. "It's near midnight and has cooled down to eighty-five degrees."

Her gaze followed his to the tall shadows of saguaro cacti illuminated in the light of the full moon as they moved down the lonely stretch of highway.

Eighty-five cool degrees in Phoenix. All in all, a nice night to die.

Not if she could help it.

Gabe ran his fingers over the massive lump on the back of his head. A headache was building, and it was going to be a doozy.

Mac's gaze darted from the road to him. "You okay, Denton? You've been awfully quiet for the last hour. Not nauseated or seeing double, are you?"

"I'm fine, except for the little hammers beating my skull. Hearing is a little better, but, man, the ringing won't let up." He turned to Mac. "Got any ibuprofen?"

"Tackle box. At your feet. Ice packs are in one of those bags on the floor by Winston."

He removed a small packet with two white tablets from the tackle box and swallowed them dry, then pulled down the visor. His eyes rounded at his reflection. Dried blood had crusted on the cuts on his face, and the frames of his glasses were still ridiculously askew.

Gabe groaned. "Why didn't you tell me I look like a home-improvement project gone bad?"

"I figured alive was good enough."

He rummaged in the back seat for an ice pack and held up a rubber chew toy.

Winston barked and grabbed the toy from his hand. "Careful. I might need my fingers."

Mac smiled. "That's his favorite toy."

"No kidding. Ah…which bag has the cold pack?"

"Sorry. The brown insulated one. There are wet wipes in there as well."

After he'd swiped at the cuts on his face, Gabe twisted his glasses into place, then applied the cold pack to the back of his head.

"So it seems you have a plan. Care to share?" he asked.

"A plan? You think I have a plan?" Mac shook her head. "We're two hours away from a car explosion. I'm still trying to answer a thousand questions. How about you?"

"I'm low on plans but chock-full of questions, too. Like…oh, I don't know. Who wants you dead?"

"I don't know, either." She gave him a quick side-glance before once again focusing on the road.

Gabe nodded slowly. She didn't trust him, which was why they were both skirting around the obvious. He couldn't blame her. After eight weeks, the Agency has a lead that Morrow is alive, Mac comes out of hiding and immediately there's another attack on her life. Coincidence? Not in his line of work. What was going on? Why did they want Mac dead? And who were *they*?

He cleared his throat. "To be clear, my only mission is to get you safely to Denver."

"Right," Mac said. "Because you're Shipman's protégé."

"And you're his family," he returned. "Which is why he made me come to Phoenix."

"As in, twisted your arm?"

"Let's just say—" he paused "—I owe him a few favors."

She nodded. "As I heard it, you don't spend much time in the field anymore. You're being groomed for greater things."

Gabe didn't deny his ambitions. Instead, he pulled in a deep breath. Mac wouldn't understand. Never had. She didn't do long-range planning. In his opinion, she was afraid to think about the future.

Well, not him. He'd worked hard for his upcoming promotion. A promotion that would secure him a much-coveted permanent position at "The Farm," the Central Intelligence Agency's training facility at Camp Peary, in Virginia. It was a safe position. One that his father approved of. And Gabe refused to allow this detour to Phoenix to mess up finally securing the old man's blessing.

Silence filled every corner of the car. Gabe knew Mac well enough to realize they were both doing the same thing—trying desperately to figure out what was going on. She was asking herself questions she wouldn't pose aloud because she wasn't certain which team he was on. And that was understandable.

They'd been compromised. Could he convince her it wasn't him?

To get a sense of the bigger picture, he needed to figure out what went down with Mac's last mission and where Morrow had been for eight weeks.

Mac glanced in the rearview mirror and hit the left turn signal.

"Someone back there?" he asked.

"I'm not sure, but the left lane is in the shadows, so I'll stay there."

"What did you see?" he prompted.

"I thought I saw lights overhead. I'm probably imagining things." She glanced at the sky, and his gaze followed. "Full moon."

"I don't hear anything. Do you?" he asked. His thoughts had immediately gone to drone technology.

"No. It was a split second of light. Could have been anything."

"Anything…" he murmured. "Think any of this has to do with your last mission?" he asked. "Care to fill in the blanks on those redactions?"

She tensed, her jaw tight. "You read my file?"

"Sure I did. You'd do the same."

"I'd like to see your file."

"Come on, Mac. I'm an open book," Gabe said with a shrug. "As always." He couldn't resist the dig. The wedge between them five years ago had intensified because Mac couldn't and wouldn't let down her guard. It seemed the song and lyrics hadn't changed much. Her walls remained erect.

"Why are we going to Denver instead of DC?" she asked.

"Shipman's been working in the National Resources Division in Denver." He resisted adding that she'd have known that if she'd checked in.

Mac blinked as if trying to wrap her head around the information. "You mean since the rehab-facility incident?"

Gabe nodded. "Yeah, he rented a house in Cherry Creek. Since the kids are both in college, he decided to get out of DC and give this try."

"He never mentioned that," she said.

"You haven't checked in since you left rehab. Shipman's been concerned." An understatement. Shipman had moved mountains to determine who was behind the attacks on Mac.

"Why Denver?" she asked, ignoring his comment.

"Why not?" Gabe said. "There are more foreign operatives than ever in the US, and Denver is centrally located. The perfect location for a domestic unit." That was the truth. It was also the truth that Shipman wanted to be close to Mac's home base.

"What about you?" she asked. "When was your last field assignment?"

"Two years ago."

"Two years!" She shook her head. "We're in big trouble."

"What do you mean?"

"You're out of touch, and I'm out of commission."

Gabe bit back a rebuttal. She was right and it stung. He'd been in various training classrooms around the country for the last two years, including his current stint at Camp Peary. Hiding. Just like Mac, though he hadn't realized it until now.

"Good thing I brought Winston along," Mac said.

At the sound of his name, the dog barked and put his paws on the console between the seats.

"Is he hungry or something?" Gabe asked.

Mac checked her watch. "Or something. He needs to take a walk."

Gabe groaned. "The clock is ticking, and we're taking doggy potty breaks?"

She pointed to the green sign on the right of the highway. "We're thirty minutes from Tucson. We can stop at a nice clean rest stop."

"A gas station?" Gabe asked.

"No. A rest stop. Restrooms, vending machines and a parking lot."

He frowned and gave a slow shake of his head as red flags waved wildly. "I don't know if that's a good idea."

"It'll be fine. They're well lit for travelers."

"Yeah, great," Gabe said. "Good lighting, so we're better targets."

Mac reached into the back seat and pulled out his weapon. "Here you go. Thirteen rounds should be plenty for any unforeseen circumstances while Winston does his duty. Right?"

"He's your dog. You tell me."

"If it makes you feel any better, I need to stop as well."

Gabe slipped his weapon back into his shoulder holster. "I guess this means you do trust me."

"I'm being practical. If you're here to eliminate me, go ahead and get it over with. If not, then I expect you to cover me."

He released a loud breath of frustration. "Relax, Mac. We're on the same team."

"Denton—"

"Gabe."

"Look, *Gabe*, I've simply learned not to expect anything from anyone."

"I see nothing much has changed in five

years." He shook his head. "That's a depressing attitude."

Mac's blue eyes faltered for a moment at his response. Then her chin rose. "My attitude has served me well."

"Has it?" Gabe paused at her words, knowing she was in serious denial. "Have you considered reckless optimism instead? It seems to work for me."

"There's nothing to be optimistic about."

Her words saddened him, and he struggled to respond. "Look, all I'm saying is that maybe you need to step outside of yourself and look at the world from someone else's point of view."

"What's that supposed to mean?"

"It's not all about you, Mac. Shipman's not exactly sleeping at night knowing you're in danger and he hasn't been able to keep you safe."

When her face paled, he realized she had no clue. "He said that?" she asked.

"Not in so many words. I think we can agree that the guy isn't real warm and fuzzy. Not unlike you."

Mac's eyes flashed and she stiffened.

"There are people who care for you, Mac. Letting them in makes you vulnerable. I get that. But, right now, it might be the only thing standing between you and the barrel of an unknown enemy's gun."

Chapter Three

Gabe kept his eye on Mac as she limped across the parking lot with her cane in one hand, the leash in the other, and the messenger bag across her chest. Winston led the way, trotting cheerfully toward the flat stucco restrooms surrounded by gravel landscaping. He supposed he should be grateful that the parking area was empty of other vehicles and they were safe for the moment.

Once she was out of earshot, Gabe dug in her ready bag and grabbed a burner phone. He turned the volume up, before punching in Todd Shipman's secure and private line. No doubt about it, once Mac found out what he was up to, she wouldn't be happy.

"Where are you? And what happened?" Shipman barked. "The Phoenix field office notified me of the explosion two hours ago."

"That was fast," Gabe said.

"Local law enforcement traced the vehicle's VIN back to the rental agency and your alias, setting off the usual red-flag alerts."

"We just pulled into a rest stop outside of Tucson." Gabe glanced at the road they'd just exited. Only the odd car zipped by on the highway that ran parallel to the isolated rest area. The night had cooled even more, down to a tolerable mid-seventy range.

"Why are you driving?"

"I can't fly. The explosion affected my ears, and she refuses to leave me."

Is she hurt?

"No. Mac and the dog are fine."

"She brought the dog with her?" Shipman paused. "Of course she did. Nothing else to do with a dog in the middle of the night, I suppose. And that animal is closer to her than any human."

"I guess you've met Winston?"

"Yeah. A few years ago." Shipman released a frustrated breath. "A bulldog. There's some irony," he muttered.

Gabe could envision his boss shaking his head. Despite Shipman's gruff exterior, the man held a soft spot for Mac.

"Does Mackenzie know anything?" Shipman asked. "Has she said anything?"

"Sir, with all due respect, I'm confused. What is it you think she knows? The woman plays her cards close. I have no idea what she's thinking."

"Find out. That's why I sent you down there."

That's why I sent you down there.

Was it? The comment gave Gabe pause, but he didn't challenge Shipman. Didn't ask the obvious. What was going on? He'd been given enough information to prep him for the trip, but hadn't been given read-in privileges on the big picture. Gabe bit back his own frustration and worked to remain calm. This was supposed to be a protective detail. Clearly, there was more to this mission.

Instead, he asked, "Any intelligence on the explosion?"

"Our people have taken over the scene, but processing will, of course, take weeks. The neighbors reported seeing you and Sharp flee the area."

"Where will that lead?"

"No need to shout. I can hear you," Shipman said.

"Sorry about that," Gabe said, lowering his voice.

"We've already sanitized the situation," Shipman said. "The follow-up will be a few lines buried in the *Arizona Republic* about a faulty electrical system in the vehicle."

Gabe opened the car door and stepped out, praying Mac couldn't see the phone or hear him talking. He continued to move in a slow clockwise circle to assess the perimeter.

The small rest area was mostly gravel with palm trees and spiny-stemmed succulent plants. At the end of the parking lot, a pergola with a red-tiled roof protected a picnic table.

"What's your ETA to Denver?" Shipman asked.

"Twelve hours."

"Twelve hours!"

"Yes, sir." He paused. "Has there been any further intel on Morrow? Have you been able to verify proof of life? Was the voice on the phone recorded or live?"

"I have nothing I can share at this time."

Gabe's jaw clenched at the confirmation of his greatest fear. "Who knew that I was coming to Phoenix?" he asked.

There was a beat of silence. "If there was a leak," Shipman said, "I'll run it down. That's all I can say right now."

If? Gabe opened his mouth to protest and stopped. What was going on here?

There was something else. He could hear it in Shipman's voice, and though he'd been with the Agency long enough to understand "need to know," it outraged him that there were layers to the situation that he wasn't privy to even though it could very well compromise the safety of the woman he'd been sent to protect.

"Anything else, sir?" Gabe asked.

"Ahh…" Shipman hedged. "As a matter of fact, there is a small problem."

"You can trust me, sir."

"I know I can. I'm just not sure you need this information right now." Shipman paused and released a breath of disgust. "We've received intel on Mackenzie as well. If true, it makes her complicit in the Toronto bank job."

Stunned by the words, Gabe glanced over at the building she'd disappeared into. There was no way Mac was involved. No way. Both he and Shipman knew that if she was a suspect, she'd been set up.

"Just bring her in, Gabe. I'm counting on you to keep Mackenzie safe so we can sort this out," Shipman said.

"Yes, sir." This time the words were a numb response. As he leaned into the car to stick the phone back into the duffle bag, squealing tires signaled a vehicle approaching.

When Gabe jerked up, his head made a solid connection with the doorframe. "Because I need another lump," he muttered as he slid his hand into his jacket to retrieve his weapon.

A black Ford panel van raced through the rest-stop parking lot, bouncing over the speed bumps. Gabe did a quick assessment. There wasn't a distinguishing thing about the vehicle. Windows in the front only. No plates. No other markings. It looked as if it had been stolen straight off the dealer's new-car lot.

In a heartbeat, the van picked up speed and headed right toward Mac where she stood outside the restroom building.

And she wasn't moving.

Winston whined and tugged on the leash while Mac stood on the sidewalk staring at the van, her face ashen beneath the overhead lights.

"Move, Mac," Gabe yelled. "Move." Could she hear him above the noise of the vehicle?

A frantic Winston barked and again yanked on the leash until she grabbed the dog and dove behind the restroom building, her cane tumbling to the pavement mere seconds before a spray of bullets echoed in repetition.

Someone dressed in black held an AR-15 and stretched out of the passenger window.

They were targeting Mac. Did they realize he was on the scene as well?

Flashes burst from the muzzle like mini explosions as rounds were emptied. Gabe's gut clenched.

Distraction. He needed to create a distraction. It was the only way to save Mac.

He counted to himself, waiting for an inevitable pause after thirty rounds. Except there was none, which meant an aftermarket magazine.

Mac was pinned by a weapon that could hold up to one hundred rounds.

As quickly as the thought raced through his mind, the firing stopped, and the distinct sound of a jammed weapon could be heard. The van stopped moving.

Reload ammo. Their mess-up was his advantage.

Gabe crouched down and approached the van, remaining in the vehicle's blind spot. Raising his weapon, he aimed for the passenger-side mirror.

Boom! The mirror and mounting shattered into pieces.

The van immediately reversed, tires squealing.

He dove to the ground and rolled out of

the way behind a trash receptacle as Mac advanced toward the retreating vehicle. Raising his weapon, Gabe fired at the van's panels, emptying his rounds, at the same time Mac began to fire. The front window imploded.

Nice shot, Mac.

The vehicle did a three-point turn and raced out of the parking lot, melting into the night.

Standing, Gabe dusted gravel from his pants. He inspected the torn elbow of his blazer. His knee protested loudly that he was getting too old for gymnastics in a parking lot.

"That's twice you've saved my life," Mac said. Her steps were unsteady, the limp more pronounced as she continued toward him with the dog in tow.

"Do I get points for that?" Gabe's hand trembled with the last traces of adrenaline as he plucked a blade of grass and a bit of gravel from her hair.

"I'll let you know," she said.

A slight smile crossed Mac's face. Exertion had warmed her skin to pink. Despite the disheveled hair and the abrasion on her chin, for the first time since he'd arrived on her doorstep, she seemed truly alive.

Gabe averted his eyes and crouched down to

give Winston a good rub behind the ears. "You did good, Lassie," he crooned.

Winston sat on his haunches, tail wagging and tongue hanging from the side of his mouth.

"I'm the target," Mac said. A statement, not a question. Her gaze moved to Gabe. "You need to get out of here while you can."

Gabe cocked his head and stared for a moment, thoroughly annoyed at her words. "Maybe you need to read my lips." He paused. "I'm not leaving you."

"Very honorable and completely unnecessary."

"Yeah?" He chuckled and put his weapon away. "Mind telling me why you froze back there?"

Mac stared out in the direction of the highway. Her face transformed, as if a curtain had been pulled. The blue eyes became dull and vacant. She licked her lips. "I thought I recognized the guy holding the rifle."

"Who?"

"The shooter from Toronto."

"You're sure?" Gabe swallowed, unease increasing in direct proportion to the headache beginning behind his eyes.

"No." Mac ran a hand over her face. "I'm

not sure of anything. It's dark, and it happened so fast."

The questions kept coming, faster than he could analyze what was going on.

The only thing he knew for certain was that Mac had no business being here. She wasn't ready. Another misstep and one or both of them might pay the price, and they both knew it.

"Where's your cap?" he grumbled, working to remain impassive in front of Mac.

She waved a dismissive hand in the air, and her shoulders slumped as if a cloak of emotional exhaustion overtook her. "Somewhere…"

Gabe slowly headed back to the restroom building, assessing the exterior damage as he walked. The black ball cap was lying on the sidewalk next to the decorative gravel. It was only by the grace of God that it wasn't Mackenzie Sharp he was picking up off the ground.

Burning anger ripped through Gabe at the destruction. For the first time in his life, he questioned the directives of Todd Shipman. What was he thinking? Mac should be in a safe house right now. Gabe couldn't accept the wisdom of putting her out in the line of fire if there was a leak at the Agency.

Was it part of proving her loyalty to the CIA?

Making sure she hadn't turned? Both ideas only added to his ire.

Gabe scooped up her cap and strode to the vending machines. Reaching in his pocket, he pulled out a dozen coins and shoved them in the machine. The candy bar caught on the metal curl, refusing to drop. He gave the machine a vicious kick. A half dozen or so chocolate bars were released. With a hat full of candy, he headed back to the car, just as several vehicles pulled into the rest area.

"We've got to get out of here before someone asks why that building is filled with bullet holes." He met her eyes. "You have anything in your vehicle besides dog food?"

"What is this for?" She stared at the bars in the cap, confusion on her face. "Hypoglycemia?"

"Reflexive anger." He nodded toward the car. "I'm asking about firearms. Do you have anything besides your Glock?"

Gabe tossed her a candy bar, and she caught the package with one hand.

"Sure," she said. "I have a few flash-bangs and assorted toys."

"This information would have been good earlier. We move our line of defense to the inside of the car."

Mac nodded and stepped to the trunk.

"Oh," he continued. "And I'm driving."

She whirled around, indignant. "It's my car."

"It's my life."

They stood toe-to-toe for a few moments, Mac's eyes locked on his. She would never back down. He'd have to appeal to her common sense.

"Look, like it or not, we're partners now. We have twelve hours to Denver. You're of no use to me as a backup without rest."

"Denver? I'll be fortunate to make it to the state line at this rate. And I don't need rest. What I need is to figure out what's going on. Now."

"We'll figure it out. Together." Gabe paused. Who would have thought when this day started that he'd be saying those words to Mackenzie Sharp? Not him.

"You landed on your leg," he continued. "It's got to be killing you. Take some aspirin and let me drive."

"Okay. Fine," she muttered, finally standing down.

"That's the spirit." He shoved the chocolate in

his blazer pocket and handed her back the ball cap. "Hey, Mac?"

"Yes?"

"You and the dog are...finished?"

"We are."

"Good. Because we won't be stopping at any other nice, clean rest stops." Gabe met her gaze. "I'm going to get you to Denver, Mac. Alive. I will keep you alive."

Gabe released a breath, praying that he hadn't just made a promise he couldn't keep.

Mac sat straight up in the passenger seat. How had she missed what was right in front of her? She shook her head and looked over at Denton. "Pull over."

"Why? We're right outside of Las Cruces." He glanced at his watch. "Once we hit Albuquerque, I'm thinking breakfast. All I've had since yesterday morning is chocolate bars and pretzels from the airplane."

"I need you to pull over now, Denton."

"Gabe. My name is Gabe."

When he turned, his intense gaze bore into her, and for a moment, Mac remembered when his name easily rolled off her tongue. She looked away. "Gabe, would you please pull over?"

"You know, you're a lot easier to get along with when you're sleeping," he muttered.

"I wasn't sleeping." The words were spoken softly. Her eyes were closed, but that was as close as she came to rest. There was no use explaining to Gabe what it was like to fear sleep and the nightmares that came in those rare times of slumber.

After he moved the vehicle off to the shoulder of the road and hit the emergency flashers, he swiveled in his seat. "What's so important?"

Mac raised her head and met his gaze straight-on. Why hadn't she put two and two together back in Phoenix? Why hadn't Gabe, for that matter?

"We've been ambushed not once but twice," she said. "How?"

"The logical conclusion is that they followed us."

Mac shook her head adamantly. She'd run through the possibilities a dozen times since Tucson. "No. I've been very careful. My guess is that you have a tracking chip on you, or there's an inside man at the Agency." She paused. "Or both."

"Inside man? Maybe. Tracking chip? Impossible." When he met her gaze, his face was void of expression, his hazel eyes shuttered.

"Think about it," she continued. "They found us in Phoenix and then in Tucson. We've been on the road now six hours and made one pit stop. But we haven't seen anything suspicious. Why not?"

"You tell me."

"Because there's no rush," she said. "They know where we are. The next time they strike, we'll be dead."

"Once again, I admire your positive attitude. However, there's a flaw in your theory." He flexed his hands. "I'm not bugged. No one has been close enough to me for that to happen."

"Look, if you aren't going to even discuss this, then I'll have no choice. I'm out of here. You're going to blink, and I'll be in the wind. Then you'll have to explain to Shipman how you lost me."

He leaned back against the seat and stared out the window with an annoyingly unconcerned expression on his face. "I found you once."

"I wasn't even trying." She exhaled. "I won't make that mistake this time."

The battle of wills ensued, and an unscalable wall of silence stretched between them. She stared at his profile for a moment and sighed. In the beginning, their covert careers had united them, along with the discovery that they shared the same interests—fly-fishing and hiking.

Things changed when she realized she was in love with Gabe. She'd distanced herself from him, like she had with the Shipmans—the very people who'd taken her in—because she was afraid. Afraid of the devastating loss that came when someone you loved was snatched away, and you thought you could have prevented it.

"Could we start from the beginning? Please, Gabe?" The gentle entreaty was a far cry from the anxiety in the pit of her stomach. "When did Shipman ask you to fly from DC to Denver?"

He looked at her and frowned. "How did you know I'm still in DC?"

"I'm good at my job." It was only curiosity that had her checking on Gabe's status every now and then. That's what she told herself.

Gabe tapped his fingers on the steering wheel and cleared his throat. "I left Washington yesterday morning. I was told to drop everything and prepare for a meeting with Shipman when I landed in Denver."

"Okay, so what happened in the meeting? Who was in the meeting?"

"Just me and Shipman. He told me about the call from whoever had Morrow."

"What exactly did they say? Did you listen to the call?"

"No. Shipman said they had Morrow. She spoke briefly to confirm that."

"Was that verified? That it really was Liz?"

"It was Morrow. Whether it was recorded or live is yet to be determined."

"And?"

"And they asked for you and said they'd be in touch."

Mac searched his face, praying for more information, but Gabe didn't give away a thing. "That's it?" she asked.

"That's it. After I told Shipman that I suspected you were in Phoenix, he had me on a plane to bring you safely to Denver."

"Safely?" Her jaw sagged as a light bulb came on. "You keep using that word, when obviously the odds are stacked against me. The Agency is using me as bait to find Liz, and whoever has her is targeting me as well."

Gabe didn't respond, but he didn't meet her gaze, either, which told her everything she'd said was spot-on. Mac crossed her arms against the invisible gut punch of reality. She stared at his profile. "Why couldn't you level with me in Phoenix?"

"Because I'm right where you are. Trying to put the pieces together. My guess is that the investigation into the mission in Toronto and the hit on you in Denver yielded information that hasn't gone vertical. Think about it. The call about Morrow is probably the only lead Shipman has had in eight weeks."

Again, a tense silence filled the vehicle. Mac's thoughts raced as she methodically put everything together. "What's the big picture here?" she asked.

"I told you. I haven't been read in, either."

"Do you think the intel is genuine?" She focused on Gabe's face, searching for any indication of what he was thinking. "Is Liz really alive?"

A tic in his jaw was the only response. "I don't know, Mac."

"Okay, okay," she said, while frantically searching for answers. "If Liz is being held... Why? And why am I being targeted?"

"I don't know that, either, Mac."

She rubbed her eyes and took a deep breath. This was a nightmare. Only she wasn't asleep. There was no way to separate the truth from an unknown plot and an endgame she had yet to figure out.

"Okay," she finally said, "so we circle back to the fact that they found us, and you're the obvious connection."

"There isn't a tracking device on me."

"If that's true, then you won't mind if we head straight to a box store, and you can toss everything. Including the holster."

"No way. Besides, that's a vintage leather holster. It's broken in. You know how many nights I've spent massaging the Italian leather with conditioner so it won't bite me?"

Mac tried not to laugh at the outrage on his face. "I'll buy you a new one." She couldn't help the tone of her voice, which clearly said he was being ridiculous.

In response, Gabe's jaw tightened. "Watch my lips. No one has bugged me."

Mac raised her palms in surrender.

A vehicle zipped past on the highway honking its horn at them. "We need to get off this shoulder." Gabe glanced at the dash clock. "We could have this conversation over eggs and toast and a large coffee. I'm thinking a cheese Danish, too. I'll buy."

When he raised his brows hopefully, Mac

nearly capitulated. Then common sense took over. "Let's finish this conversation first. Can you walk back through your day before you got on the plane in Denver for Phoenix? What was different? Did you buy anything? Was anything on your person out of your sight for any amount of time?"

"I'm telling you, I'm a creature of habit. Nothing..." Gabe paused.

She sensed the moment he figured it out. "What is it?"

He slid his wallet from his jacket pocket and pulled out an ID badge attached to a lanyard with a silver clip. "I was issued a new badge in Denver yesterday."

"Who gave it to you?"

"Some tech from the IT department." He narrowed his gaze, thinking. "Couldn't tell you his name."

The card was blue, indicating a front-door employee. Not a big deal. Yet her gut told her to check closer. Heart racing, Mac reached into the first-aid tackle box.

"What are you doing?" Gabe asked.

"I've got a razor blade and tweezers in there." She took the photo identification from him and carefully pulled apart the metal. A tiny electronic square sat in the middle.

A microchip that confirmed her suspicions and validated her instincts. She'd do well to remember that when the world whispered that she was being paranoid.

"You were right." Gabe slapped the steering wheel. "The smallest I've ever seen."

"Agency technology."

"Nice of someone to borrow toys from work," Gabe said.

"I hate to mention it, but I was right. On both counts. You were bugged, which means there is obviously a mole at the Denver office."

She shook her head. A plan was already formulating in her mind. A plan that would put her back in control. At least for the moment.

"We need to purchase a used car."

"Do you have a credit card that won't raise a red flag?"

"Yes, but cash would be a better option here."

Gabe's eyes rounded. "Whoa! You're telling me that you have enough cash in your bag to buy a decent vehicle?"

She eyed him. "That's why they call it a ready bag."

"I've been doing this all wrong. Mine has

extra socks." He glanced at the glowing red numbers on the dash clock again. "Can we go now?"

"Yes," Mac said. "We're three hours from Albuquerque. Let's stop there for breakfast."

"You got it." He pulled back onto the road. "Albuquerque straight ahead."

"Can you drive a little faster?" Mac asked.

"No. I'm trying to fly under the radar. We don't want to get stopped and tied up explaining who we are and risk information going out on a police radio."

"Fine, but there's flying under the radar, and there's driving like a little old lady."

A half smile lit his lips. "Maybe this would be a good time for you to tell me about your last mission."

Frustrated, Mac grabbed a bottle of water from the back seat and filled Winston's bowl before she took a long pull herself. "I thought you read my file."

"I told you. Most of the report on your mission was redacted."

She cocked her head, thinking. "Why would my report be sanitized?"

Gabe raised a hand from the steering wheel.

"Because Shipman suspected there was an inside person? I don't know. You tell me."

Mac released a breath. She'd been over the details of the mission so many times that she had them memorized. Two months later, the pain of what happened and not knowing why remained an open wound, and the guilt over the collateral damage ate at her until she could barely function. An asset dead and her partner's status unknown. The awful possibilities were never far from her thoughts. Not to mention the agent who died while protecting her in rehab.

Swallowing past the emotion, Mac clutched her hands together.

"I was in Toronto to investigate a bank job that occurred two weeks prior, involving a four-man armored-car detail, consisting of three Canadians and one American with dual citizenship. The American shot the other three guards and took off with twenty million Canadian dollars. None of the guards who were shot survived. The gunman surfaced briefly in the United States, and a portion of the money was linked back to an identified sleeper cell in Denver. The bulk of the stolen money was never recovered and the guard has not been picked up yet."

"So the Agency was there because of the border issue and the possible terrorist threat?"

Mac nodded.

"Why was Morrow there?"

"We were on the same task force. She had an interest in the bank job. Some connection to another asset, though I wasn't read in on the details. Shipman approved her participation. At the time, it made sense." Mac frowned. "Now? I'm not sure of anything except that someone betrayed us all."

"What went wrong?"

"My asset was prepared to share intel on the connection between the sleeper cell and the incident in Toronto. A dead drop was scheduled for Polson Pier. Our guy made the drop and we went in. Too late, I realized it was a setup. There was bullet spray—a shooter, followed by an explosion. The asset was apparently shot after he made the drop and the intel confiscated. His body was found in the trunk of his car. Divers searched, but Liz's body was never recovered, and she was—" Mac bit back the pain "—presumed dead."

Presumed dead. Such a cold and clinical term. It was the same phrase she'd heard over and over in the news reports when the embassy was bombed. Her parents, too, were *presumed dead* until their bodies were identified in the rubble days later.

Liz was her partner on the team. Her responsibility. Mac had let her down. Deep inside, a voice whispered another accusation. *Just like you let your parents down.*

Gabe released a whoosh of air. "But if the intel is correct, she is alive," he finally said.

Was she? Mac had doubts. Doubts that made her feel guilty as well. Was the intel that Liz was alive simply a ruse to get Mac into the crosshairs of the shooter?

"If Liz is alive, then I'm back at zero. Where has she been all this time? Who's holding her and why?" She looked at him. "Why didn't they kill her, and why do they want me?"

"All good questions that need answers."

Mac nodded. "Yes. I need to get back to Denver and figure out what's going on." She paused. "I have to find Liz. I owe her that much."

"Shipman is using all available resources to locate Morrow," he said.

"They've had eight weeks. Now it's my turn."

Gabe nodded slowly, as if deep in thought. Then he turned to meet her gaze. "Can you positively ID the shooter?"

Mac froze at the question, her mouth suddenly dry and her breath stuck in her chest. "I think so." Yes, she'd seen him. As she was lying on the ground that day, pain ripping through her leg, her only thought was to find cover. When she looked up, her gaze connected with the shooter.

"Mac?" Gabe called her name, bringing her back to the moment.

"I saw him briefly when he raised his weapon to fire again. Then a police vehicle pulled onto the scene blocking his line of fire. He disappeared."

"He?" Gabe asked.

"Male, white, about six feet tall. Lean. He wore a black neck gaiter over his mouth and nose, and a black cap on his head." The words were flat while Mac fought to distance herself from the terror that remembering stirred inside of her.

"And then?"

"I found myself in a Toronto hospital, and then transferred to the States when I was stable. Someone tried to take me out in rehab, killing an agent assigned to my security detail."

Without thinking, she reached down to massage the constant aching in her left leg.

"Who knew you were still alive?"

"Shipman and the shooter." Again, she shook her head. "Nothing makes sense."

"Stop trying to figure it out alone," Gabe said. "The minute you pulled out your Glock in the parking lot was the moment we became a team." His gaze remained unwavering. "We're in this together. But you have to trust me."

Together? Mac nearly softened at the word. But was she prepared to let Gabe back into her life? Five years had passed, yet one thing hadn't changed. Bad things happened to people she cared about. She couldn't—wouldn't—take that risk.

Even if her life depended on it.

Chapter Four

Gabe scrutinized the outdoor patio of the busy restaurant, assessing the threat risk. Though he'd chosen a table sheltered beneath an awning, with his back to the outside wall, he couldn't relax. His gaze lingered on the door to the restaurant, where Mac had disappeared to freshen up.

So far, nothing seemed out of the ordinary, yet his gut had him on high alert since they'd pulled into Albuquerque a little while ago.

"Everything look good?" Mac slid into the seat opposite him and put her ready bag on the ground next to Winston.

"So far." Gabe picked up the black carafe and held it over her white porcelain mug. "Coffee?"

"Yes, please." She reached for a red plastic water tumbler and took a long swig.

Gabe cocked his head and assessed her. The dark circles beneath her eyes remained, and she looked like she could fall asleep on the spot.

He recalled only too well the periods in his life when sleep seemed elusive, like the weeks spent at his mother's hospital bedside.

But there was something else besides lack of sleep. Mac seemed to be just going through the motions.

"You okay?" he finally asked.

Startled, she shot him a cautious glance and reached for the menu. "Why do you ask?"

"You look tired."

Surprise flickered in her eyes, telling him that she wasn't accustomed to anyone checking on her well-being.

"I'm fine," she said.

Of course she was. "Yeah? How about the chin?"

"My chin? I nearly forgot." She carefully touched the abrasion with her fingers and then looked at his face. "We're both a little beat-up, aren't we?"

Gabe chuckled. "Our server asked me if the other guy looked worse or better."

"What did you say?"

"I told her I didn't look back."

Unamused, Mac raised a brow. "What about your ears?" she asked. "The elevation of Albuquerque is about the same as Denver. Any pain?"

"Oh, there was definitely discomfort when we were climbing." He sipped his coffee and gave a nod. "But except for the occasional ringing and dizziness, everything is improved. Hearing is at sixty…seventy percent. Depends on your level of mumbling."

She straightened in her seat. *"I do not mumble."*

"Okay, mutter. You mutter."

Though Mac frowned, Gabe kept talking. "I ordered Belgian waffles and turkey bacon for you."

"Thank you." She didn't meet his gaze, instead fiddled with the menu in an apparent attempt to hide her surprise.

Did she think he'd forgotten Belgian waffles and turkey bacon? He remembered way too many things about Mackenzie Sharp. Like how she preferred her coffee strong and black. Or the fact that she had a weakness for French pastries.

"Did you order a plain chicken breast to go for Winston?" she asked. The dog perked up at the mention of his name, his gaze hopeful.

"Yeah. Though I forgot to ask if he wants dessert."

"What?" She blinked, confused.

"Joke, Mac. That was a joke."

"Right."

"Lighten up. I'm going to get through to you yet. You're alive. We'll deal with everything else in due time."

"Due time," she murmured. "I'm not even sure what that means."

Though he heard her response, Gabe frowned and stared at her lips to get his point across. "What did you say?"

Cringing, she met his gaze. "I do mumble. I'm so sorry, Gabe."

He offered a nod at the admission, trying not to smile or comment on the pink that tinged her cheeks. It was rare moments like this when she lowered the walls around her that he glimpsed the real Mac. The woman he'd fallen in love with when he was an idealistic officer.

Yeah. That wouldn't happen again.

Silence stretched between them for moments before Mac tucked strands of blond hair behind her ears and glanced around. "We need to dump that tracker," she finally said.

"Where?" He eyed the early-morning patrons. "Nothing but families on vacation and truckers. We should just destroy the thing."

"No. It's been seven hours since Tucson. Whoever is tracking us has relaxed. They're certain they have the upper hand." She toyed with the salt and pepper shakers, lining them up in a neat row. "I'll think of something creative." Her glance met his. "We also need to get you some clothes." She nodded toward the box store across the parking lot.

Gabe glanced down at his dark slacks and blazer and shook his head. "Why?"

"Look around you. How many guys are wearing blazers and ties in the middle of summer?"

"I'm guessing it's the clientele."

"I'm wearing jeans and a T-shirt, and I'm not a trucker."

"No, you are not." Gabe cleared his throat and did his best not to notice how the T-shirt hugged her lithe frame in all the right places. He glanced away just as the server approached the table with a fresh pot of coffee.

The woman picked up the carafe from the table and cocked her head. "Drained it, did you?"

"Yes, ma'am. This is good stuff," Gabe said.

"The best, in my opinion. Stop by Whispering Bean down the street, on Corrales Road. That's where we get our beans."

"I'll do that."

The server's grin widened. "Anything else I can get you, hon?"

"I think we're good," he said.

"All righty. I'll be back shortly with your order."

"Thanks, Anna," Gabe returned.

"Anna?" Mac's eyes widened. "I forgot what a people person you are."

"Guilty." Gabe shrugged. "Comes from my mom. Those Southern-hospitality roots. She never met a stranger."

"Your mother." Mac touched her fingers to her mouth, and alarm filled her gaze. "I didn't mention how sorry I am about your loss."

"Thanks." Four years had gone by, but he wasn't ready to discuss his mother's passing. He picked up the silverware wrapped in a paper napkin and unrolled it. "So... I've been thinking about your mission in Toronto," he said.

"And?"

"And I have a few questions." He leaned closer and glanced around. "Am I talking loud? I can't tell."

"You're fine."

"What about your asset?" he asked.

"What about him?"

"Any reason to believe he turned on you?"

"None. Though, at this point, anything is possible."

"Possible, yes. But we agree with certainty there's someone on the inside."

Mac offered a nod, and then grimaced as though the admission caused actual physical pain. "My asset and Liz paid the price because I didn't see it coming."

"Mac, you paid the price, too. You can't blame yourself. Someone had a game plan in place."

"My point exactly, Gabe. I missed something. Somewhere…" Her voice trailed off, and despair settled on her face.

"Don't go there," Gabe said.

"How can I not?"

He placed a hand around his mug. "Look, I get it. You spend any amount of time in this business, and eventually, everyone faces the dark place. We're trained to be survivors, loners. Then suddenly we're against the wall with no one to turn to because we wouldn't, couldn't, let anyone close."

"Yes," she breathed out, his words clearly hitting home.

"That's when faith is the foundation to fall back on," he said. "There is nothing else that remains when your life is circling the drain, and everything is out of control."

"I know you're right," Mac said. "I'm just not there yet."

Anna approached the table, balancing a tray of

food. She slid Mac's waffles, which were dusted with powdered sugar, in front of her and a plate filled with sausages, toast and a large omelet in front of Gabe.

Placing syrup and coffee on the table, the cheerful woman turned to Gabe. "Your hotcakes will be out in a jiff."

"Thanks. Oh, and don't forget my friend's turkey bacon."

She snapped her fingers. "I'm sorry, hon."

"No problem," Mac said.

Once she left, Gabe bowed his head and said a silent prayer. When he raised his head, Mac's blue eyes met his before she quickly averted her gaze. Gabe frowned, trying to decipher the action. Was she surprised at his moment of prayer? Mac had struggled with her faith in the past, and he could relate. Faith was a walk in the dark and stumbling happened to everyone. Despite their history, or the reason he was escorting her to Denver, he should find a private moment to reach out and pray with her.

"What are you thinking?" Mac asked.

"Shipman," he said. "How did Shipman follow up on the mission in Toronto, after things went sideways?"

Mac carefully poured a thin stream of syrup

on her waffles before looking up. "A team was sent in to evaluate the mission. But whatever the status of their investigation—" she waved a hand "—I haven't seen a report."

He arched an eyebrow. "You weren't exactly checking in, either."

"Two weeks ago, someone tried to kill me at the rehab facility in Denver. Again. A good reason not to check in."

"Here you go." Conversation paused, and they both looked up as Anna returned with Mac's bacon and another plate, stacked high with perfectly browned hotcakes. She slid the plate in front of Gabe and departed.

"You're going to eat those, too?" Mac asked.

"Absolutely. Want some?" He edged the dish across the table.

"No. But thanks."

"Eat up," he said. "Next stop, Denver."

"Denver," Mac mused.

They ate in silence for minutes, until Mac eventually sat back in her chair, apparently replete. She emptied her coffee cup and stared out at the parking lot.

What was she thinking? He had no idea. Even five years ago, it had been impossible to gauge what went on in Mac's head.

"What are we going to do about a safe house?" she finally asked.

"I've got an idea," he said.

"An idea? Does that mean a place that the Agency doesn't know about?"

Gabe nodded with confidence, though in truth, he wasn't certain. At some point, he'd need to make a quick phone call to confirm. "It's outside of Denver. Off of I-25, past Colorado Springs." He shoved a wedge of toast into his mouth, chewed and swallowed. "Close to a great little Thai place."

"A Thai place?" Her jaw sagged at his words. "How can you be so laid-back? It's not like we're on a road trip. We're running for our lives. Correction. My life."

He gave a slow shake of his head. Some things never changed. Mac would always be the pessimist—the opposite of his optimistic nature. Five years ago, he'd been certain they could overcome their basic philosophical beliefs. Now he realized how naive he'd been.

"Here's the difference between us, Mac. I'm well aware that at any moment, we could end up as a star on the wall at Langley. I won't let that keep me from enjoying life. It's too short.

We both know that." He met her gaze, and she flinched.

"Point well taken," she said. "But mission aside, you sure think about food a lot."

"Are you maligning my character?" Gabe shook his head. "Someday, I'll cook for you. I've taken a few culinary classes since the old days."

"Someday, huh?"

"You sound like you don't believe in someday, Mac."

"I don't believe in much anymore. Period."

He stared at her. The words didn't surprise him so much as they saddened him.

Mac turned her head and frowned, her gaze on the parking lot. "See that truck?"

"The black pickup?"

"Yes. It's passed the restaurant twice."

"Looking for a good parking spot? It's a busy Saturday. We had to park around the corner."

"Could be," she said. Her tone conveyed her doubt.

"Describe the vehicle."

"Black. Tinted windows. Mint condition. No passengers." Mac paused and looked around. "Do you hear that?"

"Car alarm," Gabe said.

She stood, nearly knocking over her coffee. "It's the Vic."

"Who's going to steal a car in broad daylight, in a busy parking lot? Someone probably hit the panic button by accident."

"I installed an aftermarket alarm." She pulled a sleek cell from her messenger bag. "It sends a notification to my phone if anyone breathes on the Vic."

Gabe stared at the top-of-the-line device, a far cry from the burners she kept hidden in her ready bag. The cell in her hand was a lot smarter than any phone he'd ever been issued.

Her eyes rounded as she pressed the screen of the buzzing cell with the pad of her finger. "Come on. I was right."

Standing, Gabe tossed a generous number of bills on the table. "Let me take Winston." He nodded toward the right. "I'll go around. Whoever it is won't see me approach."

He tore across the patio with the bulldog.

Mac had been correct. Two young men, Caucasian and in their late teens or early twenties, were at the vehicle. A tall skinny kid with black jeans and a black hoodie had his head in the car, and the other stood as a lookout. The lookout gave a nervous glance around and then began to play with his phone.

"Go, Winston," Gabe urged.

The dog barked, then streaked ahead, eyes on the target.

The lookout's head jerked up, and his eyes bugged out when he saw the stout and muscular animal racing toward the car. He opened his mouth to alert his partner, but Gabe ran into him, knocking him and his phone to the ground.

The other guy was halfway in the driver's side of the Crown Vic, his head under the dash, when Winston jumped into the car and held the fabric of his hoodie between his incisors. A tug of war ensued until the man peeled off his hoodie and scrambled out of the vehicle.

Undeterred, Winston followed, eager to give chase.

"Get this dog off me," the kid screamed.

"Winston. Down," Mac called.

Gabe turned to see Mac standing steady, with her Glock trained on the scene.

The younger kid on the ground groaned and rolled over.

"Don't move," Gabe told him.

"Nylon ties in the glove box," Mac said.

"Nice," Gabe said. The woman was always prepared.

After patting them down, he attached each to a metal bar on the store's cart-return corral.

"You can't do that," the younger kid complained.

"Sure I can."

Around them, curious bystanders approached. "It's okay, folks," Gabe called out. "Store security." He flashed his identification, careful to keep his face averted, in case someone was recording the incident with their phone. The last thing he and Mac needed was to have their covers blown.

"Grab their wallets," Mac said.

"Are you robbing us?" the younger kid asked.

"Wouldn't that be justice?" Gabe said as he frisked them. He took both wallets and cell phones and handed them to her. When their gazes met, he knew they were thinking the same thing. Were these kids involved in the attack in Phoenix and outside Tucson?

Mac flipped open the first wallet and looked up at the older kid. "What were you doing in the vehicle… Darryl?"

"Looking for loose change."

She shook her head. "I hope you have a better answer, Jason."

"Some guy paid us to take the car."

"Some guy? I'm going to need more information." Gabe edged his jacket open to reveal his weapon.

"Whoa. Whoa." Jason inched away. "I'm telling you the truth. He gave us a hundred bucks. These old Crown Vics are easy to pop and hotwire." He shrugged. "So why not?"

"So why not?" Gabe released a breath and bit back frustration. "What else did this guy say?"

"Drop the vehicle at the airport. Said he'd meet us there and give us another hundred."

"Did he say why he wanted you to jack our car?" Gabe asked.

"Said you have something of his," Darryl said.

Something of his? Gabe hadn't inspected every inch of the vehicle, but he'd seen the back seat and the trunk. There was nothing, to his knowledge.

Mac shot Gabe a glance that said she was as confused as he was before she put away her Glock and stepped closer. "What did he look like?"

"Big guy, like a bouncer, about six feet with blond hair." He looked at Gabe and frowned.

"Your age, I guess. All you old guys look the same age to me."

Gabe grimaced.

"Anything else?" Mac pointedly stared down Darryl.

"Look, lady, Jas and I were just hanging out. The guy pulls up in a black pickup. One of those Ford F-150s with the fancy raptor grilles. Dude makes an offer. We're no dummies."

"Yeah. He gave us one hundred bucks, man," Jason repeated.

"Crime doesn't pay, man." Gabe put their cell phones and wallets on the ground, inches from their hands. "Here you go."

"But we can't reach them," Jason whined.

"You're smart kids. You just said so. Work for it. Then maybe you can call 911 and report a crime." Gabe pointed at the parking-lot surveillance camera overhead. "I'm sure the security footage will verify your report."

Mac released the hood of the Vic and assessed the engine while Gabe got on the ground and inspected the undercarriage of the vehicle. They moved like a team. A trained team. Mac had his back and he had hers without a discussion. Whoever was gunning for them had just lost the advantage.

"Looks clean." He stood and dusted off his pants.

"Here as well." Mac shook her head. "I don't get it. What could I have that someone wants?"

"I don't understand, either," Gabe said. What had Shipman said about intel that implicated Mac? He frowned. Not enough for him to start getting suspicious of a woman he'd just labeled a teammate, his good sense whispered back.

Go with your gut. And his gut said Mac was clean.

"Whoever was in the truck could have just picked us off in the parking lot," Mac said. "Why didn't they?"

"Too many cameras and too many people," he returned.

"Still, it's definitely time to get rid of the Vic and the tracking chip." She opened the back door for Winston and then walked around to the passenger side. "Minivan, here we come."

"That's not funny, Mac."

"It's a great cover."

He glanced at his watch. "You know, we could pick up a flight to Denver. An hour and ten minutes, and we'd be there."

"How do you feel about excruciating pain and permanent disability?" she asked.

"It's starting to look attractive. That's how old this road trip is getting. Nothing personal, but I'm way too tall to be folded into any vehicle for long periods." He sighed. "You're sure about the ear thing?"

"Very certain. But cheer up. I'll have us in Denver in four hours."

"It's a six-and-a-half-hour drive."

"Not if I'm driving," she said.

For the first time in the last twelve hours, she smiled. It was a smile that reached her eyes and lit up her face, startling him. Gabe had forgotten about Mac's smile. It was a weapon all its own.

Yeah, she probably would get them to Denver in four hours if he let her.

He slowly shook his head. "No way. Shipman specified he wanted you alive. I'll drive."

Mac awoke with a start. Arms thrashing, she hit the back of the seat and the window at the same time.

Winston barked.

"Easy, boy," Gabe said. "She's okay."

Blinking, Mac sat up and reached into the front-passenger seat to soothe the bulldog, rubbing his ears and jowls.

She glanced around, remembering that she

had crawled into the middle row of seats in the ancient, baby blue minivan that they had picked up at Toad's Clean Used Cars outside of Albuquerque.

To the west, a snow-capped peak rose into the sky. "Where are we?" she asked.

"Still on I-25. Near Colorado Springs," Gabe returned.

"What?" The realization that she'd been asleep that long left her without a response. She wiped her eyes and tried to make sense of things.

"Not a morning person, huh?" Gabe asked.

"The sun is high in the sky, so it's definitely not morning. But to answer your question, I don't know what I am anymore. I haven't slept solidly in…weeks."

"Four hours is your new personal best?"

"Four hours. I slept four hours?" She checked her watch to verify his words.

"Not to be morbid, but you were dead to the world."

"Appropriate analogy." Mac stretched, noting that she felt better than she had in weeks. Someone was trying to kill her and yet, Gabe had her back. She was no longer alone.

The realization gave her pause. Did she trust

him? Apparently her head did, though the verdict was still out on her heart.

"How's your hearing?" Mac asked.

"Better. We eased into the higher altitude. That helped." He smiled. "And I can say with certainty that I heard every single snore from the back seat."

Mac gasped, horrified. "I don't snore."

"No? Ask Winston. He'll verify."

She looked at her dog. "When did Winston get into the front?"

"We started chatting about life." Gabe shrugged. "Before I knew it, he was up here, which was probably a good thing. This has been one of the most torturously boring drives of my life."

Winston cocked his head and offered an almost apologetic whine.

"He's been sitting with you for four hours?"

"You sure ask a lot of questions. Yeah, four hours with one break. I pulled over to get bottled water from the trunk and the car stalled. So I decided it was a good time for both of us to take a stroll around the car."

"I didn't think you were a dog person."

"I've revised my opinion. Winston is different. We're buddies."

She moved her leg from the seat and grimaced. When her eyes met Gabe's, she shook her head. "I'm fine. Nothing is broken. Just the usual soreness." Which was not exactly true. She'd been knocked to the ground twice since they left Phoenix. She hurt, but there was no way she'd let Gabe feel sorry for her. He'd had his own share of trauma. Besides, they were partners now, and he wasn't her babysitter.

Gabe passed her a water. "Here. I got out an extra."

Mac yawned and took the offered bottle. "Thanks."

"Oh, and we have a new trick," he said.

"We, who?" she asked, unscrewing the lid and swigging the liquid.

"Me and my copilot here. Who do you think?" He patted Winston's head, and the animal's tail began to thump rhythmically against the seat.

Gabe raised a hand. "Give me five, Winston."

The dog lifted a paw and met Gabe's palm.

Mac released a small gasp. "How did you do that?"

"Good, right? He's a quick learner."

"You've bonded with my dog." She shook her

head. "I don't get it. You seemed pretty antagonistic toward him in Phoenix."

"I was antagonistic about everything in Phoenix. Shipman pulled me from the airport boarding line on my way to a fly-fishing vacation in Ennis, Montana, for this assignment."

"What?" Mac could only stare at him. She knew how much he looked forward to his fly-fishing expeditions a few times a year.

"You'd have loved this place, Mac. Angler paradise. Streams lined with cottonwood, evergreen and willows. Then there's the lodge. Gourmet meals. Hot tubs." He gave a musing shake of his head.

"It sounds wonderful. Why didn't you mention this earlier?"

He shrugged. "There was no need."

"I'm sorry," she said. Not only had she messed with his vacation plans, but she'd also put his life in danger. Ironic, since one of the reasons she'd ended their relationship was because of the high risk their jobs entailed. Going solo through life prevented any emotional trauma, like the one that nearly destroyed her when her parents were killed.

"Don't apologize," Gabe said. "I'm over myself. Near-death experiences snap me out of self-indulgence every single time."

"If we make it out of this, I'll spring for your next trip."

"If. Again with the optimism," he scoffed and then paused. "Does that mean you'll come, too?"

"Maybe," she said. For a moment, Mac allowed her mind to wander to the fly-fishing trip they'd taken together.

It *had* been a very good trip.

When her gaze met his in the mirror, she knew he was thinking the same thing.

For a few days, she'd forgotten that her job could get someone she cared about killed.

Mac cleared her throat and pointed to a road sign for multiple traveler amenities. "How's the gas situation?"

"This baby is a gas hound, and her get-up-and-go has long gone. You should have seen me trying to pass other cars. I felt like I should put my foot outside the car to help it along."

"It's a great cover, though. Right?"

"Except for the shuddering that starts when I push it to sixty-five, the random stalling out and the door lock on the passenger side that won't open most of the time, yeah, great cover." He chuckled. "Toad saw us coming, that's for sure."

"Are you saying Toad sold us a lemon?" Mac asked with a smile.

"Yep."

A comfortable silence filled the vehicle. Then Gabe cleared his throat. "We need to check in with Shipman soon," he said.

Shipman. She'd been avoiding him since she'd escaped the shooter at the Denver rehab facility. Deep down, a slow anger simmered toward the man and the agency he represented.

They had failed her. Sure, he'd be furious that they hadn't checked in sooner, but Mac remained adamant that it was the right decision. Someone had used Gabe's trip as an opportunity to attempt to take her out. Again.

Gabe nodded at the sign that advertised gas and Golden Arches and exited the highway. He made short work of filling the tank, then drove into the parking lot of the fast-food chain next door, parking in the shade provided by a row of tall aspens.

"Looks like the perfect stop," he said. "Lots of travelers. No high ground."

No high ground meant no sniper.

One bullet and she'd be another dead CIA officer checked off someone's to-do list.

"How was the drive?" she asked. "Anything suspicious?"

"Nope."

He opened the glove box and brought out a pair of binoculars.

"Where did those come from?"

"Gas station." He got out of the minivan and did a slow one-eighty, checking the area before leaning against the van. "We're secure."

Mac eased out of the vehicle as well, biting back a groan of pain. The downside of resting was that she was stiff all over and feeling every single bruise from last night's activities. She pulled her personal phone from her messenger bag and punched in the numbers. "Here you go." She handed it to Gabe. "Shipman's secure line. On speaker."

"Sharp?" Senior Officer Shipman's booming baritone reflected relief.

"Yes, sir." Mac swallowed hard as she answered. For a moment, it was like going home. Home to that safe place before her parents died. To the time when Todd Shipman was just a family friend whose voice reminded her of all the good things life offered.

Once upon a time, before she'd been forced to erect a wall to keep herself safe.

"Denton is with you?" Shipman asked.

"I'm here, sir. You're on speaker," Gabe said.

Winston stuck his head out of the driver's-side window and barked.

"And the dog." Shipman's words were a flat commentary on his opinion of the animal. Mac let the comment pass. No one really understood her relationship with the loyal bulldog. Except maybe Gabe, she amended.

"Ah, sir," Mac began, "about Phoenix."

"I've been updated."

Mac jerked back with surprise at his words. Updated? By whom? She glanced at Gabe, whose gaze remained focused on the vehicles entering and leaving the parking lot. Maybe a little too focused.

"What's your location?" Shipman continued.

"C-Colorado," Mac stammered, her thoughts racing.

"Where in Colorado?"

She raised her palms and looked to Gabe.

"We'll be passing Larkspur next," he said.

"Renaissance festival. One hour. Joust Kitchen, inside the grounds. Brush pass."

"Yes, sir," Mac said.

"And Mackenzie," Shipman continued, "remember, a picture is worth a thousand words."

The line went dead before she could respond.

Gabe stared at the phone before handing it back to her.

"That's it?" she asked.

"One step at a time, Mac."

"Okay, sure. So what's this Joust Kitchen?"

"It's a food vendor booth."

She nodded and was silent for a moment, mulling the conversation. "Did you notice that he didn't ask any questions?" Her chest tightened, and panic bubbled up. "How did he know about Phoenix, Gabe?"

"The man is half a dozen pay grades and security clearances above us. It's his job to know things."

She paused, calculating and hating herself for where her thoughts were going. Could Shipman have sold her out? What about Gabe? And what was that cryptic comment about a picture?

Her gaze searched Gabe's, but there was nothing revealed in his hazel eyes. So if it wasn't Gabe, then Shipman somehow had tracked them. A physical ache settled in her chest, and she rubbed at the spot with the heel of her hand.

Please, Lord, not Shipman.

"You okay?" Gabe asked.

"Do you think Shipman...?" Mac paused, unable to complete the sentence.

"No, Mac. Shipman is the one person we can count on." He looked at her and released a breath. "Look, he didn't ask about Phoenix because I had already updated him. I used your burner when we stopped at that rest area outside Tucson."

"What?" She sucked in a breath. "I specifically said I didn't want to check in."

"That's you. I'm obligated to check in with Shipman. Especially when we've been compromised."

Mac's jaw tightened. The man was a total Boy Scout, and she knew that from the moment he appeared on her doorstep. She ought to be livid right now, but she couldn't fault Gabe for being Gabe and for doing his job. He had kept her alive.

So far.

Gripping her cane, she paced back and forth behind the minivan, processing.

"You're mad," he said. "I get that."

She stopped and looked at him. "If you're going to go behind my back, tell me."

"Then it wouldn't be going behind your back." He offered a grudging shrug.

Mac ignored the comment. "So why the renaissance festival?"

"Because it's close and there's no way someone will attempt a hit there. It's too crowded, and there's security walking around."

Her thoughts raced back, recalling the near-empty pier in Toronto. She could see the fog over the water, the sun rising above the shoreline. The scents of fish and sand seemed imprinted on her senses, followed by the acrid fumes of the explosion.

"Mac? You okay?"

"How crowded?" she asked, ignoring his question.

"Twelve thousand people."

"That's a lot of people," she muttered. "I don't like it."

"In and out. A simple brush pass."

"In and out was what I said about Toronto, eight weeks ago." Mac ran a hand over her face, gulping in air and willing her pulse to slow when an intense wave of anxiety threatened.

Empty pier or crowded festival. Did it really matter? It all boiled down to her and the guy holding the rifle who wanted her dead.

As if sensing her panic, Gabe pushed off the vehicle and stepped closer, his eyes locked on hers.

"Mac."

She froze, immobilized by his voice.

"Breathe. Listen to my voice and breathe."

She nodded, pursing her lips to control her respirations.

"That's it," Gabe said, his tone soothing. "We're almost to Denver. We've connected with Shipman. We're going to figure out what's going on."

Again, she nodded and began to pace once more. Then she stopped and faced Gabe.

"Shipman didn't mention Liz." She said the words that kept spinning in her head. "What about Liz?"

"He didn't say much of anything. It's only been twenty-four hours since the Agency found out about Liz. I wouldn't overthink the conversation."

Overthinking. Was that what she was doing? Overthinking and overreacting. She was trained to avoid both.

Humiliation crept over her. Mac glanced toward the front door of the Golden Arches, needing to escape. "I'm going inside to the restroom. Do you want me to pick up something for you?"

"I'll grab something when you're done."

Mac checked the contents of her messenger bag, verifying the cell and Glock remained in place before she pulled the brim low on her cap and checked the perimeter.

Winston whined and jumped into the back seat, his head popping out the window to get her attention. Mac reached into the vehicle and massaged his head. "I'll bring you back a hamburger. I promise."

The comforting aromas of salt and grease met her when she pulled open the glass door. Cane gripped tightly, Mac's steps were measured, her gaze focused as she assessed the customers on the way to the public restroom.

Any of the people in the burger place could be putting a target on her back at this moment. She picked up her pace.

When she came out of the restroom, a tour bus had pulled into the parking lot.

Talk about timing. Gabe was going to find himself behind a line of tourists. She'd go ahead and get him a burger. It was the least she could do. The guy had let her sleep for four hours.

Ahead of her, a young couple stood close,

speaking quietly to each other and holding hands. Mac stared, unsure why the sweet poignancy of the scene touched her so. She remembered the early stages of her relationship with Gabe. Before she recognized that admitting that she cared meant being vulnerable, and that was a place she couldn't go.

Biting back a sigh of regret, Mac turned away from the counter with her bag of food, just as tourists began to stream in the front door. She glanced around for another exit and spotted one to the right. Cane in one hand and food sack in the other, she maneuvered with care toward the minivan.

Gabe's back was to her as he and Winston stood outside the minivan. Mac stopped on the sidewalk for a moment and watched him. Apparently he'd used the time to duck into the minivan and change into the jeans and a T-shirt he'd picked up at the box store. Relaxed, he ran a hand through his hair. The simple gesture sent her into all kinds of what-ifs. What if they'd met under different circumstances? What if they were just two people on a road trip?

Mac smiled, anticipating his reaction when he looked in his meal bag and realized she'd gotten him a kid's toy as well.

He turned slightly sideways, revealing a cell phone to his ear.

She stiffened. Where did Gabe get the phone?

Her encrypted phone and burners were in the messenger bag, nestled next to her passport and money.

Legs leaden, Mac's thoughts exploded. Who was he calling? Her stomach took a direct hit, and her head began to spin.

Was Gabe the inside source? Right in plain sight.

Her brain began a frantic scramble, searching for a response as the adrenaline of fight-or-flight kicked in.

Run? Confront him?

She had let down her guard, and it could cost her life.

At that moment, Gabe turned, and their gazes connected. He closed the phone and slipped it into his back pocket. With quick strides, he was at her side, taking the bag. "Got it."

"Where'd you get the phone?" The words escaped in a strangled effort.

"Picked it up at the last gas station. While you were sleeping." Gabe frowned. "Mac, it isn't what you think."

"No?" She stared at him, emotion rising and

threatening to erupt. "Tell me what it is, Denton?" she said, her voice low and tense.

"I was securing a safe house."

"You had to do it when my back was turned?"

He released a breath and shook his head. "Are we at square one? Again?"

Was there anyone she could trust? Mac held the cane in a death grip. "Who were you talking to?"

Gabe crossed his arms and once again released a breath of frustration.

"Denton?" Mac persisted. *Please, Gabe, tell me you didn't compromise me. Tell me you didn't sell me out*, she silently pleaded.

"Avery Summers."

"Who?"

"Avery Summers. She was my fiancée." He looked around, not meeting her eyes. "Awkward, right?"

Awkward?

Yes.

And not the answer she expected, nor was the sudden spark of jealousy. Mac opened her mouth and closed it. No words came to mind as she processed the explanation of why he hadn't placed the call in front of her.

"Would you like to call Avery and verify the information?" he returned.

"Uh, no. Not necessary." Mac quickly back-tracked and opened the passenger door. She took the food from him and put it on the console between the seats before sliding in.

Once Gabe was in the vehicle, he leaned back and placed his hands on the steering wheel. "It lasted all of thirty days." He looked at her and then straight ahead. "I have nothing to hide, Mac. Ask me anything."

She held up a hand. Of course Gabe had a life and relationships the last five years, but she had zero business knowing about any of it. They'd been thrust together for this mission. Confidence sharing wasn't part of the deal.

"Let's just get going," she said.

"Yeah," he said. "I'm not fighting that crowd for a burger."

Mac picked up the bag of food.

"This is for you," she said. "There's a burger in there for Winston, too."

"Thank you," he said softly.

Mac nodded, now embarrassed by her actions. "Where is this house?" she asked.

"On the outskirts of Bluebell."

"Bluebell. That's between Larkspur and Castle Rock?"

"Yeah."

"And you didn't tell Shipman."

"Thought it was safer not to."

"And your fiancée is letting you stay at her place."

"Former fiancée. And, yeah, her family opens the place to friends when they aren't there. She gave me the combo to the gate and told me where the spare key is hidden."

"Just like that?" Mac struggled to process the nature of his relationship with Avery Summers.

"Yeah, just like that. We're friends. Friends stay in touch." He raised an eyebrow. "That's how it works, Mac."

Was it? That wasn't how it worked for her. She cared too much and grieved too hard. No, she and Gabe could never be just friends.

He glanced at his watch. "Twenty minutes. We better head out to the festival. It can be bumper-to-bumper."

Gabe turned the key in the ignition, and a grinding noise sounded. The minivan worked to turn over and then gave up. "Although, if this car continues to give me grief, it could take longer." He tried once again, and the engine finally purred.

"Tell me about this house," she asked. "I need a mental layout of the place."

"The cabin is close. Maybe two miles. Sits on a couple acres. Very private."

"All good."

Gabe nodded. "A two-story alarmed dwelling with a detached garage. Forest behind the property to the south. The east side leads to more forestation and then out to I-25, and the west leads to a gully."

"Once the meet at the festival is over, you can head out," Mac said.

Gabe hit the brakes, and Mac reached out a hand to stop the food from flying everywhere.

"Whoa! What? Where did that come from? Are you dismissing me?" He practically sputtered the words, his face becoming red. Behind them, a car honked several times. Gabe pulled the minivan to the side of the road and turned to face her.

"You were supposed to get me to Denver. We're close enough." She feigned a cheerful countenance. "Mission accomplished. Frankly, the only mission of late. But it's been without much incident."

"Mission accomplished?" Disbelief echoed in his voice. "In what world are an explosion and nearly being gunned down not incidents?"

She crossed her arms, refusing to back down. "I got it from here, Gabe."

"Yeah, you got it. Right. Forget that, I'm not leaving. I don't know what's going on in that mind of yours, but I'm here for the long haul. You dismissed me once, but not this time."

Mac straightened at his words.

"Truthfully," he continued, his tone relaxing, "I'm a poor sport who's annoyed that someone got the drop on me. It's a matter of personal pride that I take down whoever blew up the rental."

"And tarnished your shiny record?" Mac regretted the words the minute she'd said them. It was a cheap shot.

His jaw tightened, as though he had to bite back a response. "We can argue about this later."

The silence between them stretched.

"Mac, look at me," Gabe finally said.

She lifted her chin.

"You have to trust somebody."

Did she?

"Yeah. You do," he responded with his irritating habit of reading her mind. "This time, you can't do it alone. Someone wants you dead. You don't know why or who to trust."

The words hit their target, exploding in her chest. What was going on? Why? Why? Why?

"You can trust me," he whispered.

Mac released a breath and pushed back the emotion threatening to give way behind the fortress she'd carefully erected. "Okay."

"But?" He paused. "There's always a *but* with you, Mac."

"Don't make me regret it, Gabe. If you do, I'll take you down in a heartbeat."

A sad smile crossed his face, almost making her want to take back her words.

"I don't doubt that for a minute," he said.

Chapter Five

"Huzzah."

"Excuse me?" Mac looked up from the map on her phone and shot Gabe a questioning glance.

"Huzzah. It's Russian." Gabe pointed at a sign for the Colorado Renaissance Festival that came into view.

"Technically not," Mac said. "It says here on the festival website that it's a term of joy and awesome delight."

"Always literal, Mac." He gave a headshake that said he didn't quite get her. "Have you ever been to a renaissance festival?"

"Um, no. I never saw the point."

"The point is it's a festival. Knights and queens and kings. All things medieval fun."

Unimpressed, she continued to scroll through the information on her phone. "According to the online schedule, we're too late for both the royal procession and the knighting ceremony."

"We'll come back," Gabe said.

"I was joking." There wouldn't be any coming back. They'd be fortunate to be alive the next time the royal procession appeared. And if they were, well, she and Gabe lived in two different worlds. They'd smile and go their separate ways once the dust cleared.

"Did you find a map of the festival grounds?" he asked, glancing over at her phone.

"Yes. The place is huge. Sixty acres. Shipman chose a location close to the entrance. We enter and turn left. The Joust Kitchen is near an emergency exit."

Mac relaxed a bit at the information. Even if things went south, they were close enough to an exit to ensure a rapid retreat. At this point, she was grasping for anything that would keep today's meet from turning into a repeat of Toronto, and an emergency exit would do fine.

"Turkey legs," Gabe said.

"What?" She blinked and looked up, processing his words. "You had a burger twenty minutes ago."

"We're being targeted by someone who wants us dead. If my last meal is a turkey leg, so be it."

"Your rationale is not rational."

"According to you," he returned with a grin.

Mac stared at his profile for a moment. She'd missed verbally sparring with Gabe. There were times like now when she got a snapshot of what it would be like to be a woman without fear as her constant companion. A woman who could consider the possibility of a relationship...with a guy just like Gabe Denton.

The clicking sound of the turning indicator echoed through the minivan before Gabe directed the vehicle down the road to the festival parking.

"The parking area is packed," Mac observed.

"It's Saturday, and it's the Colorado Renaissance Festival," Gabe said. "Looks like the traffic is moving along, though."

"That's because it closes in two hours." She tapped her fingers on the messenger bag on her lap. "And we now have eleven minutes to get to the Joust Kitchen."

"Relax, Mac. We got this."

Gabe followed a small line of cars into a parking lot and then complied with the hand directions of an attendant with an orange vest, who pointed them to an open space at the end of a row.

Mac's gaze moved to a cluster of people in medieval costumes at the ticket building to the left of a brick sixteenth-century Tudor-village facade. "It appears we aren't dressed for the occasion," she said.

"Cosplay. I'm not into ankle-banded breeches and blouses myself." He reached for his blazer and holster in the back seat. "Makes it difficult to hide a SIG Sauer."

"I have no idea what banded breeches are," Mac said. She rolled up her pant leg and tucked her weapon into an ankle holster, then put her phone in her back pocket. In a perfect world, she wouldn't have to use the weapon. There were far too many people here to make that choice a good option.

After leashing Winston, she picked up her cane from the back seat and got out of the vehicle. Despite the cane, she moved awkwardly as the gravel beneath her feet shifted.

"Why don't I take Winston?" Gabe asked.

"Are dogs even allowed in the festival grounds?"

"Special Agent Winston is."

She smiled at his humor, grateful for the offer. It was humiliating that a simple task like walking across gravel required acute concentration. Would she ever again be fit for her job? Maybe it was time for a change, her mind whispered. Mac pushed aside the thought and increased her pace.

By the time she caught up with Gabe and Winston, they were at the front of the ticket line at Ye Olde Box Office.

A woman wearing a puffy-sleeved peasant blouse and a laced corset offered Gabe an inviting smile. The name tag that she wore identified her as Gwendolyn. "Welcome, milord and lady." She eyed Winston. "Would your beast be a service dog?"

Gabe pulled out his identification and quietly slid it across the counter. Mac did the same. "Right now, he's in service to his country. Winston is assisting a federal agent."

The woman's eyes rounded. "Shall I summon the boss?"

"Not necessary." He leaned close and lowered his voice. "I trust you can handle confidential information, Gwendolyn?"

"Yes, milord."

"Two tickets, then. Three, if Winston needs one." He smiled. "And, by the way, nice outfit."

She grinned. "I thank ye."

Once again, Mac admired his easy people skills as the woman handed over the tickets without further objection.

"I don't see any security," Mac said.

"Over there," Gabe said. "LEO at your one o'clock."

Mac turned casually and spotted both male and female local law enforcement carefully monitoring the stream of people walking in and out of the festival's Tudor fortress walls.

Head down, Mac followed Gabe and moved beneath the arched entrance into the crowded realm of the renaissance festival. Around them, costumed revelers walked the village-like streets, as did couples and families with strollers. Mac found herself both intrigued and confused by the costumes.

To her right, a medieval piper played while villagers danced to the music.

"This way." Gabe pointed toward a rustic sign that listed the Joust Kitchen. "Left at the fountain."

"I'm right behind you," Mac said while struggling to assess the many people she passed. Festival shop windows offered capes and hats and various medieval attire. It would be easy for someone targeting them to slip into a disguise quickly. It was already difficult to tell the festival staff from the costumed attendees, which made identifying a threat nearly impossible.

She'd almost caught up with Gabe when a barrel-chested vendor stepped into her path. The man's large, thick hands held a tall pole with bags of cinnamon-roasted almonds dangling from pegs. Dressed in a kilt and sleeveless blouse that displayed impressive tattoos, he loomed over her, blocking the summer sky.

"Almonds, milady?" he boomed.

Before Mac could answer, Gabe was at her side, taking her hand and tucking her arm beneath his. "Come on, honey. The turkey legs are this way."

"Thank you," she breathed as Gabe led her away. "That guy was a little scary."

"Yeah, but there was no way he was concealing a weapon."

"You're right. But he could have broken me in two with his bare hands."

Farther down the path, the Joust Kitchen appeared. A two-story building had been constructed to resemble a portion of a medieval village, with storefronts lined up next to each other like houses, each hosting a food vendor. A bold sign advised that the shops accepted Her Lady Visa and Master Card.

"How about if you watch the front and Winston and I circle the building?" Gabe said. When

he released her hand, Mac couldn't help but recall the easy times in the past when holding
hands wasn't part of an undercover assignment.
She'd taken Gabe's affection for granted five
years ago.

As Gabe and Winston left her line of sight,
Mac stepped into the shadows and found a position where she could observe everyone walking
by. Her back was to an oak tree, whose branches
partially concealed her.

When they reappeared on the other side of
the building minutes later, Gabe stopped a few
feet in front of her and knelt down, pretending
to adjust Winston's harness and leash as he assessed the foot traffic. Typically, the Agency sent
unknown operatives to a brush pass.

"Do you recognize anyone who could be an
operative?" Mac asked under her breath.

"Blake Calder."

She tensed. "Blake Calder? Who is he?"

"Shipman's right-hand guy. He's up there on
the food chain but he's new to the Denver office.
No one following us would recognize the guy."

"The name doesn't ring a bell."

"No reason it would. He showed up six weeks
or so ago." Gabe nodded in front of them.

"That's him. Stuffed shirt studying the chalk-board menu. The guy with the backpack."

Mac spotted him. Tall and starched with close-cropped, nondescript brown hair. Any other time and she'd have laughed at the irony. He reminded her of Gabe when he'd shown up at her door in Phoenix last night. One-hundred-percent government-issue.

"Do you trust him?" she asked.

"Shipman does. I'm guessing that's why he sent a desk jockey into the field. That and the fact that he's unknown."

"That's not what I asked."

"I don't have enough information to make that determination."

Gabe stepped up to the food building, while Mac moved to his right and got in a slow-moving beverage line.

"Looks good, doesn't it?" Calder said to Gabe as the officer continued to peruse the vendor's offerings.

"Yeah," Gabe returned. "I'm thinking about the turkey drumstick, though I've got to admit, the Earl of Bratwurst sounds good."

With a discreet nod to Mac, Calder stepped into the line next to hers, directly to her left. He casually placed the backpack on the ground next to her feet and then reached in his pocket, pulling out a wallet.

Mac took the moment to scoop up the backpack and ease out of line.

Minutes later, Calder left the counter with a plate of food in his hand. He met Mac's gaze head-on before turning away and disappearing into the crowd.

She didn't know the guy, yet there was something familiar about him. What?

"You sure you don't want a turkey leg?" Gabe asked. He stood a few feet from her with Winston.

"I know him from somewhere." Mac continued to watch the crowd that had swallowed the CIA officer.

"Calder?"

"Yes." She nodded and shivered. "And it's going to bug me until I figure it out."

"It will come to you eventually." Gabe studied the turkey leg, resting in a shallow red-and-white-checked bowl, then tore into it with his usual enthusiasm.

"*Eventually* isn't good enough. There's just so much muddled in my head. Toronto and then the Denver shooting. I was taking a lot of pain meds in rehab, too." She adjusted the backpack and looked at Gabe. "How do you know him?"

"Met him briefly yesterday, when I arrived in Denver. Most of the staff had gone home. I was serious. He really is Shipman's new right-hand guy."

Mac was silent as she tried to put together a few more pieces of the puzzle that comprised her life right now.

"Will you please hurry up and eat that so we can get out of here?" she asked Gabe.

"Almost done," Gabe said. "Something looks suspicious to you?"

"The whole world looks suspicious to me. Case in point—there's a masked man in a velvet cape eating a pork chop on a stick behind you. Then there's the guy with the chain-mail suit and a sword at my twelve o'clock. This place is a security nightmare."

"You might be overreacting," Gabe said.

She nodded toward a woman with a dragon on her shoulder. "The skirt of that dress could hide a rocket-propelled grenade."

"And you've got a vivid imagination." He tossed the remains of the turkey leg into a trash receptacle and wiped his hands. "Let's go."

As they stepped through the arch and outside the festival entrance, Mac froze, her eyes on the parking lot. "Black pickup in the front row there."

"Yeah, and there's probably fifty black trucks in this lot."

Mac rubbed her arms. It was at least ninety degrees out, yet she was suddenly very cold. "Gabe, I have a bad feeling."

"We've been here for...what? Thirty minutes? The only way anyone could have found us is if they knew we'd be here."

"What about that one? Twelve o'clock. Ford F-150 with a raptor grille. Just like our would-be carjackers described." His gaze followed hers to the black pickup, which was slowly moving through the parking area.

Gabe tensed as he assessed the vehicle, then pulled Winston back into the shadows with him. "You're right. Good call."

"Let's split up," Mac said. "You go left, and I'll go right. Meet you at the minivan."

"That's a terrible idea. You stay put, over there by the ticket building, out of sight. I'll get the minivan and pick you up."

She opened her mouth to mount a rebuttal,

but Gabe's expression caused her to rethink arguing the point.

"Mac, please. Could we do it my way, this time?"

"Why your way?"

"Because even though you're the prickliest woman I've ever known, once again you're starting to grow on me. I'd like to figure out why. And I can't do that if you're dead."

"I…" Mac sputtered, confused by his response. "Okay, fine, but we're going to have to discuss the terms of this so-called partnership. Soon."

"Nicely done," Gabe said once they were clear of the festival grounds. He shrugged out of his blazer and tossed it in the back seat before his gaze went to the rearview mirror again. "We're clear. So far."

"How did you get rid of the pickup truck?"

"Didn't get rid of him, but definitely slowed him down. I told the parking attendant that the driver had overindulged, appeared impaired. I might have suggested that he had illegal substances in the vehicle as well. The attendant radioed law enforcement and they surrounded the truck."

"Nicely done," Mac murmured.

He expected more commentary, but she turned her attention out the window. Still, he didn't regret his outburst outside the festival entrance. Keeping Mac alive was the goal here, and if he had to reveal a few personal cards along the way, so be it.

"Where's your friend's house?" she asked minutes later.

"We've already passed the turnoff for Bluebell. I'll circle back down a few of these rural roads until I'm sure we aren't being followed." He handed her his phone. "I have the directions pulled up."

They drove in silence until Gabe turned back onto a less remote thoroughfare.

Mac flipped down the mirror. "We've got a tail." She released a breath.

"The pickup truck?"

"No. Two cars back. Check out the yellow commercial moving truck. Small, maybe a ten-footer."

"This is getting old," Gabe said.

"Tell me about it." She assessed the map on his phone. "There's a left turn coming up, one quarter of a mile. It looks like it goes straight through."

"Okay, hang on."

Gabe gripped the steering wheel, braked and then made a hard left without signaling. He immediately accelerated, pulling them through the turn. Behind him, horns blared.

"He's still coming. Fast," Mac said.

"Can you see plates?" Gabe asked. "Maybe we can find out who rented the vehicle."

"Front license plate is obscured with mud."

"Can you see who's in there?"

"Male. Caucasian. Looks tall. He has a ball cap and sunglasses…" Mac paused and her face paled.

"What is it, Mac?"

"That guy could be the shooter."

"From Toronto?"

She swallowed. "Yes."

Gabe's eyes moved from the two-lane road to the rearview mirror and back again, as he prayed for a diversion.

"Train crossing straight ahead, Gabe."

He sucked in a breath as the vehicle in front of the minivan made it across the tracks before the white-and-red-checkered arms lowered, cutting them off from safety on the other side. The red lights on the arms flashed a silent warning.

"Can you hear a train approaching?" Gabe debated pulling a U-turn in the limited space and discarded the idea. If the guy had a weapon he'd easily take them out.

Mac rolled down her window and nodded. "I don't see it yet, but I can hear it."

Behind them, the moving truck revved the engine. The driver had pulled down the visor, and Gabe was unable to get a clear view of the man behind the wheel.

Mac unfastened her seat belt and crawled into the back seat, taking the messenger bag and the backpack with her.

"What are you doing?" Gabe asked.

"I'm protecting Winston, in case that guy has a weapon." She grabbed Gabe's blazer and cocooned the dog in the material.

Gabe studied the train tracks and shot the vehicle behind them a quick glance while he weighed the options. In a heartbeat, he decided. Their only chance was on the other side of the barrier arms.

"Brace yourself, Mac. I'm going to accelerate and try to get past those barrier arms."

"You mean right through them?"

"Exactly." As he said the words, Gabe floored the vehicle, gripping the steering wheel tightly when his body propelled backward, then forward, and the minivan made contact with the arms. The crunching sound of impact filled the air.

Then the minivan shuddered and came to a stop. Like spiderwebs, cracks in the windshield appeared where the arms made contact. Gabe turned to look out the rear window, where the crossing arms hung limp and defeated.

"What's happening, Gabe?" Mac called.

"Stalled." As he said the word, the rear window of the minivan exploded, sending glass into the vehicle. Gabe jerked with surprise, then quickly unlatched his seat belt. He slid down in the seat and pulled his weapon from its holster.

"Stay down, Mac," Gabe yelled. "He's up close and personal with a rifle."

"Trust me. I'm down."

Once again, Gabe tried the engine, while silently pleading. The result was a grinding noise. He hit the steering wheel with his hand in frustration.

"We have to get out," Mac said.

Gabe angled himself to look into the back seat, where he saw Mac reach for her ready bag and pull out another magazine for her Glock.

"Gabe! Are you listening to me? We can't just sit here on the tracks," Mac said. "This is not how I planned to die."

He agreed with the sentiment. Anger at the situation threatened, but he tamped it down, letting his training take over.

"If we make a run for it, we do it together." As Gabe spoke, the truck behind them edged closer and the driver's-side door opened.

Gabe opened his door, too. "Stay down, Mac." He turned in his seat and held his weapon steady, hand resting on the headrest as he prepared to return fire.

"Can you see the train?" she asked.

He shot a quick glance over his shoulder. "Not yet. The track bends around a corner. But I can hear it loud and clear."

"We need to get across the tracks." Mac's fingers worked furiously on the phone screen. "And we have about three minutes to do it before the BNSF coal train arrives."

"Lord, I could use a little help here," he muttered.

"I agree with that prayer," Mac said.

Another shot rang out, this time shattering the minivan's driver's-side mirror. Gabe jumped away from the flying glass.

"No matter what, I want you to keep your head down," he said. "I'll cover you. When I give the signal, you and Winston head to those trees on the right."

"What about you?"

"I'll be fine." He could only pray that was the truth. On a whim, he turned in his seat and tried the ignition once more.

The engine turned over.

"Thank You," he murmured on a shaky breath.

Relief was short-lived as the piercing sound of the approaching locomotive got louder and louder.

Gabe put the vehicle into Drive and floored it. His door closed by itself with the forward momentum.

The minivan flew over the tracks, kicking up a cloud of dirt and gravel when they landed on the other side. He resisted the urge to look back, and instead kept going, all the while praying under his breath. Seconds later, the train flashed past, the force and speed making the vehicle's windows rattle.

"I think I'm going to be sick," Mac said.

"You want me to pull over? Now?"

"No. No. Keep going."

Gabe accelerated, though his hands were shaking and his heart galloping. He glanced in the back seat, where Mac was lying on the floor.

It was one thing to have his life on the line, but Mac and Winston? He wasn't used to being responsible for anyone else.

"Mac, are you okay? Where's Winston?"

"Under the seat. He's shaken but fine."

Gabe grimaced when she looked up and he noted the blood on her face. He was supposed to keep her safe.

"What's that look for?"

"There's blood on your forehead."

Mac put a hand to her head, gingerly touched the area and shrugged. "Some flying glass. I'm fine." She reached into the front seat and put a hand on his arm. "Nice job, partner."

Partner? For a moment he savored the word that he never thought he'd hear from Mac. Then reality hit.

Gabe released a breath and pointed heavenward. "I've got a feeling it was our other partner who saved us."

Chapter Six

"Hang on, Mac. The house is alarmed."

At Gabe's voice, Mac stepped back from the open doorway of the home he'd brought them to. She eased down onto the wrought-iron bench beneath the covered portico and said a small prayer for patience.

Praying. That was Gabe's influence.

Winston whined and shoved his snout into her arm. The bulldog was no doubt confused. It was nearly 6:00 p.m., yet it seemed like midnight.

"I know, boy. I know." She rubbed the dog's ears and sleek brown-and-white coat before she buried her face into his neck for a moment. Oh, how she loved this animal. He'd provided unconditional love from day one, accepting her and all her antisocial quirks. Right now, while she was still trembling from the near collision with the coal train, a hug from Winston made all the difference.

Soon they both could relax and forget for a little while that nearly every moment of the last twenty hours had been disastrous. The last hour, particularly nightmarish. Even the unflappable, optimistic Gabe seemed subdued.

A beep sounded, indicating that Gabe had disarmed the system. A moment later he poked his head out the door. "Let me check the place."

"We can sweep it faster together," she said.

"I've got this." His tone was resolute.

"Fine."

It was only minutes before he returned to the front door. "It's clear."

Mac looked up and adjusted the backpack and her messenger bag. Exhaustion now paired with pain as she struggled to stand.

"Let me help," Gabe said.

When he offered his arm for her to lean on, she hesitated and then nodded. "Thanks." There was no point in being a martyr.

Gabe handed her the cane once she was standing, and she and Winston followed him into the house. Mac stepped into a huge living area and stopped.

"Gabe, this isn't even close to being a cabin."

"Did I say 'cabin'?"

"Yes. You did." She'd picked up enough copies of *Architectural Digest* in physician waiting rooms to appreciate that this house would fit right in an issue titled *Ski Lodge Decor*. While it hinted at rustic, the home was high-end interior design, from the massive stone fireplace to the vaulted, planked wood ceiling and walls.

"This place is amazing." Her gaze went to the tall windows and the double doors leading to a veranda, and she shook her head.

"You're right." Gabe addressed her unspoken thoughts. "Those windows are a concern. I think the blinds are electric." He moved to the wall. "Yeah, here's the controls, but there should be a remote around here, too."

"The woods," Mac said. She stared out the window at the dense grouping of conifers. "A hundred yards away?"

Gabe nodded, his gaze intense, as he, too, stared out at the trees.

"Hmm." A sniper in a deer blind could make the shot with even a mediocre skill level. That information would keep them awake tonight.

"What about the other windows?" she asked.

"The kitchen has a floor-to-ceiling window

as well, also facing the trees. The other windows are reinforced and much smaller."

Mac slowly strolled around the room, careful not to slip on the shiny oak floors. "Not a cabin, Gabe. This place is serious real estate."

"Yeah, it's nice," he said.

Nice? She turned around to face him, unable to resist asking a few questions. "How did you and Anne-Marie..."

"Avery."

"Avery," Mac murmured. "So how did you two meet?"

The woman was likely a physician to underserved populations while simultaneously researching a cure for a rare disease that would put her in the running for a Nobel Prize.

Not that it was any of her business or anything.

Gabe chuckled and watched her for a moment. He'd always had the unnerving ability to make her feel as though he knew exactly what she was thinking.

"Avery is a model. We met at a fundraising event my father invited me to on Capitol Hill."

Mac blinked. A model. She resisted the urge to look down at her rumpled jeans and T-shirt.

"So, um, I guess that explains that picture on

the wall." She pointed to a framed photo of several men she didn't recognize with the current President of the United States.

"Um, yeah. Her father is big in political circles."

That explained a lot, too. Yes, she could see how Gabe's father would have approved of a merger with this family. The fact left a sour taste in her mouth.

"Politics," she said. "Nice."

"Your father was an ambassador," he countered.

"To a country that no longer exists."

Mac frowned, suddenly annoyed at herself for her catty and, yes, jealous behavior. Though that failed to stop her mouth from running. "Don't try to put me in the same lane as your fiancée. She's moneyed. Her family is powerful."

"Ex-fiancée."

At Gabe's short response, she paused, horrified at her behavior, and backpedaled. "I just wondered what you'd been doing for the last five years. Now I know. Discussion closed."

"Not hardly," he murmured.

Mac pressed on, hoping to change the subject quickly. She ran a hand over the back of a buttery soft oversize leather lodge sofa and glanced around. "I'm a little nervous about staying here. What if I spill something?"

"They have a service that comes in to clean the place in between guests." He nodded toward the door. "I'll get everything out of the minivan. Including the first-aid kit. Your head needs attention."

"My head is fine, but thank you." She walked from the living area to an open-design kitchen and placed the backpack on the farmhouse table.

Minutes later, Gabe returned carrying the duffle bags and supplies. Winston followed with his food dish between his teeth, his nails clicking on the oak floor.

"Mind if I feed Winston?" he asked.

"That would be great, although I will warn you that if he identifies you as the source of food, you'll be the one he wakes up at six a.m."

Gabe chuckled. "I can deal with that."

Mac pulled a slim laptop and a thumb drive on a key chain from the backpack and put them on the table. She carefully inspected the pockets and seams of the pack for a tracking device, but found nothing.

Behind her, the sound of kibble being poured into a bowl, followed by running water, indicated Winston had been fed.

Mac powered up the laptop and examined the drives. It appeared to be clean. Once she had inserted and opened the thumb drive, she frowned at the contents.

"What's the matter?" Gabe asked.

"Well, look. I think it's entirely dog photos."

"I can see that." He stood behind her again, and she could feel his warm breath on her neck and shivered.

She pushed out a chair for him with her foot. "Have a seat."

Gabe turned the slatted chair around, then straddled it.

One by one, Mac went through the pictures, which consisted of images of the Shipman family's Labrador retrievers. One golden and one chocolate. "Why would he send me photos of Milo and Chloe?" she asked.

"They are beautiful dogs, but I'm guessing there's more here."

Mac continued to review the file until she came to the last image. It had discolored edges and a line through the center, as if folded at one time.

She nearly gasped aloud. The photo was of the Sharp family and the Shipman family sitting around a table. Thanksgiving. She remembered this photo. Shipman's children, Megan and Lance, were a decade younger than Mac, but they were like one big family. She enlarged the screen and stared at the T-shirt she wore. It was a high-school track-team shirt, with her school and the year emblazoned on the front. This photo had been taken six months before her parents died.

Such a joyous moment in time. It would be only months until their world would be turned upside down.

"You okay, Mac?" Gabe put a comforting hand on her shoulder.

She nodded. "Yes. Yes. All good."

"Where was that picture taken?"

"My house. My parents' house. They owned a place in Georgetown." Mac placed her fingers against her mouth, and for a moment was transported back. For the first time in a long time, the memories didn't trigger anxiety. Maybe that meant she was healing.

"Mac?" Gabe's gentle query pulled her from her thoughts.

"I'm good." She turned to him. "Why would he send me this picture?" And then it hit her. "That's it. Remember what he said?"

"What?"

"A picture is worth a thousand words. This is steganography. Microdots and cipher codes. It's a hobby of Shipman's. He's a real World War II cipher buff." Mac magnified the picture until she could see the tiny dots. Then she enlarged each dot.

"I see the letters. How did you know that?"

"Shipman taught me. It was a distraction after my parents died. He and I would send steganographic files back and forth. A sort of treasure hunt." She smiled. "We haven't done that in... over sixteen years." She closed her eyes for a moment and again smiled. When she was in college, on the anniversary of her parents' death, he'd sent her on a steganography treasure hunt. One that took hours and kept her from dwelling on sad memories of the day, and subsequent weeks, when her life changed forever.

Todd Shipman was a good man.

"You were pretty close with the Shipmans. I mean, you lived with them your senior year of high school and all."

"I was closest to Todd. Probably because he was so much like my father. They'd been best friends since college." Sometimes she forgot what he lost on the day of the embassy attack. The grief wasn't hers alone.

"Long time." He cocked his head. "Do you still remember the encryption key you two used?"

"Yes. It was a basic symmetric encryption."

"Basic encryption?"

"Basic with a twist that Shipman added." Mac smiled as she recalled when he first taught her the code. The world had moved to being high-tech, but sometimes the basics and old-school ciphers were all that was needed.

"Okay," Gabe said.

"He's very clever. If the laptop was intercepted it's unlikely anyone would catch this, or break the code quickly." She glanced around. "Do you suppose there's paper and a pencil in a drawer somewhere?"

"Yeah, sure." He stood and walked out of the room, returning with a pencil and notebook a few minutes later.

"Thanks." She began to scribble, transcribing the cipher, excitement building as she worked. The letters formed words and then sentences. When she'd finished, Mac gasped.

"What is it?"

"He's telling me that a bank account was opened in a Denver bank using my social security number and personal data." Mac shook her head in disbelief.

Gabe remained silent, obviously deep in thought.

"Five hundred thousand dollars was deposited into the account by wire transfer from an offshore account." She leaned back in her seat, working to take it all in.

"How would someone get that information?" Gabe asked.

"Information? Where would someone get that kind of money?" Then she paused before answering her own question. "They'd get it from the Toronto bank job. And the account was opened within five days of that mission going south."

"Yep. Launder the money through an offshore account and then send it out into the world."

"Five hundred thousand dollars would easily raise a red flag. And if not? A tip-off to the right agencies, and before you know it, I'm being investigated for a possible connection to the robbery." She released a breath and snapped her fingers. "Putting me in the crosshairs of Homeland Security."

With this information, things had gone from bad to worse, though the last thing she should do was let her emotions get in the way. It was still a mission and she was trained to handle even the most challenging assignments.

"Whoever masterminded this has a good understanding of how the system works," Gabe said. "And they're high enough on the food chain to be able to access personnel information at the Agency, is my guess."

Mac tapped her pencil on the table. "Shipman is buying me time to figure things out for myself before he has no choice but to order me to come in."

Anxiety began to rise as she stared at the paper. "I don't know where to start." She looked at him. "You said there was a security breach at the Denver office."

Gabe ran a hand over his face. "Yeah, and there's something else. When I spoke to Shipman last night, he mentioned that the Agency had received intel. Intel that, if true, could implicate you in the Toronto bank job. Now I know this is what he was talking about."

"Why didn't you tell me?" She stared, stunned by the admission.

"Shipman didn't give me details and I didn't believe it was true. There was no point adding to your stress then."

"You should have told me."

"I'm sorry, but I never for a minute even considered it to be legit intel. It hadn't been verified when he told me."

"Looks like it's been verified, all right," Mac murmured. She was silent for a moment, processing the new information. "I appreciate your belief in me," she said. "I don't deserve that after the way I treated you."

Gabe put his hand over hers. The gesture surprised her, yet she didn't move away, instead savoring his touch before looking up to meet his gaze.

"Mac, you're dedicated to your job and your country. To a fault. It wasn't until my mother's death that I began to understand where your headspace was five years ago. I get it now."

"You're a very generous man." She sighed, confused and overwhelmed by everything.

Step by step, someone was trying to silence her. If they couldn't kill her, they'd burn her career with the Agency. This new information moved the stakes to a whole new level, and she couldn't allow Gabe to get in the middle of a situation that could ruin his own career.

"You should leave," she said as she slipped her hand from beneath his.

"That's the second time you've said that. Is

there a particular reason why you're continually trying to get rid of me?"

"You have a lot more to lose than I do. A promising young man. Isn't that how Shipman refers to you? I heard he's recommended you for a position at The Farm."

"How did you hear that?" He shook his head. "Doesn't matter. I'm not leaving. If I were going to leave, it would have been in Phoenix."

"There's nothing you can do. It won't take long before the Agency directs me to come in. When I don't, I'll be considered rogue." Mac cringed at her own words. She'd spent her life up until now serving her country and that service was about to become null and void.

"We need help," Gabe said.

"We? There is no *we*."

"I thought you trusted me. Agreed we're partners."

"Partners." She said the word slowly, recalling their near-death escape on the train tracks. Her thoughts immediately went to her Agency partner, Liz Morrow. What sort of unspeakable situation was she in right now?

"What are you thinking?" he asked.

"Shipman didn't mention Liz," Mac said.

"He gave you what you need to know to

plan your next strategy. We have to trust that he's handling the Morrow situation. That's his job, and Shipman is very good at what he does."

"You're right." Mac nodded, though being right did little to assuage the guilt that haunted her about Liz's situation.

"We're running out of time here. We can't count on the Agency to help us. I'm calling my brother."

"Ben? I thought he was in the army. Army ranger training officer, wasn't it?" She'd met the older Denton brother a time or two. He was a good guy, like Gabe.

"Good memory," Gabe said. "Ben moved over to intelligence a few years ago and then got out."

"Out? After all those tours he's logged, I can't believe your brother is a civilian."

"Decided he wanted to do something in the private sector."

"Like what?"

"Security. Denton Security and Investigations is the official name."

She mulled over that information. Ben had connections in the intelligence world. Maybe he could even help them find answers about Liz.

"He's trying to get me to join him."

"What?" Mac looked up. "I'm sorry, what did you say?"

"I said that he's trying to get me to join his company."

She nodded. "And you turned him down. Why?"

Gabe raised an eyebrow in question. "How do you know I turned him down?"

Mac was silent, searching for a response. "I know you." She knew he wasn't ready to buck his father and clearly he wasn't going to discuss it, either.

He stared at her for a moment.

"Okay, yeah, I turned him down. Maybe someday."

"Someday is an illusion, Gabe."

He released a breath. "Man, next to you, I'm unicorns and rainbows."

"I'm just saying you should do what you really want. Not what someone else wants you to do."

"What about you, Mac? What do you want?"

She glanced away and fiddled with the pencil and notebook on the table. It hadn't escaped her that the advice she so easily doled out applied to her as well. Would she have the guts to do what she'd encouraged him to do?

"We aren't talking about me," she finally said.

Gabe shook his head, clearly communicating that her response was as silly as it sounded. "Why not? Don't you deserve happiness?"

Happiness. Mac nearly scoffed aloud. *Happiness* had never been a word in her vocabulary. She didn't deserve it, or expect it.

"So where is Ben living?"

"Good dodge." He picked up his phone. "He's headquartered in DC, but works all over the country. I'm going to text him."

"And I'm going to look for coffee." Her stomach rumbled as she stood. A glance at the clock on the stove reminded her that she hadn't eaten since Albuquerque.

She opened the cupboard above a fancy chrome-and-black espresso machine and found a bag of overpriced coffee beans. Mac unsealed the bag and sniffed. Stale. The date was six months ago. Ski season. Probably the last time anyone had visited the house.

At the kitchen door, Winston barked and thumped his tail on the floor.

"What is it, boy?" Mac went to the door in time to see a squirrel dancing around a tree, teasing the bulldog.

Her gaze went to the expansive yard that surrounded the house. The forest provided a silent barricade during the day. But, already, the sun was lower in the sky. Dusk would be upon them in a few hours, and then, they wouldn't be able to see what was hiding in the trees.

"Ben will be here late tonight," Gabe said. "Around midnight or so."

"That fast?"

"He's dating a commercial pilot, and she got him a standby seat on a flight to Denver."

"What did you tell him?"

"As little as possible. His phone wasn't secure. I said that I was in Denver with you, and it was urgent and classified."

"That's it? That's all you said, and he's on the next plane to Denver?"

Gabe shot her a confused look. "Well, yeah. He's my brother."

"Wow, that's loyalty. You're fortunate." As a single child, she didn't have the luxury of a sibling for support, and she found herself envious.

"Yeah, I am." He stood. "Not to change the subject, but my stomach says that it's time to eat."

"Mine, too. Is there anything to work with here?"

"They keep it stocked." Gabe pulled open the fridge, and then he turned to look at her with a sheepish expression. "Is it wrong that I'm craving pizza?"

Mac nearly laughed. "I thought you were fixated on Thai."

"That was until we passed that mom-and-pop pizzeria. We can do Thai on Sunday."

"Ugh." Mac slumped. "Is it really only Saturday night? We can't go into the field office to meet with Shipman until Monday," she said. "I can't sit around doing nothing until then."

Gabe's eyes rounded. "Going to the field office was the old plan. Shipman was warning us to stay away. If we go in, you could be arrested and I'll be charged with obstruction of justice."

She nearly gasped aloud as the truth hit home. "You're right. What are we going to do?"

"We'll head out early and monitor who goes into the field office. I want to ID the tech who gave me that security card and lanyard."

He closed the refrigerator. "Do you have a burner phone that we haven't used yet?"

"I do." She dug in the messenger bag and pulled it out.

"Cash?"

Mac nodded. "Where are you going with this?"

"I'll place a pizza order with the burner."

She perked up. "Okay. But absolutely no pineapple, Gabe."

He laughed. "You remembered."

"Who could forget?" Mac shuddered. "I'm willing to compromise here. Just no pineapple."

"Deal."

"I don't suppose we could do a grocery-store run. I've been dreaming of drinking a cup of coffee without being worried that I was going to die."

"There's got to be coffee in the cupboard to feed that beast of a machine on the counter."

"I'm particular about my coffee. The beans in the cupboard are past their prime."

Gabe shook his head. "A grocery store is pushing it. Bluebell is a small town. A baby blue minivan with the rear window shot out is not going to go unnoticed. The driver's-side mirror? Useless as well. That'll get us pulled over in a heartbeat."

"You're right."

"I'll text Ben and tell him to bring coffee."

"Really?"

"Coffee is important to you. I get that."

Yes, he did, and Mac melted a little at his words.

He smiled and went over to play with Winston, leaving Mac with the dawning realization that as much as she reminded herself that Gabe Denton was her past, her heart obviously hadn't read the memo.

Winston jumped up and gave a frenzied bark when the buzzer from the door intercom sounded. Gabe followed the animal to the front door. "Sit," he commanded the bulldog.

He glanced at his watch. One a.m. His brother had made good time from the airport.

"Gabe?" Mac called from the kitchen, her voice tense.

"Relax. It's Ben. He just texted me." Gabe stepped out to the front yard, where a trail of solar walkway lights lit up the darkness of the summer night. A warm breeze said hello, reminding him that for most of the residents of the peaceful town of Bluebell, Colorado, this was just a nice July evening.

Ben stood outside with a duffle bag and small suitcase. Gabe had always admired his brother's effortless polished look, and tonight was no different. His dark hair remained military-short, and he wore black trousers and a crisp white shirt with nary a wrinkle. He tried to emulate his big brother, but one look in the mirror always told him, once a nerd, always a nerd.

"Gabriel. Long time no see," Ben called.

Gabe grinned. Ben was the only person who got away with calling him by the full name their mother had chosen for him. "Gabriel, God, is my strength," she often said.

A surge of relief flooded Gabe, his spirit lifted at the sight of his big brother, and he let him know with a man-hug and grin. "Thanks for coming."

"Thanks for trusting me to help."

"How'd you get a rental this time of night?" Gabe asked.

"I pulled in a favor."

"Of course you did." They walked into the house, where Mac was waiting with Winston. She'd showered and changed clothes, and he found himself proud of how she stood tall and welcoming, though she had to be exhausted and hurting.

She reached out awkwardly to hug Ben and then ended up shaking his hand.

"Good to see you again, Mackenzie." Ben reached in his duffle and pulled out a small paper bag. "You requested coffee."

Gabe could smell the rich aroma of fresh beans from where he stood.

"Oh, Ben. Thank you."

"My pleasure." He looked at Winston. "Who's this fella?"

"This is Winston," Mac said.

"Churchill?"

"Yes."

Ben nodded. "Never, never, never give up." He offered the quote with a deep voice, his eyebrows knitted together as though imitating the British leader.

"Yes." Mac's face lit up at the words. "You sound just like him."

Gabe frowned at the exchange. He didn't remember them getting along so well.

"So what's the story with the clunker out there?" Ben asked. He looked at Gabe, and stepped closer, his eyes rounding. "I didn't notice your face when we were outside. Where's the bus that hit you?"

"Yeah, that's a long story."

"That's what I'm here for. Long stories." He dropped his duffle next to the couch and looked around. "Nice place."

"Belongs to Avery's dad."

Ben's eyebrows rose and his expression said

they'd talk about that later. Gabe nearly laughed out loud. Apparently Mac wasn't alone in her thoughts that it was unusual for exes to be friends. But, hey, even he and Mac had parted on good, albeit unsatisfactory, terms.

"Okay. So what's the situation?" Ben asked.

Gabe offered a fast rundown of the events that had them in hiding.

"I'm headed into Denver on Monday," Gabe said. "Surveillance of the employees entering the field office."

"I'd like to go, too," Mac said.

Gabe grimaced. "That's a very bad idea."

"I didn't ask for an opinion," she said.

"She's safer with us than here alone." Ben nodded toward the tall windows.

Was she? Gabe bit back a response. His brother didn't know Mac as well as he did. The woman was not a sideline player. That would make it difficult to keep her safe.

"Mind if we review the intel before we head into Denver?" Ben said. "I want to be sure I'm in the loop on everything."

"Sure," Gabe said.

Ben looked to Mac. "That okay with you?"

"She's already gone over everything multiple times. Maybe you and I…" Gabe stopped when his gaze met Mac's. He was doing his best to protect her from the emotional trauma of repeating her story yet again. Her face said she knew what he was doing and wouldn't be coddled.

"No," Mac said. "I don't mind. I think it would be good to have objective eyes on the information."

"Perfect," Ben returned. "We can do that early a.m."

A yawn slipped from Mac as she leaned against the couch, her head drooping.

"Mac, go get some sleep," Gabe said.

She straightened, her eyes widening. "I'm fine. Are we going to sleep in shifts?"

"Ben and I can handle security."

"I'm putting both of you at risk. I'll take a shift."

"Tell you what," Ben said. "If you wake up in the night, you can relieve one of us. Deal?"

Gabe watched the expression move across Mac's face and knew immediately that she'd agree to Ben's suggestion.

"Fair enough," she finally said.

Yeah. He probably ought to keep his mouth shut. It was clear she was on the defensive with him.

"Good night, then, gentlemen." She looked from him to Ben and slowly hobbled out of the room, with Winston following.

"Night, Mackenzie," Ben said.

There was silence in the little house as Mac left the room.

"What happened to Mackenzie's leg?" Ben asked.

"That's what started this journey. Mission gone wrong in Toronto. Mac's had a rough eight weeks."

"We have a lot of ground to cover tomorrow, don't we?" Ben observed. He paused. "Tell me again, why do you call her 'Mac'?"

"That's her name." Gabe frowned, wary of the question. "Mac. Mackenzie."

"Sure, I get that. The mascot of the Mack truck is a bulldog. She has a bulldog. *Whatever.* Still, she's a woman. No woman should be called Mac."

Stunned, Gabe could only stare at his brother. Seriously? The guy who went through girlfriends like breakfast cereal was giving him advice? "What do you know?" he sputtered. "You're not exactly a relationship expert."

"I know more than you, pal. And, by the way,

from where I'm standing, you two sound like you're an old married couple."

"That's not funny." But as he said the words, Gabe's mind flashed back through the conversation since his brother's arrival and he cringed.

"I agree." Ben folded his arms over his chest.

"I guess Mac and I are both a little edgy," he admitted, eager to disprove his brother's theory. "We've been on the road since late last night, and in that time, someone's tried to kill us or sabotage us multiple times."

"I get that. But it's obvious that you still care for her."

"She's a friend. I care about all my friends."

"Right. A friend."

"I haven't seen her in five years."

"And yet, nothing has changed."

Silence fell as his brother eyed him. He knew Ben recalled how low Gabe had been when Mac broke things off five years ago. It wasn't a good time in his life, and he didn't want to repeat the scenario.

Ben shook his head. "Be very careful, Gabe."

"Always. Always," he repeated for himself more than for his brother.

"Mind if I ask why you were protecting her a

few minutes ago?" Ben asked. "Why didn't you want her to give me the backstory?"

Gabe shoved his hands in his pockets and paced back and forth. "Look, Mac's got some PTSD. You saw her. She's a shadow of herself. Between the injuries and the stress of being on the run, I'm concerned."

"I get that, but this might be the time she remembers something that she didn't the other six times she talked about it."

"I know you're right. Just go easy on her."

"I'll take that under consideration." His brother glanced around the living area. "How come Avery let you use her house when you dumped her?"

Again, Gabe grimaced. There was no getting anything by his brother. "I didn't dump her. Merely pointed out that I couldn't give her what she wanted."

"What was that?"

"Promises."

"Promises. Okay, sure. You couldn't give her promises because you're still in love with Mackenzie."

The words, spoken matter-of-factly, hit their target with accuracy, and Gabe's head jerked back.

"Could you lower your voice?" he asked.

Lower your voice and put down your weapon was more like it. Gabe wasn't armed, and he definitely wasn't about to get into a semantics argument tonight. He cared for Mac. Friends cared for each other. Ben was way off base.

Unfazed, his brother rummaged in his duffle bag and removed a neatly folded stack of clothes. "I stopped by your place and got you a change of clothes and grabbed your spare glasses, as requested."

"Thanks."

"What happened to you, anyhow?" Once again, he assessed Gabe's face. "You look like you were in a bar fight."

"Car bomb in Phoenix."

"A car bomb. Seriously?" Ben's eyes widened at the information. "When was this?"

Gabe glanced at his watch. "Twenty-six hours ago. It was a rental-agency vehicle. The Lord and Mac's dog saved me from an untimely fate. As it was, we ended up driving to Colorado because of damage to my ears."

"How are you doing now?"

"I haven't given it much thought, so I guess it is better. I'm picking up most sounds, except low pitches and mumbling."

"So you said you've been on the road since last night?"

"Yeah. Whoever wants Mac dead has attempted three times. If I hadn't been there, I wouldn't have believed it myself."

"What's the plan?"

"After you interview Mac, let's look at a timeline of events and see if we can generate some leads. No one has seen your face, and investigation is your forte."

"Give me your gut thoughts on the situation, Gabe. Why is she being targeted?"

"Mac most likely knows something that she doesn't know she knows."

"Or she's hiding something," Ben said.

"Hiding something?" Gabe recalled the kids searching the Crown Vic in Albuquerque. Was there something to that?

"You haven't seen the woman in five years. We have to look at every angle until we rule each one out." He paused. "You're okay with me nosing around into Mac's background? Her personal information?"

Gabe nodded, knowing his brother was right, which was why he'd called him. Ben could be brutally objective, while Gabe found himself wanting to defend Mac at every turn. Ben's plan was the only way to get to the bottom of things.

"You bring a weapon with you?" Ben asked.

"Yeah. Mac is carrying as well."

"Excellent." Ben glanced around and gave a slow shake of his head. "I don't like this setup."

"I'm not thrilled with it myself, but it was the best I could do on short notice."

"I've got a few contacts in the area. I'm going to try to locate a real safe house as soon as possible."

"Thanks," Gabe said.

"Mind if I do a recon of the place?" Ben asked.

"Let me go with you."

"No. I got it. You get some sleep. You look awful. I'll do the first watch."

"You sure?"

"Yeah. I brought paperwork with me I need to review."

"Okay. I'll set my alarm for four hours from now."

"How many bedrooms in this place, anyhow?" Ben asked. "I don't have to bunk with you, do I?"

Gabe's jaw sagged at the words and he recalled his joking comments to Mac about snoring. "What's that supposed to mean?"

"You snore, buddy."

"I do not. You're the one with the deviated septum. But there are four bedrooms. You can have your own or share with Winston," Gabe muttered as he turned to leave.

"Wait," Ben said. "Any food around here?"

"There's pizza in the fridge. We ordered extra, so help yourself."

"It's not pineapple, is it?"

Gabe chuckled, remembering his pizza discussion with Mac. Forty-eight hours since he'd been assigned this mission and now everything seemed to circle back to her.

"No pineapple," he said.

"Whew."

"Your annoying big-brother attitude aside, thanks for coming."

"That's what bros are for. Besides, I figured this would be a great time to once again emphasize all the reasons why you should join Denton Security and Investigations."

Uh-oh, the big pitch was about to begin again. In truth, every time Ben pitched, Gabe lost a little more resistance to the idea.

"Denton Security and Investigations. That's still the name you're going with?"

"Yeah, the family business. Although I am open to Denton Brothers. Which do you prefer?"

"I prefer you stop selling for five minutes." Gabe tried not to laugh. "The family business, huh? Is the general aware of the family business? I can just see his face turning red and the veins pulsing in his neck."

"I'll let him know eventually. He'll get over himself if we present a united front."

"Ben, you've been out of the military for six months. How long do you think you can keep this from him?"

"He plays lots of golf these days. I'm good at least until the Thanksgiving interrogation."

"You're living dangerously." Living dangerously was an understatement. Gabe didn't want to be the one to face their father, though he could see the advantage of two of them approaching him.

"Maybe. But I wasn't talking about me. What are your thoughts on this?"

Gabe had plenty of thoughts, and most involved fear of leaving behind the only career he'd ever known. But he wasn't ready to be completely transparent with his brother, because once he did it was as good as a commitment.

"I've got a promotion coming up," Gabe said.

"There's always a promotion coming up. This is about being your own boss. Being part of something that's yours and not owned by Uncle Sam."

"I like my job."

"Great, because we're bidding on a few government contracts. You could have your freedom and your government job perks, too."

Gabe blinked at this answer. It sounded almost too good to be true, and he was once again tempted.

"What can I contribute to the family business, as you call it?" he asked.

"Plenty, with your experience. And we've been talking about opening a branch in the west. Denver would be ideal."

"We, who?"

"I've brought in a few veterans—men and women formerly in the intelligence arena. Right now, we're focused on investigation, but I'd like to branch out into security. That's where you'd come in. Training, maybe. Like you do now."

"I don't know…" Gabe hedged.

"Just tell me that you'll think about it."

"Okay, sure. I'll think about it."

And he would. Gabe headed down the hall to one of the bedrooms as he considered his brother's offer.

The idea of moving to the private sector was both terrifying and intriguing.

He tossed the clothes Ben brought him on the bed and thought about Mac sleeping in the next room. What about living in the same city as her?

Yeah, that would be the terrifying part.

Chapter Seven

Mac yawned as she stood in front of the French press. She leaned against the kitchen counter and closed her eyes, inhaling the aroma of brewing coffee. "Four minutes," she murmured.

"What are you doing?"

"Huh?" Her eyes flew open, and she whirled around, planting her face into Gabe's chest.

She jumped away, gripping the counter to steady herself. Nothing like a little humiliation to immediately wake her up. He'd recently showered and changed clothes, and he smelled good. She'd forgotten just how good. Like soap and toothpaste and Gabe.

"Easy there." Amusement filled his eyes as he nodded toward the fancy coffee machine on the counter. "Why didn't you just use that?"

"Are you kidding? Look at all those buttons. It would have taken me an hour to figure it out. I need coffee now." A soft beep sounded, and

Mac stopped the stove timer. "This takes four minutes." She gently pressed the plunger on the French press until the filter reached the bottom of the beaker. "All done. Want some?"

"No, thanks. I like a challenge. I think I remember how this works."

"Good." Ben's voice rang out. "Then you can make me a cup, too."

The two joked and exchanged barbs as Gabe made coffee, leaving Mac an opportunity to observe the brothers.

Ben looked like a soldier, tall and lean, while Gabe was solid all over and a little nerdy around the edges with his black-framed glasses.

"Here you go," Gabe said as he slid a steaming mug on the table in front of his brother. "I'm taking my coffee with me. I promised Winston a stroll."

Ben sipped his coffee. Once the front door closed, he turned to Mac. "How are you doing, Mackenzie?"

"Better. I got a few hours of sleep in. Funny, how it's easier to sleep when I know there are people in the house who have my back."

"Sleep is good." He sipped his coffee and eyed her over the rim of the mug, a question in his eyes.

"What is it?" she asked.

"Gabe is concerned that discussing the mission in Toronto may trigger some mental-health issues."

The words gave her pause. Gabe had put himself into the role of her protector and she neither needed nor wanted one. Maybe if she wasn't a trained agent, she'd be flattered. Instead, she found herself annoyed. A healing leg injury was no reason to assume she couldn't take care of herself. She needed his help to figure out what was going on, not because she couldn't protect herself.

"Mackenzie?" Ben asked. "Are you okay?"

"Yes. I'm fine," she said. "To answer your question, Gabe could be right. I can't say for certain what response might be triggered, but I want to go ahead. I can't live like this. On the run. Not knowing who or why someone wants me dead. I want my life back."

"I agree with you, one hundred percent. The sooner we figure out why you're a liability to someone, the sooner we can target your unknown enemy."

"Thank you, Ben. I really appreciate your help." She searched for the right words. "I'm sorry we took you away from your job."

He shook his head. "I'm glad Gabe called

me. And you're his friend, so I'm here for you as well."

Mac put her hands around her mug. "That's very generous of you, especially since I'm sure you must have some concerns about me."

"To be honest, it's Gabe I'm concerned about."

"Gabe?"

"He's still got feelings for you."

"No. No. It's nothing like that. We're partners in this mission. Actually, I've tried several times to get him to leave. Go back to Washington. He promised Todd Shipman he'd get me to Denver. I'm here. His responsibility has ended."

"You have to realize that he's not here because of responsibility."

Mac crossed her arms and considered his words for a moment, before quickly discarding them. This was an assignment. She and Gabe were history.

"I think you're wrong," she finally said.

"We can agree to disagree."

She could only smile at that. "The Denton brothers are a lot alike."

"Are we?" Ben chuckled. "Gabe's a good guy. I can tell you that." He paused and cocked his head. "I'm trying to lure him to the private sector. If it comes up, maybe you can put in a good word for Denton Security and Investigations."

"I can do that." She finished off her coffee. "Tell me about your company. I have to admit that I would have pegged you for a lifer when it came to the military."

"A year ago, I would have agreed with you."

"What happened?"

"I took a look at myself in the mirror and didn't like what I saw. I wasn't happy, and I couldn't remember why I was doing a job that didn't fulfill me."

She nodded, well able to relate. While in hiding for the last few weeks, she had begun to think about her career path, her loyalty and her future. Would she have the courage to veer from the known to the unknown, like Ben had? Like he wanted Gabe to? She wasn't sure yet.

"I've made a lot of contacts, and that's provided a good foundation for the company. We've got more business than I can handle."

"What is it that you do?"

"Right now, white-collar investigations, but I'm ready to expand into security. Domestic. I'd want to recruit Gabe to handle the security side. I can't expand without someone I trust partnering with me."

"Gabe would be perfect for the job."

"Yeah, I think so, too."

The sound of the front door opening and closing had both Mac and Ben on alert. Winston raced into the room ahead of Gabe. Tongue lolling, he ran in a circle, pleased with himself.

"What are you two talking about?" Gabe asked. He opened the refrigerator and took out a bottle of water.

"You," Ben said.

"I figured as much." He downed the water and leaned against the refrigerator. "This guy gave me a workout. We ran through the woods to the east of the house."

"What's it look like out there?" Ben asked.

"There are a few trails that lead out to the highway." He pulled a few brambles and leaves from his jeans. "Very overgrown."

"Another reason to get out of here soon. This place is too accessible," Ben said, his voice tense. "I'll have a place set up by Monday night."

"Are we ready to get started?" Gabe asked.

Mac nodded. "Do you mind if we sit in the kitchen? It's easier for me to get up and down from a straight-backed chair."

"Sure."

"I want to be clear, Ben," Gabe said. "What

we're doing here is a completely off-book operation. We're trying to determine who the mole is at the Agency in Denver and why Mac is being targeted."

Ben nodded as his brother continued.

"We've been unofficially provided a window of time to figure this out before the Agency will no doubt be forced to take action with intel that supposedly implicates Mac in the bank job in Toronto and then by association the explosion at Polson Pier."

Ben nodded. "The bank account that was opened in her name."

"Yeah," Gabe returned. "Which would signal the FBI and Department of Homeland Security, who would begin an internal investigation."

"Understood. Let's start at the beginning," Ben said. "Gabe gave me a quick briefing, Mackenzie. But I want to hear it in your own words. Tell me everything that happened before Toronto."

"This is a highly classified, need-to-know op," Gabe said.

"Look, Boy Scout, you contacted me. If I'm going to help Mackenzie, I need to know."

Mac's eyes rounded at the interaction between brothers. So she wasn't the only one who'd noticed Gabe's propensity for following the rules. He only glared at Ben.

"Gabe, your brother is right. The advantage here is Ben can be objective and hopefully see things that I've missed."

"I know. I know," Gabe said. "This is just new territory for me."

"I get that," Ben said. "But someone on the inside is gunning for both of you. You don't have a choice, except to color outside the lines." He turned to Mac. "Go ahead."

"I was read in on the case in early spring. The bank robbery had just happened. Three dead guards."

"Why was the Agency interested in this incident?"

"They'd been monitoring a sleeper cell in Denver and activity indicated that funds from the Toronto bank job were funneled to an account managed by the leaders of the cell."

"How much are we talking?" Ben asked.

"Twenty million, though only one million showed up in the account. The rest is unaccounted for." She shared the details without emotion. These were the facts, and as a professional she'd learned long ago to compartmentalize in an effort to remain objective.

Gabe's brother offered a low whistle. "That's a lot of reasons to want you dead."

Mac released a breath at his words. He was right. There were nineteen million reasons to want her dead.

"Why were you chosen for this assignment?"

"I'm fluent in French, and I'm based in Denver. Shipman sent me to meet with a potential asset. A roommate of the missing bank guard. The asset agreed to provide information in return for a visa into the US."

Ben nodded. "I'm just tossing out ideas, but is it possible you were chosen for another reason?"

"Another reason?" The question flustered her for a moment.

"I'd say anything is possible." Yes. Anything was possible. Her mind raced at the thought. Had she been played? Set up in an elaborate plot as the fall guy? The idea both terrified and angered her.

"Go ahead," Ben prompted.

"I...um." Mac cleared her throat and worked to tuck the premise Ben suggested into its own box so she could focus on his questions.

"Are you okay?" Gabe asked.

"Yes." She gave a firm nod. "Once I established that the asset had credible intel, we set up the meeting. Evaluating that information would determine the next step."

"Who else was involved in this mission?"

"Several analysts monitored the case, and Elizabeth Morrow was brought in and accompanied me to Toronto."

"Morrow. How well did you know her?"

"We weren't exactly friends. Liz is a loner." Mac paused and looked at Gabe and then away. "Yes, I know I'm considered a loner," she added. "But Liz, she's in a different category. We'd gone through training together and we've been together on a few missions, but I have to say, she isn't a talker. I know more about the barista at my local coffee shop than I do about Liz. However, I always thought we had a good working relationship."

"She never talked about growing up or her parents when you were working together?" Gabe asked. "Her file says she lost her parents when she was a freshman in college."

"I know what her file says. I asked for it when Shipman debriefed me. But there was one odd incident. I ran into her around the holidays, here in Denver, over a year ago. She's based here as well." Mac took a breath. "I was at a local restaurant getting takeout. Liz was sitting at the bar and I got the impression she'd been there a while drinking. I asked her if she was going home for Christmas. Liz said she didn't have a home, and that she was raised in foster care. She looked me right in the eye and said I had no idea what that was like."

Mac frowned, recalling the incident with regret. She should have tried harder to push past her own fears to connect with Liz on an emotional level.

"That was it?" Ben asked.

"No. When we were in Toronto, somehow family came up again. I think she brought up the embassy bombing. I hadn't read her file at that point, and I mentioned that she told me once that she was raised in foster care. Liz became really agitated, and raised her voice, telling me I didn't know what I was talking about." Mac paused. Recalling the incident continued to disturb her. She glanced between Gabe and Ben.

"It was as though she was another person. Then she gave me the verbatim story that's in her file about her parents dying when she was in college."

Mac shook her head. The incident had left her second-guessing herself. Now, she realized that it was a huge red flag and she should have listened to her gut. She wasn't imagining things.

What was the truth about Liz's past? And did it affect the events that unfolded with the mission? Was there a connection she was missing?

"That's very strange. Did you trust Morrow?" Ben asked.

"That's my job. To trust my team. Although, right now, I'm starting to think that every person attached to the task force could be culpable." She raised a brow. "Should that old saying apply to operatives?"

"What saying?" Gabe asked.

"No honor among thieves. I'm starting to think it's true." She sighed and tapped her foot nervously on the floor, then detailed how the Polson Pier dead drop had gone bad.

"Tell me about your informant," Ben said. He reached for the notebook on the table and tore out a piece of paper. "Any idea what information he had?"

"Abrak Taher was his name. He claimed that he had the hard drive of a computer that was jointly used by several roommates in the apartment, including James Smith, the American bank guard. It was never recovered."

Gabe turned to his brother. "Ben, you should

know that on Friday, Shipman received intel indicating that Morrow may be alive and held hostage. Shipman asked Mac to come in to protect her," he said. "I'm beginning to wonder if whoever has Morrow used her to lure Mac out of hiding."

"So, if the intel is correct, Morrow didn't die on the pier." Ben made a note on the paper. "How far has the Agency gotten with tracking her down?"

"Nowhere, as far as we know," Mac said.

"Mackenzie, have you considered the possibility that Morrow was the inside person?" Ben asked.

"I've considered that everyone was an inside person." She'd been awake night after night trying to figure out who had set her up and why. "If it was Liz, then she was working with someone else at the Agency," Mac continued.

"What makes you think that?" Gabe asked.

"The GPS on you, for one. That IT staffer was working at someone's direction, someone with system admin access who could help them slide under the radar."

"You're right," Gabe said. "But that staffer is the direct link to our answers."

"Yeah, I agree," Ben said. "Did either of you get a visual on the guy in the black truck or the commercial moving truck?" Ben asked.

"Not close enough to be helpful," Gabe said. "We don't even know if both drivers are the same person."

Ben looked at Mac. "Could he...they be the guard from Toronto or the shooter on the pier?"

"It's impossible to say," she returned. "Neither Gabe nor I can ID the drivers. And I wasn't close enough in Toronto to provide a positive ID on a man who for the most part was hidden beneath his hat and sunglasses. Afterward, I didn't want to think about him." She didn't admit that for the last eight weeks, the shooter at the pier had kept in the shadows of her nightmares. Thinking about him when she was awake wasn't something she'd dared to do up to now.

"Could you think about him now?" Ben asked gently.

"I can try."

The only sound in the kitchen was the hum of the refrigerator. Mac said a silent prayer before she closed her eyes. She went back to the pier, back to that day. A shiver ran over her arms, and she licked her dry lips. She had to remember.

Her life depended on remembering something about this shooter.

She visualized him, his face covered to his nose by a black neck gaiter and his head hidden by a black cap, the eyes anonymous behind dark aviators. He raised the rifle without hesitancy. Then, his left hand moved to lift the brim of his cap, his right index finger never leaving the trigger.

"Tattoo," Mac said. Her eyes popped open, and she gasped at the same time.

"What?" Gabe asked.

Mac wiped away the bead of perspiration that had formed on her upper lip. "He had a tattoo on his left forearm. Something circular." She blinked. "A lion's head."

"Bingo," Ben said. "I have a friend who can check the FBI tattoo recognition database. It may yield something that could help us." He looked at Mac and offered a nod of approval. "And I'll see what I can find out about Morrow's background."

They were one step closer, yet fear bubbled up inside of Mac. For eight weeks, she'd been running, always on the defensive, to stay alive. Now they were about to go on the offensive, straight to the enemy. Was she prepared for the consequences?

★ ★ ★

"You okay back there, Mac?" Gabe asked. He checked the rearview mirror of Ben's rental, glancing to where she and Winston sat in the back. "You're looking a little stressed."

"She has to be worn out from yesterday's interrogation," Ben said from the front passenger seat. "I know I am."

"Are you sure this is the right way?" Mac asked. "You haven't lived in Denver in a while."

"Nice try," Gabe said. Mac was an expert at evasion, and he was determined to call her on it, every single time. He hadn't done that five years ago, but instead had allowed her to continue to build her wall. The wall that eventually destroyed their relationship.

Gabe met her gaze in the mirror once again. "That wasn't the answer to my question," he said. "But, yeah, I know where I'm going."

Ben snickered. "The guidance thinks you missed your turn, too."

Gabe gave his brother the side-eye. "Thanks for the support there, big brother."

Ben raised his hands in response. "Just saying. The guidance doesn't lie."

"I'm doing some diversionary tactics to ensure we aren't being tailed," Gabe said.

Ben turned to her and winked. "Translation. He's lost."

Mac laughed, her voice warming Gabe. He'd gladly volunteer to be the target of all their jokes if it meant hearing her relaxed laughter more often.

"Make a right up ahead," she said. "It's a one-way street. Then circle back to Santa Fe."

"Nothing much changes in Denver, does it?" Gabe observed. It seemed as if he'd never left the Mile High City.

"Sure it does," Mac said. "You've passed at least four new businesses. The Colorado Ballet relocated down here to the arts district a while back. That's newish."

"Were you raised in Denver, Mackenzie?" Ben asked.

"Mostly. My family moved overseas when I hit high school."

"That's right. Gabe told me your father was an ambassador."

Gabe shot his brother a warning look. This wasn't the time to bring up a subject that might trigger the memories associated with her parents' deaths.

"What?" Ben returned.

"Gabe," Mac said gently, "it's all right. I'm

almost thirty-four. I can talk about my parents without breaking down."

"Did I put my foot in my mouth again?" Ben asked, his gaze going from Gabe to Mac in the back seat.

"No. You're fine," Mac said. "When I was a freshman in high school, my father took the ambassador post."

"So no moving every three years like we did?" Ben continued.

"No," she said.

"We moved six times while we were growing up," Gabe interjected. "The only good part was Ben always had my back, and I had his."

"I always wished I had a brother or sister," Mac said. "Although, Megan and Lance Shipman are like siblings to me."

"It's got its advantages and disadvantages," Ben said. "We'll have to compare notes sometime. I know all Gabe's secrets."

"Cut it out, Ben," Gabe said. He was half-serious. Ben did know all his secrets, and a few could really cement the fact that he really was a nerd.

"There." Mac waved a hand into the front seat. "You just passed the field office."

"Yeah. I know. I was here on Friday. Remember?" Gabe said.

This time it was Ben who shot *him* a look. With the raising of his eyebrows and the quirking of his lips, Gabe recalled his comment about him and Mac acting like they were married.

He took a deep breath and resisted the urge to give his brother's shoulder a shove. "I'll go around the corner, and Ben and I can get out," Gabe said instead. He glanced around. "That bakery across the street from the entrance is a good location to watch for my IT tech buddy."

"Gabe, remind me what the target looks like," Ben said.

"Tall, lanky, Caucasian male. Dark, curly hair, glasses. Approximately twenty-five." Gabe shrugged. "No distinguishing marks."

"Got it." Ben glanced around. "I'll be at the bus stop."

"What about me?" Mac asked.

"What about you?" Gabe returned. "We're trying to keep you safe, so keep circling the block, but don't be obvious."

"Don't be obvious?" She practically snorted at his words. "I'm the one who's been in the field. Remember?"

"Sorry about that," Gabe said. The irony of

the situation didn't escape him. Here he was back in the field again. He hoped it was like riding a bike.

"Everyone on comms?" Ben asked as Gabe pulled the vehicle to the curb.

"Yes," Mac said. She connected her head-phones to the burner phone.

"Yeah." Gabe put the wireless earbuds into his ear and then dialed his brother's phone. "Okay, let's do this."

Ben was first to depart. He circled the rear of the sedan, glancing up and down the street. Gabe opened his door and stepped into the street. Around him, 7:00 a.m. traffic had begun to pick up, as the RTD, Denver's transit buses and light rail, moved early-morning commuters into the city from the burbs.

When Mac got out of the car, Gabe tapped the brim of her ball cap as she headed to the driver's seat to replace him. "Be careful," he murmured.

Her blue eyes met his, and a sweet smile curved her mouth. Gabe's heart stuttered.

"Me?" She shook her head. "I've been ordered to remain in the vehicle."

"You're also the one someone is trying to

kill." The one who should have stayed in Bluebell away from potential danger.

Winston barked as if he'd read Gabe's mind.

"I've got protection sitting in the back seat," Mac continued.

His gaze swept her features, memorizing the round eyes and full lips. He leaned near enough to smell the mint on her breath. Any other situation and he'd take a chance and close the distance between them.

But this wasn't the time or the place to consider the risks of letting Mac into his heart.

"Don't take any chances, okay? I'd like to see you again. In one piece."

She placed a hand on his arm and looked up at him, her eyes warm with something he didn't want to analyze. "Ditto, pal."

With a final look at the vehicle before he turned the corner, Gabe said a quick prayer. "Keep her safe, Lord."

Long strides took him down the street to the popular bakery and coffee shop, where Gabe ordered a plain joe and a scone to fit in with the urban crowd moving in and out of the place. He sat at a table next to the window, pretending to check his phone with rabid devotion, like every other patron. His position provided a perfect view of the field office.

The building was nondescript brick with no signage to identify the tenants. It might appear empty to the undiscerning eye, but it held the offices of the domestic division, at least as of his visit Friday. There were no windows on the first few floors, and when the front doors pushed open, two security guards were visible in the building's entry, monitoring everything that went in and out of the building.

"I've got eyes on the building from the bakery," Gabe said.

"Ten-four. I'm at the bus stop to your left," Ben said.

"Mac, you all right?" Gabe asked when Mac failed to respond.

"Yes. Yes. Winston needed a break."

Behind Gabe, loud laughter broke through the buzz of chatter as a group of women entered the bakery. Behind the women, two young men slipped into the shop.

"I've got him. Target just entered the bakery," Gabe said.

There was no doubt at all that the kid who walked in was the IT staffer who'd given him the security card a few days ago. Gabe stepped in the tech's path and crossed his arms over his chest, doing his best to appear menacing.

"Hey, how's it going?" Gabe asked.

"I…uh…" The kid's Adam's apple bobbed, and his eyes darted around. He was clearly desperate to escape.

"That good, huh?"

The guy who came in with the tech puffed out his own chest and frowned. "Ribinoff, you know this guy?"

"Sure he knows me. I met Ribinoff on Friday," Gabe said. "You gave me my badge and security card. Right?"

The other guy narrowed his gaze. He looked from Ribinoff to Gabe. "Have we met?"

"We are right now. Gabe Denton. I'm here from DC to handle a special project for Senior Officer Todd Shipman." He frowned. "You know Shipman, right?"

Both men paled at the mention of Todd Shipman.

"I'm in serious trouble," Ribinoff mumbled. He shoved a table toward Gabe, startling the patrons as he bumped into people in line and sped out the doors, knocking over a trash receptacle as he made a hard left.

Gabe followed, pushing open the glass doors

and racing onto the sidewalk. "He's on the move. Heading north."

"Eyes on him," Ben said.

"Kid's name is Ribinoff."

The tech then crossed the street with a quick dash through traffic, over and around cars. Horns blared as he dodged a city dump truck.

"He's fast," Gabe said.

"You got this, old man," Ben said in his ear.

Gabe trailed him, then he stopped and looked to his rear. Someone was following him. He was sure of it.

"He's yours, Ben. I've got a tail."

"Be careful," his brother said.

"I'm coming up the street from the other direction," Mac said.

"No. Mac," Gabe said, unable to hold back his irritation and concern. "You're supposed to stay in the car."

"I'm a CIA operations officer. I don't stay put in cars," she said. "I'll be at your back door in five minutes."

Gabe ducked into an alley and picked up speed until he passed a dumpster. Then he stayed out of view, crouching against the wall behind the metal container. The hard, rough edges of the brick poked at his back through his shirt as he waited.

Moments later, he heard heavy breathing.

Whoever had followed him was definitely a civilian with the stealth skills of a large animal. From the sound of his footfalls, he was at least two hundred and fifty pounds, and panting to keep up as well.

When the guy passed the dumpster, Gabe jumped out and pinned him against the wall.

Yeah, he was a big guy, all right. Big and out of shape, a white male, in his late thirties, with short blond hair, wearing a T-shirt and jeans.

He swung a massive fist toward Gabe.

And missed.

Gabe landed a blow to the guy's gut.

He crumpled, but quickly rebounded to elbow Gabe hard and pin him to the wall next to the dumpster, knocking the Bluetooth from his ears.

"Who are you?" Gabe asked while the guy pushed him into the unyielding brick.

"I'm the guy who's going to kill you unless you tell me where Mackenzie Sharp is."

"Why do you want Sharp?"

"Because she has our money."

"What?" Gabe jerked back, working to push

the weight off him. "Whose money?" His thoughts flashed to the attempted carjacking in Albuquerque. He fought to keep his thoughts objective, to stay focused, though he couldn't deny all the indicators pointing at Mac.

The guy tightened his hold on Gabe and his face reddened with anger. "Ask Sharp. She has the money."

"What about Morrow?" Gabe asked. "Is Morrow alive?"

"She died on that pier in Toronto, and I'm thinking Sharp killed her. Last thing Liz said to me before she went to Toronto was that Sharp double-crossed her and had the money. *Our money.*"

For a moment, Gabe froze. Mac and Morrow working together? He didn't believe it. Couldn't let himself believe it.

A surge of anger at the implication was all it took for Gabe to slip from the guy's grasp and grab his arm, twisting it behind him. "That's why you're trying to kill Sharp?"

"What are you talking about?" he panted. "We don't want her dead…yet. We just want our money."

"We? Who's we?"

The guy gave a vigorous shake of his head. "I told you way more than I should."

Gabe pulled the guy's arm higher.

"Oww," he yelled. "Okay. Okay. Ease up. 'We' is me and Ribinoff."

"So that was you in Phoenix and Tucson," Gabe returned. It seemed the more information he got, the more confused the situation became. "I thought you said you didn't want Sharp dead."

"Nope, not me. I didn't start following you until Tucson. That van thing, in the rest stop? I saw it, but it wasn't me. I can claim responsibility for trying to jack your Crown Vic in Albuquerque. Just looking for what's mine, dude."

The Bluetooth on the ground vibrated, causing Gabe to turn his head and loosen his hold briefly.

"Get. Off. Me," the guy screamed. He pushed himself off the wall and threw his full weight against Gabe.

As the two flew across the alley, his elbow struck Gabe's face, knocking off his glasses.

"That was unnecessary," Gabe muttered to the blurry and retreating form racing down the alley, kicking up loose bits of gravel on the way.

Before the guy reached the end of the alley,

the muffled sound of a gunshot filled the morning air.

"What?" Gabe's pulse pounded out of control, as he rolled out of the middle of the alley and pressed himself flat against the wall. He made a frantic search of the windows and the roof. No sign of the shooter.

Minutes passed.

"You shot him?"

Gabe looked up to see Ben standing over him. "He was hit?"

"Yeah."

"No, I didn't shoot him." Gabe grabbed his glasses and the Bluetooth earpiece from the gravel before doing another visual sweep of the area.

"Somebody did," Ben said as Gabe struggled to his feet.

"You get Ribinoff?" Gabe asked.

"That kid is part monkey. Scrambled over a wall and took off." Ben shook his head as the two raced down the alley to the body.

Gabe crouched down and checked for a pulse on the big guy, who was facedown on the ground in a puddle of blood. He shook his head. "Whoever hit him was a professional. A single shot." His eyes searched the buildings that formed the alley. Plenty of windows. Plenty of opportunity.

"Yeah," Ben agreed. He slipped two fingers into the man's back pocket and pulled out a wallet. "Meet Wade Masterson."

"Masterson. Doesn't ring a bell."

"I'll check his background," Ben said.

"Thanks."

"You want to tell me what happened when you went off comms?" Ben asked.

"He took a swing at me."

"No, Gabe," Ben said. "I know you, and something else happened."

Gabe looked at his brother. It wasn't that he didn't trust him, but repeating what Masterson said out loud would make it real and he was still stunned by the information. He hoped he could make it disappear.

"Gabe?"

"Masterson talked before he was shot. He said that Morrow was connected to the stolen money."

"Morrow?" Ben's eyes popped at the info. He nodded slowly. "Okay. That makes everything fall into place. She's the inside person."

"There's more." Gabe hesitated, dreading what he was about to say. "He indicated that

Mac was involved as well and that she's responsible for Morrow's death." He shook his head and released a breath. It was almost a relief to be able to share the information with someone else.

"Your agency says Morrow is alive." Ben shook his head. "What about Mackenzie being involved? Do you believe him?"

"Come on. You know I'm in an impossible situation here." An understatement at best. He had an obligation to follow up on the intel, no matter what he believed. Ben knew that as well as he did.

"What do you want me to do?" Ben asked.

"I'm going to need you to dig a little deeper into both Mac and her partner's activities for the last eight weeks. Probably longer."

"You got it." Ben paused. "You didn't answer me. Do you believe him? I mean, about Mackenzie?"

"I don't know what to believe, and it's tearing me up."

"What happened?" Mac asked as she approached them from the other end of the alley with Winston.

Both Ben and Gabe turned at the sound of her voice.

"You were supposed to stay in the car," Gabe

barked. "There's a shooter out there." Again, his gaze spanned the buildings looming over them. Masterson had been shot. Mac would be an easy target. "At least stay against the wall."

Mac raised a hand. "Easy, Gabe." Then she pressed her back against the brick and offered him a tissue from her messenger bag. "Ah, your nose is bleeding."

Gabe nodded his begrudging thanks and wiped the blood from his face.

"Mackenzie, do you recognize this guy?" Ben asked. He examined Wade Masterson's left arm. "No tattoo."

"No. Are we going to leave him?" she asked.

"That's the plan," Gabe said. "There's nothing we can do here."

"I'll call 911 with one of the burner phones," Mac said.

"Okay, but we need to get out of here. Now. And stay on comms," Gabe returned.

"Where's the car?" Ben asked as they headed out the other end of the alley.

"Two blocks down. Some guy pulled out, and I snapped up the spot."

"I'll keep my eye on Mackenzie," Ben said. Head down, he crossed the street.

Gabe kept to the right of the sidewalk, with

Mac and Winston a distance behind. He began to process Wade Masterson's words. *Sharp has the money.*

Each footfall on the cement beat the words into his brain.

Sharp has the money.

Sharp has the money.

The compelling words of the dead man continued to shake Gabe's confidence in Mac's innocence, and he hated himself for his thoughts.

"I don't see the car," Ben said.

Gabe's head jerked up, startling him from his reverie.

"It's right…" Mac gasped, the sound echoing in his ear. "The car is gone."

As they approached the open parking spot along the curb, she let out a breath and stared down where glass littered the ground. Then she turned and walked over to the storefront window behind them and feigned interest in the display.

"It's a rental," Ben said. "It's insured, and there wasn't anything of value inside." He walked to the corner and pressed the pedestrian button at the crosswalk.

"I can't believe it," Gabe said.

"Let's face it," Mac said. "Since Toronto, everything I touch turns into a dumpster fire."

Ben cleared his throat. "I'll call the rental agency to get another vehicle, then file a police report. This is going to take a while."

"We'll find a way back to the house," Gabe said.

"Are you sure?"

"Yeah."

"Stay safe," Ben said. His gaze connected with Gabe's for a long moment in an unspoken message that said, *Watch your back.*

Gabe nodded, though his brother was already gone.

"We just need to get back to Bluebell without anyone following us," Mac said.

"Any suggestions?" Gabe asked.

"I've got a ride-share app on my personal phone," she said.

"That's forty miles. You have cash, but do you have a disposable credit card?"

"Yes," Mac said. "Plenty of cash and cards."

An ominous dread filled him at her words. Gabe turned on the sidewalk and stared at Mac as she stood beneath the awning of a local business with Winston at her side. She patted her messenger bag and smiled.

At the gesture, his stomach turned. He debated telling her what Masterson said in the alley and decided to wait. Wait and see. For what, he didn't know. Mac's vindication, perhaps?

"Gabe?"

"I hear you. Let's go. We have a lot to process."

That much was true. Maybe the only truth.

Gabe worked to comprehend the possibility that everything he'd thought was the truth when he landed in Denver on Friday and met with Shipman could be a lie.

Logic reminded him that, at minimum, Mac deserved his trust until she was proven guilty. The problem was the clues were starting to be stacked against her. The offshore account and now a dead man's confession.

The only thing certain was that Gabe didn't have a clue what he was going to do next.

Chapter Eight

"Have you heard from Ben?" Mac asked. She filled a glass with water from the tap, pausing to glance outside, where dusk had settled, before she eased into a chair at the kitchen table. "I thought he was coming back here after he took care of the rental car. It's almost dark. Should we be concerned?"

Gabe's back was to her as he waited on the coffee machine. "Ben can handle himself. Right now, he's reaching out to his contacts, and running checks on the Ribinoff kid and Masterson." He stared out the kitchen window without turning toward her.

Mac nodded. "Who do you think shot Wade Masterson?" The question had plagued her all afternoon, though she hadn't said anything.

"Someone who didn't want him talking to me," Gabe said.

She frowned. Had she imagined the edge to

his voice? Maybe he was concerned about Ben, but was trying to hide it.

For a few minutes she was quiet, as she turned over the events of the morning in her head.

"I don't get it," she finally said. "We keep adding more players, but we don't seem to be able to figure out what's going on or where Liz is. Nothing makes sense."

"No. It doesn't." The words were flat and without emotion.

Mac rubbed her arms against the chill in the room.

Something had shifted since the incident in Denver this morning, and she didn't know what. Gabe's easy banter and amusing comments were all but gone. Several times, she felt his gaze on her. She'd look up to find that he was watching her.

Weighing. Measuring. Why?

"We're on the outside looking in without the Agency resources," Mac said. "If we could connect with Shipman without the inside person finding out, we might be able to stop this cat-and-mouse game."

Once again, Gabe was silent.

Winston padded into the room, the soft jingling of his collar and tags alerting her to his presence. He put his big head on her lap and looked up at her with his soulful eyes, begging for attention. Mac complied and rubbed his velvety ears. At least the bulldog still liked her.

Frustrated, Mac cleared her throat. "What's going on, Gabe?" she asked. The words slipped from her lips before she had a chance to consider the wisdom of the question.

Gabe turned from the counter. His hazel eyes searched her face, though he didn't respond.

But Winston did.

The bulldog barked and moved to the kitchen door. Snout pressed against the glass, he released a low, ominous growl.

Gabe dropped to the floor. "Get down, Mac! That dog can sense danger. We need to pay attention."

"Come here, boy," she commanded. Winston was at her side in a heartbeat.

As she, too, moved to the floor, the sound of glass shattering had both Mac and Gabe jumping.

Mac held Winston by the collar as she turned to see razor-sharp shards of glass hanging from the kitchen window over the sink.

"Our shooter is back and he's closer than those woods," Gabe said. "I'm guessing he was waiting for nightfall. We have to get out of here. Now. Before he gets any closer."

"Can we make it to the minivan?" Mac asked.

"We better try." He tossed her the keys. "I'll distract him. Head out the front door and don't stop."

She nodded and reached for Winston's leash from where it dangled on a kitchen chair. "Okay, but I'm not going anywhere without you." Mac scooted on her bottom to the living room, where she grabbed her messenger bag. Using the couch arm as leverage, she stood. There was no way she could crawl out the front door. Her leg simply would not bend that far yet.

Gabe stood as well and inched along the wall to one of the bedrooms. A moment later, she heard a window opening, and a gun blast followed by return fire.

Yet another shot rang out as Mac exited the house with Winston at her side. In the gravel drive, the pitiful minivan, with its blown-out rear window, now had four slashed tires.

Mac pulled out her Glock and moved quickly behind the branches of a wide blue spruce with Winston. With only the rising moon to illuminate the area, she waited for Gabe.

One. Two more shots sounded. Then, in the

distance, the wailing of police sirens could be heard, coming closer.

"Come on, Gabe. Come on," she murmured. Her heart banged in her chest, the sound getting louder and louder, along with her anxiety. "Oh, Lord, please, keep him safe."

A moment later, the door opened, and Mac released a small gasp at the sight of Gabe racing across the drive to her, kicking up gravel as he moved.

"What's happening?" she asked.

He caught his breath and glanced around. "Gunshot sounds carry pretty far. One of the neighbors must have called the police."

"Where's the shooter?"

"I don't know. My guess is that whoever is out there heard the sirens and is retreating. Hopefully, they're going to be on the other side of the woods. But there's no way to be certain."

"What do you want to do?" she asked.

Gabe turned to look at the house, thinking. "I tried to reach Ben, but he didn't pick up. We'll hitch a ride to a public place and then call him again."

"Okay," Mac said.

"There's a trail behind us," Gabe said. "Let's go. Fast."

"I don't do fast," she said.

Gabe frowned. "You do now. Get on my back."

"You must be joking." She stared at him in the fading light.

"Get on my back."

"What about my cane?"

"Leave it. We can get another."

Mac glanced at the woods to the east of the house and then at Gabe, anxiety rising. "You can't carry me through there."

"This isn't a discussion. Get on." Gabe stooped down and Mac positioned herself on his back, holding tight to his shoulders.

"Winston. Come," Mac commanded. The bulldog followed them into the darkness, where the trees enveloped them.

Mac tucked her head into his shirt, narrowly avoiding a branch. "How can you see?"

"I've hiked the trail a few times and walked Winston through here."

"Not with a body on your back."

"You're a lightweight." He said the words without pause.

"If you say so," Mac murmured. She raised her face, only to have her cheek slapped by the brush and her ball cap plucked from her head.

Mac released a small sound of surprise as the cap disappeared.

"What?" Gabe asked, not breaking stride.

"Nothing. Nothing." Caps were replaceable. She tucked her head down again and tightened her grip on his shoulders as he passed through a narrow path.

Minutes later, Mac heard the rhythmic whooshing and thumping of cars driving on the highway.

"I hear vehicles," she said.

"Yeah. It won't be busy this time of night. That will help. The problem is going to be flagging someone down in the dark."

"There's a flashlight in my bag," Mac said.

"Ah, the messenger bag," Gabe mumbled.

Mac noted his odd comment but said nothing.

Gabe stopped at the edge of the wooded area and crouched down to let her off his back. Then he pointed to the grassy incline that led to the road below. "We need to slide down there to the highway." He looked at her. "Think you can do that?"

"Yes." She'd do whatever it took at this point.

"Okay, I'll take Winston and go first." He half walked, half ran down the incline, and then called Winston, while gently clapping his hands. "Come on, boy. Come on."

The dog whined and looked at Mac.

"You can do it, Winston," she said, giving him a small nudge.

Winston barked and raced into Gabe's arms like a kid on a slide.

"Your turn, Mac," he called.

Mac assessed the angle of the incline before she sat on the ground and inched her way down, managing to get caught on shrubbery twice along the way. If she kept her injured leg raised, it wasn't painful, merely embarrassing.

At the bottom of the incline, Gabe held out a hand and pulled her up. She bumped into his chest and froze before awkwardly stepping away to brush dirt from her backside and legs.

"Flashlight?" he said.

Mac unzipped the messenger bag and rummaged inside. "Here you go." She handed Gabe the flashlight.

"You and Winston wait there behind the guardrail. I'll flag someone down."

Traffic was slow on a Monday evening, as he'd predicted. A few cars zipped past, and an occasional truck. When a large produce truck rumbled around the corner, Gabe stepped into the road and waved the flashlight.

The pneumatic hissing of the truck's brakes competed with the vehicle's horn as the driver pulled to the shoulder of the road. The driver leaned over to the passenger side, and the window opened. "You okay, pal?" he called out.

"My wife and I have a disabled vehicle on the other side of the woods. Can you give us a lift down the road?"

"Sure."

When the driver leaned over to push open the passenger door, the light from inside the cab illuminated his smiling, weathered face. "I'm Harley."

A friendly face. The man's demeanor alone was enough to slow Mac's breathing.

"Gabe and Mackenzie," Gabe said.

Gabe helped Mac over the guardrail, and she held his arm in a death grip, determined not to trip and fall in the darkness.

Harley frowned and looked at Winston trailing behind. "He bite?"

"Not unless I tell him to," Mac said.

That elicited a hearty laugh from the trucker. "Fair enough."

"Mac," Gabe said quietly next to her ear.

"I'm going to boost you into the cab and then Winston."

"I can do this." And she would. She'd had enough awkwardness for one day, riding on Gabe's back. Holding on to the frame of the door, Mac used her right leg to step up and raised her left leg slowly into the cab. "Got it."

"You hurt that leg, little lady?" Harley asked.

"It's an old injury. No big deal."

"Here comes Winston," Gabe said. He hoisted the bulldog by his posterior until he was on Mac's lap.

"Come on up here, puppy," Mac murmured while Gabe jumped into the truck next to her. When his leg touched hers, Mac inched away. Nearly shot and killed, and then embarrassed to death. That's how she'd remember today.

"Where you headed?" Harley asked. He glanced into his mirrors and signaled.

"Depends," Gabe said. "Where's the nearest truck stop?"

"Oh, there's a place about twenty miles from here."

"Perfect, could you drop us off?" Gabe returned.

"Surely."

Winston raised his head and glared at Harley, his upturned jaw and drooping eyes almost comical. Then he shifted to grace Mac with a generous and slobbery kiss.

"Maybe you'd be more comfortable with your dog in the back seat," the trucker said.

Mac glanced at the extended cab's second row of seats. Yes, that was an excellent idea in theory, but her leg wouldn't be happy, and Winston wouldn't be persuaded without her.

"He won't leave me," she said.

"That might get uncomfortable," Harley said.

"Tell me about it." She sighed and wiped her cheek as Winston settled on her lap, his wrinkled face nestled in the crook of her arm.

Gabe looked at her and frowned. "I can hold Winston."

"It's okay. We've done this before."

From around the bend in the road, two police cars appeared, racing in the opposite direction, their sirens loud and insistent. Harley glanced in his side mirror. "Wonder what that's all about?"

"No clue." Gabe tensed, as did Mac. His expression said they were thinking the same thing. They needed to fly under the radar until Ben could pick them up.

"How far did you say that diner is?" Mac asked.

"We're about twenty minutes from Francine's

Truck Stop," Harley said with an enthusiastic grin. "Best peach pie on the Front Range."

"Sounds wonderful," Mac said.

Gabe turned to the driver. "We sure appreciate this."

"No problem. I'm heading home, and Francine's is on the way." He leaned forward and looked at Gabe. "You all live around here?"

"We got in from Phoenix on Friday for the renaissance festival," Gabe said. "We spent the night at a friend's rental, and our minivan decided to breathe its last when we went to leave."

Mac was reminded of Agency training as Gabe replied. Keep the story as close to the truth as possible. It's easier to remember the truth than a lie.

"That's a shame. Mighty dangerous to be walking this road in the dark." Harley turned on the radio, and the soft crooning of a country-western song wrapped itself around them.

Winston let out a soulful sound in response, and Harley burst out laughing. "I see your dog likes country music."

"Apparently so," Mac said with a chuckle. She held the animal close and stared out the window as the night flowed past them.

The neon lights of Francine's Truck Stop

came into view fifteen minutes later, just as Harley promised.

"There it is. Now you tell Fran that Harley sent you, and she'll give you a discount." He signaled and pulled into the wide drive of the truck stop.

"Thanks, Harley. You really saved the day," Mac said.

"Aw." Harley grinned. "Happy to help. Now you two be safe."

"We will," Gabe said. He opened the door of the truck and jumped down. "Come, Winston."

The bulldog eagerly jumped into Gabe's arms.

Gabe turned to Mac. "Need help?"

"I've got it," she said.

"Mac," he murmured with a smile for Harley. "A fella is supposed to assist his wife."

"Oh!" She took Gabe's hand. "Of course."

Once she stepped to the ground, Gabe put an arm around her shoulder, and together they waved at Harley as the friendly trucker pulled away. Just like they were a real couple. A normal couple.

While a part of her savored Gabe's touch, Mac nearly laughed aloud at the thought of her ever fitting into the mold of normal. She released a sigh of regret. Gabe deserved so much more than she and her emotional baggage could offer him.

When the vehicle was out of sight, Mac gave Gabe an awkward smile. "Sorry about that. I nearly messed things up."

"No problem." He pulled the burner phone from his back pocket. "Why don't you go in and grab yourself a coffee? I'll wait out here with Winston and try Ben again."

"Gabe, your arm," Mac said.

"What?"

"It's bleeding."

Gabe glanced down at his right arm. "Superficial. I ran into a branch in the woods."

She handed him her messenger bag. "I put a small first-aid kit in there."

"Mac, I'm fine."

"Take it." She shoved the bag at him and headed into the restaurant with slow steps.

Mac scanned the room, silently taking in every single face. The couple seated at the window, laughing. The gray-haired guy in the corner with his back to her. She pulled the minivan keys from her pocket and purposely dropped them to the ground so she could get a look at him. The guy in the corner eyed her curiously before returning to his book. Nothing concerning about him.

"How can I help you, sweetie?" the woman at the counter asked.

"Two black coffees, a water and..." She glanced at the glass pastry case. The assortment of baked goods reminded her that she hadn't eaten. But her stomach was so knotted up, she didn't think she could eat anything right now. "And two muffins."

"What kind? We have blueberry, oat, banana and cinnamon-raisin."

"Banana, please." She remembered that Gabe once brought her banana bread he'd made. How odd that she should recall that right now. It had been an autumn day, and they hadn't seen each other in weeks while on separate assignments. She was only going to be home for the weekend. Saturday morning, he brought her the newspaper and banana bread. They'd walked over to Cheesman Park, read the paper and talked.

A smile lit her face at the memory.

"Is your husband okay out there?"

"What?" Mac blinked.

The woman nodded toward the door, where Gabe and Winston sat outside on a bench.

Her husband. "Oh, yes. He's fine. Our van broke down, and a trucker gave us a lift. He doesn't want to leave the dog alone."

"I don't blame him. Animals are like our children, aren't they?" She kept talking as she filled the cups with coffee from a carafe. "You two have any kids?"

"Kids?" Mac shook her head. "No. No, we don't."

The woman put lids on the cups and placed them in a carrier. She slid a white pastry bag across the counter. "Here you go."

"What do I owe you?"

"On the house. You look like you've had a tough night." She offered a gentle smile. "I remember what it was like to be young and just starting out. If it's not the car, it's the washing machine breaking down." She chuckled. "But trust me. If you can make it through the hard times, the good times will be all the

sweeter."

Mac mused on her words as she pushed open the door. What would it be like to have a normal life and be married to someone like Gabe? A solid rock. Dependable. A man who loved the Lord.

She couldn't imagine a regular life and was afraid even to consider it. That was for other people, not her. Besides, guys like Gabe would want a family. She hadn't allowed herself to go down that road. It was far too terrifying.

Winston was her family.

Before the door had closed behind her, Gabe was at her side, taking the coffee tray. "Let me help you."

"Um, thanks." She met his gaze. Okay, what had changed since his almost hostile comments at the house?

"Everything look good in there?" he asked.

"Yes. Nothing out of the ordinary." She glanced around at the parking area.

Gabe placed the coffee carrier on the bench. "Quiet out here, too."

"But he's out there, isn't he?" Mac stared into the darkness. There was a shooter who wouldn't stop until she was dead. How long until he hit his target?

"Think positive. We're alive."

"What about the house?" Mac asked. "What's Addy going to say when she finds out it was shot up?"

"Avery," he said. "It's Avery. And I'm sure insurance will cover it." Gabe looked at the white sack. "What's in the bag?" She handed it to him.

"Your reward for carrying me through the woods."

He peeked inside, and his eyebrows lifted. "Nice. I should do chivalrous things more often."

Mac smiled slightly at his enthusiasm, though she remained confused at his change in attitude.

Gabe nodded toward the bench. "Have a seat. Ben didn't pick up. I left him a message, but he hasn't returned my call yet."

"I'd rather stand."

"Are you hurting?" He leveled her with a gaze that held so much concern that she had to tell him the truth.

"Yes."

"I'm sorry."

"As you said. We're alive." She took a coffee from the carrier and removed the lid. The strong aroma of beans perked her up. "I still can't believe you carried me down that trail."

"You probably weigh less than Winston."

At the sound of his name, the bulldog perked up, looking back and forth between her and Gabe.

Gabe bit into a muffin. "Whoa, this is good. Want the other one?"

"No, thank you. Interestingly enough, while facing death gives you an appetite, it does the opposite for me." She looked around for her messenger bag and grabbed it off the end of the bench.

Digging inside the bag, Mac found Winston's small collapsible bowl. She opened a plastic zip bag and poured kibble into the bowl. The dog wasted no time chowing down.

"Is there anything you don't have in that bag?" Gabe asked, his gaze watchful and cautious again.

Mac looked out into the night once more. She took a long breath and released it. "Answers. I don't have answers."

"Ben." Gabe stood and paced in front of the bench as he held the phone to his ear. "Finally. Where are you? I was getting concerned."

"Right outside of Bluebell. Sorry it's taken me so long to get back to you. Between the car-rental issue and returning calls to my sources, the day is shot."

"As long as you're okay."

"I'm fine, and I've got intelligence regarding some of those leads."

Gabe moved out of Mac's earshot. "Great.

And, um, what about that other thing I asked you to look into? Anything?"

"I've got contacts in the intelligence community with top-secret access checking on Mackenzie, but so far, everything has come back clean."

Relief caught him right between the eyes. Gabe sent up a silent prayer of thanks. He was ashamed of doubting her. Yet, his training told him that thoroughly investigating every single person attached to the mission in Toronto was procedure.

"Thanks, Ben," he said.

"Don't thank me. All that means is I haven't found evidence that she is involved. I haven't proven she's innocent."

"I get it."

"Good. Because you've still got to figure out how you're going to explain withholding information to Mackenzie. She won't be pleased, and I don't want to be around when a woman with a Glock is annoyed."

"I'll handle Mac." He paused, glancing around to be sure he hadn't been overheard. "What about Morrow?"

"I haven't found anything the Agency wouldn't

have uncovered. No activity on credit cards in eight weeks. I'll keep digging."

"Thanks."

"I'll be at Avery's in about ten minutes," Ben continued.

"We aren't at the house. We're at Francine's Truck Stop. It's on I-25, just north of Bluebell."

"Why?"

"Our shooter friend stopped by."

"Then it's good that I found a safe house." Ben paused. "I take it you and Mackenzie are okay, or you would have led with that info."

"Yeah. More or less." If *okay* meant he'd held off a shooter, all the while paranoid that the woman he was protecting could be the enemy. Then he was okay.

"Stay that way," Ben said. "I'll see you in about twenty minutes."

"Thanks, Ben." He disconnected, walked back to the bench and sank into it, emotionally exhausted.

Mac looked up at him. "Is he okay?"

"Yeah. He's been following leads on Masterson and Ribinoff. He'll be here in about twenty minutes."

"Thanks." She nodded over her shoulder. "There's a small convenience store on the other side of the diner. I'm going to go check out their amenities. We left everything but my messenger bag at your fiancée's house and I could at least use a clean T-shirt."

She's not my fiancée, Gabe mentally shot back.

"Take Winston with you, would you?" he said instead. "Flash your badge if anyone has dog issues."

"Okay." When Mac's gaze met his, Gabe grimaced. They'd been on the road since Friday, and he hadn't done anything to ease the bone weariness or pain he saw on her face. Guilt ate at him. Guilt for having doubted her loyalty even for a second and for not finding out who'd put her in this position.

"It'll get better, Mac," he said.

"Will it? It seems all we're doing is running, and we're only barely a step ahead of whoever is trying to kill me. We're trained government agents. We should be ahead of this situation."

"Tomorrow will be better. Ben said he has information."

"I hope you're right," Mac said. "Because so far, every day has only provided more obstacles and more questions."

Gabe sat down on the bench to finish his coffee as she headed to the convenience store. Yeah, he hoped he was right, too.

A few minutes after Mac and Winston returned, a dark sedan pulled into the parking lot and flashed its headlights at them.

"That's him," Gabe said.

Mac stood slowly and slipped the messenger bag over her head.

"Need any help?"

She gave a weary shake of her head. "I'm fine."

He ignored her refusal and grabbed her plastic shopping bag, then opened the back door of the sedan.

"Thanks for coming, Ben," Mac said as she slipped into the vehicle. "Come, Winston." The dog crawled over her and settled on the seat by her side.

"All three of you look exhausted," Ben said. "Sorry things went south. I got here as fast as I could."

"We're alive," Gabe said. "Everything else is gravy."

"So this is gravy?" Mac murmured to herself.

"What's the status of the house?" Ben asked.

"A few windows damaged, and a couple of bullet holes," Gabe said. "But relatively intact."

"I'm sure Avery will be glad to hear that."

"Don't remind me. I'll need to take care of that eventually."

"I'll want to go back and retrieve my duffle and suitcase when it's daylight," Ben said. "But for now, I've found a cabin."

"A real cabin or another *Architectural Digest* layout?" Mac asked.

Ben laughed. "A real log cabin. In fact, the place is vintage seventies era."

The drive was silent, the rhythmic sounds of the road nearly lulling Gabe to sleep, until Ben tapped his arm and pointed to the back seat. When Gabe looked over his shoulder, both Mac and Winston were asleep. The dog was snoring lightly.

"It's been a long, four-day weekend," Gabe said quietly.

A few minutes later, Ben pulled into a gravel drive leading to a simple A-frame log cabin. "This is it. There's a man-made lake behind the house, lots of shade trees around the lake and about a mile of pastureland. No one is going to sneak up on us."

"How did you get this place?" Gabe asked.

"I called a vacation-rental company. They weren't going to let me have it without checking references. But the owner has a soft spot for newlyweds. I'm officially on my honeymoon."

"That works."

"Are we home?" Mac yawned and got out of the car.

Gabe's gaze followed hers as she peered at the A-frame log home. The front featured a wraparound porch illuminated by two hanging bronze lanterns. Clay pots filled with red geraniums flanked the front door.

"Now this is a cabin," she finally said.

"Yeah," Gabe said. "I wouldn't mind retiring to a place like this. A little fishing and no people."

"You'd never survive without people," Mac said.

"She's not wrong," Ben added.

He shrugged. If being social was a flaw, he could live with it. Far better to take chances than to live a life in fear of getting close to people. If he could only convince Mac of that.

"Being social has its advantages when it comes to information gathering," Gabe finally said. "And speaking of being social. How many bedrooms?"

"Three. Two on the first floor and the entire second floor is a bedroom and office."

"Score," Gabe said to his brother.

"I called earlier and asked them to stock the place with basics so we won't have to drive into Bluebell," Ben said.

As they stepped toward the door, Gabe turned to Mac, but she held up a hand. "I know. I know. Wait here, while you and Ben do a sweep of the cabin. I'm too tired and sore to argue."

"Sorry," he returned. "I know it's been a tough day."

"For all of us," she said.

"Nice place, right?" Ben asked him as they moved through the cabin.

"Yeah. It is," Gabe said. "Functional. Not fancy. Like me."

"All clear," Ben called to Mac. He turned to Gabe. "I'm going to get some stuff from the rental car."

Winston followed Mac inside, sniffing the room with interest.

"What do you think?" Gabe asked her.

Mac stood in the center of the living area and glanced around. "Nice." She moved past the island separating the living area and the kitchen to a scarred oak table and eased into a chair.

"You okay?" he asked.

"Uh-huh." She rolled up her left pant leg,

revealing the pink scar that ran down her calf. "Sometimes the leg needs a good massage."

Gabe stared at the evidence of her trauma in Toronto. Shame swept over him as the depth of her injury became real. Once again, he chastised himself for giving credence to the idea that she was involved in the bank job. If not by virtue of her moral character, surely the injury she'd suffered and continued to endure was evidence that she was innocent. In reality, he knew they'd need much more than her injury to clear her name.

"Ouch," Gabe murmured.

"My scar?" She shot him a weak smile as she rubbed the muscle. "It's so much better than it was."

"Are you in pain?"

"Yes, but it's the mosquito bites that have gotten the best of me." She glanced at the wrought-iron rooster clock on the wall. "Would you mind if I took a quick shower before we talk with Ben? I want to clean up and get some cortisone cream on the bites. The itching is overwhelming."

"You don't need to ask." He glanced around the compact kitchen and spotted a drip coffee maker. "Take your time. I'll make some coffee."

A few minutes later, Ben came into the kitchen with a paper shopping bag in his hand. "I'm going to do a quick check of the perimeter and set up cameras on the driveway and back door."

"You bought cameras?"

"I picked them up for Avery's place while I was in Denver. A little late, but they'll come in handy here."

"Good thinking."

Gabe opened the cupboards and found coffee and filters. He had the electric coffee maker gurgling within minutes. When the carafe had spit out the last drops of brew, he poured himself a cup and pulled out a chair.

"That smells good," Ben said from behind him.

"You're fast," Gabe replied. He sat down and took a cautious sip of the hot beverage. "Cameras set up?"

Ben nodded. "Yeah. The app is downloading to my phone." He glanced around. "Where's Mackenzie?"

Gabe looked past the living room to the hallway. "Taking a shower. You want to tell me what you found out about the money?"

"I had a friend check the paperwork on the

account that was opened in her name eight weeks ago. Someone obtained a copy of her driver's license and other documentation to open it. I can't get information on the offshore account that wired the money into this new one."

"What about her other financial assets?"

"Everything is legit. She has a hefty inheritance and hasn't touched any of it in years. In fact—"

"Why didn't you just ask me about my finances? Why go behind my back? I have nothing to hide," Mac said.

Gabe's head jerked back when he realized Mac was standing in the entrance to the kitchen. She wore a clean T-shirt and sweatpants with the Francine's Truck Stop logo on them. Her damp blond hair had been combed back, and a red flush of anger brightened her face. She turned to Ben with steady, almost dangerous eyes.

"Would you take Winston for a walk, please? Gabe and I need to talk."

"Yeah, sure." Ben backed out of the room with a pitying glance at Gabe.

When the front door closed, Mac pinned him with her gaze as she leaned against the wall.

"After the death of my parents, I was the sole beneficiary of a substantial life-insurance policy and their modest estate. The government provided a generous settlement amount as well. Todd Shipman oversaw the funds until I turned twenty-one."

She sat down in a chair and folded her hands. Gabe swallowed, but it failed to help his dry mouth. He had never seen this scary calm behavior in Mac, and it rattled him.

"When I joined the Agency, twelve years ago, I withdrew a healthy amount of my inheritance and placed a portion of it in a floor safe in my condo. The rest of that withdrawal is in a safe-deposit box with my passport, in case I ever need untraceable funds. I emptied the safe before I left Denver for Phoenix." She looked at him. "The remainder of that withdrawal remains in my safe-deposit box. You never know when you'll need to disappear. Right?"

The insinuation was clear. He'd better come up with a good response or, as she promised on Friday, Mackenzie Sharp would be in the wind.

"Ben ran your financials at my request. Everything came back clear. If you were in my position, wouldn't you have done the same?"

"I'm not sure I understand the question." She tilted her head and looked at him. "At what point did you decide you couldn't trust me?"

Touché. She was right, and he'd feel the same way. Gabe took a deep breath, knowing that he was about to jump without a safety net.

"I received information this morning that I was obligated to follow up on. Before he was shot, Wade Masterson told me that he was the guy in the black pickup in Albuquerque and was following us in the Colorado Renaissance Festival parking area. The implication was that he worked for Morrow in some capacity related to the bank job. I didn't get the details before he was shot. But he did tell me that Morrow told him that you had the missing bank-job money."

Mac's eyes rounded and she released a quick breath. "You withheld information from me. Again. I thought we had a deal." She paused. "You told me I had to trust someone. I chose you."

Gabe's gut burned at her words. Yeah, he did. He'd promised her they were partners. Now, when a shadow of doubt was presented, he'd become judge and jury and convicted her.

"I'm sorry, Mac. I was following protocol." Silly as it was, protocol was his only excuse.

"We're off-book. There is no protocol, except trust."

Silence maintained a tense standoff between them as the rooster clock ticked off the seconds.

"Everything okay?" Ben approached the kitchen island.

"Getting there," Gabe said.

Mac frowned, communicating that she didn't agree.

"Did Gabe update you?" Ben asked.

"Yes, but there's so much to unpack, I don't know where to start."

His brother reached for the coffee carafe and poured a cup before sitting down at the table. "Let's start unpacking," Ben said.

"Why was Wade Masterson trying to kill me?" she asked.

"If Masterson was telling the truth, it's someone else who wants you dead," Gabe said. "Masterson was working with Ribinoff. They were tracking us to locate the missing money from the bank job, not kill you."

Mac scowled. "Why would they, or Liz, for that matter, think I had the money?"

"Morrow told them you double-crossed her and took it."

She nearly jumped up from her chair at that. "Liz? Liz told them that?"

A play of expressions raced across Mac's face,

until her eyes rounded with understanding and she met his gaze.

"Masterson and Ribinoff thought I was in on the bank job? They were working with Liz? He followed me, hoping I'd lead him to the money?"

Gabe nodded.

Mac opened her mouth and closed it, looking as stunned now as he was in the alley. "Is Liz alive?" she asked.

"Masterson believed she died on the pier," Gabe said. He didn't add that the man also believed Mac was responsible. Though he would certainly pay the price for the omission, right now, there was no point heaping more coals upon her head. She had enough information to digest.

"And do we have any idea who shot Masterson?" she asked.

"I think we should look into the guard, James Smith," Ben replied. "We may never get a match on the lion tattoo. It's the identifying symbol for several criminal groups. I checked, and Smith's background shows no criminal record. It would have to be clean to get him hired as a bank guard."

"I'm still trying to wrap my head around the

idea that Liz was actually involved in the bank job. Is she connected to Smith somehow?" Mac asked.

"A very good question," his brother said. "My intelligence sources tell me that all of them, Smith, Ribinoff and Masterson, aged out of foster care. If Liz did grow up in the system, as she accidentally revealed to you, it's very likely all of their paths crossed hers. My guess would be that she recruited them."

Gabe considered his brother's theory for a moment. It made sense, but they couldn't actually prove any of it.

Unless they got Ribinoff to talk.

"I don't understand," Mac said. "Why didn't the Agency or Canadian law enforcement pick up on this?"

"Why would they?" Gabe responded immediately. "The bank guard is who they were looking at. Masterson and Ribinoff, and even Morrow, weren't on their radar. There was no reason for law enforcement to dig into the foster-care angle. Ben is the first one to connect the dots that no one even noticed until today. So it wouldn't have come up on a background check."

Once again, confusion had Mac frowning. Gabe related. They had plenty of information but not enough answers. He'd already come up with many of the same questions Mac had.

"What are you thinking?" he asked Mac.

"If the foster-care connection is valid, who altered Liz's file?"

"Someone with admin access," Ben said.

"Like Blake Calder." Mac looked to Gabe and he nodded.

"Recently transferred to the Denver field office. He's the number-two guy under Shipman. He'd have admin access." Gabe gave a slow shake of his head. "That would explain how the shooter found us at Avery's house. The laptop Calder gave us."

"That I can agree with," Mac said. "The rest... I'm not so sure. I mean, think about it. The Agency tracks every access on the intranet. They require regular polygraphs and annual investigations. How did he pull off a plan this big?"

"No intelligence-gathering network is perfect," Ben said. "Once again, I'm speculating. I believe that whoever is involved is playing a long game, requiring patience." He paused and sipped his coffee. "Every instance of access into files would have been a small tweak, so no one noticed. They built their game one move at a time over a long period of time, without calling attention to themselves."

One piece at a time. Gabe nodded. Yeah, it would require months of focused patience with an eye on the prize. Twenty million dollars.

"It would be helpful if I could remember where I've seen Calder before." Mac stood, moved to the island and poured coffee into a cup.

"You could have seen him anywhere." Gabe shrugged. "While he's new to Denver, Shipman told me he's had assignments in several field offices in the States and abroad."

Calder had experience, but he was a benign enough character to move anonymously on a daily basis. Plus, he was high enough in the food chain to have the access needed to pull off the heist undetected.

Mac nodded, her gaze directed out the window, apparently thinking. "So, how is Ribinoff connected?"

"If Ben's theory is correct, then it makes sense that Ribinoff and Masterson were following someone's instructions. Masterson admitted that Ribinoff was his inside guy," Gabe said.

"Ribinoff just happened to get a job with the Agency?" She shot him a doubtful look.

"We can't prove anything yet," Ben said. "I'd theorize that someone in authority paved the way for Ribinoff to be hired."

Calder again, Gabe surmised.

"Who killed Masterson?" Mac asked.

"Once again, our shooter strikes," Ben said. "My money is still on James Smith."

"Do you think Liz was involved with the bank job from the start?" Mac asked.

Ben cocked his head and gave a quick shrug. "We can't prove anything, but it sure smells like both Morrow and Calder were the masterminds."

"And do you think Liz faked her death on the pier?"

"That's the twenty-million-dollar question," Ben said.

Mac looked from Ben to Gabe, her expression bleak, and he knew what she was thinking.

All this time, she'd carried the guilt of the death of her team member and the asset. If they could find Morrow and prove she was involved, Mac could be released from her self-inflicted prison.

Gabe turned to his brother. "If Morrow masterminded the bank job and faked her own death, why didn't she just walk away? Disappear?" He raised his palms in question. "I keep circling back to that."

"Because Mackenzie is a loose end." Ben narrowed his eyes. "She's the only person besides Calder who can connect Liz to the foster-care system and to Smith, Ribinoff and Masterson."

"Do you think that's it?" Mac asked.

"Yes," Ben returned. "It may not seem like much, but you can connect the dots. You just didn't know it."

Mac's eyes widened. "Does that mean Liz is alive?"

Once again, Gabe's brother shrugged. "We don't have enough information to make that determination."

"He's right," Gabe said. "There are still too many variables."

"Shouldn't we get this intel to your boss?" Ben asked.

"Not yet," Mac said. "We don't have proof of anything."

"What about Ribinoff?" Gabe turned to Ben. "What did you find out?"

"I have his last known address. Tomorrow morning, we should stake it out."

"We need Ribinoff," Gabe said. "I'm sure we can get him to talk if we offer him a deal."

"We're running an unauthorized operation here. We don't have the authority to offer anything," Mac argued. Once again, her voice was chilly.

"He doesn't know that," Gabe said.

Ben stood and reached into the shopping bag on the table and pulled out two packages of burner phones. "Next order of business. You two need to destroy any phones you have. I picked up a couple of new burners for you."

"Thanks." Gabe looked at the rooster clock. "What time are we leaving in the morning?"

"Sunrise is five forty-five a.m.," Ben said. "I'd like to stop at Avery's to grab my stuff, and arrive in Denver before then."

Gabe groaned.

"Could we find my cane?"

"If you bring that handy flashlight of yours we can," Gabe said. "I mean, since my brother's plan has us out the door in the middle of the night."

Ben laughed at his words and stood. "I'm taking a shower. And I'll take the first watch." He offered a short salute. "Night, all."

A flash of pain crossed Mac's face as she slowly got up as well. Without looking at him, she went to the counter and poured herself more coffee. Now was the time to reach out to her and hope that she could see things from his side of the table.

"I'm sorry, Mac," Gabe said. "I hope you'll forgive me."

"Oh, I forgive you. I don't know where we stand with the whole trust thing, though." She turned. "Tell me. Did you really believe I had gone rogue?"

"When that shooter showed up at the house, I knew I had to make a decision." He met her gaze. "Wade Masterson's words rang in my head. He said you had the money. I had to decide if I believed you were part of the plot. Had you taken the money from Morrow as he was convinced?"

"And?"

"I went with what my heart and my head were telling me. There was no way the Mackenzie Sharp I knew could be involved. Period. Still, it was in your best interest that we find out how you'd been implicated. Ben's investigative work provided paper evidence that someone else opened that offshore account. Your financials show that you've had a substantial portfolio for some time. While that isn't proof for the Agency that you weren't involved, it's enough for me."

She stared at him with enough concentration to start a small fire. Would his admission end the tension between them?

"Why didn't you leave me in Phoenix?" Gabe took a deep breath. "Leave me on the ground when the SUV exploded? You weren't sure you could trust me. But you went with your gut and gave me a chance. It's the same thing."

"Is it?" She offered a curt nod and picked up her cup. "Good night, Denton."

Denton.

They were back to square one. For the fourth or fifth time. Gabe ran a hand over his face and prayed for patience.

Chapter Nine

"This is Ribinoff's place?" Mac asked.

Ben nodded as he drove past the apartment complex.

Mac grimaced. Fiesta Apartments in the light of a Tuesday dawn in Denver was nothing to celebrate.

Two floors of units and every apartment door had a view of the parking area. Streetlamps at the corners of the building cast more shadows than light. Not even the arrival of daylight in another thirty minutes could alter the drab appearance of the apartment complex.

"I'm depressed just looking at it," Mac said.

"Great place to stay if you want to keep a low profile," Ben said.

"Which apartment is his?" Mac asked. Once again, she directed her questions and comments to Ben. It was early. She hadn't had coffee, and cranky had settled on her like a scratchy sweater.

While she'd forgiven Gabe, she wasn't ready to let him off the hook for his acute episode of protocol yesterday.

"Last apartment on the right, first floor," Ben said.

Mac said a silent thank-you. Her leg wasn't prepared to handle stairs yet, and her pride wouldn't allow her to admit that fact.

Gabe pulled out his binoculars. "The lights are on. All of them."

"Maybe he's a morning person," his brother said.

"This isn't morning," Gabe groused. "But let's park the car and find out."

"You say that like there's a place to park." Ben glanced around the dark street.

"The alley looks good," Mac said. "It's too early for trash collection."

"Good idea." Ben eased the vehicle into the alley.

"All clear," Mac said as she exited the car.

Gabe approached the door to Ribinoff's apartment first, weapon raised, while Ben positioned himself on the other side of the door. Mac remained in the parking area, eyes on the apartment.

Suddenly, the door burst open, slamming

against the building's exterior wall with a reverberating bang. A tall man ran out, knocking Gabe to the ground. Head down, face hidden by a hoodie, the light from the streetlamps reflecting off the 9 mm in his right hand.

"He's got a weapon," Ben yelled.

Mac's cane clattered to the ground as she hit the pavement behind a parked car and withdrew her Glock from the ankle holster. Tension kept her fingers tightly gripping her weapon.

"In pursuit." Ben raced through the parking lot after the fleeing man.

Gabe scrambled to his feet and whipped around. "Mac?" His eyes connected with hers.

"I'm okay."

"Are you carrying?"

"Yes." She held up the Glock.

"Can you cover the apartment while I cover Ben?"

"Go. Go. I can handle this." Mac inched to a half-sitting position and eyed the perimeter. The door to the apartment was open. There was no movement inside. With a hand on the car's bumper, she struggled to stand, searching for her cane.

Minutes later, Ben and Gabe returned.

"Lost him," Ben panted.

Gabe stood hunched over, hands on knees, catching his breath. "I'm too old for this. I want a nice cushy office job."

"Like managing partner of Denton Security and Investigations, perhaps?" Ben asked.

Gabe only glared at his brother.

"Was it Ribinoff?" Mac asked.

"No way," Gabe said. "The guy who ran out of that apartment was tall and muscular. He fits the physical profile of the Toronto shooter. James Smith."

Mac swallowed hard at the words. If he'd seen her, would he have turned that 9 mm on her?

"You're looking pale, Mac. You okay?" Gabe asked.

"Fine. What about you? He knocked you down."

"Yeah, he did." Gabe nodded and rubbed his back. "And I'll be feeling that tomorrow."

"The door is still open," Mac said. She motioned toward the apartment building.

Gabe followed her gaze. "That's not good."

"It's also not good that lights are coming on all over the complex," Ben said.

The three of them cautiously approached the open door, with Mac taking up the rear.

Gabe entered first. "Clear," he called out from the living room.

"Any sign of your tech?" Ben asked.

"Not yet," Gabe said. "Kitchen is clear."

Mac entered the first bedroom, weapon ready. The bed was rumpled but empty. He'd been here. She pulled open the closet door using the edge of her T-shirt and then checked under the bed.

Pausing, Mac backtracked to get a better look under the bed. Was that a dust bunny? Left leg awkwardly extended, she knelt on her right knee. A cell phone? She pulled a tissue out of her pocket and grabbed the phone.

"Bedroom is clear," she called out.

In the hallway, Gabe and Ben had positioned themselves outside another door. Gabe nodded, and Ben pushed open the door to what looked like an office. Mac followed behind cautiously as they entered the room.

A crumpled body lay next to the desk.

Though high-end electronics and computer equipment fought for space on the desk, nothing seemed amiss in the room.

Except Ribinoff.

Both Ben and Gabe knelt next to the body.

"Poor kid." Hands trembling, Mac looked away. Another death and for what end? Money?

"He's still warm," Ben said. "Single GS to the back of the head. He probably didn't even see it coming."

"The kid didn't deserve this." Gabe shook his head and ran a hand over his face, visibly shaken. "Some days, I hate my job."

"Someone is tying up loose ends," Ben said. "We need to find them before they find Mackenzie."

"Let's get out of here," Mac said. "We can make an anonymous 911 call in the car."

The drive back to Bluebell was solemn. Mac wrestled with her thoughts. Her job had been about intelligence gathering up to now. Ever since Toronto, everything had changed.

The only way to stop the domino of events was to get ahead of the situation. Then maybe no one else would die. She pulled the cell phone wrapped in tissue from her pocket and stared at it for minutes. Maybe there was something here that would help.

When Ben turned into the gravel drive of the A-frame cabin and parked the car, Mac cleared her throat. "I have Ribinoff's cell phone. It was under his bed."

Gabe turned in his seat to look at her, his expression appalled. "You took the cell phone?"

"I borrowed it. It's not like he'll need it." She looked at him, annoyed. "Seriously, Gabe? We're running blind here. We don't have access to the Agency resources and we're trying to stay one step ahead of some very bad people. This might tip the odds in our favor."

"I get that. What I don't get is why you're just saying something now."

"Because she knew you'd object to removing something from the scene," Ben said. "Let's take it inside. I have gloves."

"So I like to follow protocol," Gabe grumbled as they entered the cabin and went into the kitchen. "Some people find that quality admirable."

Mac ignored him. "There's a voice mail on this phone." She sat at the kitchen table and donned the gloves Ben gave her. Then she pressed the voice-mail button.

"You've called in sick for the next few days, Ezra," a voice rang out. *"I've taken care of everything. Just stay low until I call back. I'm arranging your flight."*

"That's Calder," Gabe said.

Mac shivered. "Calder, again. And I still

can't figure out why that guy seems so familiar. Maybe he was in Toronto."

"Was he on the flight you and Morrow took to Toronto?" Gabe asked.

"We flew commercial. It's possible, but I didn't notice him in the boarding area."

"Slow it down, Mackenzie," Ben said. "Small memories can trigger big memories. You remembered that tattoo. You can remember this."

She nodded. Ben was right—she'd pushed everything from the last eight weeks into a drawer that she'd locked away. Opening it up and carefully sorting through each memory could yield valuable information again. Though it came with risks, she was willing to try.

"Give us a play-by-play of the day you left for Toronto."

"I took Winston to the boarding place."

Mac closed her eyes for a moment and concentrated, but all she could hear was the accelerated thump of her heart pounding in her head. She took a deep breath and, using the biofeedback techniques she'd learned long ago to ease anxiety, slowed her breathing and heart rate.

"When I got home, I called a ride-share service to get to the airport. Which is a good thing, or my car would still be in long-term parking."

"You and Morrow didn't go to the airport together?" Ben asked.

"No. Never. She always declined the offer to carpool."

Mac was silent for a moment, rubbing the bridge of her nose. "Airport departures." *One by one, the driver had passed each airline drop-off point before pulling to the curb in front of mine.*

She released a small gasp as the memory materialized. "That's it!" Mac worked to control the trembling of her voice. "That's where I saw Calder. At airport departures. My ride-share dropped me off, and I stood at the curb, adding the tip to my ride. I looked up and saw Liz arrive farther down." She nodded. "Calder exited the same vehicle as Liz and handed her a suitcase from the trunk. Then he kissed her. It was an intimate kiss."

"You saw his face?"

"Only in profile. But I'm certain it was him. Absolutely certain."

"So Calder has...or had a relationship with Morrow," Gabe said. "Who is giving the kill orders?"

"Good question," Ben said.

"Do you think Shipman knows Calder is the mole?" Mac asked.

"I don't think so. He trusted Calder to meet us," Gabe said.

"We should call Shipman," Mac insisted.

"No," Ben said. "You're already a liability to Calder. If he somehow intercepts a phone call and finds out that you can ID him with Morrow, who knows what he might do."

"But Shipman needs our intel." Withholding info from each other had been getting them nowhere, and Mac wasn't going to keep Shipman out of the loop any longer. "In person. Tonight. After dark."

"You're going to Shipman's house?" Gabe looked at her. "Is that wise?"

"Wisdom isn't part of the equation. Expedience is, if we're going to stop them," she said. "I might not agree with how this situation is being handled by the Agency, but I still trust Shipman."

"Okay. Then we're going to talk to him," he said. "Together."

"Once again, you don't trust me?" Mac sighed and gave a slow shake of her head.

"I don't trust the shooter who wants you dead."

"He's right, Mackenzie," Ben said. "You have to take backup with you. I'll stay here with Winston."

"Fine," she said. "We leave at midnight."

"Because getting sleep at night would be out of the question," Gabe muttered. Winston trotted into the kitchen and put his head on Gabe's lap.

Mac couldn't help but notice how her dog was becoming more and more attached to Gabe.

"The first thing I'm going to do when this is over is find some good sushi and then sleep for a week." Gabe looked at Winston. "What are you going to do, buddy?"

The dog whined and flopped down on the floor.

Mac stood and looked from the dog to the man. Winston was going to miss Gabe when this was over. She empathized with her dog. Despite his trust missteps, she feared she would feel the same way.

She offered Gabe a nod. "I'll see you at midnight."

"Have you thought about what we're going to do once we get there?" Gabe asked. He glanced at Mac in the passenger seat. She'd been less antagonistic since they'd left Bluebell. And silent for the most part, which he chose to interpret as a step toward reconciliation of their friendship.

"Yes," she answered. "I'll text him using my new burner."

Gabe turned into the Cherry Creek neighborhood and noted the neighborhood-watch and security signs.

"This is where he lives now?" Mac asked.

"Yeah. He's leasing a place."

"Leasing in a nice neighborhood. Old money mixed with new money," she observed.

"Pretty much," Gabe said. "I haven't been to his home since he and Mary moved." He handed her his phone. "Directions are on here."

"Keep going straight." Mac leaned forward in her seat, eyeing the street signs. "Slow down."

"Sorry."

"Turn left into the next cul-de-sac." She pointed as he turned. "That's it, the second house on the right."

Gabe parked in front of the house and got out. He assessed the neighborhood as he stood in the street. While not a mansion, the Shipmans' two-story brick Tudor home indicated affluence. He wouldn't be surprised if there were hidden cameras beneath the eaves. Shipman could very well have already been alerted to their presence.

Mac sent a quick text and moved behind the shadow of a looming Douglas fir.

"He got your message." Gabe motioned toward the second floor, where lights now glowed behind the closed blinds.

"Duck, Gabe," Mac said.

"What?" He tensed and glanced around before stepping into the shadows right before the headlights of the neighborhood rent-a-cops swept past. "Thanks."

A few minutes later, the front door opened, and Todd Shipman stepped outside. His graying hair was mussed, and he wore a crisp dark dress shirt and jeans. "Mackenzie, Denton. Glad to see you both in one piece."

"Sorry to disturb you and Mrs. Shipman, sir." Gabe was already regretting Mac's midnight rendezvous plan.

"Not at all. I expected you to visit long before this." He paused. "Though I'll admit, I was surprised when the cameras went off and I saw you two in my drive." Shipman nodded toward the side yard. "Let's go around to the back. Voices carry out here."

They followed him through a fence to a backyard lush with pots overflowing with blooming flowers. A gentle light lit up a cobblestone patio that held more furniture than he had in his whole apartment.

"Please, sit." Shipman pulled out chairs at a glass-topped table. "You're safe here. Two of my neighbors are law enforcement, and another is a martial-arts instructor. I have them on speed dial." He pulled a Glock from his waistband and set it on the table. "And I still manage to qualify on the range, once a year."

Of course he did. Gabe nearly laughed aloud. This was typical Shipman. Formidable with a dry sense of humor that caught you off guard.

Mac sat down across from Gabe.

"How's your leg, Mackenzie?" Shipman asked.

"Fair to middling, sir."

"What do you two know about Ezra Ribinoff's death?" Shipman's change of topic had Gabe's head spinning.

"I…um…" Mac stuttered and turned to Gabe.

"There's no proof yet, but we believe he was working with the team that pulled the Toronto bank job," Gabe said.

"That's a shame." Shipman shook his head. "Always regrettable when one of our own is lost." He took a deep breath. "Any idea who turned him?"

"Only a theory," Gabe said. "An investigation will no doubt alert the inside person."

"Blake Calder," Shipman said with a knowing nod.

Gabe and Mac looked at each other in stunned surprise.

"I am the head of the Denver office of the Central Intelligence Agency, people. And I pride myself in staying a step ahead."

"But how did you figure out Calder?" Gabe asked.

"Found a listening device in my office today. No one else had access except Calder and my secretary. She's been with the Agency through so many presidential elections that I've lost count. Unlikely that she'd risk her pension."

"What are you going to do about Calder?" Mac asked.

"For now, I have agents watching him." He turned to Mac. "Does Elizabeth Morrow play into your theory?"

"Yes, sir." She paused and looked at Shipman beneath the pale glow of the back porch, then glanced at Gabe.

She was hesitant to share, and Gabe didn't blame her. Shipman himself suspected Calder, which helped their case. Would he believe Morrow's involvement when they had nothing but unsubstantiated intel?

"It's possible that Liz used her past in foster care to recruit at least three of her former foster-care brothers that we know of into this plan," Mac said. "James Smith, Ezra Ribinoff and Wade Masterson."

"Masterson. The man shot in the alley, blocks from the field office," Shipman said.

"Yes, sir." Mac nodded.

"Morrow's file doesn't indicate foster care," Shipman said.

"We believe Calder altered her file and paved the way for Ribinoff's employment with the Agency," Gabe began. "Either Morrow or Calder, or both, assisted James Smith in getting the bank-guard position, and masterminded the entire robbery."

"That's an elaborate plan, and as you said, there's no evidence. At least not yet, correct?"

"Yes, sir," Mac said.

"This is day five and the Agency hasn't been able to verify Morrow is alive. In fact, except for her Agency footprints, we haven't been able to find much of anything." Shipman frowned. "Do you two have any insights?"

"Very few," Gabe said. "Ribinoff and Masterson were under the assumption that Morrow was dead. They were told that Mac was in on the robbery and took the money from Morrow."

"Mackenzie." Shipman nodded slowly as though contemplating his words. "Which explains framing her with the offshore account."

"I, um…" Mac paused. "I hope you don't think I had anything to do with that."

Shipman shook his head. "There are an inordinate number of unknown variables, Mackenzie. You are not one of them."

"Thank you, sir."

Gabe shared the audible relief he heard in Mac's voice.

"What about the shooter?"

"We think he shot Masterson and Ribinoff and has been after Mac since Toronto."

"Sounds like someone is tying up loose ends to me," Shipman said.

Exactly their thoughts. Gabe nodded. Good to know they were on the same page as Shipman.

"Any idea who the shooter is?" Shipman continued.

"Possibly James Smith, the bank guard," Mac said.

"As I recall, Calder reached out and recommended Morrow for the Toronto assignment before he was even moved to the Denver office." Shipman was silent for a moment. "Do we have anything on him?"

Mac pulled a plastic bag from her pocket. "Ribinoff's cell phone. Though he doesn't identify himself, Calder is on a voice mail left yesterday. There are multiple phone numbers that we believe are Calder's and Morrow's."

"I'll need a warrant to obtain the phone records," Shipman said. "And I'm going to have to do that without Calder finding out." He picked up the plastic bag gingerly. "I don't want to know how you obtained this, do I?"

"It was just lying around, sir," Mac said.

"I see." He looked from Mac to Gabe. "At best, this is circumstantial evidence. However, it may help me convince Calder to flip and talk to Homeland Security. But that won't change the fact that there is still a shooter out there."

"Yes, sir," Gabe said.

"Why are you being targeted, Mackenzie?" Shipman asked.

"I stumbled upon the truth about Morrow's background without realizing how important the information is. I know enough to raise questions that could ultimately put Smith, Calder and, if she's alive, Morrow behind bars."

"I'll have their passports red-flagged as a precaution. They won't be able to leave the country." Shipman frowned. "You both understand we never had this discussion."

Gabe nodded.

"Yes, sir," Mac said.

Shipman looked at Mac, his eyes filled with concern. "Mackenzie, be very careful. Whether Morrow is dead or alive, someone is trying to kill you."

"Yes, sir."

Gabe followed Mac back to the car. She was silent as she got in and fastened her seat belt.

"What are you thinking?" he asked.

"I think it's time to go after Calder."

"Shipman will handle Calder."

"Yes, I'm very familiar with the speed at which the wheels of bureaucracy move. I want to follow Calder now and see if he leads us to Liz or James Smith."

"I get that, but I won't let you use yourself as bait," he said.

She looked at him.

"No, Mac, that option is off the table."

The dogged expression in her eyes said that she hadn't agreed to anything.

Hours after the meeting with Shipman, Mac stepped into the living room, where she found Ben reading. An old-fashioned kerosene lamp sat on the table next to him. Outside, rain danced on the windows, and in the corner, Winston had sprawled on a rug, and was softly snoring.

"Mackenzie, did the storm wake you?" Ben closed the book in his lap and stood.

"No. I've been thinking about the meeting with Shipman and I couldn't sleep. Why don't I take over now? There's no use both of us being awake."

"Sure. Okay. Thanks a lot." He motioned to the lamp. "Power is out. I imagine that happens a lot here. It'll probably be back up by morning. I cracked a few windows to create a cross breeze."

Mac nodded. As Ben turned to leave, she touched his arm. "Thank you."

"For what?"

"For coming, for putting yourself on the line."

"Friends do that. Gabe would do it for me and for you, too."

"Friends," she murmured. "He doesn't seem to trust this friend."

Ben met her gaze, his eyes searching. "Haven't we already had this conversation? My brother cares for you more than a friend, which is why he tends to overreact to issues that concern you."

"I know you mean well, but is it possible you're working with old data?"

He started laughing, his eyes crinkling with amusement, just like Gabe's. "The data is current," Ben said.

Mac raised a hand and then dropped it to her side. What could she say to that?

"You know this job isn't exactly conducive to caring."

"Yeah, I get it. The job, always the job. Which is why I got out. I want a future and a family, and I want that family to come first." He paused. "Not the job. God and my family, and then my country and the job. It's the only way that works."

Mac nodded, mulling Ben's admission. She'd dared to consider a life outside of the Agency in the last few weeks. That was a huge step. Could she follow through and take a chance on the possibility that someone like her could have a family? Once again, the idea terrified her.

"Don't hurt him again. I'm not sure he could handle it a second time."

"Gabe was engaged. Clearly, he moved on," she countered.

"No. Not really. Fortunately, he figured that out before the wedding." He winked. "That's between you and me."

"Thank you, Ben. I appreciate your honesty."

He nodded and left the room.

Though her response to Ben had appeared calm, inside she was overwhelmed with confusion. She turned over his words again and again, with no idea what to do about them. She and Gabe couldn't go back.

Could they go forward?

The only sound was the clock on the wall. Mac stood at the window, staring out at the rain falling on the small lake. Each droplet created a dance of circles.

She cranked the window open a little more and inhaled the earthy scent of soil after the rain.

A chilly breeze rushed past, mixing in the smell of pine from the big tree next to the cabin.

Mac glanced at the coffeepot in the kitchen. No electricity, but she could boil water on the gas range and make tea. She carried the kerosene lamp to the kitchen table and began opening cupboards, until she found a small pot.

Staring mindlessly into the pan of water on the gas burner, she waited for the bubbles to simmer on the bottom and break the surface.

The pantry held several choices of tea bags. She chose chamomile, poured the hot water into her mug and sat down.

Her dream would be to live in a place like this. Away from people, away from threats and away from the Agency.

What did retired operatives do with the rest of their lives? It sounded like a bad pun.

"Couldn't sleep, huh?"

Mac turned around at Gabe's words. He wore a disheveled T-shirt with jeans, and his hair was totally mussed, which made him an adorable nerd. She glanced away.

"Where's Ben?"

"I relieved him." She glanced at the rooster clock. "It's four a.m. What are you doing up?"

"My internal clock is confused. From DC to Denver, to Phoenix, and back to Denver." Gabe smiled and opened a cupboard.

"What are you looking for?"

"The beans." Pulling out a silver package, he rolled back the packaging and sniffed. "Nice."

"Isn't there ground coffee? The electricity is out."

"There must be a grinder around here."

"You'll wake Ben."

Gabe frowned and opened a few more cupboards until he pulled something out. "I'm talking an old-fashioned hand grinder." He carefully measured out the beans and dumped them in the grinder. Turning the handle, he stopped periodically to evaluate the grind.

"Perfect."

"But the coffee maker doesn't work."

"If there's a kerosene lamp—" Gabe nodded toward the one flickering on the kitchen table "—then the electricity goes out regularly." He pulled out an aluminum stove-top coffeepot from the cupboard, lifted the lid and filled it with water, before adding the ground beans to the basket.

Five minutes later, the smell of fresh coffee filled the kitchen.

"Mind if I trade my tea for a cup of that?"

He laughed. "You're drinking herbal. That might be a good thing."

"Herbal tea isn't going to slow down my mind. Things are about to blow wide open. It's like the still before a tornado. I feel it in my spirit." She looked at him again and her heart ached with concern. "I couldn't handle it if something happened to you because of me, Gabe. It would be my fault again."

"Again? You're talking about your parents?"

Mac nodded. She'd held everything inside for so long. Even from Gabe. Especially from Gabe. Now, here she was rambling and couldn't stop. "I have so much…guilt about that night."

"Stop looking back. There was nothing you could have done to prevent the bombing. Nothing."

"I snuck out of the house on a dare." She swallowed a sob, intent on her admission. "I don't deserve to be alive."

"Don't say that. You were a kid, and you know there is no causal relationship between what happened at the embassy and your youthful activity."

Mac reached for his hands as anxiety choked her. "I can't do it again. I can't handle it if someone else I care about is killed."

"You can't live your life worried that people are going to die, either. They are. This world is only a stop on the way to forever, Mac. People die. God is our only hope."

She looked down at her hands in his and pulled hers away. Now she was being foolish.

Gabe cupped her face with his palm. It would be easy to lean into the comfort he offered, but that wouldn't be fair to him.

"Talk to me, Mac." Gabe's warm voice slid over her skin, and she shivered.

Again, she edged away from his touch. Despite their ongoing trust issues, when she looked into Gabe's eyes, she was unable to deny how much she cared. So much so, that she feared she was close to falling in love with him again.

"Ever think maybe it's time to get out?" she asked.

"Sure. All the time," he said.

"Don't tell Shipman, but if we get out of here alive, I'm thinking about turning in my resignation." *There, she'd said it. For the first time in her life, she was considering putting her past behind her to grab the possibility of a future.*

"*When.* Not *if* we get out of here alive," Gabe corrected with a frown. "And I have to tell you, Mac, you are the last person I would have ever guessed would leave the Agency."

"Things change. People change."

"I'll agree with that." He looked at her as

though both confused and intrigued. "What are you going to do next?"

"I don't have a clue." She stared out the window at the lake.

What would it be like to have a normal life? Everything came down to whether or not she had the courage to find out.

Chapter Ten

Gabe checked his watch and kept his eyes on the front door of the Denver field office. Well after 5:00 p.m. on a Wednesday and yet, no Calder.

He adjusted his Bluetooth and spoke to his brother again. "Nothing yet."

"Where are you?" Ben asked.

"Mac and I are parked across the street from the parking garage in a black minivan, Texas plates," Gabe said.

"Another minivan?" Ben noted.

Gabe chuckled. "They blend in. What can I say?"

Mac turned in the passenger seat to face Gabe. "How'd you get Ben into the Agency parking garage?"

"I gave him my pass."

"You have a parking pass?" she sputtered. "I park on the street."

"I'm a VIP visitor. I have to turn it back in when I leave for DC." Gabe bit back a laugh at the expression on Mac's face.

Minutes passed until, finally, Gabe spotted a group of employees leaving the building across the street. "Here he comes."

Gabe and Mac both slid down in their seats.

"I've got my eyes on his parking stall," Ben said. "Silver BMW with vanity plates."

"Roger that," Gabe said.

"So what we're going to do is follow him and hope he leads us to Smith or Morrow?" Mac frowned.

"Do you have a better plan?" Gabe asked.

"Yes. I vote for confronting him."

"So he can disappear?" Gabe shook his head. "All we have is a bunch of theories. We need more information."

"Exiting parking garage in the BMW and turning left," Ben said minutes later. "I'm two vehicles behind in the black sedan."

"Here we go." Gabe started the minivan and turned to Mac. "Seat belt."

She buckled up and checked her mirror as he pulled into traffic. "Do you think Winston is safe at the cabin alone?"

"Ben has cameras set up. Winston is safer

there than here, where he could take a stray bullet if things go south again. You can't worry about him when you're supposed to focus on keeping yourself safe."

"You're right. I know you're right. I still hate leaving him."

"Calder's parking garage is two blocks ahead, on the right," Ben said.

Gabe glanced at Mac and her expression said they were thinking the same thing. Would he lead them to Smith or possibly Morrow, if she was alive?

"Hang on a minute." Gabe narrowed his eyes and assessed the traffic in front of him. "Ben, Calder has another tail."

"You've got to be kidding me," his brother returned.

"I'm four vehicles behind you. A burgundy pickup truck pulled into traffic. He's moving fast and coming up next to you on the right. It looks like he's going to try to edge in behind Calder."

"I see him," Ben said. "I'm not going to let him in."

Gabe signaled left. "I'm diverting to a side street. You stay with Calder. No one can ID you. We can't take the chance that they'd make

Mac and me. Just keep me updated on your location and I'll stay in the vicinity."

"Calder just turned into underground parking. I'm going to follow."

"What about the truck, Ben?" Gabe asked.

"He's right behind me on the entrance ramp."

The sound of shots firing echoed in Gabe's ear and had him swallowing, as adrenaline surged.

"Ben!" Jaw tight, Gabe clenched the steering wheel.

"Ben, what's going on?" Mac asked.

"It's Smith. He's got Calder pinned down inside his vehicle."

Gabe made a hard right into the next lane, jerking both him and Mac sideways.

Horns blared as he cut off a cabbie, who was now behind him.

"Come on. Come on. Come on," Gabe muttered, fist pounding on the steering wheel. He had to get to that parking garage.

"What do you want me to do?" Gabe asked his brother.

"Block the exit. Maybe we can get a twofer. Keep Calder alive for Shipman and grab Smith."

"Okay, but I'd like to keep us alive, too."

"I'm all for that," Ben said as another shot rang out.

"On my way." Gabe said a silent apology as he cut off another vehicle and turned onto the entrance ramp of the parking garage. Gripping the steering wheel, he did a quick three-point turn to block the exit.

He looked at Mac. "I know you hate to hear this, but please stay in the vehicle. Smith will pick you off like cans on a fence if you're walking down that ramp. Hide on the floor in the back in case he rams the van out of the way, and have your weapon ready."

"What about you?" she asked, her face reflecting concern.

He unfastened his seat belt and opened the door of the minivan. "I'm going to run up to the next level and assess the situation. Smith won't know I'm there."

"That's your plan?" Mac grimaced.

"I'll improvise and pray." He pulled out his weapon and eyed the ramp.

"I'll be praying, too."

His gaze met hers and he gave a nod. "Thanks." It didn't escape him that Mackenzie Sharp, who seemed to be having a crisis of faith, had offered to pray for him. He was going to be the one to pray with her, yet she'd taken the lead. Gabe nearly laughed aloud as he jumped out of the vehicle.

"Keep her safe, Lord," he murmured.

Mac got out of the minivan, removed the Glock from her ankle holster and slipped into the back. "Stay on comms, Gabe."

"Will do."

A gunshot rang out, ricocheting off the walls of the garage, its sound amplified in the cement structure.

Gabe took off running, his eyes everywhere. Thankfully, there were no civilians in sight.

The smell of exhaust and gasoline wrapped up in the heat of the day greeted him as he raced uphill to the second level of the parking garage.

"Where are you, Ben?" he panted.

"Ground floor. Section B. I've got eyes on Smith and Calder. Both are inside their vehicles."

"Does Calder have a weapon?"

"It doesn't appear that he does. He hasn't returned fire. Smith has a sniper rifle. I can see the fat barrel when he pokes it out the window."

Gabe eyed the walls for section numbers. He found section B and moved slowly to the yellow barrier rail. Looking down to the ground floor, he spotted Calder's BMW sideways against the cement wall, as if he was going to turn the vehicle around but stopped. He could see Calder on the floor of the Beemer.

Ben's rental sedan was the only thing between Calder and the pickup. The driver's door was open, and the vehicle was now minus his brother.

The pickup truck was right beneath where Gabe stood.

Where was Ben?

Gabe scanned the area, searching between vehicles until he finally spotted his brother, weapon ready, crouched down next to his rental vehicle, with a clear line of sight to both Smith and Calder.

"Look up," Gabe said softly.

Ben did. He smiled and gave a thumbs-up.

"What are you doing?" Gabe asked.

"I'm doing my best to keep Smith from killing Calder. Every time Smith opens the door of his pickup to get out, I fire. Then I move to another position. He's pinned in his truck."

Gabe tensed with anger as he recalled Masterson and Ribinoff lying in puddles of their own blood.

"I'm convinced this is the same shooter who took out Masterson and Ribinoff and nearly killed Mac and me on the train tracks," Gabe said. "It's time to shut him down."

"What do you have in mind?" Ben asked.

"I'm going jump into the flatbed. Cover me."

"No, you can't do that. Smith will nail you."

"Extended cab. I'll roll toward the window, and he won't even be able to see me from the driver's seat. While he's trying to figure out what happened, you get Calder out of his car and into the elevator."

"I won't be able to cover you, if I do that."

"Once I'm in the back of the truck, I'll be fine."

Ben was silent for a moment and he knew his brother was calculating. "Okay. I don't like it, but I don't have another plan."

Gabe looked down at the truck, gauging the distance. He climbed over the barrier and stood on the edge with one hand on the metal rail.

He looked down at Ben. "Ready?"

His brother nodded.

"One. Two. Three…"

Gabe pushed himself off the landing into the back of the truck, purposely pounding hard against the metal. The sound of his shoes hitting the flatbed reverberated like thunder. He dropped to the floor of the truck and then rolled toward the window, making himself as small as possible.

The back window of the truck exploded as a shot hit the glass.

Gabe covered his head and his ears, praying the distraction had worked.

"I've got Calder," Ben said. "We're in the elevator going to street level. Are you okay?"

"I'm fine. He can't reach me unless he gets out of the truck."

Suddenly, the pickup truck jerked to life.

"Whoa," Gabe murmured.

Smith backed up and then slammed the brakes.

Gabe braced his legs and arms against either side of the vibrating metal of the bed, using all his strength to keep from bouncing out of the truck. At the same time, he prayed for an opportunity to pull out his weapon.

Smith floored it, shooting the vehicle forward. The sound of a spray of bullets indicated Smith hadn't forgotten his primary target. The BMW.

Then he backed up and did a one-eighty. Metal crunching metal drowned out squealing tires as Smith continued to hit parked cars as he headed back to the entrance. Burnt rubber filled Gabe's nostrils.

He dared to lift his head and peek over the side of the flatbed to where the minivan blocked the entrance.

Why did he think that was a good idea?

"Brace yourself, Mac. He's going to plow past the minivan."

"I've got this, Gabe." Her voice in his earbud was steady.

A single shot rang out.

"Mac!" Gabe's heart thudded as adrenaline shot through him. *Not Mac. Please, Lord. Not Mac.*

The truck swerved, the left rear bumper tagging the minivan before it crashed into the cement divider. Gabe slid forward and then bounced back against the tailgate.

Then the truck stopped.

"He's down," Mac said. The words were low and flat.

Gabe jumped out the back and staggered toward the minivan, then dropped to a knee. Relief was bittersweet. Another person dead. But Mac... Mac was alive.

"Are you all right?" Mac's breath was warm

on his face. She slipped an arm beneath his and helped him to his feet.

"Yeah. I'm good. My equilibrium is pretty messed up, from bouncing around back there, but I'm okay."

"I'm glad," she said.

"Me, too." He met her gaze and smiled. "Very glad."

"What happened?" Ben asked through the bud in Gabe's ear.

"Smith is dead," he returned.

"What a waste." Ben sighed.

"What's happening with Calder?" Gabe asked.

"He's safe. We'll meet you in his condo. Second floor. Number twelve. Take the front entrance on Broadway. The door code is twenty-eight thirteen. He's kindly offered to host our next get-together."

"Nice job, Ben," Gabe said.

"Thanks. Would this be a good time to mention Denton Security and Investigations again?" his brother asked.

"No, it's not." Gabe went to the truck and checked for a pulse. Then he pulled up Smith's left sleeve. The lion tattoo, as Mac had described it.

He walked back to her. "Smith is your Toronto shooter. Lion tattoo, left arm. We should call Shipman. He'll send a team in to clean this up."

"Already called him." There was a tremor in her voice and her face was pale.

"Are you okay?" Gabe asked.

She wordlessly shook her head and glanced back at the truck. "I didn't want to do that," she whispered.

He pulled the Bluetooth from his ear and tucked it into his pocket. Then he wrapped his arms around her and pulled her close. "I know, Mac. I know."

"Morrow sent her shooter after you, Calder. Give her up," Gabe said. Calder grimaced, but said nothing.

Mac assessed the rogue agent from her position against the wall. Was that grimace a confirmation of Gabe's accusation, or of Liz's death on the pier? He wasn't cooperating and she might never know. Mac tucked her shaking hands under her crossed arms. She hadn't stopped trembling since she'd fired the Glock in the parking lot. The loss of life on this mission staggered her, and would for a long time.

Calder turned his head in Mac's direction and stared at her for a moment, his eyes unreadable, before he turned away. There was no malice. No, instead she thought she saw a glimpse of pity, which only confused her.

"Don't look at her," Gabe said. "I'm the one asking the questions."

"I have nothing to say, Officer Denton."

Gabe shrugged. "Fine. Homeland Security is on the way."

The agent sat in a wooden chair at his kitchen table, his hands restrained with flex-cuffs Mac found at the bottom of her messenger bag.

Gabe had been asking questions for thirty minutes and Calder had yet to respond. He knew his rights. They couldn't even arrest him, let alone persuade him to talk. Calder held tight to the knowledge that CIA agents have no law-enforcement authority in the United States. They'd have to wait for DHS to arrive.

Mac glanced around the room. "What happened to Ben?"

"He slipped out to talk to the car-rental place." Gabe raised his eyebrows. "Two rentals in less than a week. Ouch."

She nodded. They hadn't done any better.

A total of four vehicles since leaving Phoenix last Friday.

Mac walked around the living room, unable to relax. The intimate kiss she'd observed at the airport between Calder and Liz told her that Liz had no doubt been here many times. A quick check of the condo when they arrived had revealed no evidence of her presence. Still, the place made Mac uncomfortable, almost nauseated. She had to get out soon.

"When can we leave?" she asked Gabe.

"When Shipman gets here."

"If Calder doesn't talk, what is he going to be charged with?"

"Treason. He knowingly altered CIA files. Shipman has no doubt already tracked his computer access. That should be enough to make him decide to talk."

A knock at the door had Gabe tensing, on alert again.

Mac's phone buzzed and she pulled it out of her pocket. "It's okay. It's Shipman and Homeland Security. He sent me a text."

Gabe opened the door, and Todd Shipman entered with two DHS agents.

"Nice work, Sharp, Denton."

"Thank you, sir," Gabe said.

"I've promised our friends at DHS that the two of you and your brother will make time to return and provide written statements. All standard procedure. Tomorrow work for you?"

"Yes, sir."

"Good." He handed Mac a set of keys. "I understand you like minivans. There's one parked at the curb. It's a rental. Keep that in mind when you return it to us in the same condition."

She tried not to smile. "Yes, sir."

They were silent on the elevator down to the ground floor. When they got in the minivan, Mac released a long breath, relieved to be on the way home to Winston.

"Do you think Calder will cooperate?" she asked. "He does have some leverage because there are still a lot of unanswered questions." She said the words more for herself than anything else.

Gabe nodded. "You're right. A lot of answers that went to the grave with Smith, Masterson and Ribinoff. We don't even know what happened to the money."

He signaled and merged into expressway traffic.

Mac's eyes were on the road ahead, and she didn't even notice the mountains to the west or the trees lining the roadway. Her thoughts were on Liz Morrow. They hadn't found her. Had she gone off the grid, was she being held by someone intent on finding the missing money, or was she dead?

"Calder was arrested. Smith is dead. Yet we still don't know anything about Liz." Her heart pounded in her chest as she spoke.

"Whoa, Mac, take a deep breath. It's going to be okay." Gabe reached out to hold her hand and squeezed gently.

"Is it?" Mac asked. "I've been in limbo for eight weeks..." She did a mental calculation. "Almost nine now. When will this nightmare end?"

Chapter Eleven

"Good boy, Winston." Mac caught her breath as she walked up the gravel drive to the log-cabin rental. While Ben and Gabe went to pick up the Thai food for dinner, she had gone for a stroll with the bulldog to clear the cobwebs from her mind.

She'd walked a little farther today. Not as fast as Winston preferred, but she was making progress.

Despite walking with a cane, her steps were lighter knowing the shooter who'd followed her for weeks was no longer a threat.

This morning, she, Ben and Gabe had provided their statements to DHS. There was no new intel on Liz, and so far, Calder hadn't co-operated with the authorities.

She couldn't hide forever. Maybe it was time to accept the fact that Liz was dead and move on. That meant Gabe would return to DC. Her steps slowed at the thought and emotion clogged her throat.

Mac reached in her pocket for her key to the cabin. As she did, Winston stopped and sniffed, then growled low and deep. Pay attention to Winston. That's what Gabe said.

Out of habit, she patted the Glock tucked in her ankle holster. She could reach it quickly if needed.

"Lord, be with me," she prayed before unlocking the door.

Winston growled again as they walked into the entryway, where Mac held his collar with one hand, her cane with the other. "Sit." The dog whined, but obeyed.

"Hello, Mackenzie."

Mac whirled around and a jolt of adrenaline raced through her at the voice. Liz Morrow's voice.

Across the room, Liz sat on a stool drinking coffee from one of the cabin's mugs. A Glock rested on the counter within reach.

"You certainly are a lot of trouble." Liz smiled.

"Liz." Confused, Mac searched the woman's face for answers. But Liz merely cocked her head and assessed Mac in return.

"I've been waiting for hours for your friends to leave," Liz said. "Now it's just you and me."

A shiver ran over her as she confirmed that her guilt had been misplaced. Liz hadn't been kidnapped, and certainly wasn't dead. Her heart pounded in her ears and her chest tightened as she looked at the Glock on the counter again.

Nine weeks, and Liz was lovelier than ever. The dark hair tumbled to her shoulders and she seemed fit and healthy. She certainly hadn't suffered any sleepless nights.

"Nothing to say?" Liz taunted.

"What do you want me to say, Liz?" Mac fought to control her breathing and push back the fear. She wouldn't give her the satisfaction of a response.

"You could start by apologizing, dear Mackenzie. You spoiled everything."

"Did I?" Mac asked. "Why didn't you take the money and run?"

"Because you knew. You knew enough to connect me to the crime. When you blathered on in Toronto, I realized you had to go, so my plan could play out. I won't let you keep me from my spoils. I earned that money."

"Blood money?" Mac returned, spurred by outrage. So many had died because of Liz's greed.

Liz narrowed her eyes. "I hear that disdain in your voice. Spoken like a woman who knows nothing about growing up without anything. Not a name, not a past, a present or a future. Nothing. You will never understand what it's like to be alone in this world. To have all your worldly possessions fit into a paper bag from the grocery store."

"Oh, I know what it's like to be alone. We really aren't all that different."

"We have nothing in common," Liz sneered.

"Sure we do. Except you killed innocent people, Liz."

She raised a shoulder in dismissal. "All for the greater good."

"Shipman knows," Mac said. "And Calder is already in custody."

"Blake will never give me up. That leaves you. The key witness. Anything else is hearsay and conjecture. There isn't a shred of evidence." She grinned. "I'm that good."

Mac's stomach heaved at the words.

Liz glanced at her watch. Then she eyed Mac again. "How's the leg?" She shook her head. "My apologies. He was supposed to kill you. Not maim you."

Mac gripped her cane tightly.

"You look like you're in pain. Why don't you have a seat over there, in front of the window? I want you to be able to see me shoot your boyfriend, and that's a good spot."

"Go ahead and shoot me now. Denton isn't part of this."

"Maybe not, but you've managed to take almost everything from me in the last week. I'm going to return the favor."

Mac moved toward the rocker, her grip tight on the cane. Her pulse raced and her mind continued a desperate scramble for a plan.

"Wait," Liz called out.

Mac froze.

"Put your weapon on the floor and kick it over to me."

Mac released a breath. Liz was one of the few people who knew she had an ankle holster. She withdrew her Glock and kicked it toward Liz. Then she began to turn again.

"No. Don't move."

"You're going to shoot me in the back?"

"Of course not. Only a coward shoots someone in the back." She smiled. "I thought I heard something. But I guess I was wrong." Liz waved a hand toward the chair. "Sit. Sit. Get comfy."

Mac rocked slowly, her gaze taking in the

landscape. Beside her, Winston sat watchful, as if waiting for permission to strike.

Liz Morrow was absolutely going to kill her. There was no trace of ambivalence in her voice. Only determination. If she could get her to talk, maybe she could distract her.

"So Calder was the one who planned everything, I assume."

Liz's eyes widened and she offered a bitter laugh. "Calder? He doesn't have the brains to plan an operation like that. I've been planning for two years. Two years. Bit by bit, so as not to call attention to myself or anyone else. Everything orchestrated down to the moment I dove off that pier."

"Calder's statement indicated the opposite," Mac lied.

"He's lying to you. I'm the brains. Calder doesn't know enough to tell anyone anything. Everyone gets a piece of the information pie. No one but me gets the whole pie."

"I guess you managed to hide the money as part of your plan," Mac said.

"You'll never know, will you?" Liz shook her head, dark eyes glittering with anger.

Winston tensed at the rising tone of Liz's

voice. He got to his feet and paced back and forth across the living room, ears perked, listening.

"Mackenzie, get the dog to settle down, or I'll shoot him."

Winston barked, confused, looking to Mac for direction.

"I mean it."

"It's okay, boy," she soothed. Though it wasn't. Nothing was okay.

Minutes ticked by. The window was open, but all Mac could hear was the splash of a duck on the pond, its wings flapping as it flew from the mirrored surface, into the sky.

Again, Liz looked at her watch. "What's taking him so long? I have a private jet waiting on me. The captain agreed to stow me aboard for a nominal fee." Once again she offered a satisfied smile. "Money can buy anyone and anything."

"Where are you going?" Mac asked.

"Montenegro. Did you know they don't have an extradition treaty with the United States?" She grinned. "Of course you didn't. It's beautiful. Quiet secluded beaches. The perfect place to become permanently invisible. And without you, I won't even have to look over my shoulder."

"It sounds lovely. Going alone?"

Liz laughed. "Look at you, trying to get intel from me. Maybe you should call your boyfriend instead. If he doesn't get here soon, I'm going to have to move on to Plan B. Not nearly as much fun."

"Why wait for Denton?" She stared at Liz, trying to understand what drove the woman.

"I told you. It's payback time." A faint smile touched her mouth. "Go ahead. Call him," Liz insisted.

"I don't have a phone. He took it with him." Mac eyed her messenger bag on a peg next to the door.

"I knew you were going to be a problem." Liz turned and reached for her cell phone on the counter.

When she did, Mac jumped from the rocker and grabbed her cane. She swung, and the metal rod connected with Liz's head with a thud and a crack.

Liz moaned and fell to her knees, swaying. "I'm going to kill you for that."

"Not if I can help it," Mac muttered. She grabbed her messenger bag and pulled open the door. "Come on, Winston."

The dog followed.

"Good boy. Now all I have to do is hobble faster than I have in my life."

"Do you hear that?" Gabe asked. He glanced around the floor of Ben's rental. A luxury vehicle, it was a dozen steps up from the minivan Shipman rented him and Mac yesterday.

"Buzzing," Ben said, his eyes on the road.

"My phone is in here somewhere."

"We're five minutes from the cabin. You can find it when we get there. Do I need to remind you that this is my third rental since I landed in Colorado? I'm keeping my eyes on the road and the vehicle away from criminal elements." Ben cleared his throat. "Speaking of the cabin. Maybe we should talk about what's next before we get there."

"Next? What do you mean?"

"It's Thursday. Calder has been arrested. What's next?"

"Oh, that next." Gabe nodded. He'd been asking himself the same thing. "I've reached out to Shipman to find out if he's gotten any intel on the Elizabeth Morrow situation. But nothing yet."

"Calder isn't talking."

Gabe shrugged. "Guess not."

"Let's chat with Mackenzie about it, and we can go from there," Ben said.

"I'm putting 'chat with Mac' on my schedule." The buzzing sounded again. "Can you pull over? This is annoying me. Could be something important. Maybe Shipman is trying to reach me."

Ben signaled and moved to the shoulder of the road. "I'll help you look. Just be gentle with the vehicle."

Gabe lifted the mats from the back seat with no results, then stuck his hand under the passenger seat and hit a rectangular object. "Found it." He got back in the car and put on his seat belt.

"Is it Shipman?" Ben asked.

"No—voice mail." Gabe pulled up his text messages and read the brief message from Mac. A guttural sound slipped from his lips, and he grimaced at the sucker punch that knocked the air from his lungs.

"You okay? What is it, Gabe?"

"Morrow is alive and she's at the cabin intent on eliminating Mac." Fear wrapped its hands around his neck and squeezed.

"She's alive?" Ben gripped the steering wheel. "What do you want to do?"

"Look, is that Winston?" Gabe pointed across the field adjacent to the cabin.

"Sure is," Ben said.

"Then Mac must be close by. Stop here, Ben. Let's ditch the car and approach on foot."

"Will do," Ben said. He guided the sedan off the road and pulled out his phone. "Sound is off. I must have turned it off accidentally. I've got those cameras on the cabin." He tapped the app and then the front-door feed, and checked the image captures. "Nothing out of the ordinary in front. The capture shows Mac and Winston entering the cabin."

"Do you have a camera on the back door?" Gabe asked.

"Yeah." When an image capture of a woman appeared on the screen, Gabe grabbed the phone.

"Ben, isn't that Morrow? You saw the file photos."

"Yeah. That's her. She's got a Glock in one hand, and..." He paused. "Whoa. That's Mac coming out the door. And look at the next image. Morrow. She's leaning sideways. I'd say she's injured."

"How did she get to the cabin? I don't see a vehicle." Gabe pulled out his binoculars and did a 360-degree sweep. Lots of trees. No vehicles.

"I don't see one, either," Ben said. "She must have parked to the north and come in on foot."

"Let's go," Gabe said.

"What's your plan?" Ben asked.

"If only I had one." The only plan he had right now was to keep the promise he'd made to himself to protect Mac. His stomach burned when he thought about Morrow's deadly determination.

"Take comms," Ben said. "Morrow is armed, and we can't be sure Mackenzie is."

"Good idea." Gabe reached in his pocket for his Bluetooth.

"Gabe, look at me."

"Yeah?" He met Ben's gaze and drew a deep breath at the concern on his brother's face.

"You're going to be useless to Mackenzie if you let your emotions get in the way. You're a trained operative. This is a mission. Focus."

Gabe nodded, grateful for the words of wisdom. "You're right. I know you're right."

"Okay. Now, let's split up and take Morrow down," Ben said.

"Now you're speaking my love language. Why don't you come around the other side of the house?"

Gabe pulled his binoculars from his pocket

again and searched the landscape around the lake, hoping to see Mac. Her leg injury would slow her down, and Morrow's bullet would find its target if she tried to outrun the rogue agent.

Mac was one of the smartest people he knew. She'd hide. That's what he'd do.

Now all he had to do was figure out where.

Winston raced back and forth along the trail around the lake. Protected behind the wide base of a blue spruce, Gabe released a low whistle, as soft as he dared, without alerting Morrow. The bulldog's ears perked up, and he looked around. Gabe stepped out, and the dog saw him and came running.

"Good boy," he soothed. "Now, where's Mac?"

"It's clear on this side of the cabin," Ben said. "I can see into the living room from the side window. No sign of Morrow or Mackenzie, but there's blood outside the back door."

Gabe's heart lurched at that information. "We know Morrow is injured. I pray Mac isn't also."

A gunshot rang out. Gabe froze in place, trying to determine the direction of the sound. But the geese scattering on the pond drowned out every other sound with their angry honks and flapping wings as they dispersed.

"Someone is shooting at us," Ben said in Gabe's ear.

"Where did that come from?" Gabe asked.

"Other side of the lake," Ben said. "I'll take the trail from the east."

"Come on, Winston." Gabe kept a close eye on the dog as they took the west side of the lake.

Another bullet whizzed by. This time, much too close. He couldn't risk Winston taking a bullet. Gabe slipped between the branches of a blue spruce and pulled Winston into the tree with him. The dog whined in protest.

"I don't like it, either, pal." He tapped his earbud. "Where are you, Ben?"

"To your right, behind that oak."

From the corner of his eye, Gabe saw a flash of light. He reached for his binoculars and swept the landscape. There it was. A flare. Right in front of a thicket of tall blue spruce.

Mac carried flares in her messenger bag. Why would she throw out a flare, which would only put a target on her location?

"I have eyes on Morrow," Ben said. "She's moving toward that flare. Weapon still in her hand."

"I see her," Gabe said. "She'll pick us off if we get any closer."

"Where did the flare come from?" Ben asked.

"It's got to be Mac. We don't have a plan, but it seems she does."

A scream cut through the quiet. Then a gunshot.

"Go, Ben! I'll meet you at that flare."

"Come on, Winston." Gabe picked up speed, racing around the lake to the apex. From a distance, he could see two women fighting. Mac had her cane across Morrow's shoulders, pinning her down.

Gabe's relief was immediate. *Go, Mac.*

Ben came running around the corner a moment later. He stopped short and blinked as if he couldn't believe his eyes.

"Not that she needs us," Gabe said, "but let's give her a hand."

The two of them subdued Morrow's legs while Mac used flex-cuffs to restrain the woman's hands.

Gabe grabbed Liz by her clothing and pulled her to her feet. An angry Elizabeth Morrow lunged toward Mac. Winston growled, threatening to attack.

"Get that dog away from me," Morrow screamed.

Ben stepped forward, his weapon trained on the rogue agent. "Give me an excuse, lady."

"Winston. Come," Mac called. The bulldog immediately obeyed, returning to her side.

"How did you get the jump on Morrow?" Gabe cocked his head and stared at Mac. Even injured, she was a force to be reckoned with.

"Literally." Mac pointed to the tree next to them. "I climbed the tree. Tossed the flare and then jumped her."

"You climbed a tree with your leg?" Gabe glanced up through the dense branches of the tree in disbelief.

Mac dusted the dirt and pine needles from her clothes before she looked at him. "It was either that or die. I'm not ready to die."

"The gunshot I heard?" Gabe asked.

"It went off when Liz hit the ground. Fortunately, I wasn't hit."

"Whose blood was that on the porch?" Ben asked.

"Liz's. I hit her with my cane and took off."

Gabe continued to shake his head, amazement warring with pride. "How's your leg now?"

"It's fine. I landed with my weight on my right foot and my fist in her stomach."

He nodded, still stunned that she'd taken down the mastermind of a bank heist and the puppet master who'd manipulated at least four men to do her bidding.

"So basically, you didn't need us," Gabe said.

Mac looked up at him. "Oh, Gabe. I'll always need you."

Ben started laughing. "Mackenzie Sharp, you're okay."

Gabe shook his head. He had to agree with his brother. Mac was more than okay.

Chapter Twelve

Mac sat down in a chair facing Senior Officer Todd Shipman's desk and waited for him to arrive. She propped her cane against her legs and wiped her moist palms on her black dress pants. The spacious office had multiple framed awards and degrees on the wall. Her gaze stopped at a simple wall calendar.

Monday again. So much had happened in a mere eleven days. Her life would never be the same. After today, that would be truer than ever.

"Sorry to keep you waiting." Todd Shipman entered the room and closed the door.

"Good morning, sir." She moved to stand, but he was quick to wave a hand.

"Don't get up." He took a seat behind his massive desk and offered a welcoming smile that helped Mac relax.

She couldn't help but note that her father would have been the same age if he was alive.

Perhaps with the same gray that now dominated Todd Shipman's hair.

Don't look back, her mind warned. *Don't look back.*

"The Agency let you down, Mackenzie." Shipman released a breath. "I let you down." He steepled his fingers and grimaced as if in physical pain. "I'm sorry. More than I can express."

"I don't blame you. I should have seen beneath Liz's facade."

"You can't blame yourself. We were all fooled."

Mac shook her head. So much loss because of Elizabeth Morrow.

"The Director has already initiated a full investigation," Shipman said. "Protocols were in place, and yet both Calder and Morrow managed to misdirect and bypass procedure. It should have never happened."

"What will happen to Calder?"

"He's agreed to a deal and has implicated Morrow. His career is over, but I can't say what will happen next."

Mac digested that information. "And Morrow?"

"DHS is still working on the charges against

her. Interestingly enough, the money hasn't been found."

Mac shook her head at the irony. Liz would be in jail for a very long time, unable to enjoy the money, wherever it was.

"I assume you're going to be able to finish rehabilitation on your leg, and then you'll be back with us," Shipman said.

"Rehab starts again this week. I hope to see more of you and Mary and the kids in the future," Mac said.

"I can start you on desk duty if you like?"

She took a deep breath. There was no need to hesitate, the decision had been thought out and prayed over. "Sir, I'm not returning to the Agency."

He frowned in confusion. "What am I missing here?"

Mac pulled an envelope out of her messenger bag. "I'm submitting my resignation. Effective today."

Shipman's face reflected surprise. "You're one of our best operations officers. You have a bright future."

"Thank you, but I'm ready for a new direction for that future."

"I see." He offered a slow nod as though processing the information. "Have you considered a career as an analyst? We have an opening for a technology-and-weapons analyst in Los Angeles."

"With all due respect, sir, it's time to walk away. Don't think I don't appreciate everything you've done for me."

"Nothing was done out of obligation, Mackenzie. It was because you're someone that I can rely on. I never had to think twice when you were on assignment. You've always been a valuable asset to the company."

She bowed her head. He wasn't making it any easier. "Thank you for that."

"If you'll be seeing the family more often, does that mean you're staying in Colorado?"

"Yes. I love Colorado. I'm going to find a house in the country so Winston can run. I'll spend time catching up on my reading and maybe do a little fishing." Just saying the words brought a smile to her lips.

"There's always a place for you at our table, metaphorically and literally." He leaned back in his chair. "Megan is home from college for a few more weeks. We'd love to have you for dinner this Sunday."

"Thank you."

"I'll tell Mary and the kids. They'll be delighted."

Mac stood and offered her hand, but Shipman shook his head. He came around his massive desk and embraced her. "You're a civilian now, Mackenzie. Family. I can hug you."

Mac choked back emotion at the embrace.

Yes. Family. It was time to let people in, as Gabe had reminded her.

Mac picked up her cane and started toward the door.

"Mackenzie."

She turned. "Sir?"

"Your parents would be so proud of you."

When she met Todd Shipman's gaze, his eyes were moist. Her heart swelled with emotion. "Thank you. That means so much."

He nodded and returned to his seat. "Would you send Denton in for me?"

Denton? She hadn't seen him since Thursday. The last few days had been a whirlwind of being debriefed and medical examinations.

"Yes, sir," she returned.

Gabe waited outside, chatting with Shipman's new assistant, a leggy blonde. The woman smiled up at him, and Mac couldn't help a tiny twinge of longing. There wasn't anyone Gabe couldn't strike up a conversation with.

She'd had her chance once. There was no reason for regrets.

Mac cleared her throat. When he turned in her direction, she nodded toward Shipman's office and he offered a quick nod of acknowledgement in return. As Gabe passed by her, he touched her arm and paused. "Did you drive here?"

"Um, no. I took a ride-share. I was running late and didn't want to deal with parking."

"Wait for me. I'll give you a lift home."

She opened her mouth to protest, but he spoke before she could, his hazel eyes warm with entreaty.

"Please."

"Sure," she said softly. "I'll be outside."

Mac didn't do goodbyes. They hurt, and saying goodbye to this man wouldn't be easy. Not when he'd managed to bluster his way past all her objections and convince her heart that she was capable of trusting…and loving.

Yes, Gabe Denton deserved a few minutes of her time before they went their separate ways.

Mac took the elevator to the lobby and nodded to the guards before pushing open the glass doors. She stood on the sidewalk, letting the sunshine warm her face, watching morning traf-

fic and busy people with places to be hurry past.
Life continued to move on as though nothing
had happened.

Her phone vibrated, and she checked the
screen. It was a text message from Mary Shipman.

Todd says you're joining us for dinner on Sunday. I'm so glad.

Mac laughed. It had been all of ten minutes,
and already Shipman had given his wife Mac's
new phone number and told her about their
conversation.

Thanks, Mary. I can't wait.

And she couldn't. It would be good to see
the Shipmans. She was moving on, but that was
okay. It was time. Time to make peace with the
past and begin to carve out a future.

She'd spent years feeling guilty because she
hadn't died with her parents in the embassy
bombing, instead of appreciating the fact that
she was alive.

Thankful.

That was the word that popped into her spirit.
Mac smiled. Very thankful.

"Ready?" Mac turned at the sound of Gabe's voice behind her. He stood there blocking out the sun, yet she felt warm in his presence.

"What are you looking at?" Gabe asked. "It's the clothes, right?" He glanced down at his dress shirt and pants. "You haven't seen me in anything that wasn't wrinkled, torn or bled on since I arrived."

"You look very nice," Mac said. "And your bruises are fading. How are your ears? Have you had your hearing evaluated?"

"I'm cleared to fly." He grinned. "The doc says I made a wise decision to drive from Phoenix."

"Yes, you're very wise." Mac couldn't help but laugh.

He nodded toward the left. "Car's parked around the corner."

"I thought you had a coveted parking pass," Mac said.

"I'm leaving. Had to turn it in."

"Right." Another reminder that he'd be gone soon.

They walked to a black SUV, not unlike the one that exploded in Phoenix, and he held the door for her before getting in.

"Rental?" she asked.

"Yeah." He turned in his seat to look at her. "We've come full circle, haven't we?"

Mac smiled. "Yes. I guess we have."

Gabe put on his seat belt and gestured toward Mac's leg. "Any issues with medical for you?" he asked.

"No. I'll be back in rehab tomorrow."

"Then what?" he pressed.

"I've got that inheritance from my parents. I've been thinking about buying a little land."

"A little island?"

She laughed. "No. A little parcel of land. Something with enough room for Winston to run. Maybe out in Larkspur. Despite the past week."

"That's a long commute."

"No." She shook her head. "Sorry. I wasn't clear. I'm not going back to the Agency. I'm done. I want to taste normal."

"Normal. Is that really what you're looking for?"

"I'm not sure. But it's a start."

"You're seriously leaving the CIA?" Gabe slowly shook his head. "What will you do?"

Mac shrugged. "Maybe I'll do nothing for a while. Nothing sounds really good."

"Don't forget. You owe me a fly-fishing trip.

I'll expect an email regarding your availability soon."

She smiled once more. It was good to be able to joke with Gabe. She'd missed their repartee the last few days.

"You're the one who still has a job," she answered. "Let me know when you have time off."

"Oh, I will."

"What about your day job, anyhow?" Mac asked. "Promotion finalized?"

"Yeah. I'll be back at The Farm in time for the incoming recruits."

"Great. I'm sure you're good at your job. You have a lot of patience."

"Do I?" He glanced at her.

"Yes," she returned. "What about Ben?"

"Back to DC. We're flying out together this afternoon."

"You're still not interested in joining Denton Security and Investigations?" She peeked at him from the corner of her eye. It was too much to hope he'd stay in Denver and join the family business.

"Oh, yeah. I'm definitely interested. My heart says yes." He paused. "But my head is wavering."

"I can relate. That's what took me so long to

decide to leave the Agency. Stepping out into the unknown is never easy."

"Look at you, talking all philosophical," Gabe said.

"I'm not being philosophical. What I'm trying to say is your brother's company sounds like a great future. I think your father will be proud."

"That's because you don't know the general." He started the car, turned on the AC and drummed his fingers on the steering wheel as the cool air blew in. "I'm a coward."

"I didn't say that."

"No. I did."

He backed up the SUV and headed down Santa Fe. Mac kept sneaking looks at Gabe as they drove in silence to her condo. When would she see him again? Five years? Ten? What regrets would she have then?

"I never noticed that dog park before." Gabe signaled and pulled up to the drop-off area in front of her building.

"It's fairly new. The city added it a few years ago. I guess they knew Winston was coming to live with me."

"He likes it?"

"Loves it. We're there several times a day."

Gabe nodded, a smile touching his mouth. "I'm going to miss you and Winston."

Mac looked out the window. She didn't know how to say the words that were locked inside of her. How could she possibly ask him to stay?

"We're going to miss you, too, Denton."

"Are we back to that?" He cocked his head and gave her a censuring look.

"Gabe." She reached for the door handle, looked at him, and then away. "Gabe, I…"

"What?" he asked.

"Thank you. For everything."

She opened the door and carefully stepped onto the sidewalk, using her cane to keep her steady, though she felt anything but steady right now.

"Be safe," Mac said before turning away.

Because I care for you. I always will.

Gabe verified his departure time on the flight-information display and wandered to a bookstore. His phone buzzed, and he pulled it out.

A text from his brother.

In TSA line. Join you shortly.

Disappointment hit Gabe.

What was he expecting? Mac to call and beg him to stay?

Yep, that was exactly what he wanted. Waited his whole life for. Mac was his future, but she couldn't see it. Maybe never would.

A quick stroll around the bookstore proved fruitless. After nearly bumping into several harried customers in a rush to get in and out, he left. The truth was, he didn't need a book or a magazine.

He needed Mac.

Gabe headed back to the gate. Walking down the long corridor, he spotted Ben and waved his arms. Ben jogged to meet him.

"Thought I was going to miss the flight."

"Where were you?" Gabe asked.

"Pacing the parking lot and arguing with the insurance company. Do you know how hard it is to explain that your vacation rental was destroyed by a rogue government operative and get someone to believe you?"

Gabe's head jerked up at the words. "Naw. Tell me you didn't say that."

Ben laughed. "I didn't, but all the same, it was time-consuming."

Overhead a speaker crackled, and the first boarding announcement rang out.

"I take it Shipman booked us first class," Ben said.

"Keep dreaming," Gabe said with a laugh. "It's good to have dreams. The boarding pass indicates we're in the last row, next to the restroom."

Ben groaned. "That means I sit with my knees under my chin for four hours." His brother cocked his head and looked him up and down. "What are you doing on this flight, anyhow?"

"What do you mean?"

"Why are you leaving Denver?"

"Because I have a job in DC. Any other silly questions?" Gabe leaned against the wall and frowned.

"Yeah, but Mackenzie is here." Ben narrowed his gaze. "And you're in love with her."

Gabe stared at his brother. He considered denying the accusation, but what would be the point? Ben saw far too much.

He released a sigh. "My being in love with Mac doesn't change the situation."

"Are you going to wait another five years before your paths cross and you have a third opportunity to do something?"

"Do something? Ben, I can't keep banging my head against the wall around her heart."

"Sure, you can. This is it, man. We all could have been killed at any time in the last week. No guts. No glory. No risk. No reward." Ben raised his hands. "How many more pithy quotes do I have to recite? Life is short, man."

"What if she doesn't...?"

"She loves you."

"How can you be sure? I'm never certain what Mac is feeling from one moment to the next."

"Trust me. It's in her eyes when she looks at you."

Gabe took a deep breath, as he considered his brother's words. Could Ben be right? He'd been waiting five years for her. Was it a foolish dream to think Mac might change her mind about them?

"I know that dog loves you. And if a woman's dog loves you, then the woman does, too."

"So I should try, one more time, because of a drooling one-hundred-pound bulldog?"

"That, and there's the fact that she called me and asked if I was still considering opening a Denver office."

"What? When was this?"

"On my way over." He shrugged. "She wants to invest her inheritance in the company."

"What?"

"You already said that."

"Pardon me, but I'm stunned."

"Yep. I was a bit surprised, too. My theory is that if Mac didn't want anything to do with the Dentons, she wouldn't have called."

"None of this makes any sense," Gabe said.

"It's love. It's not supposed to make sense."

Gabe narrowed his eyes. "How is it you're the expert?"

"I listen to a lot of podcasts when I'm on the road."

Gabe burst out laughing. Overhead, another boarding call was announced.

"They just called for all passengers seated next to the restroom," Ben said. "You better make a decision."

Gabe glanced at the lines of people funneling past the gate agent. "I guess I could always get a later flight if she says no."

His brother grinned and gave him a thumbs-up. "That's the indomitable Denton optimism. Mom would have been proud."

"Thanks, Ben."

"Sure. I'd expect you to kick me in the seat of my pants if the situation was reversed."

Gabe gave his brother a man-hug. "Seriously.

No matter how this turns out, I appreciate you. I'm glad you're my brother."

He pivoted and headed back down the long corridor of the airline terminal. At the elevator bank, he punched the button for ground transportation. He'd already turned in the rental car. How was he going to get to Mac's place?

A cab. More expensive, but cabs would be lined up and waiting.

Warmth surrounded him as he passed from the air-conditioned doorway to the outside sidewalk. Another hot day. Though not as hot as Phoenix, he reminded himself. And certainly not as hot and humid as DC.

Denver was a nice town. Crossing the street to the cab station, his gaze took in the mountains to the west. God's country. He could see himself waking up to those mountains every day.

It all depended on Mac.

He found himself more terrified of her response than he'd been at that last standoff at the cabin. Except when he thought Liz had killed Mac.

That was a moment he never wanted to face again.

Gabe waved a cab over.

Ben was right. He'd never stopped loving Mackenzie Sharp.

Now he prayed she felt the same.

"Go get it, Winston," Mac called. The chew bone sailed across the grass, and the dog eagerly chased it. Right now, she was the only one at the dog park, so Winston had the luxury of being off his leash without being in the designated play area and he was enjoying himself. He jumped in the air and caught the toy, then rolled on the grass wrestling with it.

Mac glanced at her watch and then at the sky. It was almost dinnertime. Gabe would be on his way to DC by now. She swallowed. That was good. He got the promotion. Great for his career. She wouldn't be surprised if he was sitting behind a desk like Shipman's the next time they ran into each other. And he deserved it.

But where would she be when Gabe was getting on with his life without her?

Mac hadn't a clue. She had let Ben know that she was interested in Denton Security and Investigations if a Denver office panned out. Her college degree was in economics with a French-language minor. Maybe she'd teach. Maybe she'd take a trip to France.

There wasn't a rush to make a decision. She had a few weeks of physical therapy ahead of her. Though even that looked promising. Despite the trauma of the last week, the orthopedic surgeon said her leg was healing well. He'd assured her that once she'd finished treatment, the cane most likely wouldn't be needed.

That thought cheered her up.

Winston picked up the chew toy and raced toward her.

And right on past.

"Winston? Where are you going?"

Mac whirled around. "Stop." She blinked, certain she was hallucinating. But, no, it really was Gabe striding across the grass in her direction. Winston kept running joyously toward him.

When Gabe crouched down, the dog leaped into his open arms and knocked him over. Winston began an enthusiastic inspection of Gabe's face with his tongue.

"Winston. Stop," she called. The animal ignored her.

Gabe raised himself to a seated position and adjusted his glasses. He chuckled as he rubbed Winston's head and ears.

"Hi, Mac," he said.

"Gabe? What are you doing here?"

"Good to see you, too." He lifted an eyebrow. "I guess you didn't miss me."

"I just saw you this morning." She checked her watch. "You're supposed to be on your way to DC."

"Missed my flight."

"Oh," she murmured. "I'm sorry."

"On purpose."

Mac's chin lifted, and she stared at him, confused. "What did you say?"

"Someone pointed out to me that taking a chance and being shot down was better than never taking a chance at all."

"Um…" She swallowed, her breath stuck in her throat. "I don't know what to say to that."

"Glad to hear it." Gabe nodded toward the bench. "Let's sit down."

He scooped up Winston's chew toy and pulled back his arm. The rubber toy sailed a distance twice as long as Mac had pitched it minutes before.

Mac sat on the bench and folded her hands on her lap, uncertain of the protocol here. Was this the part where she told him that she'd been the coward? Or the part where she begged him to stay?

"Here's the thing, Mac." Gabe sat and stretched out his long legs. "I'm in love with you."

"I—I…" she sputtered and worked to catch her breath.

"I know. I know. Imagine how surprised I was. But, when you think about it, it's not a surprise. When you find the right person…" He shrugged and sighed loudly. "Why keep looking? Right?"

Mac's knees trembled and goose bumps danced up her arms.

Gabe Denton just said he loved her.

She glanced at him, leaning back with his arm across the back of the bench.

How could he be so relaxed? This moment would define the rest of her life.

"So here's the thing," he continued. "I'm not willing to close the door on us a second time until you tell me that you don't love me."

"Um," she squeaked.

He raised a hand. "I'm not done yet. I practiced this speech on the way over, so you may as well let me get it out of my system."

"Okay," she murmured.

"The thing is, I don't think you can use that fear-of-someone-you-love-dying rationale for not living your life. Not after the last week. We both could have died. Several times. But we didn't. We made it, Mac."

He turned to her. "There are no guarantees. I'd rather live my no-guarantees life with you by my side than without."

"Me, too."

Gabe's eyes popped open. "I wasn't expecting that. I have at least two more persuasive arguments."

Mac smiled slowly. "You came prepared."

"Yeah, I did. I'm not letting you go this time."

"I love you, Gabe." The words came naturally. Probably because she'd wanted to say them for such a very long time.

"Oh, thank You, Lord," Gabe said. He closed the space between them and then stopped and pulled back. He removed his holster and placed it on the bench.

Mac laughed as his lips met hers.

"Stop laughing so I can give you a proper kiss."

She wrapped her arms around his neck and complied, her lips meeting his for a sweet kiss.

"Looks like I can tell Ben we're opening a

Denver office of Denton Security and Investigations."

Mac brightened. "You're going to stay in Denver?"

"Absolutely. Welcome to the family business, Mackenzie Sharp."

Winston whined and nosed his face between them. "You're part of the family, too, boy." Gabe leaned down and gave the bulldog a loving head rub.

"What happens next?" Mac asked.

"I'm starving," Gabe said. "How do you feel about sushi?"

Mac laughed. "I'll follow your appetite anywhere, Gabe Denton."

He leaned close, his breath warming her face. "I thank God for you, Mac. Every single day." And then he kissed her again.

★ ★ ★ ★ ★

Romantic Suspense

Danger. Passion. Drama.

Available Next Month

Colton Mountain Search Karen Whiddon
Defender After Dark Charlene Parris

....

A High-Stakes Reunion Tara Taylor Quinn
Close Range Cattleman Amber Leigh Williams

 LOVE INSPIRED

Baby Protection Mission Laura Scott
Cold Case Target Jessica R. Patch

Larger Print

....

 LOVE INSPIRED

Tracking The Truth Dana Mentink
Rocky Mountain Survival Jane M. Choate

Larger Print

....

 LOVE INSPIRED

Treacherous Escape Kellie VanHorn
Colorado Double Cross Jennifer Pierce

Larger Print

brand new stories each month

Romantic **Suspense**

Danger. Passion. Drama.

MILLS & BOON

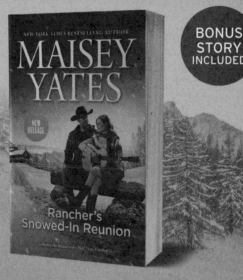